Perfect Storm

Arne Weinz

Defiance Press & Publishing, LLC

ISBN-978-1-963102-82-6 (Paperback)

ISBN-978-1-963102-81-9 (eBook)

Published by Defiance Press & Publishing, LLC, www.defiancepress.com

Bulk orders of this book may be obtained by contacting Defiance Press & Publishing, LLC., publishing@defiancepress.com

C1 Prologue

Prologue: Sweden

Early Summer 2032

Rumors swirled through the streets and workplaces of Sweden, whispers of impending war echoing in the air. Would it be the military seeking to reclaim control with an iron fist? Or would it be the hundreds of thousands of what the Muslims called the *Holy Warriors* poised for a coordinated strike across the nation? Speculation ran rampant, but certainty eluded all.

Amidst the uncertainty, the populace witnessed a steady stream of skirmishes, street battles, and clandestine clashes, claiming lives with chilling regularity. Yet, the media remained eerily silent, forbidden to report on the escalating violence that gripped the nation.

Night after night, the tranquility was shattered by the ominous sound of detonations—hand grenades and explosive charges piercing the air. While official narratives pointed fingers at Nazi factions, most Swedes harbored suspicions of a different origin: Muslim terrorists. The police and Swedish Secret Police, SÄPO, remained tight-lipped, withholding information in a bid to deny the perpetrators any advantage.

But it was the specter of suicide bombings that struck fear into the hearts of the people. The constant threat of sudden, violent death hung heavy in the air, casting a cloud of suspicion and paranoia over daily life. A mere glimpse of traditional Middle Eastern or African attire was enough to send crowds scattering in terror. At the same time, any sudden movement or shout sparked panic like ants fleeing their nest.

In the wake of this pervasive fear, public spaces lay deserted, once-thriving arenas and concert halls echoing with silence. Weekend shopping excursions became a relic of the past, as malls and department stores stood eerily vacant. Once bustling with activity, public transport ran empty, its passengers opting for isolation over the risk of danger.

The genesis of this descent into chaos lay in a historic misstep—the result of an irresponsible migration policy. In the early 2010s, Sweden's doors were flung open to asylum seekers from the Middle East and North Africa, a flood of humanity welcomed with open arms by politicians eager to burnish their humanitarian credentials.

Yet, as the years passed, this humanitarian gesture became a tidal wave of migration, inundating the nation's borders with an influx of unknown proportions. With lax border controls and scant oversight, Sweden transformed itself from a bastion of stability into a battleground, its streets haunted by violence and uncertainty.

The solution seemed simple enough—a mass issuance of permanent residence permits, swiftly followed by citizenship without scrutiny. Yet, beneath the veneer of generosity lay a ticking time bomb, primed to explode with each passing year.

Despite assurances from politicians of a strict immigration policy, each year, they brought a fresh influx of arrivals, swelling the ranks with a motley crew of lifestyle criminals and known terrorists. The Swedish Migration Agency was restricted by mandates to maintain order at all costs. With a preponderance of Muslim caseworkers, loyalty often trumped duty, as regulations from Swedish leadership were brushed aside.

Then came the summer of 2029—a turning point cloaked in surprise and trepidation. Refugee boats from the Middle East and North Africa altered course, setting sail for Sweden's shores with unprecedented boldness. Upon arrival, they were met not by welcoming committees but by the silent dread of abandonment, left to fend for themselves as the wheels of bureaucracy ground to a halt.

Behind the scenes, a shadowy coalition of global influencers pulled the strings, funding the influx through covert channels. The Open Society Foundation and secret funds controlled by the World Economic Forum, through a conspiracy of clandestine organizations like the Bilderberg Group, the Trilateral Commission, and the Rome Club, conspired to destabilize Western Europe, using mass immigration as their weapon of choice.

The coalition government, which governed Sweden since the temporary state of emergency was introduced during the Second Intifada in 2029, struggled in vain to calm the situation. Tensions were high, the rhetoric was harsh and uncompromising, and everyone realized that some form of outburst was inevitable sooner or later. Yet, the Muslims had gotten exactly what they wanted.

The Muslim party *Nyans* gained traction with its demand for increased immigration of selected quota refugees. Since 2028, the 284 autonomous enclaves have been governed by Sharia laws without interference from Swedish authorities, except for the extensive financial support – a forced tribute paid by Swedes to avoid violence.

Without this tribute of money and resources, the 2.7 million Muslims would lack food, healthcare, and schools. Politicians deemed it best to pay the tribute without complaint to prevent civil war.

By 2032, the tribute amounted to sixteen percent of the state budget. Yet the Muslims demanded more, believing that as good Muslims, they had the right to live at a higher economic standard than Swedes.

Submitting constantly to Muslim demands only fueled the flames of discontent. Each concession served as a temporary remedy, followed by a fresh onslaught of grievances. The list of demands seemed endless, an ever-growing testament to the erosion of Swedish sovereignty.

The most painful concession for the Swedes was the Equality Act of 2030, also known as the "trade-off," when Sweden introduced Arabic as an official language alongside Swedish and simultaneously changed its national standard. The proposition passed with a narrow majority in the parliament, stated that the Swedish standard could no longer be adorned with a cross, as the Christian cross was perceived as an insult to a large part of the Swedish population. Sweden was officially a secular country without a state religion, making the decision logical and justifiable. From July 1, 2030, Sweden's flag was three vertical fields in blue-yellow-blue colors. The three fields were to be associated with Sweden's ancient national symbol, the Three Crowns.

The "trade-off" was followed a few weeks later by the blasphemy law that made all criticism of Islam prohibited by law. Non-Muslims who criticized Islam were automatically sentenced to a minimum of six months in prison for blaspheming Islam.

The alarm clock that finally woke the Swedes up and made them realize that they were indeed on the verge of losing their country forever was the "Little Civil War" that raged for nine days in the fall of 2030, shortly after the election. When the war ceased, through a ceasefire agreement and a general amnesty, 1,249 lives had been claimed.

After the "Little Civil War," the Swedes finally realized that there was no other option but to arm themselves and prepare for another civil war, which risked being much more extensive. In November 2030, the parliament decided to transform the National Response Force into a paramilitary force of nine thousand soldiers equipped with armored vehicles, grenade launchers, and machine guns tasked with securing the streets and being able to engage in direct combat.

The Home Guard, the leading citizen militia that had long sought to become a nationwide organization, was granted status as the umbrella organization for all local citizen militias through a parliamentary decision in December 2031.

It is said that the lack of bread always triggers revolutions, and that situation seems to be drawing closer. The first sign that the economy was on the brink of collapse was when the welfare systems ultimately failed in the fall of 2029 after years of dysfunction. Healthcare had year-long waiting lists. Pension payments could only be made at seventy-five percent of what was supposed to be paid. Salaries for public employees were only paid sporadically. The cause of the economic chaos was a combination of the wealthiest Swedes leaving the country and millions of new Swedes being supported through welfare benefits.

As always, in economies gone haywire, the Central Bank increased the speed of the money printing presses and granted commercial banks expanded mandates to create new digital money, resulting in inflation skyrocketing to one hundred fifty percent. Sweden was mockingly called "the Venezuela of the Nordics" in the world's financial media, and the krona plummeted like a stone among currency traders.

In January 2032, the US dollar cost forty kronor, sharply declining Sweden's imports. This led to food, medicine, fuel, and consumer goods shortages. Many industries shuttered or operated at reduced capacity due to the need for more inputs. The so-called just-in-time deliveries, which had worked well for forty years, had left industries with minimal inventories, barely enough for a couple of days of production. The situation worsened with the recurring power outages, resulting in constant production halts.

The stream of wealthy Swedes emigrating trickled to a halt as it became impossible to finance establishments abroad due to the crashed krona, and assets in Sweden could only be sold at fire-sale prices. However, half a million of the wealthiest had already managed to flee the country, resulting in significantly reduced tax revenues. Thousands of businesses closed or were left to their fate after their owners went into exile. Sometimes, the employees attempted to continue operations as best they could, but it was rarely sustainable.

On the international front, dramatic changes occurred, with the most significant for Sweden being the dissolution of NATO in December 2031, followed by the withdrawal of the last American troops from Germany after eighty-seven years of presence since the end of World War II.

In Southern Europe, the collapse of the EU led to the end of the democratic era, as military juntas replaced parliaments through largely bloodless coups in France, Spain, Italy, Portugal, Croatia, Slovenia, and Greece. The juntas garnered strong popular support as the democratically elected leaders, with the EU leadership at the forefront, were blamed for the reckless Islamization policies.

Sweden stood alone in a tumultuous world, grappling with insurmountable internal problems. The ever-rising spiral of violence was impossible to halt. The once wealthy Swedes were now patiently queuing at soup kitchens funded through international aid.

The tribute to the Muslims could no longer be fully paid, further escalating tensions, with increasing unrest on the streets in the form of Muslim mass demonstrations that often descended into outright clashes with the police and the National Guard.

Dark clouds gathered over the Kingdom of Sweden, and the wind whispered more sparingly. As the Swedes embarked on their long vacations in the early summer of 2032, they harbored forebodings that everything might not be as usual when they returned. Everyone knew that something terrible was about to happen. It was shaping up to be a Perfect Storm.

CONTENTS

Chapter 1

An almost sleepless night

July 17, 2032, 2 a.m.

Sleep eluded him, even as the clock struck past two in the dead of night. Ahmed's entire body hummed with a sense of urgency; a distinct tension that announced the task bestowed upon him by Allah. Years of meticulous planning would unfurl into action in just a few hours. The world would reel in shock and awe soon. After centuries of disrespect, Western exploitation, and humiliation, now was the time for retribution. Ahmed savored the prospect of etching his name into the walls of history, a legacy destined to resonate through the ages.

Stubbing out his cigarette beneath the heel of his military boot, Ahmed drew in a lungful of crisp night air. The tentative embrace of dawn could already be felt on the distant horizon to the northeast while the colossal cruise ship plowed steadfastly through the Kattegatt Strait, bound for the port of Gothenburg. Gliding at fourteen knots, he had deliberately reduced speed to avoid premature arrival. Trailing in his wake were two RoRo ships packed with armored vehicles, tanks, and mobile artillery, their lights and lanterns casting an eerie glow visible from Ahmed's vantage point on the bridge deck.

Ahmed's mind drifted back to the winding alleys of his childhood in Casablanca's ancient city, with its whitewashed facades whispering tales of yore. As the youngest of eight siblings, Ahmed had been the apple of his parents' eye. His talent transcended the ordinary, complemented by a natural charm that disarmed everyone he met. With a face of striking symmetry, wise and expressive eyes, and a smile that could charm the stars, many believed Ahmed was destined for greatness—as a model, perhaps, or a soccer prodigy. When Ahmed was fifteen, his coach said he was the best of his age group in Casablanca, where they had organized soccer leagues. Yet Ahmed aspired to more than the confines of sweaty locker rooms and raucous teammates. Ahmed was acutely aware of his unique talent. He sensed a greater purpose, a destiny appointed by Allah.

Ahmed's humble fruit vendor father worked tirelessly to provide for his wife and eight children. Despite the perpetual scarcity of essentials, their plight wasn't any different than that of their neighbors. From a young age, the children were thrust into the workforce to contribute while their mothers scrimped and saved every meager penny they could earn.

Yet, the Ben Barka family was somehow upheld and respected in a way their neighbors weren't. They were distinguished. It was because of politics. Ahmed's uncle, who had been a leader of the opposition against the draconian regime in Rabat, had achieved martyrdom since the agents from the Moroccan General Directorate for Territorial Surveillance, also known as the *DGST*, assassinated him during his forced exile in London. Ahmed vividly recalled the spring day of 2001, when his father returned home, pale and tear-streaked, bearing the tragic news to the family.

As was customary, the focal point in the modest living room of a Moroccan family wasn't a portrait of King Muhammad VI. Instead, there was a black-and-white photograph of a strikingly handsome and astute man. His smile gentle yet mysterious, adorned with a silver frame, commanding attention. It was the portrait of the great pan-Arabist and former Egyptian President, Gamal Abdel Nasser, who held pride of place—a constant source of contention between Ahmed's parents. While his mother fretted about the photograph bringing trouble if the police would pay a visit, Ahmed's father unwaveringly admired Nasser's vision of Arab unity, which he believed held the key to their salvation.

"That photograph will be our downfall," Ahmed's mother warned weekly. Ahmed's father, unfazed by his wife's jabs about the idealized pan-Arabism on the worn dresser, had his grievances. "If only our Arab brethren could unite and stand firm, the Westerners wouldn't stand a chance," he lamented. "We possess incredible strength, and Nasser illuminated our path. But when Allah called him, we were left with a crooked successor who betrayed our cause for alliances with Jews and Americans." His frustration resounded as he added, "Sadat wasn't even a true Arab. Just a damn Nubian with a Christian mother to boot. What could one expect from him?"

Ahmed's heart surged with pride, much like his father's and every Arab's, as he reflected on the remarkable history of the Arab world ingrained in him since childhood. From the Atlantic's shores to the Shatt al-Arab's banks in the Arabian Gulf—what the heathens dared to call the Persian Gulf—Arabic endured, a testament to the unity awaiting the nations in an imposing caliph.

As he swung open the door to the small cabin off the control room, preparing to unfurl the prayer rug one final time before docking, Ahmed couldn't shake the notion that perhaps this day would mark the dawn of the golden era all Arabs had yearned for—an inevitable destiny, just past the horizon.

Despite his reservations toward Shia, the prayer rug remained Persian. It was crafted from the finest turquoise silk and adorned with natural gold threads intricately woven into the fabric. Despite their religious deviations, the Persians excelled in carpet weaving—a fact undeniable. This particular rug, reserved for the elite echelons of society, bore witness to their craftsmanship.

"Show me your prayer rug, and I'll tell you who you are," the saying echoed in his mind as he knelt and bowed forward. "Today," he thought, "the great Prophet would surely be proud of me."

"Oh, great Prophet, see us today and guide us in the battle against the heathens," Ahmed whispered as he bent over, his forehead touching the floor.

With his forehead, he felt the subtle vibrations coursing through the floor, resonating from the ship's engine. Despite the room's elevated position, the low hum of the massive engines reached his ears and relaxed his body. The convergence of vibrations and hums evoked a sense of divine purpose within him. It was comforting to envision the unstoppable force propelling the ship towards a future of glory—a force unstoppable.

After expressing gratitude to Allah, he rose from the floor and sat into one of the plush, dark green leather armchairs. Leaning his head back against the neck rest, he shut his eyes. Images of Casablanca raced through his mind, and he drifted into a deep sleep. Forty-five minutes later, he awoke with a clear mind, his body rested and ready for action. Today was the pinnacle of Ahmed's existence and could not be wasted.

A sharp and urgent knock interrupted his thoughts as he prepared to act. Opening the door, he was met by his loyal deputy, his face alive with excitement.

"Trouble brews for the Luleå Squadron, sir—it's urgent," the deputy exclaimed.

Unperturbed, Ahmed gestured for him to proceed. "Come, Hassan, my friend. Tell me what has happened."

Chapter 2

Embarking Gothenburg

July 17, 2032, 3 a.m.

Ahmed breathed in the cool night air out on the deck once again. The Swedish summer night was chilly but somehow warmer than the biting cold desert nights in North Africa, where the warmth disappears within a few minutes after the sun sets.

He smoked another Moroccan *Sobranie* cigarette as he traced the ship's route in his mind, as he had done many times in the simulator. The dawn broke quickly, and now he could see the contours of Gothenburg from his position at the very front of the bow. He noted that they were passing the Vasskären island on the starboard side. A few nautical miles ahead in the bow's direction, Hunneskärs lighthouse blinked its eternal signal: long-short-short ... long-short-short ... a pulsating heart of guiding light. Soon, he could see the waterway entrance to Gothenburg, Göta Älv. The large cruise ship would dock at Skandia harbor in less than an hour. That would be the defining moment. If the Swedes had been alerted by intelligence reports, their navy would have already attacked, as Ahmed's small convoy had been in Swedish waters for hours. Perhaps a Swedish submarine of the A26 type was lurking in the depths beneath them. The world's quietest submarine had an air-independent Stirling engine that was barely audible even if you put your ear directly to the engine—a technological marvel.

Perhaps they had already locked onto one of their state-of-the-art, target-seeking, twenty-feet-long, three-thousand-pound Torpedo 62s, which would soon detonate in the ship's hull and send the boat to the seabed within ten minutes? Or was an A26, the submarine without a periscope, lurking just below the surface observing them through its optronic mast? Ahmed's eyes scanned the water's surface as far as he could see, even though he knew it was virtually impossible to detect the optronic mast, not even if he were to look directly at it.

It was no coincidence that Sweden was among the world's leading weapons exporters. Swedish engineers were at the forefront of the global arms industry despite Swedes proclaiming themselves the World's Conscience. But why willingly give away their country, Ahmed wondered? Why? He couldn't grasp it. Neither could anyone else. It was a mystery. Perhaps everything had gone awry simply because they were too well off. Nothing to fight for. Like a spoiled child tossing away a nice toy, confident a new one would arrive soon. But there was only one Sweden. All they had was their land, yet they didn't seem interested in defending it. At the same time, they exported large quantities of weapons to those who wanted to protect their countries. Nothing made sense, not at all. Ahmed shook his head, thinking about the peculiar Swedes as he had done many times before.

"If a Torpedo 62 was to be fired, we're done for," thought Ahmed, taking the final drag on his *Sobranie*. "The same goes if any Swedish JAS Gripen planes would suddenly appear on the horizon and launch an attack. There would be no chance of escaping. The planes wouldn't even need to appear over the horizon to fire their missiles, which with almost one hundred percent certainty would hit bull's-eye thanks to active targeting. Torpedo or missile, it wouldn't matter. We would be dead in a minute," Ahmed thought again. "Then we'll all be swallowed by the black depths beneath us and end our time on Earth as martyrs in a frigid sailor's grave." He shuddered at the thought. He wasn't afraid to die and meet Allah, but preferably not like that. The black abyss felt foreign and terrifying to Ahmed with its cold water, nothing like the warm, blue waves of the Mediterranean that he had plunged into so many times. Or, maybe an ambush was awaiting them just as they were about to dock? If so, the entire operation would be a failure. However, neither the observers on site, in the ports, nor the Muslim Brotherhood's infiltrators in the Swedish military and intelligence services had noted signs that the Swedes were prepared for what was to come; no abnormal activity was present.

However, some warnings had popped up from the leading Swedish intelligence agencies, FRA and MUST. They seemed concerned with what they thought were isolated incidents, a few out of hundreds of pieces in the big puzzle. The Swedish Secret Police, SÄPO, had reported abnormally high activity among Swedish Salafists and unusually high attendance at the recent Friday prayers. Despite all their infiltrators in the mosques, they did not draw any conclusions about the increased activity.

Since the Muslims had infiltrated all parts of Swedish society, including the security services, they knew about most of Sweden's infiltrators, but time was running out for them. Defectors are the worst of the worst, thought Ahmed, and they should be captured and punished without mercy. If the Swedes managed to stop a couple of isolated attacks – out of a hundred or so – it wouldn't change the overall picture. Ahmed would give the naive and sleeping Swedes the biggest surprise of their history, not vice versa.

Meanwhile, as the squadron approached Gothenburg, two nearly identical squadrons, consisting of a cruise ship and two RoRo ships, were heading towards the east coast towns of Stockholm and Luleå. The report from the Luleå squadron was concerning. Still, it was a matter of pushing on and improvising based on the new circumstances—like the great Saladin would have done, and to an even greater extent, as the Prophet had so successfully done—every time something unexpected happened.

The report stated that the cruise ship in the Luleå squadron had encountered some technical issues and was forced to proceed at reduced speed. The two RoRo ships could not arrive in Luleå ahead of the cruise ship, so they, too, were compelled to slow down. The squadron wouldn't reach Luleå until around 5:15 a.m., an hour and a half behind schedule. By that time, alarms would sound across Sweden. This could mean that the targets in Luleå would have time to organize some defense. In the worst-case scenario, combat-ready soldiers would be on site in the harbor at Southern Harbor or at the unloading docks in Victoria Harbor upon landing at Luleå. But even so, there would probably be a maximum of thirty to forty older men and women from the Swedish Home Guard. They would be armed with automatic rifles or, at best, semi-antique submachine guns, or "k-pist," as the Swedes called them; mere pea shooters compared to modern automatic rifles. A snack for Ahmed's well-trained and battle-hardened elite soldiers. Fighting down their resistance might take an additional fifteen to twenty minutes, he thought.

But nothing would unfold as Ahmed anticipated. And no one could predict the unpleasant surprise awaiting Ahmed's *Holy Warriors* at the landing in Luleå.

The Brotherhood's meticulous analysis of Sweden's defense organization showed that it would take at least forty-eight hours before anything resembling defense kicked in, and by then, it would be too late for the Swedes. Operation Perfect Storm would be launched during the Swedish vacation season when most decision-makers were at their summer homes. Many would be in for a surprise tonight while sleeping in their beds. Tonight, many of Sweden's leading figures would be murdered by Muslim agents, and the killing was taking place at this very moment. Wasn't this how the Prophet had taught *jihad* to behave, perhaps? 'We smile at our enemies while at a disadvantage to strike quickly and mercilessly when the time is ripe.'

The Prophet's infinite wisdom was timeless and applies just as well now as it did fourteen hundred years ago, thought Ahmed. 'Always attack just before dawn when the unbelievers sleep soundly in their beds!' The unsuspecting Swedes had never dared to face the truth head-on, even though deep down, everyone knew what would eventually happen, and now they would pay the price. And the Swedish decision-makers still abroad would remain there out of cowardice. Even if they were brave enough to travel for Sweden's defense, all airports would still be under Ahmed's control.

Ahmed felt they couldn't afford to risk the element of surprise, which was the foundation of the careful planning. Via the radio, he ordered 150 armed *Holy Warriors*, waiting in and around the neighborhoods of the new al-Hakim mosque in Herts Island in Luleå, to initiate the attack on F21—the largest of Sweden's three air convoys—at 3:45 a.m.

At the same time, thirty *Holy Warriors* would attack and detonate the enormous Facebook data buildings, a small bonus that would cripple the Internet in large parts of northern Europe. To secure the landing, the remaining one hundred *Holy Warriors* would discreetly spread around the docks in civilian cars. Forty-five of the *Warriors* were dispersed as reserves in five civilian minibusses with different company names and logos, one each in one of the neighborhoods with exotic names like Mjölkudden, Bergnäset, Bergviken, and Svartöstaden, where they cruised slowly and as discreetly as possible.

All the *Holy Warriors* were dressed in blue overalls, just like factory workers. No one would think they were other than Muslim laborers on their way to and from their shift. Together, they constituted a significant fighting force that could quickly deploy where and when needed.

Ahmed was not one to leave anything to chance. He knew the entrance to Gothenburg harbor in detail, better than most seasoned sailors, just as he knew the city maps better than most residents of the towns Gothenburg, Stockholm, and Luleå. He had also visited the cities multiple times as a tourist to soak up the atmosphere and physically orient himself through the city streets. As the commander of 'Operation Perfect Storm', he needed to make quick decisions. For that, he needed to know the terrain, the street grid, and all the significant buildings, which Ahmed did because Allah had blessed him with a photographic memory. All he needed to do was close his eyes, and he saw the city maps with the street names printed. He didn't read the books line by line but page by page. His eyes took photos and registered everything he needed to know to recall a particular scene instantly.

Ahmed sometimes thought about the scholarship that so radically changed the course of his life. He had dreamed of a future as a researcher in fusion power or astrophysics. At sixteen, he was admitted as a doctoral student at the Mathematics Department at the University of Rabat, where he taught mathematics to students ten years older than he. Then, the Muslim Brotherhood's scholarship offer fell upon him like a gift from Allah. Within a few weeks, he found himself in Alexandria, enrolled in the Arab world's leading military academy. He had free housing, a car with a private driver, and a considerably higher salary than he could have imagined. What could be better than studying and living life in the city of Alexander the Great? It was completely different from his homeland, where he felt he was constantly being watched, like the national celebrity he had involuntarily become. "Morocco's own Einstein," as the newspapers had written. But who wanted to be likened to a Jew, regardless of the scientific discoveries he had made? Didn't the journalists know that the Prophet had stated that the Jews were the lowest of the infidels, pure vermin to be eradicated? Hadn't they absorbed any of the Quran during the many years of mandatory study of the holy book? Ahmed's father had taught him that the entire Arab world was their homeland, and Egypt was still the cultural and intellectual center of the Arabs, even though economic and military power had shifted eastward to the other side of the Red Sea, where the wealthy oil states lay.

Ahmed knew he wouldn't disappoint his benefactors. Year after year, without exception, he graduated at the top of his class without exerting the slightest effort. Now, the day had come for payback. If he succeeded with Operation Perfect Storm, the doors would be open to the highest power in Egypt and the entire Muslim world. Ahmed Ben Barka was visibly and unmistakably a perfect creation of Allah.

But one thing disrupted the image of this brilliant and ideal Arab man. Ahmed was holding a secret he would never tell anyone, which could never be revealed. And if it were shown, it would disappoint his proud parents over their son, the chosen one.

Chapter 3

Landing in Skandia Harbor

July 17, 2032, 3:45 a.m.

Ebba Hansson had seen better night shifts. She was in a terrible mood. Her vacation had been abruptly interrupted in the unpretentious, charming little cottage she had inherited, way out on the point on the western Öckerö island in the Gothenburg archipelago. There, she used to sit and sip on a glass of red wine with her husband while the sun slowly sank into the sea on the horizon. That scenery was magnificent. "Stunningly beautiful!" as her beloved husband, Kalle, always said. The evening before, she had waved goodbye to him and the kids entering her worn-out old Volvo V60, the last generation "gas guzzler."

When Chairman Lindberg called and said there was a situation at work and that she should catch the last ferry to the isle of Varholmen, she could only obey the orders. If Lindberg hadn't checked the timetable, she would have lied to him right to his face, Ebba thought as she sat in front of the computer to see which boats were docked and which were on their way in. It was what it was, and now she had a job to do.

Ebba had been the operational harbor master of Skandia Harbor for a couple of years now. She was looking forward to the day when she would hopefully assume the role of permanent harbor master, which would double her salary. Above all, being in charge seemed to promise a much calmer existence, at least from a distance. But to get there, you had to endure the rocky times and show loyalty. Hopefully, the job was worth pining for. After eleven years in the harbor, Ebba was deeply tired of all the strikes and work slowdowns that never seemed to end. It had been decades since communism had been defeated, but that didn't apply in Gothenburg, especially not in the Skandia Harbor. Here, the old communists still ruled both the union and the workers. "Damn them," she thought as she unconsciously pounded harder on the keyboard, making the keys clatter loudly.

The approaching cruise ship, which strangely enough had registered with the Swedish Maritime Administration only thirty hours before arrival, had been assigned and received mandatory towing assistance in accordance with the standard procedure. With some difficulty, the passenger giant was eventually docked at the pier. But there was no activity on the ship, no people on deck. No gangway was laid. Wholly dead and silent. There was something strange about this Panama-flagged giant sailing under *Hymn of the Seventh Galaxy*. It sounded like Hindu or something, Ebba thought as she continued to search the records intently.

When she checked international records, no ship was registered under the *Hymn of the Seventh Galaxy*. Perhaps the boat had been renovated and renamed? It was not uncommon, but it had never happened before that the name had no registration record during her eleven years in the harbor. Usually, ships of this size have some history or documentation to go on.

Many factors need to function when several thousand passengers are entering the port. But here, there were no waiting buses, no waiting cleaning companies, no food deliveries, no request for refueling. Strange. *Hymn of the Seventh Galaxy* had yet to submit any waste declaration, which had been mandatory for many years. Still, at least Ebba could see that the preliminary advance payment of the harbor fee had been made in the system. However, it was impossible to see if a recognizable company name had deposited the money. It was just one of those things.

Everything about this ship was a mess, and Ebba and her colleagues could be forced to clean it up—as if they needed more work.

"This shipping company, whoever it is, will have to pay for its mistakes," Ebba remarked bitterly, turning to her closest colleague, the young assistant Glenn. "There will be the highest possible penalty fees here, mark my words!"

"They certainly deserve it," Glenn replied shortly. "But now we have new troubles coming up."

He pointed to his screen, where the self-steering harbor cameras focused on a RoRo ship coming in just a few minutes after the cruise ship.

"Okay, what's the problem?" Ebba wondered, feeling the stress begin to rise inside her.

This shift seemed worse than usual. The situation was as far from a typical day at work as possible.

"Check out this vessel with a Georgetown flag," Glenn told his boss. "It seems to be called *Inner Worlds*, by the way. This group of boats all have very strange names."

"It was only reported an hour before the deadline, which looks odd. I can't find it in any of the international systems, and the information they provided to the Maritime Administration seems incorrect. It's supposed to be 29,500 tonnes under mandatory towing assistance, but this ship is MUCH bigger than that!"

"I can tell with my ass that she's at least 100,000 tonnes," Ebba remarked, leaning sideways so she could see Glenn's screen. "Call them up and put me on the line when they answer!"

"Roger that, ma'am," Glenn replied sluggishly, with theatrical calmness, but then hesitated and suddenly exclaimed, "Wait, what now? Alert camera 1 shows another RoRo incoming parallel to the Knipple Isles. She isn't even reported to have arrived, at least not as far as I can see! Let me check the name... hmm... No records exist either!"

"Another ghost ship? I can't believe this! What the HELL is going on HERRRRE?" She rolled her Rs with a typical Gothenburg accent, as Gothenburgers often do when they want to emphasize something.

"Call up the planning unit; I need to speak with them immediately!"

"Bettan is on vacation, so it might be a little tricky," Glenn replied resignedly. Some student from Chalmers University is holding down the fort now, so it's probably not worth it."

Ebba's headset beeped. Now, she was in contact with the captain of the first RoRo ship. After eleven years, Ebba's maritime English was excellent, and she knew exactly how a professional harbor master should speak. This time, she got straight to the point and skipped the otherwise obligatory "Welcome to friendly Gothenburg, at the front side of Sweden."

"Harbor captain, here. You need to register the size of the vessel correctly. Mandatory towing assistance applies here. We'll send out towing assistance immediately. Please confirm."

A few seconds of silence, then an unusually polite and cultivated voice that sounded more like an airline pilot than a sea captain:

"We don't quite understand what could be wrong. We'll sort it out when we dock. Towing assistance confirmed!" The voice was calm and confident, with a sharp accent they couldn't quite identify.

"We have many concerns. Your ship needs to be registered; its name is unknown. What's going on? You haven't paid the harbor fee required to dock."

"Not registered?" The calm voice sounded genuinely surprised.

"It sounds like you have a problem with your data systems. That's happened before. Relax, and we'll resolve this as soon as possible. Of course, the harbor fee should be paid. If something's gone wrong, we'll fix it right away. We'll continue docking."

"Okay, you have my permission to dock even though you've broken the rules. That's it!" Ebba concluded, turning back to Glenn.

She wished she had time to investigate properly, but now her adrenaline was pumping full throttle, and she had no time to think clearly before tackling the next problem.

"Have you called the other RoRo, Glenn?"

"She's not answering. The line is completely dead. But I've seen on the screen via the cameras that her name is *Love & Eternity*—another strange name, by the way—and she's going under a Filipino flag. What do we do now? They can't just dock without answering calls. But she's already on her way in, and they can't exactly turn around now."

"Yeah, what the hell do we do now?" Ebba replied with an elevated tone. "I wish we could send some torpedoes at those bastards!" Ebba felt a growing stress, approaching panic.

"There's something creepy going on here. Look at the cruise ship; no soul is on deck even though they've been there for over ten minutes. Look at the RoRo ships. Nothing adds up. We have THREE unknown ships at the same time, big ships. This is eerie! What should we do, what should we do?" she repeated frantically to herself.

"It looks like a full-on assault," Glenn replied calmly. But I'm sure there's an explanation, you'll see, and they're civilian ships, after all. Should I call 911 and raise the alarm? According to the manual, that's what we're supposed to do in this situation. I just finished the course, part two," he added.

"Yes, Call 911 now! Look, gangways are being set up from the cruise ship! I'll go down there as quickly as possible and speak with them. You hold down the fort here, Glenn! Make sure the police send some cars with sirens, one to each ship. We must show these bandits that we don't play around here!"

Ebba took the three flights down in a few quick leaps and hopped on her electric scooter. She could see the cruise ship about half a mile away. She cruised down the dock, past stacks of containers and equipment, as fast as possible without colliding with vehicles and dockworkers. After a minute and a half, she was there. She parked the scooter in front of the central gangway and began walking up the ramp briskly, but she was suddenly stopped by a civilian-dressed man who stood in her way.

"What can I do for you, madame?"

"I need to speak to the captain. Immediately!"

"From whom may I say?" said the civilian-dressed man a bit coolly and took out his communication radio.

"From the harbor master. Tell him it's critical and urgent!"

The man nodded and began to speak into the radio in what Ebba perceived as Arabic, but she needed clarification. It sounded like when her neighbors from Syria talked to each other. That coarse language that always sounded aggressive – even when they talked about everyday things. Ebba hated listening to them, especially when the man yelled at his wife, which he did often. They were partly why Ebba and her husband decided to move out of that apartment building to a house, for the children's sake, if nothing else.

A couple of long minutes passed. Ebba looked around. From her place on the dock, she could see that the towing assistance was about to complete the docking of the first RoRo ship. It's nice that it's not windy, she thought. They only had three tugs available in the summer season. Fortunately, the docking was going smoothly, and the towing assistance would soon be off to get RoRo number two. If they answered Glenn's call, that is. I wouldn't be surprised if they just docked themselves without assistance. Today, it seemed like anything was possible.

Suddenly, the captain stood before her in an impeccable navy-blue uniform, a white shirt that looked freshly ironed, and a white, superb cap with a gold embroidered anchor on the front. He was very good-looking, Ebba reflected despite her upset state.

At that moment, soldiers in khaki-colored combat uniforms began disembarking via the other gangways. Most seemed to be Arabs, but many were black Africans, and some appeared to be from Central Asia, with straight black hair and slightly slanted eyes. Yet others were obviously from the Far East, perhaps Indonesia or Malaysia, thought Ebba, an experienced world traveler since her teens. There were hundreds of soldiers just pouring out onto the dock. No, there were thousands!

"What the hell is going on here?" Ebba shouted, agitatedly, straight into the captain's face, without bothering to shake the captain's extended hand. "This looks like an invasion!"

The captain appeared completely unruffled, except for raising his left eyebrow slightly to indicate he was attentive and accommodating. It was Ahmed playing the role of the sea captain, and he flashed his most charming smile while holding up his right hand at his hip and waving dismissively and apologetically.

"Ah ha, yes, it's supposed to *look* like an invasion," Ahmed replied. "Otherwise, it wouldn't be realistic! It seems like you're not informed, which surprises me. Really? Have you not received information about the military exercise *Polar War*? It is due to be carried out all over Sweden right now. Soon, you'll see fighter jets coming in at low altitude," Ahmed lied, all to establish credibility and create uncertainty in Ebba.

Ebba couldn't believe her eyes. The embarking soldiers seemed never-ending. They just kept marching, like mechanical dolls, in Santa's workshop on Christmas Eve. The disembarking queue was never-ending. All were in full combat gear, with helmets on their backpacks and automatic rifles slung over their shoulders—Kalashnikovs, as far as she could tell. She recognized the typically curved magazines from numerous war documentaries that her husband always insisted they watch.

She glanced at the RoRo ship, *Inner Worlds*, which had opened its ramp. She saw that the ship was loaded with green-painted military vehicles, which were obviously about to disembark. She felt dizzy and nauseous, wondering if this was all just a strange dream. None of this was happening.

"I don't give a damn about your so-called exercise that I haven't heard a damn thing about! I'm the boss in this port!" Ebba screamed, jabbing her right index finger quite forcefully against the captain's chest. "Order all soldiers to return to the ship immediately! Do it now!"

"I can understand your frustration," Ahmed said calmly and kindly while gently moving Ebba's arm aside. I'm sorry to put you through this, but it seems to be a regrettable communication oversight by my Swedish friends. It's not my fault, you must understand. I suggest you join me onboard and meet Sweden's minister of defense in person, so you'll get all the information you need."

"Is the Swedish minister of defense on board? Really?" Ebba was in shock.

"Yes, absolutely, a very charming and nice man! Plus, you'll get to meet Sweden's Supreme Commander, Daniel Gyllenstierna, and some other leading persons in Sweden's defense staff. They're all sitting with me in the captain's cabin, which serves as the command center throughout the exercise. It will calm you down. You haven't done anything wrong at all! Come, follow me, my friend!"

Ebba glanced to the left at the RoRo ship as she followed Ahmed up the gangway. About twenty military vehicles had already driven onto the quay, with long lines of vehicles waiting their turn—armored cars, tanks, and motorized artillery pieces or anti-aircraft guns. She was sure something serious was going on.

To the right, she saw flashing blue lights quickly approaching them from what appeared to be a small convoy of four police cars. Suddenly, she heard the discharge of automatic gunfire directed at the police cars, which had been shot, and she could see the last blue light extinguish before her eyes.

With horror, she turned to the captain, who now had a silver pistol in his right hand, its barrel pointed straight at her heart.

"I'm sorry. You are such a beautiful blonde woman," Ahmed said calmly, and he pulled the trigger, shooting her straight in the heart.

The small, sharp sound was entirely absorbed by the increasing crescendo of thousands of marching boots, roaring diesel engines, and the squeal of metal against metal as fifty-tonne tanks moved out of the RoRo ships' ramps and onto the quay.

No more bullets were needed. Ahmed blew the gun smoke out of the barrel just as he had seen James Bond do and calmly returned the weapon to his shoulder holster. Then he picked up his communication radio hanging at his hip and pressed the transmit button. Now, his voice was firm, powerful, and commanding.

"Attention, all units, attention! The Muslim swords will soon fall upon the necks of the infidels. The time for revenge and vengeance has come. Let us show the faithless and cowardly Swedish dogs what kind of men we Muslims truly are. Let us all seek martyrdom and earn our place in paradise! In the name of the great Prophet Muhammad: Forward! With God's will, we shall prevail! *Inshallah*!"

Ahmed stood thoughtfully with the communication radio close to his mouth for a few seconds. There was no turning back now. Everything depended on his ability to lead the operation and the morale and determination of the *Holy Warriors*. It felt monumental to make history here and now. Suddenly, he felt invigorated! Finally, action, after three long years of planning. Ahmed's own plan, ninety percent of his own ideas. No, this was not one of the war games they had practiced. This was for real!

He felt exhilarated and confident as he hurried back to the captain's cabin, where his loyal adjutant Hassan had packed his belongings. Hassan always knows exactly what I want and need, Ahmed thought. How would I survive without my Hassan? But the best thing about him is still his brilliant cooking skills. The landing in Gothenburg had gone smoothly. No one could stop them now. Hassan's succinct reports indicated that things were going well in Stockholm, where the Swedish *Holy Warriors* had secured the docks, and the unloading was largely undisturbed. Only a few policemen had been quickly eliminated when they attempted to intervene, unaware of the overpowering force they were facing.

The only thing causing slight concern was the delayed operation in Luleå, but it would probably turn out fine. In the long run, Luleå wasn't a strategic area for Operation Perfect Storm; it was just about quickly taking out two key targets. Then, whatever happened with the territory up there in the north didn't matter much. In almost all the war scenarios they had simulated, the *Holy Warriors* in Luleå were eventually overtaken. They were already on their way to paradise, Ahmed thought, but they didn't know it yet, and before they had the joy of meeting Allah, they had a critical mission to carry out.

The other operations, which collectively involved 127,300 *Holy Warriors* and which he had just given the go-ahead, weren't worth expending energy on. Each of them had their local Muslim leader acting independently according to plans Ahmed had been deeply involved in. He was the only one who knew exactly what would happen in the next few hours. After that, only Allah knew. There were five more masterminds: his right-hand man, Mahmoud, and four leaders in the Brotherhood, who had access to the complete plan. For Ahmed, however, it was just a matter of closing his eyes and looking at all those thousands of pages of text and sketches that his eyes had photographed and stored in his brain's memory.

Attacks against the nine military centers across the country had now commenced, aiming to destroy and paralyze the entire Swedish defense network in one fell swoop. Vital communication centers, both physical and digital, were being taken out. Within an hour, no media would be functioning. Airports, railway stations, and bus terminals would be bombed and shut down. At the same time, 353 leading decision-makers were being murdered in their homes across the country in a simultaneous attack carried out by exactly 706 *Holy Warriors* – two for each person to be eliminated.

Soon, the naive and cowardly Swedes would awaken from their slumber and, to their surprise, find that their secure existence was no longer. They would wake to an ongoing war. Once they had rubbed the sleep from their eyes, they would gather in streets and squares to try to understand what was happening and what to do. That's when the suicide bombers would spring into action, further fueling the chaos and instilling terror into the minds of the Swedes.

In just a few days, they would realize that all resistance was futile and that now and forever, they would kneel before their Muslim masters. But ordinary people who converted and chose to live as good Muslims would be spared and could continue their everyday lives. Christians and Jews – the people of the book – who refused conversion would be forced to live an uncertain existence under special laws that emphasized their subservience to Muslims.

Naturally, they would also have to pay *jizya*, heavy taxes that all non-Muslims must always pay to the ruling Muslims. But only for a transitional period of fifteen to twenty years until no opposition was left and absolute control was achieved.

That's the plan, thought Ahmed, but considering the fierce hatred towards Jews that the *Holy Warriors* harbored, Sweden's twenty thousand Jews would probably feel the whip much more than the Christians. And that was how it should be. According to the Great Prophet, everyone who had read their Quran properly knew that, *aw kayf*. Ahmed glanced at his diamond-faced gold watch, which showed 4:16 a.m.

Chapter 4

Embarking in Port of Stockholm and attacks on selected targets

July 17, 2032, 3:49 a.m.

The docking of the 750-foot-long cruise ship, with the intriguing name *Between Nothingness & Eternity,* was completed at 3:49 a.m. She was now stationed at the accessible quay 2 on the pier in Frihamnen Harbor, where the most significant ships usually docked. There was plenty of space as the pier measured a whopping 1,350 feet.

The Swedish Maritime Administration had received the arrival notification four months earlier, on the same day the harbor fee was paid. No source of funds was specified, but that didn't matter now that the money had been deposited. Everything appeared completely normal, except that a ship named *Between Nothingness & Eternity* was not to be found in the registers.

Värtan Harbor was crowded as the RoRo ship Love Devotion docked close behind the large cruise ship. Considering the dense traffic of the Finnish shipping company Silja Line and its ferries, it was not unusual for large vessels to share space in the larger part of the harbor. The ferries from Finland were quite substantial vessels, although they couldn't compare in size to the large cruise ships. *Love Devotion* was positioned at Pier 5.

Inside Port Control, activity was high as the two large ships arrived almost simultaneously. Some confusion arose as the registry had no record of the ship's names.

"Love Devotion," exclaimed Sune, who was well seasoned and the traffic controller during this night shift. "Yet another quirky name. When I started in the ports, boats had names like *M/S Helsinki* and *M/F Kvarnholmen*, but times have changed," he sighed. "Times certainly have changed, and I am an old man." he lamented. "But I'll be retiring soon!"

Sune had been counting the days to his long-awaited retirement for the last five years. He was tired of this job with its eight-hour-a-day shifts, which he increasingly viewed as a stint in jail. Quite often, he would sneak into the handicapped restroom to take a few sips from his little hipflask to brighten up the monotonous nights. Tonight had been no different. It was no secret; everyone knew what was happening, but no one bothered Sune since he never messed up. He was often quite heavily intoxicated, but he kept his breath fresh by constantly chewing on throat lozenges. Like many other alcoholics, he had "throat issues."

"Leave Sune alone and let him retire with pride and respect," Sunes' boss used to say when his alcohol abuse was mentioned. The job duties ran on autopilot after a whole career in the field. He never needed to think clearly to do his job. He often referred to himself as a drunkard with maintained control, which he used to boast about somewhat self-deprecatingly. It would have been more accurate to call Sune an alcoholic, as his consumption had steadily increased over the past few years. But Sune was not ashamed of it.

"Aha, apparently it's the night of funny names, boss," replied his younger colleague, Anna. "Look, here comes *Birds of Fire*, another RoRo with shipowners who fancy themselves poets. Have you noticed that none of the boats appear in any registry?"

"What are you talking about? Not in any registry?" said Sune with a calm voice. "That doesn't seem right, sweetheart. But as you know, all that matters to me is if the payment is made to our account. The board always wants the funds, and they've always gotten that from me, not that anyone has ever thanked me for it," he sighed, disappointed. "The rest will probably sort itself out in due time," he remarked calmly. "And I'm retiring in less than a month. So, who cares, anyway?"

"Wait a minute!" exclaimed Anna suddenly as she received a news flash on her phone. "Shooting in Skandia Harbor in Gothenburg," she read aloud. "Ten police officers killed. Many foreign military and military vehicles are on the quay. More information is coming shortly. The end of the message was received at 4:12 a.m. This is a bit scary. Are we being invaded now, or what? By whom, then? Thank goodness it's in Gothenburg and not here, at least!"

"Yeah, it almost sounds like it, little Anna, but now you need to call *Birds of Fire* so we can get this docking in order. She'll take Pier 3. Lucky, we weren't full before this lot arrived."

Ten minutes later, the pier was filled with a swarm of soldiers in khaki-colored field uniforms and combat gear. At the same time, both RoRo ships had opened their bow doors, after which hidden vehicles rolled out onto the quays in a steady stream.

"It appears it's not just Gothenburg being invaded!" shouted Anna. "I think I'm going to lose it!"

Sune dug out the hipflask from his briefcase, opened it, and sipped a few hefty swigs in front of his colleague. He looked utterly terrified as he drank from it.

"Let's get out of here, now!" he shouted, rising abruptly from his office chair with the hipflask in a firm grip. "Anna, you got your car with you today, right?"

The two flew down the stairs at a speed that defied their age and ran across the parking lot to Anna's little Tesla.

"Pedal to the metal, Anna. That's an order from your boss!" chuckled Sune, grinning broadly. Finally, there was a bit of drama in his dull and uneventful life. Drunk as he was, he didn't feel the slightest fear—everything was like a Hollywood action movie. The Tesla accelerated almost silently, and the main harbor street quarter mile was covered in seconds. Still, at the ferry terminal, the road was blocked by a hundred or so black-clad individuals wielding assault rifles. Not a situation one dreamed of ending up in. Anna hit the brakes in panic. Would she be raped first before being killed?

"Oh man, now we're screwed," Sune remarked calmly. "Seems like the Arab population of the suburb ghetto of Rinkeby is on the loose, and they seem to have dressed up for a carnival!"

Right in front of the car, a large man with the longest and biggest beard shouted out a couple of orders in Arabic, which were then repeated in Swedish by someone who seemed to be his assistant. Suddenly, the crowd parted while the assistant waved the little Tesla forward energetically. Many soldiers gave thumbs up and raised their Kalashnikovs to the sky. Others laughed loudly and saluted the two Swedes in the car as they passed through the crowd.

Like a soccer team on tour, the soldiers looked happy and confident, mostly young men in their twenties to thirties. A few gave the impression of being upwards of forty years old. Most had beards or were unshaven with thick stubble. Many wore black berets, seemingly doing their best to resemble Che Guevara, while others had black headbands. The scent of revolutionary romanticism was unmistakable. Anna noted that most seemed to come from the Middle East and North Africa, but a group of darker-skinned guys stood in a separate cluster, who – as far as Anna could tell – were Somalis.

Sune rolled down the window and cheerfully waved to the soldiers with outstretched arms. Some held out their palms and slapped them with Sune's in a high-five. Suddenly, it was a victory parade—instead of the funeral procession, it had seemed to be just seconds before.

"Drive, baby, the age of miracles isn't over! I never thought ISIS would be this cool. Maybe a caliphate wouldn't be so bad after all!"

Sune laughed as Anna sped up. They continued the southern route of the harbor, towards Stockholm's northern link in the north part of town, speeding as fast and as far away as possible. Suddenly, the sky lit up, followed by a loud, piercing explosion. They felt the shockwave even though they were inside the car, albeit with the passenger-side window open. "The blast came from the Stockholm Olympic Stadium," Anna thought as she, in hyper-concentrated mode, maneuvered the Tesla sixty miles per hour on the narrow road.

"Well, that was the 'Dorkagon'," said Sune trying to explain his joke. "That blast was right above The Swedish Pentagon for the 'Dorks', or the Swedish National Defense Headquarters as some would call it. This doesn't look good. Maybe we can turn the game around in the second half?" He raised the half-full hipflask and emptied its contents in three hearty gulps, then casually tossed it out the window, a routine he had undoubtedly done many times before.

Suddenly, they saw the road was blocked six hundred feet ahead by thirty to forty soldiers, who appeared to be the same type of black-clad soldiers as at the first barrier. They stood passive and heavily armed. To the left, they could see some soldiers taking cover by the building belonging to the TV stations TV4 and Canal Digital. Two more minor explosions were heard only a few seconds apart. Anna slammed on the brakes and made a U-turn. Full speed ahead again, right onto a bridge over the railroad tracks, left onto the road Tegeluddsvägen, and quickly up to seventy miles per hour. They were almost in the harbor again, just a bit higher up from the water this time. To the left, they could see about fifty military vehicles moving around the port area. Some turned right onto the Southern Harbor road, where Anna had just driven, while others turned left at the ferry terminal onto the road leading towards central Stockholm. Fortunately, they hadn't reached Tegeluddsvägen yet, where Anna's Tesla was racing forward at full throttle.

Soldiers who had just left the cruise ship were boarding buses parked in a long line in the port area. Most parked buses were charter buses with different company names on the sides. More buses kept arriving, mostly regular blue city commuter buses picking up waiting soldiers. As Anna slowed down, she noticed that almost all bus drivers were dark and that most wore berets, caps, or headbands.

Anna turned right onto the minor road of Lindarängsvägen towards the big boulevard, Valhallavägen. Something was happening on the big recreation field in Gärdet, but she wasn't able to see it; she was so focused on driving. She could see thick black smoke rising into the sky from the building of Swedish Television, which was on fire. Along Valhallavägen, several of the Armed Forces buildings were ablaze. Just as they reached the roundabout at the beginning of Valhallavägen and rounded it at a risky speed, the car narrowly missed an explosion just three hundred feet to their right.

"Well, now they've also blown up the pub named Headquarters, too," Sune pointed out. That's where I usually sit and watch soccer in the evenings. What the hell is going on? Can't they tell the difference between a pub and a military headquarters? Where will I hang out now in the evenings when I'm retired?"

When she turned onto the big parade street of Strandvägen, it was almost deserted. In the distance, they saw flashing blue lights from blue-and-yellow police vans and regular police cars forming a roadblock at the bridge of Djurgården. Stopped In front of the roadblock, a small line of cars had formed.

Police officers with automatic rifles had taken cover behind the cars. Some lay on the ground by the canal, their weapons aimed at the Sweden National Television building. Several more officers pressed behind the corner of Narvavägen, running down towards Strandvägen, unaware of the masses of enemy soldiers coming their way. Soon, their blood would be shed in vain.

At the end of Narvavägen, up at the lush roundabout of Karlaplan, Anna could see masses of flashing blue lights, and she devised that it was another hastily set up roadblock. The police have sent out all they have, she thought, but when will the military wake up? And where are the National Task Force and the Home Guard? Sussie Anna wasn't religious, but suddenly she was clasping her sweaty hands under her steering wheel and murmured, "Dear God, please help us!" The police were thorough, shining flashlights into each car. People in the buildings above stood on their balconies, awakened by explosions and blue lights, wondering what was happening.

"Look, one of the radio masts in Nacka is falling," exclaimed the sharp, nasal voice of an elderly woman clad in a burgundy dressing gown, gesturing south towards where Sweden's towering radio masts once stood. "What on earth is going on? Can someone please tell me? And now the other mast is falling, too. Oh dear, what is happening?" The frightened old lady was in tears.

Suddenly, they were let through, and Anna breathed a sigh of relief, glancing at the car clock, which showed 5:01 a.m.

"I think we're in the clear, but the question is, where can we go?" she said, finally turning to Sune who had fallen asleep, snoring softly with his chin against his chest.

Chapter 5

Assassination Attempt on the Chief of Defense

July 17, 2032

When his mobile phone read 3:45 a.m., Mahjabeen ascended the four steps in two strides and firmly pressed his right index finger against the doorbell. He stood on the entrance steps with the railing against his back, less than three feet from the old brown double doors, each with a rounded glass pane covered with white curtains.

The doorbell obediently responded with a loud "ding-dong," echoing in the quiet summer night, disturbed only occasionally by shouts from a drunken party in the neighborhood. Even though he was thirty feet away, Abdikadir could hear the doorbell chime, kneeling against the car parked on the other side of the narrow street. Abdikadir's Kalashnikov was unlocked, the stock resting against his shoulder.

Mahjabeen and Abdikadir were devout Muslims who abhorred alcohol and drunken revelers. Abdikadir thought it would have been more fun just to kick down the party's door and pepper the drunk Swedes, but that wasn't part of their mission in Torekov.

They both knew that the target assigned to them was of the highest distinction—none other than Sweden's Chief of Defense, Daniel Gyllenstierna. They also knew they had been chosen because they were considered top-notch—skilled snipers with nerves of steel, having killed many times before and gotten away with it. They were genuinely proud that they, as being Somalis, had been tasked with eliminating the highest-ranking officer in Sweden's defense forces.

"You don't mess around with us Somalis," they used to say with no exaggeration. Everyone knew their words were valid. Somalis were met with more fear than anyone else because they were known to be particularly "trigger-happy." One word to a Somali, perceived as condescending or ironic, could have dire consequences.

It only took a few minutes to find Gyllenstierna's tax declarations through the Swedish address register online, where the property designations were listed for both his residence and summer house. As a precautionary touch, they searched the Transport Agency's vehicle register, which provided information on Gyllenstierna's two vehicles: an anthracite gray Mercedes GLE 450 AMG and a black BMW X4.

"That's not a bad car collection," said Abdikadir. The old man has some cash! That Mercedes has a V6 engine, you know! Maybe we should rob him and take the car while we're at it?"

"Haha, you're insane, buddy," replied Mahjabeen. "Then we would be next in line."

When Mahjabeen dialed the defense headquarters in Stockholm, the summer stand-in at the switchboard calmly informed him that Gyllenstierna was vacationing at his summer residence in Torekov, where he planned to stay for two weeks. Mahjabeen graciously expressed gratitude in his most charming tone while smiling at Abdikadir. Bingo. It couldn't have been easier.

Two days earlier, the two friends had scouted the modest, whitewashed Skåne-style house at the end of the street Christopher Barfoths gata number fourteen, determining a suitable spot to park the motorcycle they had previously stolen in Halmstad. To avoid suspicion, they had slapped false plates on the Triumph and sprayed the gas tank black because the original yellow tank stood out too prominently.

To seamlessly blend in with the Swedish elite at their summer retreat, they sported helmets and dark visors, giving off the vibe of two bikers enjoying a getaway. Despite the scorching heat, they refused to remove their motorcycle gloves, determined not to be confused for mere burglars scouting the area or kidnappers on the prowl for their next target.

Recently, the Swedes in the area had become increasingly suspicious, especially in Torekov, following the kidnapping of a business executive last summer. It had been Somali kidnappers, so they realized they should downplay their looks in Torekov. They knew who the kidnappers were and who had executed the victim when the ransom was not paid on time. Within their network, they had heard about the incident and that the police had never managed to find the perpetrators.

In a recent article, they found online in the defense force's own newspaper, they learned that Officer Daniel Gyllenstierna took a morning stroll to the bathing jetty in Torekov at half past six every morning during his vacation. This was invaluable information. Gyllenstierna himself was depicted in a photo: freshly bathed, with wet hair and a wide grin, sporting a ratty bathrobe, gray terrycloth, and blue plastic bath shoes.

Among those who frequented the bathing jetty for their morning dips, arriving in a worn-out old robe was considered the epitome of status, hinting at ancient ties to Torekov, robust self-assurance, and, at least during vacations, a carefree attitude toward material things. When he bought the house seventeen years earlier, Gyllenstierna had found the old robe in a closet. It was now in such poor condition that he barely dared to launder it anymore. If Mahjabeen and Abdikadir had their way, they would have dealt with Gyllenstierna on his walk to the bathing jetty. However, their orders were to strike precisely at 3:45 a.m., making a hit on the bathing jetty Plan B if Gyllenstierna failed to appear when they rang the doorbell at the appointed time.

If Gyllenstierna didn't show up by seven o'clock, they would break into the house by smashing one of the large glass panes of the front doors, step inside, and execute him. And they would only leave Torekov once the target was hit. Failure was not an option for this duo. They had never failed before, except for in school, which they both dropped out of in the eighth grade. However, for them, dropping out of school early was hardly a failure. They had other plans. A regular job had no appeal to them. Didn't pay much either. You needed cash, flashy cars, the best weed, and a cool style to impress the right girls.

Mahjabeen pressed the doorbell again, and it chimed for the second time. Nothing happened. Maybe they would have to resort to Plan B. Just as Mahjabeen lifted his foot to descend the stairs, he heard footsteps inside the double doors. The light flickered on, a hand drew back the curtain, and Gyllenstierna's startled face appeared behind the glass.

"Be ready," Mahjabeen hissed softly in Somali. *Diayarisay*!

"Why are you ringing my doorbell in the middle of the night?" Gyllenstierna asked sharply without opening the door.

Through the glass pane, Mahjabeen could see that Gyllenstierna was concealing something in his right hand behind his back, probably a handgun. Mahjabeen didn't have a good answer for Gyllenstierna's question, so instead, he sidestepped and leaped down the stairs smoothly. Abdikadir unleashed a barrage of gunfire, sending Gyllenstierna forcefully backward in a shower of glass shards, disappearing from sight.

"That's enough!" Mahjabeen shouted, raising his arm to stop Abdikadir. He moved back onto the front porch, whipping out his mobile phone to take the pictures the boss required. The glass pane was gone, revealing the lifeless body lying face up, making it easy for Mahjabeen to snap the photos without even entering the house. Then he bounded back down the street, sprinted to the motorcycle, swung his leg over, and fired up the engine. "Hurry up, we've got to go – u*gu dhakhsaha badan!*"

They rounded the corner and gunned it up the main street, where they encountered a group of youngsters who had heard the gunfire and pressed themselves against the wall in fear. As the two killers roared past, Abdikadir whipped out the Kalashnikov and let loose a short burst at the group but missed due to the rapid acceleration.

Soon, they were cruising down county road 115, headed back to the little village of Andersberg outside Halmstad, where they shared an apartment with four other Somali buddies. Abdikadir patted Mahjabeen on the shoulder, leaning in and yelling into his ear, "*Halkaas what ku slight Swede* – There goes the darn Swede nerd, hahaha!"

Abdikadir was practically bursting with joy, while Mahjabeen tried to stay focused on driving as best he could.

"Not a chance he's making it out alive, hahaha! *Waxaan nahay kooxda horyaalka*, we are the champions!"

As they approached the village of Gulbränna, cruising steadily at one hundred miles an hour on the highway, Mahjabeen spotted two police cars ahead of them with their blue lights flashing. He alerted Abdikadir. Normally, they would have swiftly pulled over and ditched the highway, but today was no ordinary day. They knew the war was starting on this very day, and they were about to join their brothers waiting at their mosque in Halmstad, where they would return as heroic Muslims, as *God's Holy Warriors*.

Mahjabeen pulled in between the rear of the police cars so Abdikadir could pepper both officers with gunfire. Then, with a sudden burst of speed, they unleashed shots at the cops leading the way. Abdikadir looked back and saw both police cars veer off the road and crash, one in each direction.

"Hahaha!" He erupted in laughter again. "First time I've taken these cops down, fuck that was cool. *Sebbisch!* I'm almost *giddy*! Hahaha!"

Exiting the highway onto Laholm, they spotted a bus stop where a group of people were waiting. Abdikadir signaled for Mahjabeen to stop beside the little shelter.

"Go check out who's Muslim and pull them aside. I'll handle the rest!"

Mahjabeen hiked up to the bus stop, where he noticed five potential Muslims among the crowd, while the rest seemed like drifters, except for two Gypsy women. After a brief exchange in Arabic and Somali, Mahjabeen separated four others who, without a doubt, were Muslims.

From a distance, Abdikadir observed the fifth person, who appeared to be of Pakistani, Indian, or Bangladeshi descent, hesitating before finally joining the group and stepping aside. Maybe he sensed something was off. Perhaps he caught sight of Abdikadir swapping out the magazine behind the motorcycle earlier.

Abdikadir strode up to the bus stop and shouted "*Allahu Akbar*" in a commanding voice while raising his Kalashnikov. The people waiting stood frozen, staring in terror. None dared to make a move, fearing they'd be shot. Perhaps the only hope of survival was to stand still with their hands raised. Abdikadir hesitated momentarily, then signaled the two Gypsy women to step aside.

"You've done us no harm. But you filthy Swedes has!" he bellowed, mercilessly spraying bullets at the eight people in front of him, emptying the entire magazine.

Approaching the group of Muslims, Abdikadir noticed a young man, initially hesitant, trying to hide behind the others. His face, of olive complexion, had turned ashen.

"Muhammad, Muhammed," the poor young man stammered, pounding his chest repeatedly. "Muhammad, Muhammed," he repeated in despair.

Abdikadir motioned for him to unbuckle his belt and lower his trousers. The young man hesitated, then shook his head vigorously, "No, no, no..." he uttered in what seemed like an attempt to speak English.

Without warning, Mahjabeen lunged from behind, delivering a heavy blow to the young man's head with the barrel of his Yugoslav Army pistol.

The young man collapsed, moaning with both hands on his head.

Abdikadir squatted down, undid the young man's belt, pulled down his trousers and underpants, then pointed at his genitals, shaking his head.

"An unfaithful dog, I knew it," observed Abdikadir, nodding towards his companion. A Christian pig pretending to be a nice Muslim! Damn! Or worse, such a goddamn polytheist!"

Mahjabeen aimed the gun at the man's face and fired a shot that struck the bridge of his nose. The sound of his skull hitting the pavement transformed the area into silence.

"Now, we're headed to the Mosque on Fredsgatan! Peace Street! Freeeedsgaaaataaaan, here we come!" Abdikadir exclaimed.

"*Allahu akbar*! What a glorious day it is!" Mahjabeen cheered.

The war couldn't have started any better.

Chapter 6

Operation Manhunt

July 17, 2032

July 17, 2032, would be a monumental date, charting a new course for this northern country, with its naive and decadent people in dire need of governance and guidance. "A Muslim rule under *Sharia* laws would be beneficial and formative to these blonde, blue-eyed bastards who seem to lack any form of morality," Mahmoud thought to himself as he worked to prepare *Operation Manhunt*. Initially, blood would be shed, but it would be good for the Swedes. They would be eternally grateful once they experienced the joy of living as the Prophet had decreed. Mahmoud felt pride in being one of those who brought the light of the Koran to this cold and godforsaken land.

Mahmoud was unequaled to oversee Operation Manhunt. His excellent organizational skills, manic determination, and lack of empathy made him the first to come to Ahmed's mind when appointing this fierce operation. Yes, Mahmoud was the obvious choice. Moreover, he was Ahmed's right-hand man and successfully executing the operation was pivotal to a swift victory over the Swedes.

Mahmoud had worked out every detail of this assault, whose origin and framework belonged to Ahmed. Ahmed had not changed a single detail in Mahmoud's scheme, which aimed to kill 353 prominent Swedes, all the while the invasion of Gothenburg, Stockholm, and Luleå was underway.

The list of the 353 names was drawn up by Basir Kalpan, who had previously been Minister of Foreign Aid in the Swedish government, then later as a parliamentary representative of the Left Party. Kalpan had been expelled when he was found to have close ties to Muslim extremists. Kalpan's detailed list was later refined and further developed by Karim Musama, who had previously been the leader of SUM, Sweden's Young Muslims, the extremist organization secretly founded by Kalpan.

Kalpan's and Musama's lists were compiled based on the detailed criteria Mahmoud had worked out. The list included politicians, government officials, military personnel, fighter pilots, corporate leaders, cultural personalities, news anchors and presenters, the royal family's closest heirs to the throne, revered sports heroes, and some leading opinion makers.

The idea behind Operation Manhunt was to eliminate all individuals who could possibly emerge as leaders and unify forces for the Swedes. Without trusted leaders, the Swedes' morale and defense capability would quickly and effectively be burst. Just the knowledge that so many prominent and well-known individuals had been murdered would be terrorizing enough.

The goal of Operation Manhunt was to break the stamina of the Swedish resistance before they could organize anything. The massacre would be conducted ruthlessly and without limitations, aiming to crush the Swedes quickly. Ahmed had planned for the war to be won within six to eight weeks, but with some luck, the Swedes would unconditionally surrender after a few weeks. A surrender required some political decisions, but it was doubtful the Swedes could make decisions quickly with their political leaders eliminated. A likely and often discussed scenario was that the fighting would subside from place to place and result in a ceasefire when the Swedes realized they were in a hopeless situation. In practice, this would be a Swedish surrender and treated as such.

At 3:45 a.m. on July 17, hell broke loose in hundreds of places around Sweden and, in some cases, abroad. Mahmoud had appointed two Swedish *Holy Warriors* as executioners for each of the 353 individuals to be eliminated, totaling 706 warriors on a mission. In most cases, it was a straightforward affair that a single warrior could have handled, but there were still significant advantages in having two on each mission. The likelihood of success increased significantly with two individuals, and the reporting became more reliable. The supply of loyal Jihadists was unlimited in carrying out this task.

Everything related to Operation Manhunt was organized in cells, where the warriors did not know other cells existed. Each warrior duo knew they were tasked with eliminating a particular person. Many suspected they were part of a larger unit, but to believe is not the same as knowing, especially if someone were one of SÄPO's infiltrators.

All the targets were surveyed by each pair of warriors, discreetly following them and knowing where to find them in their homes or vacation residences. Passport photos of all targets had been ordered to avoid any mix-ups. The approach was the same everywhere, as the warriors had clear instructions on what to do. They were ordered to dress in regular clothes, specifically jeans and a summer shirt. They were also instructed to be freshly shaved and groomed, giving the targets a false sense of security when the situation arose so they would voluntarily open the door when called upon. Great emphasis was placed on selecting warriors with a generally appealing appearance, while psychopaths and individuals with threatening appearances were screened out.

If the designated target opened the door when called upon, they would be immediately shot in the heart with the Yugoslav Army pistol carried by the *Holy Warrior*. If necessary, multiple shots would be fired at the heart. Then, the face of the lying target would be photographed. Finally, the victim would be shot in each eye. Nothing would be left to chance, as always when Mahmoud was responsible for the planning.

If the target did not open the door but stood at a window to inspect the person knocking on the door, they would be shot with a hail of bullets by the other warrior who was hidden in a suitable location, behind a hedge or similar.

If the target stood behind the door without opening it, asking who it was, the hidden warrior would shoot at the door at chest height with a burst of bullets from their AK-47. Bullets from an assault rifle go straight through any wooden door, except for security doors with a built-in steel plate, which were deemed to be rare. Then, the building would preferably be breached appropriately for photography to be done and to ensure that the target was genuinely dead. If there were no response after the doorbell was rung, the warrior would force open the door or smash a window, enter, and shoot the target inside the residence.

Regardless of circumstances, the deceased would be photographed with a close-up of their face as evidence of a successful operation. Failure to obtain a photo would be considered a failed mission. In cases where family members or neighbors intervened, they would be immediately killed by shots from *Holy Warrior* number two. After ensuring the successful completion of the mission, the warriors would quickly leave the scene in the manner they deemed best, which often meant using mopeds, bicycles in urban areas, and cars or motorcycles in rural areas. In one case, a jet ski was used when the target was at their summer residence on a small island.

Ahmed and the other six command staff officers received a summary of Operation Manhunt's outcome by eleven o'clock on the same day, with Mahmoud delivering the news. They were in the captain's cabin onboard the *Hymn of the Seventh Galaxy*, which remained docked in Skandia Harbor in Gothenburg. Deputy Hassan served them a much-needed lunch while the operation's results were analyzed.

Of the six officers, one, like Mahmoud, was Egyptian, while the other five were from Saudi Arabia, Kuwait, Syria, Jordan, and Chechnya. They were all profoundly devout Sunni Muslims, holding high positions within the Muslim Brotherhood's most secret committee, "The Holy Committee." Its existence was known only to a few. The command staff should have moved to "Suite Belle" at the Hotel Pigalle, situated in the part of the city called Nordstan, which was better located from a security perspective. Still, Ahmed hadn't had time to move because the difficulties in Luleå had kept him busier than expected.

The Hymn of the Seventh Galaxy was a sitting duck for both air and sea attacks, but reports of successful attacks on the airports in Sotenäs,

Ronneby, and Luleå led Ahmed to believe the risk of being attacked was low. In the chaos throughout Sweden, the risk of anyone identifying the target and launching an attack was unlikely. Battles were raging in twenty-eight locations throughout Sweden, so who would have time to take an interest in this cruise ship?

Mahmoud projected a picture with numbers and pedagogically designed tables in different colors on the large screen before them. It would have been enough for Ahmed to know who had yet to be eliminated since he had a handle on every one of the 353 people on the Kalpan list. But since the brain capacity of the others had limitations, they needed a total rundown. Mahmoud tucked the package of honey cakes with sunflower seeds into his breast pocket, swallowed the last bits of the cake, and wiped his mouth with the back of his hand.

"Operation Manhunt has been carried out as planned and with the expected outcome," he began. "I don't think I'm exaggerating when I call the operation an undoubted success, but unfortunately, not quite one hundred percent— I'll get back to the missing percentage shortly. I'll cut to the results since we all have important matters on this historic day. Feel free to interrupt me if you have any questions."

The seven men in the room nodded quietly to Mahmoud, eager to hear the results.

"Out of the 353 targets, 319 have been confirmed dead, resulting in a success rate of over ninety percent, slightly higher than expected. In addition, we have five likely dead but without photo evidence. We have reached over ninety-two percent success rate if we include these five.

"Bravo, the Swedes will never recover from this!" a voice from the small audience said. "A great success, congratulations, Mahmoud. Now, let's hear the details!"

Ali, the Saudi, praised Mahmoud appreciatively as he nibbled on a lamb kebab. Ali, Ahmed, and Mahmoud wielded the most influence in the group.

Mahmoud stepped closer to the screen and pointed with his thick index finger at the tables and numbers, which listed the number of eliminated targets and under what circumstances it had occurred.

- A total of 184 enemies were killed in summer residences, many on sites like Fårö, in Torekov, and scattered places in the Stockholm archipelago, Roslagen, and Skåne.

- Of those, 103 were killed in their homes, about half of them in

Stockholm.

- Twenty-three were killed in hotels or other vacation homes around Sweden.

- Nine were killed abroad.

- Five have been shot but not confirmed dead—lack of photo evidence.

"In a moment, you'll each receive a list where you can study the results for each of the three hundred and fifty-three targets, along with their bios, if you want to amuse yourself. I won't waste your time reviewing the whole list here and now, but I wanted to give you a quick summary," Mahmoud continued.

"Among the 319 eliminated, most belong to the government, including the prime minister, foreign minister, finance minister, and defense minister. Only a few of the less significant ministers remain. Additionally, we have fourteen eliminated state secretaries. In the military, we have confirmed the elimination of the supreme commander and the chief of the Swedish air defense. The chief of the navy may be among the five likely eliminated, but photo confirmation still needs to be provided. There is uncertainty about the correct person being eliminated here."

At this point, Mahmoud could hardly know that the Swedish supreme commander was alive, as a mix-up had occurred, and the Supreme Commander's younger brother had lost his life in his place. By pure chance, the chief of the navy also happened to survive because of a case of mistaken identity, which would later be revealed.

"As for the business sector, the CEOs of Ericsson, Saab, SCA, SKF, and Sandvik, as well as the head of the Confederation of Swedish Enterprise and the two most influential members of the Wallenberg finance family, were all eliminated."

"Good job, Mahmoud. I knew I could count on you as usual," praised Ahmed. "But let's hear about the twenty-nine who escaped and why they managed to do so. We want to know what you meant by the missing percentage before we wrap up this meeting."

Mahmoud happily savored the praise and resumed speaking while his listeners eagerly indulged in pita bread dipped in traditional Bedouin lamb stew, falafel salad, bulgur, and other delicacies.

"Twenty-nine of the targets could not be located, as they had either disappeared without a trace in the days before or, for unknown reasons, were not where they should have been sleeping. We know that at least five of the twenty-nine are on their own or others' private boats and cannot be located. If they return to their regular boat berths, immediate elimination awaits, but we believe that at least one has landed in Denmark, and one is heading towards Finland. Most likely, they will hear about this on the radio by now. We must assume that at least four of these five will get away."

Mahmoud surveyed the audience, visibly pleased with what he had to say before continuing.

"Two of the targets are hiking somewhere in the mountainous regions without being able to be located. A handful are on vacation abroad, where we need more local representation.

Do you have any questions? None? Then, in conclusion, I'll address the missing percentage that we need to be completely satisfied. It concerns the royal family, where the three adult siblings were to be eliminated." He took a deep breath.

"Queen Victoria unfortunately found herself at a charity conference in Kuala Lumpur, protected by an army of Malaysian security guards, impossible to reach. We believe she will stay a few days there, considering Sweden is at war. But we can reach her through our local supporters everywhere in Malaysia, at all levels. Since we have people in the kitchen of the hotel where she is staying, we will attempt poisoning. Ongoing reports will follow."

Mahmoud paused again and took a honey cake from his pocket, which he returned without tasting it. For the first time during the presentation, he looked slightly uncomfortable. He glanced nervously at Ahmed as he continued.

"Prince Carl Philip, the queen's oldest sibling, was found in Saint-Tropez, but he cannot be located. Our operatives lost track of him as the prince's entourage unexpectedly left with the prince's boat around 11 p.m., which was too early for us to act since the operation started at 3:45 a.m. We expect to get him when he returns to his house in Sainte-Maxime unless he gets alerted beforehand. Our people are waiting for the prince at his boat dock and the residence. Princess Madeleine, the youngest of the three royal children, is at a luxury resort in the Polynesian archipelago, specifically on an island called Bora-Bora, where, unfortunately, we don't have any of our warriors on-site."

"Those royals should be skinned alive and boiled in oil. Don't let the prince get away with just a shot; he should be tortured first and set as an example!"

"Hmm, yes, it's not good news about the royals. I feel Prince Carl Philip is as important as the Queen, while Princess Madeleine is less significant," Ahmed remarked.

"In thirty minutes, we will relocate to a new leadership venue, a Pigalle hotel. Armored cars will be waiting at the gangway. Pack your things now and make sure to be there on time!"

Mahmoud thanked everyone as he began to nibble on another honey cake. The eight men concluded the meeting by kneeling, pressing their foreheads against the carpet, and praying for Allah's assistance.

Chapter 7

Assassination attempt on Prince Carl Philip of Sweden

July 17, 2032

The narrow and winding streets that steeply ascended to the top of the hill, where the well-known house of the Bernadotte royal family stands, were not an easy hideaway. Carl Philip's father, Carl XVI Gustaf, the King of Sweden, had inherited the house from his uncle, Prince Bertil, who had no children. Now, the house was jointly owned by the three adult siblings. The higher up the hill one was, the less traffic there was. Half an hour could pass without cars driving by on this dead-end street, where parking was prohibited. Two men sitting for hours in a parked car would inevitably attract attention.

High fences surrounded the grand villas. It was impossible to hide in the gardens, considering the risk of being detected by cameras and alarm systems. Perhaps there were also dogs and security guards with sharp eyes. Not even a consideration. On the way down towards the sea, the two assailants could not help but admire the magnificent view over the Golfe de Saint-Tropez, with the famous party town visible on the other side of the bay. This was a place fit for royalty.

The two assailants decided to park at the foot of the hill, where there was a parking lot with about fifty cars, some shops, and a bustling pizzeria promising the best pizzas in Sainte-Maxime. From their spot, just ten meters from the road to the prince's residence, the two assailants expected to recognize the prince when he arrived. Via their mobile phones, they kept in touch with two other assailants who were monitoring the prince's boat berth in the marina. They suspected that the boat would be driven home by someone other than the prince, as after a night of revelry, it might be more convenient to get home by car, and they turned out to be correct.

At 3:45 a.m., a car appeared. A white BMW SUV Electric slammed on the brakes and turned left onto the driveway right before them. They could see the face of the prince, his characteristic gray beard, and that he had a female passenger who was likely his wife. There was no doubt. They rolled out and positioned themselves two hundred feet behind the BMW. Now, it was just a matter of following the prince's car up the winding journey up to the top of the hill to the moment the prince would turn left onto his driveway and stop while the automatic gate opened. There and then, it would be easy to jump out of the car and spray the BMW's driver's seat with a barrage of bullets. The prince wouldn't stand a chance of getting away.

The journey proceeded slowly uphill, with several intersections where they turned left or right. They followed at a respectable distance. Some road sections were switchbacks, allowing them to occasionally catch sight of the prince's car above them as vehicles met on different levels. The prince seemed to study them for as long as he could each time he had them in his sight. Was he suspicious? They had the feeling that the prince was vigilant and sensed something. Just as the BMW approached the last turnoff at the top of the hill, the prince's car suddenly accelerated and surprisingly continued straight ahead, on the road leading down the other side.

"He's onto us. Catch up to him, and I'll take him out with my AK through the side window!"

The BMW sped off at a breathtaking pace, weaving through curve after curve. They did their best to close in on the vehicle, but no matter how hard they tried, the distance increased with each passing meter.

"Damn, he is speeding like a race car driver!"

Behind the wheel, Massoud was no slouch of a driver himself, an experienced car thief from Le Cannet. He had eluded the French police many times in various luxury cars he used to steal along the Croisette in Cannes. But to his surprise, the Swedish prince was a sharper driver than any of the French cops he had ever outrun. And sharper than himself, he began to realize slowly. He didn't know that the Swedish prince was a successful racing driver with plenty of experience from numerous competitions.

The distance had now widened to nearly three hundred feet, and there was no indication that they could catch up to the prince. "Just keep driving as fast as you can, I'll get them in the next right turn when I have a clear shot," said Massoud's passenger, extending the tip of the AK's barrel through the side window.

They found themselves on a straight stretch, speeding a hundred miles per hour on the one-lane gravel road, where passing wasn't an option. But the prince drove even faster and disappeared in a cloud of dust, out of sight around a left curve. Just before the pursuers reached the curve, a flash emerged from the bushes on the left side of the road.

A herd of wild boars, quite large specimens, suddenly ran themselves in the middle of the road. The collision was brutal. The heavy thuds against the animals' bodies sent the car into a spin, flipping sideways straight ahead through the metal poles that snapped like matchsticks, unable to stop the two-ton vehicle. It continued over the cliff and fell two hundred feet below the small mountain plateau.

The prince had eluded Mahmoud, responsible for Operation Manhunt, and it wouldn't be the last time. Now, Prince Carl Philip was forewarned and harder to eliminate, but Mahmoud and Ahmed could only imagine the decisive role the prince would play just a week later.

Chapter 8

Attack against F21 in Luleå

July 17, 2032, 3:43 a.m.

At 3:43 a.m., the heavy truck barreled at forty miles per hour straight into the locked gates of F21 in Luleå, Sweden's largest airbase. With a deafening crash, the gates were torn from their hinges while the truck continued for five hundred feet, sparks flying from asphalt in an ear-splitting screech.

The attack surprised the two half-asleep rookies in the guard booth. They didn't notice the heavy truck rapidly approaching with its lights off until the dull sound and the rough vibrations of the eight-cylinder sixteen-liter diesel engine was roaring at them at full throttle. When they realized what was happening, the truck was seconds away from the gate, and they had no chance to activate the security barriers before it was too late. One of the soldiers had the ingenuity to press the large red alarm button, setting off alarms blaring across the entire airbase. Simultaneously, all exterior and interior airport lighting flickered to life, including the red siren lights flashing everywhere. The alarm automatically notified the guard force barracks and the emergency services at number 112. The attack occurred two minutes before the scheduled time and marked the very first act of aggression of the Muslim offensive on Sweden.

In the truck's wake followed a convoy of fourteen minibusses and SUVs, transporting 175 *Holy Warriors* through the open gates. The vehicles dispersed across the airport, racing towards hangars and buildings, where they immediately took action. All visible aircraft and helicopters were sprayed with bullets from the warriors' automatic rifles. Hangar doors were blown apart with Swedish-made grenade launchers m/49 Carl-Gustav, after which fire was directed towards the JAS Gripen aircraft that were parked inside the hangars.

It took eighty-five seconds before the guard force came rushing out of their barracks. Almost everyone assumed it was an unusually intense exercise, with harmless explosions and gunfire with blanks, but they would soon realize it was for real. Many were surprised and hadn't even had time to dress properly; buttons were unbuttoned, belts hung loosely, boots were untied, and some lacked helmets. But they were armed with their AK 5 rifles, and their pockets weighed down by five magazines each.

Normally, there would have been two squads, totaling twelve riflemen, to defend the airbase, but there were twice as many on this day. During the handoff, no gap in security was allowed; as a precaution, the outgoing guard always stayed overnight after the incoming guard had arrived. The twenty-four riflemen spread out in a fan formation, dropping to the ground, and immediately began firing bursts of live ammunition at the unknown vehicles and attackers. Within seconds, a dozen of the attackers fell, either fatally wounded or dead as they hit the ground.

When the attackers realized they were under fire, they dropped to the ground and returned fire towards the guard force. Amidst the inferno of whizzing bullets, staying pressed against the ground was crucial. The attackers outnumbered the defenders, which was countered by the fact that the riflemen were significantly better trained. The riflemen's bullets hit their intended targets, while most of the *Holy Warriors'* bullets created long holes in the air, far above the defenders' heads. Fierce resistance wasn't part of the attackers' calculations; they had been informed they would encounter little to no pushback. Now, they found themselves suddenly engaged in a violent gunfight, significantly depleting their ranks before they even realized they were under attack. The tables had turned. The attackers themselves were now the target of a surprising assault.

"All mobile units to Luleå Airport!" shouted the highest-ranking officer of the attackers excitedly into his communication radio. This was directed at the five minibuses circling around different parts of Luleå, each carrying nine warriors.

"Abandon the vehicles outside the gates where two of ours will meet you. Hit the enemy from behind! Hurry up! We're in trouble!"

Meanwhile, in Hangar 3, integrated with the guard force barracks, preparations were underway to get four JAS Gripen aircraft ready for takeoff. Hangar 3 had not yet been attacked by the assailants, who believed it to be an office building. The four JAS aircraft, operating in pairs called flights, were scheduled to take off at 4:30 a.m. for sea-target training flights. Since missile launches constrain the budget, the aircraft would take off unarmed. Per routine, the pilots were already in the hangar to personally check and verify the final steps before being helped into the cockpits. The pilots savored every moment in the air with their fighter jets. Feeling the power of forty thousand vibrating and roaring horsepower behind their backs was a pure and simple love affair between the pilot and their aircraft.

While the firefight raged on with intensity, the gates to Hangar 3 were opened, still shrouded in darkness. Technicians had turned off all lights in the hangar and its vicinity, though the action made little difference as the sun had begun to rise in the northern sky. The two tow vehicles pulled out each plane, their engines idling, and parked them side by side. The pilots throttled up, accelerated, and took off with a deafening roar before the attackers realized what was happening. The two remaining fighter jets, parked side by side in the middle of the hangar, revved up their engines. Technicians had already left the hangar to avoid exposure to the jet blast. The attackers now directed fire toward the hangar's door. The pilots throttled up, swiftly passing through the hangar door, down the runway, lifting off simultaneously.

As they reached an altitude of sixty feet, the left plane suddenly downturned on its side, and as its wing touched the ground, it exploded into a blaze, swallowing a dozen of the attackers. After a few more minutes of combat, the first two attackers' mobile units arrived. The eighteen *Holy Warriors* moved in a bounding march through the open gate, shooting at the reclining defenders from behind while still on the move. Because they were firing from a standing position toward the low-level soldiers, the angle of the shots was effective and deadly. It was devastating for the defenders, who had already lost over half of their men and were running low on ammunition, prompting some to race to the barracks for resupply. Just as the attackers' third mobile unit arrived on the battlefield, the gunfire ceased, with all twenty-four defenders silenced for good.

The attackers could now systematically destroy all aircraft and set fire to buildings and facilities. Of the 45 JAS Gripen E aircraft stationed at F21, forty-two and all six helicopters were damaged. The operation was considered a significant success because almost half of the Swedish Air Force had been neutralized on the ground. However, it had cost the attackers seventy-seven casualties and around a dozen gravely injured.

At the air bases in Sotenäs and Ronneby, all JAS Gripen E aircraft had been destroyed, with minimal losses for the attackers. The Swedish Air Force had been eradicated before it took to the skies. Three JAS Gripen E managed to take off and escape from F21 in Luleå to Kuopio in Finland.

One of the planes turned out to be so damaged by the gunfire that it couldn't be repaired. It was a miracle that the aircraft had made it across the Bay of Bothnia and landed in one piece.

Another facet of the attack on Luleå was the ambushing of the massive Facebook data centers. The unfortunate employees of Facebook's largest facility outside the USA were shot on the spot unless they had managed to hide in the vast server halls. After the bullet parade, the engineer warriors rigged hundreds of pounds of explosives to the building, which were then blown out in a single magnificent blast, causing internet outages across most of the Nordic region.

According to the plan of the Muslim commander Ahmed Ben Barka, F21 satellite bases in the town of Jokkmokk and the village of Vidsel were to be attacked at 3:45 a.m., simultaneously with all other targets. Muslim infiltrators within the Air Force could confirm that there were no JAS Gripen aircraft currently stationed in Jokkmokk, which was corroborated by on-site observers, leading to the cancellation of the attack on the

Jokkmokk satellite base. However, the infiltrators also knew to report that two Gripen aircraft were stationed at the missile base in Vidsel.

At Vidsel, or FMV Vidsel Test Range, as it's known internationally, there were two JAS Gripen E aircraft. They were conducting test firings with the latest radar-homing missile, Meteor X, powered by a variable ramjet engine instead of just a simple rocket like most missiles. At the same time, the gathering of Swedish and European weapons engineers took the opportunity to conduct an unofficial first test with the new cruise missiles, Taurus KEPD 375, from the initial test series.

The Vidsel missile base, Europe's largest and most sophisticated testing area for instrumentation, was the obvious choice for testing Meteor X, a collaborative project between five European countries. The JAS Gripen E would be used as the platform. Military weapons engineers and mathematicians from Germany, France, Italy, and the Netherlands were present on this significant evening to analyze the large amounts of measurement data generated by the tests and their Swedish hosts. The missiles were tracked by high-speed cameras and sensors, second by second, until they hit their targets. Everything was recorded and played repeatedly until the engineers knew everything about the missiles' journey to the targets, which were up to eighty miles away. The variable ramjet engine provided endless possibilities to control the missiles' trajectory, involving wide swings far out in the terrain and rapid ascension before finally diving and hitting the target with a substantial explosion. The weapons engineers were ecstatic, like children on Christmas Eve. Everything worked perfectly! Tonight, the champagne would flow at the mess.

The attack on the missile base in Vidsel would ultimately fail due to misunderstandings in the rushed and overly wordy communication between the leader of the attack group and the Muslim Supreme Commander, Ahmed Ben Barka. When Ahmed informed the leader that the fleet squadron en route to Luleå would arrive approximately an hour and a half behind schedule, the leader of the attack group interpreted it as meaning that the attack on the missile base would commence an hour and a half later than planned.

FMV Vidsel Test Range is situated in pure wilderness, out in the marshlands, approximately thirty miles from the inconspicuous village of Vidsel. The rugged and barren marshlands are completely devoid of buildings, which was precisely why the missile base was established in 1958 for tests of the then state-of-the-art firefighter Saab 35 Draken.

Parking a bus with forty *Holy Warriors* near the missile base on the only road available would risk detection, so the bus departed from Boden, where a sizeable Muslim congregation lived. The driving time from Boden to Vidsel was just under an hour. The alarm triggered during the attack on

F21 in Luleå at 3:43 a.m. automatically triggered an alarm at the missile base in Vidsel, where security barriers were immediately activated. A group of six riflemen guarding the base took position in the bunkers at the security barrier, where two heavy Swedish-made model Ksp 88 machine guns were set up, loaded with long belts of armor-piercing ammunition. The riflemen received information that battles were ongoing at F21 in Luleå and that they should be ready for combat, as the enemy could appear at any moment. The situation was described as extremely serious. After an hour, they received a report that an enemy bus was approaching and that any trespassers should be eliminated.

It was a beautiful summer day, completely calm. The only sound the riflemen could hear as they took position and lay waiting in tense silence was the buzzing of wild bees busy sucking nectar and pollinating the flowers of the marsh.

"It looks like it's going to be a good cloudberry year," thought the twenty-four-year-old second lieutenant who led the group. As he swept his gaze over the red-yellow-white cloudberry plants that would soon ripen and transform into coveted gold on the restaurant plates. He loved being out in mother nature, he thought to himself. Just a few feet from the bunker, the lieutenant had observed very fresh droppings from one of the brown bears active in the area. Most likely, the bear had been drawn there to feast on the remains of the moose carcass he had seen nearby. Decent antlers, a fourteen-pointer, the kind any German tourist would be overjoyed to find. Then, his thoughts returned to the present situation he found himself in. Soon, he would lead his group into battle – for real – and it felt surreal. This was not what he had imagined when he decided to join the military at seventeen.

After over an hour of tense waiting, the rumble of rubber tires rolling on the gravel road suddenly broke the silence. However, no engine noise could be heard from the electric bus. The bus was not visible, but the defenders could hear it approaching the small hill that concealed it from their eyes, right where the sparse and stunted pine forest transitioned into open marshland.

"When I fire the first shot, you deliver the second fire with the machine guns," shouted the young lieutenant in a tense, slightly shrill voice. Cover the entire bus, back and forth!" To be safe, he motioned the sweeps with his AK5 rifle. But not until I shoot, understood? The rest of you hold your fire and cover us if needed!"

They spotted the bus with the *Holy Warriors* on the top of the small hill, almost quarter of a mile ahead of them. When the bus got closer, the lieutenant squeezed the trigger and fired a short burst of bullets at the driver's side. His round had barely finished before the machine guns rattled to life, with the triggers tightly squeezed by fierce shooters with clenched teeth. The bus was showered with a rain of heavy-caliber ammunition, firing at a rate of over one shot per second from each side diagonally to its front. The bus quickly veered left at the lieutenant's first burst, which pierced the driver's chest and neck, and came to a slow stop on a steep incline with the wheels on the bus's right side in the shallow ditch. The relentless and deadly shots of the machine guns continued for a few minutes. The heavy ammunition pierced right through the bus, massacring all of its passengers in a merciless bloodbath without the slightest chance of escape. The few who managed to reach the exit door were shot down by the other riflemen from their position beside the road.

"Cease fire!" shouted the lieutenant. "Cease fire!"

Suddenly, it was quiet again. The riflemen remained in position for a minute to observe and be prepared if they encountered any shots back at them. The only sound was the whispering of blood flowing from the bus's doors, forming small red waterfalls that dripped to the ground where the red rivulets merged, growing into a bubbling stream of blood flowing in the ditch.

The lieutenant was the first to reach the bus. He approached the heavily damaged vehicle through the door by the driver's seat. The sight was horrific. Hundreds of armor-piercing bullets had been fired, disfiguring all human life inside. The lieutenant waded through blood flowing in a stream, his boots stepping on torn bodies and fragments of bones, brain matter, fingers, eyes, and intestines. Those who were hit in the face had parts of their heads blown off.

A nauseating smell of blood and human excrement made him rush out of the bus, where vomit sprayed from his nose and mouth. It was an unexpected reaction for him, the hunter, who had believed himself to be immune after gutting and dismembering many different slain animals throughout his life. But this was entirely different.

He caught his breath, stood upright, and said with a pale face, "Good job, men. But, next time, we might want to save a bit on the ammunition. This bloodbath was a bit overkill."

"Good thing we're not undertakers in Älvsbyn." joked the group's leading humorist, trying to lighten the atmosphere.

No one laughed.

Chapter 9

Embarking in Luleå

July 17, 2032, 5:15 a.m.

The handful of cruise ships that visit Luleå every summer usually dock at the quay of Svartö, a polluted former ore harbor in the middle of an industrial area. However, the seven-hundred-foot ship *Apocalypse* was granted special permission to dock at the South Harbor, a cleaner quay right next to the city center, just a thousand feet from the main street.

The reason for the harbor boards' good nature towards the *Apocalypse* was that the cruise ship's passengers were believed to consist of hundreds of wealthy and money-spending Arabs – not thousands of soldiers waiting to invade Luleå. Southern Harbor was clean, tidy, and devoid of people, which the ship's command noted with satisfaction. Suddenly, the embarkation of the 3,600 soldiers was in full swing. They left the boat in long rows and sat down to take a break on the quay. The soldiers marveled that it was already full daylight and pleasantly warm. Apparently, they were not as far north as they thought. Most soldiers thought it was dark and cold up at the North Pole, so this weather was an unexpected welcome surprise.

Icebergs hadn't been spotted, so they must be somewhere else. Hopefully, they will know their whereabouts after the seventeen-day journey. They had all sworn to serve Allah through the *holy war of jihad*, and many of them looked forward to martyrdom. In paradise, seventy-two virgins awaited each martyr, and a harem for pleasure awaited.

Around South Harbor, about a hundred local *Holy Warriors* lingered in various vehicles, awaiting orders to take action in case there were defenders. But there had not been any resistance so far. No Swedish defense in sight, despite the alarm about the invasion going out an hour and a half ago.

The Swedish Home Guard had managed to deploy twenty-three lightly armed men, women, and young teens around Luleå Airport, which the Muslims held after they defeated the Swedish guard force in intense firefighting. With their inadequate weaponry, the Swedish Guard soldiers could only wait and hope that military resources were on the way. Meanwhile, in the confusion of the early morning, no one had suggested defending Luleå's ports, despite reports that both Stockholm and Gothenburg had been invaded from the sea.

Many who should have read the reports and could have acted were still asleep or just pouring a cup of morning coffee, only beginning to realize something was seriously wrong. As they sat down to watch the morning news, they found the TV screen remaining black and silent. They then felt a growing sense of unease as they discovered that the internet and their phones were not working.

The last few minutes of the journey into the Southern Harbor allowed everyone on the *Apocalypse* to witness the spectacle at Luleå Airport. Buildings were on fire, and thick smoke rose towards the blue sky. Sporadic gunfire could be heard clearly. At a distance past the city center, a large plume of smoke rose from the location of the Facebook buildings. The smell of smoke irritated their noses as they began to organize their embarkment into groups on the landing.

From their position in Southern Harbor, the attackers could see the first vehicles starting to leave their ship on the RoRo ramp in Victoria Harbor. Around Victoria Harbor, about fifty assigned *Holy Warriors* were hiding in their hideouts, waiting to act, but there were no defenders to fight there either. From the captain's cabin on the *Apocalypse*, the five-member operations team could observe the developments, or rather, the lack of events,

"They say war isn't a picnic," said the operations leader, an experienced colonel from Jordan of Bedouin descent. "But this is nothing but a picnic, hahaha! Look at our guys on the quay; how cozy they are!" Just as the colonel spoke, the situation changed dramatically as they heard the roar of passing fighter jets.

"What's this? All Swedish planes are supposed to be eliminated. Where are these coming from?"

The operations leader couldn't imagine that the forty *Holy Warriors* assigned to attack the robot base in Vidsel had failed. They had failed to such an extent that they didn't even have time to send a message before being massacred by machine gun fire.

The entire operations team rushed to the row of windows on the starboard side, from where they could see two JAS planes turning wide over the bays and returning in their direction. Suddenly, the team panicked, storming out of the captain's cabin and down the stairs to leave the ship before it was too late. They didn't get far.

It was a well-coordinated pair of two JAS planes that gained an overview of the situation by making a wide turn over the harbor area and the inner archipelago before deciding on their attack strategy. This time, they had to do it without ground control, managing their own air traffic control.

"It's the same as in Stockholm and Gothenburg, as we were briefed," said Lindroth, the lead pilot to his relatively new wingman, Lännholm. "The passenger ship in the Southern Harbor is offloading soldiers, and there are two RoRo ships with vehicles. The first one is unloading in Victoria Harbor."

"Are you sure they're not our own guys?" asked Lännholm.

"Yes. I saw the military vehicles. There are no Swedish ID marks at all. They are all a much lighter color, the kind you see on TV from the desert wars."

"OK."

"The second boat is coming in through the strait of Malmporten out at Klubbviken," Lindroth continued with his slow Lappish accent. "We're taking all three. We have four missiles with us, Thank God."

"Did you see the rubber boats inside the pier? What are they up to?" Lindroth continued. "Packed with soldiers."

"I didn't see any rubber boats," replied Lännholm.

"You didn't? But you saw what those bastards did to our workplace?"

"Yes, I did. They will pay for this, believe me."

The only ammunition they had was two Meteor X missiles on each plane, which was all that was available in Vidsel as the test firings were coming to an end. Additionally, they had automatic cannons, though they were only loaded with twenty percent ammunition, as usual during exercises. Before takeoff, the rate of fire had been changed from exercise mode to combat mode, which enabled firing five times faster.

Lindroth seemed to take pride in speaking slowly but always with good audibility. As calm as a cucumber, no matter the situation. Like those Americans from the deep south he'd seen on TV, who seemed nonchalantly half-asleep while extinguishing lives by firing drones from the other side of the earth. Despite his passive tone, his perceptiveness was lightning-fast. Like all combat pilots, he had an exceptionally good ability to keep track of many things simultaneously, with simultaneous processing skills of the highest caliber.

"I'll take the passenger ship with two hits," said Lindroth. "It's big, one won't be enough. You take the boat in Victoria Harbor with one hit, then go out and take the other. Okay?"

"Understood! I'll take the one in Victoria Harbor, then the one at Klubbviken."

"Make sure you target the right one at Klubbviken," Lindroth continued. There's another cargo ship behind it, so the one closest to the dock is the target."

"Confirmed. I'll take the one closest."

"Then we empty the load of ammunition. I'll take the Southern Harbor and the rubber boats. You take Victoria Harbor. Aim for the vehicles, not the boat."

"Understood. I'll target the vehicles in Victoria Harbor with the cannon."

"Make a turn before you attack and fly from the city towards the water so you won't shoot towards the city."

"Ten-four. I'll attack from within the city."

"Seeing what Meteor X can do in real combat will be interesting. Here we go!"

Half a minute later, the two fighter jets thundered towards Luleå at a speed of almost a thousand knots, formed in a flank-right formation with the wingman forty-five degrees aft, to the right. Just as they passed above their old workplace burning, Air Base F21, the planes split apart to fire the missiles just seconds later.

Lindroth's missiles hit *Apocalypse* with two sharp explosions slightly above the railing, the first closer to the stern, the second closer to the bow, causing maximum damage. Large parts of the superstructure were blown away, and *Apocalypse* was instantly transformed into a blazing inferno. Next, the RoRo ship in Victoria Harbor suffered the same fate, a direct hit by the Meteor X missile launched by Lindroth's wingman, Lännholm.

Lindroth banked left, tracing a wide circle of condensation trails, to return for another attack along the wharf and over the rubber boats. As he completed the circle, he saw the explosion from his wingman's second Meteor X, hitting its target by the bay of Klubbviken, destined to send the RoRo ship to the bottom of the sea within minutes.

Approaching the jetty, Lindroth noticed that the rubber boats, six in number, had already dispersed and were heading away from Southern Harbor. On the ground, he saw scores of dead soldiers, and he could see many others desperately seeking cover or fleeing as fast as they could. He pressed the button, causing the plane's German-made Mauser cannon to unleash a barrage of twenty-seven-millimeter caliber grenades at a rate of twenty-eight rounds per second. He hit the last two rubber boats before finishing off the soldiers on the wharf with automatic fire as long as the ammunition lasted.

Lindroth made one final pass to photograph the scene. The devastating firepower of the Mauser cannon had taken out numerous soldiers. He estimated the number of scattered bodies to be around a hundred. At the same time, he could see his wingman emptying his cannon on the military vehicles in Victoria Harbor, and he observed that most of the visible vehicles were knocked out by the bursts of fire raining down from the sky. The vehicles were sprayed with hundreds of mini grenades within seconds. None of the vehicles will survive that firestorm, Lindroth thought.

"Fantastic job Lännholm! Remember to take pictures of your targets—or what's left of them, hehehe. See you in Kuopio! It will be a few cocktails with our Finnish pilot friends tonight," Lindroth exclaimed.

"Or maybe a couple of bottles of Koskenkorva vodka. This day has been hell," Lännholm concluded.

"Flying fighter jets might give you a high, but there is nothing like firing live rounds at real people", Lindroth thought as he banked a wide turn to the southeast. He let out a big exhale, slowly feeling his pulse return to normal.

Chapter 10

RIB Boats going to A9

July 17, 2032, 9 a.m.

When Rune woke up as usual at five o'clock and pulled up the blinds, he saw smoke rising from air flotilla F21, where he had been commander for a few years in the 1980s.

What's going on? He hadn't heard any explosions. His triple-glazed windows were too well soundproofed, and his hearing wasn't what it used to be. He had vivid dreams of war and battles the night before, and it had been years since he remembered any of his dreams. Did it mean something?

Despite his ninety-four years, Rune Larsson was still in good shape and as active as a seventy-five-year-old. But Rune wasn't just average. Rune was a legendary fighter pilot, sometimes compared to the famous American test pilot Chuck Yeager. Putting his life on the line, Rune worked as a test pilot developing Saab's fighter jets, the Draken and the Viggen. Of course, Rune had also flown Saab's classic planes Tunnan and Lansen from the early era of jet propulsion, but that had been for fun. Due to his age, Rune wasn't allowed to fly anymore. Chuck Yeager and Rune became good friends when Chuck visited Saab to fly the Draken under Rune's supervision. Chuck's insights and comments were an important contribution to further developing the Draken and the Viggen aircraft.

From his living room window, at the top story of Residensgatan 6, the long-retired air force colonel could observe the activity in the Southern Harbor. Rune was puzzled by what he saw. Large numbers of what appeared to be foreign soldiers disembarking. Neither their uniforms nor their appearance suggested they were Swedes. Six RIB boats, vessels with fiberglass-reinforced hulls and rubber pontoons carrying soldiers, were being prepared to depart. Who were these soldiers, and where were they going?

Suddenly, the two JAS planes sweeping over the harbor caught his attention. How wonderful it would be to fly these high-tech marvels, he thought. He couldn't even dream of their performance and technology back in his days—pure science fiction. Computers and a bunch of systems control everything nowadays, he thought. It differs from my time when it was about the pilot's skill. It might have been more fun back then when the pilot wasn't a slave to the controls, he thought.

With growing concern, Rune observed a sudden increase in activity on the dock immediately after the JAS planes flew by. Everyone began moving and running, and congestion formed around the gangways as people tried to disembark. Officers shouted orders and pointed their arms in directions.

Suddenly, the entire house shook from a powerful detonation. He could feel the floor vibrating under his feet as he watched the large cruise ship shudder and transform into a sea of flames. It engulfed the fleeing passengers who hadn't yet made it off the boat. Those were my boys, Rune thought, referring to the pilots who had fired the missiles. Rune realized what he was seeing was indeed a battle. But if Sweden was at war, who were we fighting? And why?

Rune watched the six RIB boats, which were rapidly trying to leave, as the dock suddenly shook with gunfire from the JAS pilot Lindroth's automatic cannon. The last two RIB boats, which hadn't gotten out yet, were hit while their passengers, dead and alive, were thrown into the water. Those still alive were quickly dragged beneath the surface, weighed down by combat gear, automatic rifles, hand grenades, and loaded magazines. Suddenly, Rune realized the targets of the four remaining RIB boats. It could only be the military regiment A9 in Boden, where all Swedish artillery was gathered in one place. He had to sound the alarm!

As quickly as his old legs could carry him, he hurried into the hallway and lifted his old phone, the design classic model Cobra. Rune had never bothered with a smartphone; his fingers were too thick and clumsy. And even if his fingers had worked as before, the numbers and letters on the screen would have been far too small for his ninety-four-year-old eyes.

He could still handle the keypad on that old Cobra telephone, as he dialed 112 as quickly as possible. Busy signal. He stood perplexed, with the quirky-designed Cobra in his right hand and his left index finger hovering over the keypad on the phone's underside. Where should he call? He still knew the number for F21 by heart, even though it had been nearly forty years since he retired. He dialed the number—but the line was dead.

Then he remembered Hugo, the hunting leader for the moose hunting team in Unbyn, ten miles up the river, halfway to Boden, where A9 was located. The RIB boats would pass there in approximately half an hour. It had been eight years since Rune's last moose hunt, but the list of numbers for the hunting team was still there, taped on the top of the telephone table. He dialed the number for the good old Hugo, who still dropped by with a box of moose meat every fall.

"Hi, it's Rune. This is an emergency! It's urgent and very important. Please listen to me."

Unconsciously, Rune had switched to his old, commanding military voice, which Hugo had never heard Rune use before.

"Rune! I'm here, and I'm all ears," Hugo replied.

"Sweden is under attack. The battle is already raging on the dock in Southern Harbor outside my window. Four RIB boats with soldiers took off the river to attack A9. You must round up the hunting team and try to stop those boats when they pass!"

"Damn, my boy just came home from his shift and said it looked like there was fighting at F21, but he thought it might be an exercise!"

"You only have twenty to thirty minutes. Go now and get as many as you can," said Rune as he replaced the Cobra back on the telephone table.

Thoughts raced through Hugo's mind as he tried to think clearly and consider the options available. He would do his duty as an old reservist if Sweden were at war.

At first, he thought they should gather at the ferry landing in the village of Avan to use the ferry as a platform and partially block the fairway, but he realized there was not enough time. After a few more seconds of consideration, he made three short calls to his most skilled hunting buddies, creating a phone chain. It was early Saturday morning, and almost everyone was at home.

"It's the real deal. There is no time for questions. We're at war. Grab your rifles and several magazines and get down to Brinjan by the river as soon as possible. We all need to be there within fifteen minutes!"

Hugo and his son dashed across the yard with their hunting rifles and two magazines stuffed in their jacket pockets. They jumped into Hugo's dented old Volvo and hit the gas, racing the short distance to the river. When the road ended, they jumped out of the car and ran the short distance to the beach, stopping and scanning downstream toward Luleå. No boats in sight. Hugo glanced at his wristwatch and noted that it had only been twelve minutes since Rune had called. Pray the others make it in time, he thought as he loaded the magazines with four rounds each.

They loaded one shot each into the barrels of their rifles, allowing for five shots before they had to change magazines, which took a couple of seconds. After nine relatively quick shots, it would take twenty seconds to load a new magazine with four shots, and by then, the boats would likely be gone. Hugo and his son pushed their fishing boat into the water together and started the old ten-horsepower motor, which idled smoothly. They usually used the boat for duck and goose hunting, but this time, they had different targets in mind.

Soon, more hunters arrived, full of wonder and questions.

"What's going on? Is this a war, or have you gone mad, Hugo?"

Hugo looked at his watch and realized it had been eighteen minutes since he received Rune's call. There were only seven rifles, including his own. He had hoped for a few more.

"You guys get in the boat and lay low towards the other side," Hugo commanded, pointing with his whole hand at two of the hunters and then at his son, who was used to operating the boat.

"That way, the enemy boats will keep close to this side of the river, where the rest of us are hidden," Hugo continued. "When they approach, you move the boat slowly towards us so the enemies will be forced closer. Those of you in the boat concentrated fire on the first boat, and we shooters on the shore will take the second. I don't think we'll have time for more. Aim for the driver. And keep track of your shooting directions so we don't hit each other, but you're used to that!"

Hugo gave the boat with the three hunters a shove, then stood still for a couple of seconds, watching it float away towards the other side of the river. After that, he took a few steps up the shore and settled into the bushes to find a good support for his rifle.

After ten minutes of waiting, they wondered if this was a false alarm. Two more hunters arrived, bringing the number of rifles to nine. They hadn't brought any communication radios in their hurry, so they could not talk to the trio out in the boat, slowly cruising back and forth to avoid being carried away by the current.

Suddenly, Hugo's son waved frantically with his right hand before disappearing under the railing.

"Get ready; here they come!" Hugo shouted.

They were ten miles upstream, where the river narrowed to a width of a couple of three hundred feet. Further down at the mouth, the river resembled a calm bay. They had chosen a good spot to attack the boats, Hugo thought, as the boats slowly came into view for the hunters hunkered down in the bushes.

Four RIB boats were in a row, a hundred and fifty feet between each. Hugo estimated that the heavily loaded boats were moving at about twenty-five knots. Not an easy target for amateur hunters with hunting rifles, especially for those shooting from the boat, Hugo thought.

The driver of the first RIB boat, who was leading the operation, seemed to know the route well. As expected, he saw the river narrow. The boats hugged close to the right bank, having planned to choose the right side when passing the low-lying little island in the middle of the river.

As they passed the island, he spotted a small, open, white recreational craft with a lone driver in the middle of their path. A recreational fisherman, he thought and adjusted their course slightly towards the left bank where there was more space to pass. Just as he adjusted course, annoyingly, the recreational craft started moving towards the left bank, and now it would require quite a sharp turn to pass to the right of the recreational craft. So, he decided to stick with the course to the left of the boat. He thought there should still be enough room for the last boat. In the worst-case scenario, it'll just have to stay to the right of the recreational craft, no problem.

When they were about three hundred feet from the recreational craft, he saw the boatman lying down, while he noticed other movements suggesting more people were in the boat. Before he could think more, bullets started whizzing around them, and two of the soldiers in his boat collapsed while the others threw themselves down, seeking cover as the boat continued to rush forward.

They were now almost even with the recreational craft, and he saw one of the soldiers in front of him get hit in the head, which exploded in a cascade of blood and brain matter, splattering over his face and temporarily obscuring his vision.

He had passed the boat, and he hastily wiped his face and spat out bone splinters from his comrade's skull while warm brain matter dribbled from the side of his face. In shock, he slowed down and turned backward to see what was happening. He saw the boat behind them veer towards the left bank at full speed. It was out of control, and the driver slumped over the steering wheel.

At the same time, the third RIB boat steered toward the white recreational craft, which was peppered with bullets from automatic carbines, before the RIB turned away and continued forward.

The fourth and last boat continued straight ahead without being shot at.

The last thing the boat commander saw of the boat closest to them was that it was hitting the shore at high speed, rolling over into bushes where it stopped. Civilians with rifles emerged from the bushes and began shooting at his men, who had been thrown out of the boat and were now scattered on the beach and in the bushes.

The boat commander decided to continue forward without engaging in combat with the armed civilians on the beach. He signaled for the three dead soldiers in his boat to be thrown overboard.

On the beach, two surviving enemy soldiers were captured. Paralyzed by their injuries, they lay on the beach awaiting the mercy shot that never came. One appeared to be Arab, while the other had a darker complexion. When addressed in English, they responded with headshakes.

"I think they're those damn Muslims," said Alf, who was Hugo's assistant during hunts. "Annika Lundgren is married to one of those bastards. Let's bring them in and see if they can talk to each other!"

The shot-up and half-sunken fishing boat drifted slowly downstream on the river. They all knew there was no hope for the three in the boat's survival. The six men watched the drifting wreck in complete silence. No one dared to meet Hugo's gaze.

"My little boy was only nineteen," Hugo muttered almost inaudibly, sitting on the bank, his face buried in his hands. "Why didn't I drive the boat myself?" he shouted. "Why didn't I? I should have realized it was the most dangerous place to be!"

Hugo stood up, wiping the tears with his fingertips, and again assumed the hunt leader and reservist role. "There is no time to mourn now. You two take care of the prisoners," he said, pointing his whole hand at two hunters. Alf, please retrieve the boat so our boys can have a decent burial. The rest of us are heading to the power plant. The boats will dead end there. We need to keep killing these bastards," Hugo concluded, striding quickly toward the car.

Within half an hour, the war had shattered Hugo's life. The war had become a highly personal matter.

A few minutes later, they turned and abandoned the narrow asphalt road along the river's south side, speeding onto Bodfors Road. They took the back roads on the last stretch to the Boden Power Station. They had to hope the enemy had yet to have proper surveillance. Hugo stopped at the forest's edge to avoid revealing their presence and turned the car around in case they needed to leave in a hurry.

They jogged the distance to the power plant and then crouched to minimize their visibility. A few feet from the shore, they took cover in some brush. The river was only two hundred feet wide at the power station, and the three moored RIB boats were on the opposite shore.

Two soldiers stood up on the bank among the birch trees. Further up the road, they could see the other soldiers climbing onto the flatbeds of two large trucks, which would take them the remaining mile to Artillery Regiment A9, where all of Sweden's artillery was gathered.

On the other side of the road, which ran on the dam wall of the power plant, half a dozen soldiers dressed in black overalls were standing. They had mounted a machine gun in the middle of the road, effectively blocking the crossing.

"Heden Bridge is probably guarded, too," Hugo whispered to his two buddies. "We won't make it to the other side, so we'll have to do our best from here."

"You take the guard on the right and the one on the left," he continued, pointing to his two comrades.

"I'll shoot at the guys by the machine gun, and you both do the same once you've taken out the guards. If we get the chance, we'll shoot up the boats, but if they manage to get the machine gun going, we run for the car and get out. We're more useful alive than dead. I'll count. On three, we shoot together. Okay?"

The three hunters settled in to find a good foundation on the ground. The distance to the guards was barely three hundred feet, almost impossible to miss if they had a sound footing. They barely breathed as they carefully aimed their rifles, ensuring the targets were in their scope crosshairs.

Hugo counted, and the shots rang out simultaneously. The two boat guards, along with the Jihadist nearest to the machine gun, were immediately killed. Their chests were pierced by bullets of 30.06 caliber, causing exit wounds as large as egg yolks on the victims' backs.

Moose rifles are designed to take down much more prominent and sturdier creatures than humans. A shot to the torso or head means instant death. A shot to an arm or a leg results in extreme bleeding, which leads to death within a couple of minutes.

Hugo managed to fire off a second shot, hitting another one of the soldiers manning the machine gun before the others could jump down onto the asphalt. The hunters continued to shoot at them, but the position wasn't ideal, as they were several feet below the level of the dam wall. They saw the machine gun pivot towards them. Luckily, before it started firing, they had raced through the thicket, jumped into the car, and sped away back to the village of Unbyn.

Chapter 11

The attack on A9

July 17, 2032

The attackers' plan was to stage a surprise assault on regiment A9 in Boden. One hundred and fifty local *Holy Warriors* had discreetly gathered at the Al-Masjid Mosque by the lake Bodträsket the day before.

The idea was to transport the *Holy Warriors* in four buses via Hedenbro Way directly to A9. There, they would launch their attack simultaneously with their fellow elite soldiers, who were due to arrive by RIB boats from Luleå.

However, the attackers' plan did not work out as intended. The JAS Gripen fighter's automatic cannon shot down two of the six RIB boats as they left the Southern Harbor in Luleå. Gunfire from the elk hunting team in the village of Unbyn halted another RIB boat midway. Just over half of the force, comprising thirty elite soldiers, made it to the power station in Boden. Even more disappointing was the lost element of surprise. When the thirty Muslim elite soldiers left the RIB boats and boarded the two trucks at Boden's power station, four and a half hours had passed since they initiated the attack on F21. The delayed and unsuccessful landing in Luleå gave the locals in Boden time to launch a defense. The trucks transporting the elite soldiers along the path of Åberg came under intense fire from soldiers of the Home Guard's Norrbotten Battalion. They had taken up positions at the intersection of the path of Åberg and Svea Road, equipped with AK-4 rifles, KSP-58 machine guns, M48 grenade launchers, and anti-tank artillery.

The attackers were fortunate in that some defenders revealed themselves too quickly, allowing them to retreat and get out of sight without being hit. But they barely had time to stop before they were subjected to gunfire from behind, where more Home Guard soldiers suddenly appeared on the road. The Muslim elite soldiers quickly abandoned their trucks and sought refuge in the small, forested area west of the little stream of Bodån. Around a thousand feet into the woods, they found a trench that provided shelter from enemy fire. Unfortunately, they were trapped there, surrounded by the river of Luleå, Bodån, and a hostile battalion. There was no turning back; by now, the Home Guard soldiers controlled the RIB boats at the power station. The Muslim elite soldiers could only hope that the 150 *Holy Warriors* due to arrive would tip the balance in their favor, but there were no guarantees.

At the roundabout of streets Hedenbrogatan and Garnisonsgatan, the fighting was in full swing between the Home Guard soldiers and the *Holy*

Warriors. Both sides were firing wildly into the air without bothering to aim. Although the Home Guard soldiers numbered only thirty-five, there was no indication that the *Holy Warriors* would succeed in forcing the defenders, who were more heavily armed than the attackers, who were only equipped with AK 47s.

There was a short pause in the rain of bullets when reinforcements were delivered from the infantrymen of the regiment I19. The *Holy Warriors* decided their best chance was to retreat to the Al-Masjid Mosque, where they could take up better defense positions.

One of the Home Guard's rifle groups was positioned by the entrance of the Migration Agency, from where they could see a handful of their wounded and dead countrymen lying motionless on the ground. As the *Holy Warriors* withdrew, the rifle soldiers stood and looked around.

"God Damnit!" suddenly roared one of the overexcited soldiers, who had just survived his first firefight, and let loose a round towards the Migration Agency's large sign above the entrance.

"What are you doing? Stop immediately!" shouted the group's leader, agitated.

"That's where those bastards come from!" yelled the soldier who fired first, emptying the rest of the magazine straight through the glass doors. "What the hell are they doing in our country?"

It was as if the first shooter had opened a floodgate by expressing what they all were thinking. All at once, the Migration Agency was bombarded with anti-tank artillery, grenades, and gunfire from their machine guns and assault rifles. The responsible officers had no chance in preventing what was happening.

"This is what I've been waiting to do for years, hahaha!"

"Now those bastards get what they deserve!"

A few minutes later, thick, black smoke rose into the sky from the bombed-out building. Fortunately, it was Saturday, and the "Miggs", as the staff was called, celebrated the weekend in the peaceful comfort of their homes, completely unaware of what was happening at their office.

"Remember, if anyone asks, it was the Muslims who did this!" shouted the squad leader.

The *Holy Warriors* were now entrenched in two different locations, unable to move. The Swedish defenders had weathered the initial storm but did not yet have a plan in place to launch an attack on the entrenched Muslims.

However, more soldiers in full combat gear were constantly joining the fray. Most of them were enlisted servicemen who lived in Boden. As the day continued, more Swedish infantrymen began to organize, even the special operation force I19's rangers from the old military town Arvidsjaur were arming and heading to fight.

At times, it seemed like the Swedes had the situation under control, with steadily growing resources, but appearances were deceiving. Later that same evening, two battalions of 450 Muslim elite soldiers arrived in armored vehicles and troop carriers from Luleå, tipping the balance of power in their favor.

The Battle of Boden raged with sporadic fighting for over three months, and neither side gained full control of the city.

Finally, it took a deluge to liberate Boden on November 2, 2032. When the rain lifted and liberation finally came, the city lay in ruins, shattered and submerged under water.

Chapter 12

Military depots emptied

July 17, 2032, evening

There was no time to lose. A9 was under attack, and Hugo knew that thousands of soldiers had invaded Luleå. As a reservist, Hugo was very experienced in the military's operations, and he realized that it would take several days before an organized defense could be established. It was now a race to the weapon depots—and being first would make or break their outcome.

At the same time, Hugo and his two hunting companions conducted their little raid at the Boden's power station; much was happening in the village of Unbyn. When they returned, the courtyard outside the school building was filled with men and women wielding defense weapons. Hugo calculated the number of guns alone to be around sixty.

He recognized some of the faces from the moose hunting team in the neighboring village of Avan. Unbyn and Avan were in an everlasting and historic feud dating back to medieval times. The documents in the village records from the district court testified to a conflict that had lasted for hundreds of years. The friction typically involved land boundaries and who had the right to release their animals into lush meadows or allow them to drink from disputed springs. But on this day, the hatchet had been buried; the enemy of my enemy is my friend.

A few of them sat on the benches, tinkering with AK-47 Kalashnikov assault rifles they had confiscated from the attackers in the stranded RIB boat. They found the weapons to be straightforward, not much different from Swedish assault rifles except for their appearance and caliber, of course.

As Hugo Engman stepped out of his dented Volvo S90, a loud murmur broke out, and a few men strode purposefully toward him. It seemed like everyone was waiting for him. Then he spotted the person he was looking for, the dignified Allan. Allan had been a long-lasting military employee all his life, and above all, he had been responsible for the weapon depots in the area until he retired a couple of years ago.

"Allan, you're an angel sent from heaven. We need to secure the weapon depots, and you're the one with the keys!"

"Well, Hugo, I already have a plan. There are three large depots around the mountain of Rödberget, which we should focus on. The others are on the north side of the river, and they will be difficult to access."

"Can we blast our way in?"

"Well, it's possible, but we're talking about steel doors that are ten inches thick, and I don't think we have explosives for that. But it's not necessary. I've called my two successors, who gave me the codes. They are meeting me with their keys, which we also need for access. We are going to Rödluvan depot, but you probably need to find out where that is because only a few people do. There are eight thousand AK-5 rifles, light and heavy machine guns, about a thousand hand grenades, a couple of tons of explosives, and several anti-tank weapons. The other two depots are smaller but contain the same type of equipment."

"Is everything in working order?"

"Oh yes, I can guarantee that! I've been in charge of maintenance for twenty years. We've been conducting spot checks with functional tests on a rolling schedule, so there shouldn't be any functional issues, although I suspect the hand grenades might have passed their expiration date. The only issue I can think of is how we will transport this many weapons out of the depot."

Hugo looked around and spotted Alf, who stood listening without saying anything.

"Alf, have you secured the boat with the bodies?"

"Yeah, all three," Alf responded softly, with an avoiding gaze. They're in the moose cooler. It's not a pleasant sight, I can tell you."

"Good! Now, I want you to arrange all the available vehicles in the village—flatbed trucks, tractor-trailers, anything that can carry weapons! Johansson's Trucking has two large trucks; make sure we get them. We'll gather down the road in half an hour and caravan towards Boden, understood? Allan will lead us to the weapon depots. We need all available hands to carry and load. Everyone needs to help!"

As Hugo stepped out of the car, outside the lodge with the cold storage room, he noticed small pools of fresh blood on the ground. He slowly opened the heavy door and paused in the doorway as he saw his wife kneeling with her back to the door, gently caressing the cheek of the nearest body.

The three bodies lay side by side in the middle of the floor, hands clasped over their chests, or at least what remained of the bloody fingertips. The bodies were severely maimed and riddled with countless bullets. The closest one was their beloved boy, their only child. Egon's face was utterly unharmed, unlike the crushed and bloody visages of his two comrades. Their little boy looked like a peacefully sleeping angel, with his rye-blond hair neatly in place, but his innocent blue eyes were wide open, staring blankly at the ceiling. He was beautiful even in death.

The caravan started their journey towards Boden. The flatbed trucks led the way with Allan and Hugo in the first one, while the tractors with trailers immediately behind. They had to navigate using Allan's hand-drawn maps, but signposts would be stationed at critical intersections in the forest to help them find their way.

After fifteen minutes, the first truck approached the Rödluvan depot. They were surprised when they were three hundred feet from the massive steel gate, which they could see behind the camouflage nets. Several massive concrete blocks blocked the road, forcing them to stop. A handful of soldiers emerged from the bushes, pointing their automatic rifles at the driver's cab.

"Out of the truck! Lie face down on the ground! Who are you, and what are you doing here?"

The young female officer's voice was sharp, aggressive, and piercingly high-pitched. The three men dropped to the ground face-first.

"We're here to ensure that the depot doesn't fall into enemy hands," Hugo yelled. I'm a captain at I19."

"Look what they have in the cab!" shouted one of the soldiers, holding up two Kalashnikovs towards the officer.

Out of the corner of his eye, Hugo could see the young sergeant with her finger on the trigger, pointing her AK5 straight at his head. Then he felt the barrel pressed firmly against the back of his head, pushing his face into the ground. He was sweating profusely, hoping the sergeant had her nerves under control.

"Captain at I19? Since when did the Swedish army start using Kalashnikovs?" she sneered. "Tell me who the hell you are before I blow your brains out! Got it?"

Before Hugo could answer, the rest of the flatbed trucks began to arrive, lining up along the road. In a few moments, the sergeant's squad was surrounded by fifty hunters with their rifles ready. A few of them carried the same Kalashnikovs the sergeant had just pulled from the cab.

"Let him up. We're on your side!"

"And we sure as hell don't look like Arabs!"

The young sergeant took the barrel away from Hugo's head and looked suspiciously at the group of hunters.

"Well, I can see you're Swedes, at least."

Hugo stood before the young sergeant, placing his right hand on her shoulder while wiping mud off his face with his left hand.

"Good job, just as you're supposed to do! Good. But now, young sergeant, you'll hand over command to Captain Hugo Engman of the Norrbotten Regiment I19. Attention, and execute!" he shouted.

The sergeant and her five riflemen took up individual positions.

"I'm handing over command to Captain Engman!" the sergeant shouted.

"I'm taking command! Your task now is to watch and secure the road here while we secure the armory. Execute and move!"

Then, the six youths jogged down the road to find a hiding spot for an ambush in case the enemy showed up.

When Hugo turned around, the gates were wide open, and a bright row of industrial lights illuminated the entrance to the cave.

"Yeah, it looks just like when I handed it over," he heard Allan's calm voice. "Everything's in order. Let's start with the heavier weapons at the back and in the boxes to the right. Over there are pallet jacks and trucks, and there should be a loaded forklift. We'll begin by loading up the two big trucks. I can drive the forklift."

Allan had voluntarily taken on the role of logistics chief, and soon, strong arms were lifting and carrying with all their might while Allan shuttled the yellow forklift back and forth to the trucks. Twenty minutes later, the first truck slowly drove off, weighed down with heavy cargo, heading towards Unbyn.

Chapter 13

Sweden establishes Defense Headquarters

July 20, 2032

In the event of war, Sweden's civilian and military leadership have a plan to convene in a top-secret headquarters seldom mentioned, and when it is, only by its nondescript name, Zone 1. Very few individuals are fully aware of the exact location of Zone I. For security reasons, only about a dozen politicians and an equal number of top military officials are fully informed.

Slightly more people are aware that Zone 1 exists and understand the overall purpose of the headquarters but do not know its location and specific details. No written documentation of Zone 1 exists for fear that a foreign power, namely the Russians, might obtain the information. If Zone 1 cannot be used, Zone 2 will serve as the alternate headquarters. Zone 2 is located in the northern landscape of Dalarna, in the sparsely populated area called the "Finnish forests", not far from the village of Noppikoski. Even fewer people know that Zone 2 exists.

Both defense headquarters were established in the 1950s, during the Cold War. Sweden prepared them to withstand a nuclear attack from the Soviet Union. The work was carried out by an unknown private company supposedly engaged in mineral exploration. The Swedish state-owned the company through a front. The workers believed they were conducting test blasts for potential mining operations. Work crews were rotated regularly to prevent anyone from acquiring too much information. Under strict confidentiality, the final installations were completed by military personnel who had obtained the highest security clearance.

Yet, the Russians were already aware of Zone 1 and Zone 2 from the outset, not to mention the invading Muslims, who had infiltrated Sweden at all levels over decades and were fully informed about every detail of the ongoing maintenance and modernization of the headquarters.

The government's national security cost-cutting, which naively and recklessly abolished Sweden's invasion defense in the early 2000s, had never impacted Zone 1 or Zone 2, as these locations were for the safety of top politicians. Both headquarters had been continuously modernized and were prepared to accommodate around two hundred people without notice, sustaining them for three weeks with no supplies from the outside world.

Zone 1 and Zone 2 are guarded round the clock by a company of 120 infantrymen, who have yet to learn why they are training there specifically. The soldiers are well-fortified and equipped with heavy machine guns and autocannons. The attacking Muslims knew better than to attempt an attack solely armed with assault rifles. Zone 1 and Zone 2 are formidable fortresses and were not part of the invasion for the time being. Not even a thousand *Holy Warriors* would have had the slightest chance of breaking thru.

In the nuclear-bomb-proof headquarters of Zone 1, deep within Tiveden National Park in Östergötland, in bedrock 250 feet below the surface, Sweden's political and military leadership finally managed to convene on the third day of the war. That is, what remained of the leadership, as most had been murdered three days earlier by Mahmoud's assassination squads. It was a battered and bruised assembly of twenty-two people who settled around the oval conference table with cups of instant coffee. Most of the exhausted attendees had barely managed to get there alive, and the shock and stress of the last three days were evident on their faces.

Sweden's Supreme Commander, Daniel Gyllenstierna, well-known and respected by all present, opened the meeting. Contrary to the others, he looked as fresh and alert as ever.

"I welcome my fellow officers despite our country's current difficult situation. I'll give the floor directly to Minister of Justice Anna-Lena Beckstedt, who will start by providing us with a brief overview of the political situation."

"Hello to you all. My name is Anna-Lena Beckstedt, and I am Sweden's minister of justice, which you already know because I have met all of you at our security strategic meetings."

Everyone around the table nodded in agreement. "Of course." "Certainly."

"Based on our rather limited information, a significant portion of Sweden's leadership was assassinated in their homes the night of July 17. This includes the prime minister, foreign minister, finance minister, and defense minister, who were also my close friends."

Anna-Lena Beckstedt wiped a tear from the corner of her right eye with the back of her hand and continued:

"As far as I know—I'm not entirely certain which I, as minister of justice, should be—I am fifth in the line of succession, making me Sweden's prime minister. I will now take the helm of our country's political leadership. If someone higher in the line of succession should appear, I would be grateful to hand over the reins to them, but as it stands, this is the situation. Does anyone have any objections to this? There must be no uncertainties about who holds the ultimate decision-making authority. Can we agree that, for now, and until further notice, it's me?"

The silence in the bunker was so thick it could almost be felt. The tensions between the military Sweden supporters and the political Globalists who governed Sweden—and whom the Sweden supporters believed were working to destroy and Islamize Sweden—had been intense for decades. This mutual suspicion made cooperation between the military and politicians dysfunctional, as both groups viewed each other with deep mistrust.

Among the political cadre, Beckstedt could be more trusted. She was the typical career politician who had risen through the ranks via the youth organization. She had limited knowledge, a low intellectual level, and a two-year high school education as her most notable qualification. Yet, she was a cunning and cynical player, armed with sharp wit and a remarkable knack for sensing prevailing attitudes and aligning with those in power. Her accurate political instincts had now propelled her to the highest political position.

After a few seconds, faint and somewhat hesitant political voices began to be heard until they were interrupted by the booming voice of Army Chief Anton Brännström.

"What is needed now is military competence and only that! At every strategic security meeting over the past decades, we have warned that this would happen, but you politicians have brushed off the warnings and played right into the hands of the Muslims. So please don't talk to me about taking the helm because you've intentionally run the ship aground with eyes wide open!"

"May I ask the Army Chief to choose his words more carefully," said the self-appointed prime minister. "First of all, we are not talking about Muslims but about radical Islamists. We have many good and loyal Muslims in our country, and perhaps even in this room right now, which is especially important to remember. And I forbid any other insinuations!"

"I am at war with Muslims. Call them whatever you want," Brännström continued. "Our country has been in a state of emergency for three years. We make the necessary decisions here and now in this group without seeking support in parliament. We don't need politicians who are out of touch with reality and think they're in control when they're not!"

The self-appointed prime minister stared at Army Chief Brännström.

"That sounds dangerously close to high treason and an attempted coup! Is the Army Chief aware of the consequences of this? Let me add that we are now applying martial law, and all it entails."

Supreme Commander Gyllenstierna interjected loudly.

"There's no time for internal disputes, damn it! Then we certainly lose. Anton, I want to tell you something as your good friend for many years, but perhaps most importantly now as your superior: Do your job and let others handle politics! To Madame prime minister, I want to convey that no one can replace the competence that Army Chief Brännström possesses. Anton is essential for the defensive war that we must immediately initiate. Can we proceed? There's no time to lose."

"Alright, let's move forward." said Brännström. "There's not much politics left to manage anyway. It's possible we don't even have a country left to manage anymore. No politician should come and talk to me about treason. We all know who has betrayed Sweden, and it's not us Sweden nationalists. We'll see who will be held accountable for treason in due time! And, by the way, Anna-Lena, what mandate do you imagine you have as a self-appointed, maybe, prime minister?" asked Brännström, making air quotes with his index and middle fingers.

"Now we'll hand over the floor to Lieutenant Colonel Alfred Baksi, the acting chief of staff responsible for compiling and analyzing our intelligence. He has assembled as much information as possible. Please proceed, Ali!"

Alfred Baksi, who belonged to the well-known Kurdish political family Baksi, was born in Diyarbakir, southeastern Turkey. He came to Sweden at the age of two years. Ali had never felt anything other than Swedish, and in a futile attempt to also be perceived as entirely Swedish by the Swedes themselves, he changed his name to Alfred Baklander. But when a girlfriend pointed out that his last name sounded like a well-known pastry in the Middle East, he renamed himself Alfred Baksi, which was somewhat impractical since most people persisted in calling him Ali, much to his annoyance.

Alfred felt he would never be seen as a true Swede because God had given him thick black curls, strongly marked eyebrows, and a jet-black beard. But nowadays, he believed it didn't matter anymore, as Sweden had transformed into a country that resembled the Middle East more than the Nordics. Alfred Baksi sometimes joked about his looks, calling himself "the guy who put a face to the term 'blackhead.'"

Alfred still wished that Sweden had retained its Nordic identity and, thereby, its political stability and economic prosperity. After all, his family had once fled the Middle East. But the Middle East and Islam followed the refugees, which was a trauma he shared with many other secular Muslims and even more so with the Christian refugees. They had all fled the Muslim dictatorships to live in freedom in the wealthy, secular, and oddly tolerant country up north, but now everything had changed.

Like many other immigrants, he and his family had long considered leaving the deteriorating country of Sweden behind. They didn't have strong roots in Sweden, so the idea of leaving and living far from Islamization and the European civil war in the USA or Australia was appealing. Still, it just hadn't happened yet, and nowadays, getting visas for Swedish citizens was difficult. If he could invest two million US dollars, they would be welcome in the USA. The question was how he would come up with the money now that Sweden was at war and their house was unsellable.

Alfred walked up to the front of the room and quickly began his presentation by showing image after image on the big screen.

"Starting early on the morning of July seventeen, Sweden was invaded by a foreign power. We don't know who this foreign power is, but we know it solely involves a composition of Muslims from many countries. We believe it's an organization rather than a country; most signs point to the Muslim Brotherhood. We know they identified Sweden as their priority target a long time ago, and their interest has remained and increased with the Islamization of Sweden. Around three hundred of our political, military, and economic leaders were murdered in their homes on the night of July seventeen. As you've already heard, the majority of those killed are part of the government and military leadership. Stockholm, Gothenburg, and Luleå have been invaded from the sea, where the enemy has landed around four thousand soldiers and hundreds of armored vehicles in each city. They faced no resistance in Stockholm and Gothenburg. But in Luleå, the enemy suffered significant damage, with up to half of the landing soldiers killed and most of the armored vehicles destroyed."

Alfred paused briefly and looked at his audience. "Any questions so far?" Everyone remained silent, struck by the gravity of the situation. Alfred continued his presentation.

"According to our intelligence, the nine invading ships departed from nine different ports. So far, we have identified Tripoli, Alexandria, Rabat, Qatar, and the Saudi cities of al-Jubayl and Yanbu. We have no information on the departure points of the three ships, but we think our Israeli friends at Mossad will be able to provide us with that information soon. Mossad has provided a brief and describes the invading soldiers as battle-hardened elite troops with experience from many of the places where Muslims wage war. Many appear to be Moroccan mercenaries who have long served as security forces for the Saudi royal family. In case you weren't aware, soldiers are Morocco's largest export. Our Swedish Muslims seem to cooperate with and support the invading forces fully. We estimate that there are now perhaps two to three hundred thousand armed *Holy Warriors,* as they call themselves. There are currently around two and a half million Muslims in our country, and the majority are men of fighting age. These warriors are passionate, enthusiastic, and willing to sacrifice but lack military training.

They only have access to lighter weapons such as automatic rifles, machine guns, hand grenades, and to some extent, anti-tank weapons."

Suddenly, a lively discussion broke out in the room.

"How on earth have they acquired such vast weapons secretly?" asked the minister of education. "What have our intelligence services been doing?" he exclaimed, clearly upset, speaking in his hometown dialect.

"I might be able to shed some light on that," said Bertil Wiklund, the head of the military intelligence service, MUST, who had narrowly escaped Mahmoud's assassination squads by being out sailing on Lake Vänern in his small private boat.

"We've known that large weapons depots have been built up in the autonomous enclaves for years. We suspect now that virtually every mosque has functioned as a depot. But, as you also know, since politicians have not allowed any patrol in these autonomous Muslim areas, we are not certain. They were too worried about unnecessarily provoking the Muslims and sparking a civil war. Our previous estimate from 2030 was around thirty thousand automatic rifles in these depots. Still, it's become increasingly difficult to gather information as the enclaves have been closed off and all access denied to non-Muslims."

"Thank you, Bertil," said Gyllenstierna. "For those of you who naturally aren't familiar with our secret intelligence services, few people have had as significant an impact on the nation's security as Bertil Wiklund, who is the head of MUST."

"The Islamists have plundered some of our weapon depots," Wiklund continued. "But even more have been plundered by Swedes, which we'll get back to."

"We within SÄPO largely agree with MUST's assessments," responded Bianca Popovic, who had just been appointed as the acting chief of the Security Service, SÄPO, after the assassination squads had killed her superiors.

"That must mean that upwards of ninety percent of the weapons used by the *Holy Warriors* came from the invading ships, supported by the testimonies and images we've received. We have reports of the unloading of approximately one hundred containers. We can probably assume that the landed armored vehicles were also fully loaded with weapons. The number of *Holy Warriors* skyrocketed from what we believed to be manageable in case of a civil war to ten times that number. I can't understand how we will handle these masses of *Holy Warriors*. What do we have to respond with?"

Commander-in-Chief Gyllenstierna had to keep the discussion on track.

"We will get to the response part soon, I promise," said Gyllenstierna, gesturing with his arm and pointing his whole hand at Army Chief Brännström, who sat to his right. "Continue now, Ali!"

"The *Holy Warriors* have taken over all the towns where these regiments are located, which largely coincide with the locations of their mosques," Alfred Baksi continued. "In many towns, like Malmö and Helsingborg, they didn't even need to fight since they've long held control of the streets and silenced the opposition, leaving no meaningful resistance. As it stands now, the following towns and regions are under the control of the Muslims – sorry, the Islamists. Starting from the west: all of western Skåne, large parts of Halland with Halmstad at the center, the Gothenburg–Borås–Trollhättan–Uddevalla area, Växjö, Kalmar, Jönköping, Norrköping, Skövde, Karlstad, Stockholm western suburbs, Uppsala, the Eskilstuna–Västerås–Arboga-Köping area, Falun-Borlänge, Gävle, Sundsvall, Härnösand, Umeå, Skellefteå, and Luleå-Boden."

"Well, that sounds like almost all major city centers," said the sixty-seven-year-old minister of agriculture, sipping his cold coffee. But why not Linköping? The beards in Skäggetorp are known to be the most militant of our dear Muslims, which says a lot."

"I can answer that," exclaimed the acting Air Force Chief, William Wennergren, a lifelong resident of Linköping. "I was there. 'The Beards' had the misfortune of having half the Swedish National Task Force on a major exercise in Ljungsbro and Motala. The Islamists had to contend with over four thousand task force soldiers who entered and defended the city center. It was over in a couple of hours. When a few hundred 'Beards' lay dead in the streets, the rest surrendered and raised their arms. So now three hundred and forty 'Beards' are interned in Medevi Brunn, an internment camp. I have a message from Björn Väster, the head of the task force. He would like to know if he can get permission to execute the prisoners."

"Execute the prisoners? Is he completely insane?" exclaimed the self-appointed prime minister. "We must, of course, always respect the Geneva Conventions! Sweden has a proud tradition to uphold within the UN. That despicable Nazi Väster needs to be removed, and quickly. He's a security risk!"

"Thank you for the information, William. Let's move on, Ali," said Gyllenstierna, ignoring the prime minister's comments.

"I believe I'm done for now," said Alfred. "There's endless information to go through, but we can revisit it later."

"Very well," said Gyllenstierna. "Let's see what countermeasures we have, which will be presented by the heads of the Army, Air Force, and Navy. Anton, you start, as you'll likely have the most to carry out in the next few months!"

Anton Brännström sat at the computer by the large screen and began with some background information in his characteristic Luleå dialect.

"As you may understand, the situation is still somewhat unclear, but we must work with what we currently know. Despite the additional recent enrollment, the number of combat-ready soldiers could be better. However, those available are highly motivated, well-trained, and well-armed. Our available infantry and ranger soldiers are on par with the invading *Holy Warriors*, who now seem to number around ten thousand. Look at the numbers; one of our soldiers is likely as effective as at least ten *Holy Warriors* in combat. Many of our soldiers have combat experience from all our missions as peacekeeping troops in Africa, the Middle East, and Central Asia. What's different and new for us now is that we'll be fighting in urban environments. We don't want to destroy our communities. Our combat strategies are designed for battles at sea, in the air, and in rural areas. Our defense capability relies on high-tech weapons with great destructive power that isn't particularly personnel intensive. We now need boots on the ground, classic infantry soldiers. The kind our politicians never thought they'd need again."

Brännström lit up the first of his three images.

"Let's start with our elite units, the ranger soldiers—the Amphibious Regiment in Berga, known as the Coastal Rangers, tallies around eight hundred. K3 in Karlsborg has twelve hundred regular paratroopers and an airborne rapid response unit of four hundred. F17 in Kallinge consists of five hundred rangers. Lastly, we have the ranger battalion at I19 in Boden, at about three thousand soldiers, of which around eight hundred are stationed in Arvidsjaur at the old K4. We have just over six thousand ranger soldiers available right now. The number could double within one to two weeks when we get the reservists."

"But, my God, is six thousand all we can muster against the enemy's three hundred thousand?" groaned the self-appointed prime minister.

"Yes, it's all the result of thirty years of defense budget cuts, decisions that you and your political colleagues have pushed through," replied Brännström. "But I did say twelve thousand rangers within a maximum of two weeks. In addition, we're mustering around twenty thousand regular infantry soldiers in the near term and double that within a couple of weeks."

"Note, if you didn't already know, that more than a fifth of our soldiers – both rangers and infantry – are women. They are highly motivated and fully on par with their male counterparts, if not better. We will have twelve thousand rangers and forty thousand infantry soldiers available within the next two weeks. This should be compared to the enemy's ten thousand professional elite soldiers and perhaps three hundred thousand *Holy Warriors*. Many will likely be stuck in Muslim-controlled areas, so in the worst case, the number could be significantly fewer than this number. In addition to the above, we have nine thousand within our paramilitary National Task Force, the only soldiers trained for urban combat, which has already proven very useful in Linköping. Daniel and I have discussed how these resources should be used. We'll get back to this."

"It's never going to work!" the prime minister exclaimed. "Never. We need international assistance. And the National Task Force is – and should remain – under civilian leadership; there can be no doubt about that. We've allowed the force to expand and upgrade to counterbalance your growing military power."

"Who would come to our aid now that war is at our doorstep or has already begun across Western Europe?" continued Brännström. "No, we'll have to use the available resources for now. But there's a glimmer of hope that we can level the numbers against *Holy Warriors*. We've received reports that large quantities of weapon depots have been looted by Swedes, especially in Stockholm, Gothenburg, Norrköping, Skövde, and Boden. The reports suggest that there are probably thirty to forty thousand armed Swedes currently forming local defense groups that we can't control at present but who will undoubtedly fight on our side against the Muslims."

"Islamists, if I may," objected the prime minister. "It sounds like we're about to get uncontrollable warlords. We can't have that. Those who have looted weapon depots must be arrested and brought to justice."

"In this situation, I welcome all possible forces fighting on our side," said Brännström. "But you can try to arrest them if you think it's a good idea for us to invest our limited military resources in fighting Swedes. If you are to be interpreted correctly, it is apparently on the side of the Muslims that we are to fight – against our own countrymen."

"On the side of the Islamists you mean," the prime minister stubbornly retorted, glaring hatefully at Brännström.

"May I have Colonel William Wennergren, acting air force chief, provide his assessment of the situation?" said Gyllenstierna.

"I'm afraid I don't need to show any pictures," Wennergren quickly stated. "We have no Air Force left. All our planes have been destroyed on the ground by the enemy, except for five JAS Gripen Es now located in Kuopio, Finland. It's uncertain if these planes are combat-ready. In any case, they lack armaments, which can probably be arranged with the help of our Finnish friends. But that will take time. Swedish technicians from Linköping are already on their way to Kuopio. I'll get back to you on that matter soon. Thanks to the excellent work of the National Task Force, the aircraft factory in Malmslätt was saved. The Task Force arrived just as the Islamists launched their attack. Thank goodness we have leaders like Björn Väster! I estimate there should be three or four planes in the final stages of assembly, which might be operational soon. Maybe. Some planes are there for essential parts replacement or upgrades that could be combat-ready within short. I'm awaiting information on this soon. In the best-case scenario, we'll have seven or eight combat-ready JAS Gripen Es within a month unless the Muslims manage to take and destroy the factory in Malmslätt. Thank you!"

"Thank you, William. We had all hoped for a more favorable situation for the Air Force. Let's turn the floor over to Fred Bergström," said Gyllenstierna.

"We in the Navy have fared relatively well compared to the Air Force," began Bergström. "Both naval bases in Berga and Karlskrona have indeed been attacked and, to some extent, partially destroyed. However, we've been fortunate. Brännström is confident that the remaining Islamists can soon be eliminated from Berga and Karlskrona, and I'm inclined to believe him. Only one of our seven corvettes has been destroyed. Three were at sea and are completely unscathed, while the remaining three have minor damages from gunfire and armor-piercing shots. If they aren't already combat-ready, all three can quickly be repaired. In total, we will have six corvettes available, along with about thirty smaller traditional surface vessels with varying armaments. Unfortunately, these vessels rely on outdated twentieth-century technology but can still be lethal in combat. One of the minesweepers was destroyed by fire, and the other was already undergoing long-term repairs and upgrades, which means we have only three operational minesweepers. We have a new A26 submarine that is fully operational. The A26s weapon systems are world-class, and as you probably know, they can be used offensively for ground operations and combating sea targets with super torpedoes. It carries thirty American-British Tomahawk cruise missiles that can be fired vertically underwater. Additionally, we have six recently upgraded medium-sized submarines of the Gotland class with decent combat capabilities. Interestingly, we have recently launched a group of eight self-operating boats of various sizes. The group, or 'pod' as we call it, is called the 'Orcas' and is fully intact but not quite fully tested. We already have orders for these boats with different configurations and armaments. Ironically, all of the orders come from Saudi Arabia and Qatar, which likely had a hand in this attack on our country. This has been a top-secret project, so I assume you're unfamiliar with the details. We are the first in the world to have self-driving combat boats controlled from the command center in Berga. We initially offered to have the Arabs operate their pods from the Berga command center with their personnel until they built their centers. I guess that's probably not going to happen now... If the lead boat is removed, another immediately activates as the new lead, coordinating the operations. The group can execute complex, coordinated operations, provided the targets are programmed into the system. Thanks to these small, high-speed, well-armed boats, we can achieve previously unknown flexibility and carry out operations we could only dream of without risking a single human life. Seeing what the Orcas can do in a real-world scenario will be extremely interesting. Swedish naval technology is rendering large surface ships obsolete for all future operations. The smallest boats in the pod are only eight feet long but carry enough explosive power to take out an aircraft carrier. The largest Orca is 150 feet long. The next phase is to create a pod that includes fighter jets, drones, and submarines to carry out unmanned, autonomously targeted, highly flexible, coordinated, and multiple maritime, underwater, and aerial attacks."

The audience shifted uncomfortably and glanced at each other.

"Name one enemy that can defend against mass attacks by super-fast and intelligent attacking vessels. It's like trying to fend off an angry swarm of bees with a fly swatter. I can tell you that Saab in Linköping is already test-flying a fleet of aircraft called the Wild Geese. They should have a multifunctional fleet of coordinated combat forces operational within three to four years.

Berggren looked visibly pleased and had become animated when discussing his favorite subject. However, he suddenly looked up and fell silent, realizing that his technological enthusiasm and visions for the future had led him slightly off-topic.

"I hope that wasn't too futuristic," Berggren concluded.

"It's reassuring that our naval capabilities are relatively intact," Gyllenstierna noted. "But we should probably hold off on future scenarios and focus on the combat forces we currently have available. This means we can at least prevent the enemy from bringing in reinforcements via sea. Unfortunately, naval forces aren't helpful for future fighting in urban areas."

"No," replied Berggren. "But I can sink all of the enemy's invasion boats still docked in Stockholm and Gothenburg at any time. But now they are empty civilian vessels, so the question is, what good would it do? It's possible we'll find them more useful when we retake the ports. *If* we retake the ports," he added with hesitation. "Well, we can block the sea entrances to our major port cities. It's a shame our fixed mine installations were removed. We could use them now."

"There is no point crying over spilled milk," Gyllenstierna concluded. "We have to deal with the situation. Anton, how are we doing with our artillery and anti-aircraft defenses?"

"All artillery and hundreds of armored vehicles are gathered at A9 in Boden. About 150 local *Holy Warriors* attempted to attack with support from the Muslim elite soldiers who came up the Lule River in RIB boats. But A9 is now secured. We estimate that ninety percent of our resources at A9 are operational. As everyone knows, I've been a major critic for years of the decision to gather all the artillery in one place, significantly far away from the areas where it would be needed. How can we move the guns now when the enemy controls the railway junctions and several cities along European Highway 4? The weapons are stuck there. From a military standpoint, it wouldn't have mattered much if A9 had been destroyed. As for our anti-aircraft defenses, the thinking was that our Air Force would be so effective that we hardly needed any anti-aircraft guns. But we do have six mobile Patriot batteries available. They are equipped with the most efficient missiles on the market, the Israeli ones. With these, we can combat enemy aircraft and incoming missiles of both the cruise and ballistic types, which currently seem like rather unlikely events."

Gyllenstierna stood up and looked each person present in the eye, one by one.

"We're concluding this meeting and transitioning to work in smaller groups, where the military will have full authority to make decisions without political approval. I would like each branch's chief to report directly to me. Isn't that right, Madame prime minister?"

The prime minister looked troubled but nodded briefly and cautiously under everyone present's scrutinizing and critical gazes. "What would happen if I refused?" she wondered to herself.

"Could Madame prime minister inform Björn Väster that the National Task Force will now be under the army's command and that Väster himself will report directly to Army Chief Brännström? Ask Väster to join us as soon as possible. He's a competent person who urgently needs to be in this room. Tomorrow and every day after that, we'll meet in this room at the same time to go through updates from the outside. Let's do everything in our power to win this unjust, unprovoked, and unwanted war. Let us all do our duty for Sweden, for freedom and democracy! And for the Queen!"

"For Sweden, until the last bullet is fired!" exclaimed Brännström, quickly seconded by the entire group, including the prime minister, in a resounding "For Sweden!"

"For democracy and the multicultural society!" added education minister Gustav, drawing disapproving glares from everyone in uniform.

From now on, it was clear who was in charge, even though democracy stayed alive. The meeting was over, and everyone began to leave the room in small groups, engaged in intense discussions.

Chapter 14

Meeting at the Defense Headquarters

July 24, 2032, Zone 1

"Now we're starting to get a reasonably reliable picture of the situation," said Alfred Baksi, the Chief of Staff's information officer. "We've had a lot of help from satellite images from Kiruna, where everything seems to work fine, at least for now. But most of our useful information still comes from local reporters nationwide. It will get even better when we access the National Reconnaissance Office, NRO spy satellites. They've already redirected the satellites. I've been in touch with a US military attaché, a good friend, for a long time. She's promised us full support from the NRO, DIA, the Defense Intelligence Agency, and the CIA. Even though the US has withdrawn its military presence from Europe, no one surpasses them in intelligence, except perhaps the Russians. I also know that Rudolf Enbom, the head of the Swedish Defense Radio Establishment, FRA, has scheduled a meeting on the radio link with his American counterpart at the NSA, the National Security Agency."

"Sweden's cooperation with the NSA dates to the end of World War two and is characterized by great openness from both sides. The US has benefited from Sweden's strategic location for signals intelligence against the Russians. Sweden has had the advantage of consistently having access to the best technology. The FRA has been a branch of the NSA since its inception in 1942."

The door opened, and the stainless-steel serving cart rolled in, a welcome sight for the tired and hungry attendees. Gyllenstierna pointed at stacks of simple plates and light-yellow plastic mugs.

"Today, we are having Swedish potato pancake with bacon and lingonberry jam, and I think we're all pretty hungry by now. Let's grab some food while we continue."

A small line quickly formed in front of the cart. The bacon slices and the potato pancakes looked as limp and tired as the meeting participants, and to make matters worse, the food was no longer warm.

"What, do you eat bacon, Ali?" the minister of agriculture asked as he pressed the lever, filling the light-yellow plastic mug with ice-cold milk flowing generously from the two-gallon box. There's still milk from Swedish cows," he exclaimed happily, toasting toward Alfred Baksi.

"Tasty and nutritious! Truly delicious! Milk from Swedish lowland cattle, nothing less than Swedish Holstein. I can feel those beautiful black and white animals."

"Yeah, what do you think? We celebrate Christmas at home with ham and everything, and we've done that all my life."

Ali avoided commenting on what he thought about milk as a meal drink.

"That was a surprise to me!" said the minister of agriculture, surprised.

"There's a lot you don't know and even more that you think – without knowing," replied Alfred sarcastically. "During Ramadan, we fast. The whole family. So that you know."

Gyllenstierna chose the vegetarian option, with fried soy steaks burnt around the edges like potato pancakes. If the Swedish military needed upgrading and modernization, cooking was certainly one of the first areas to deal with. Could the vegetarian options be extended beyond just soy steaks? As he was scanning the buffet, he questioned whether pork-free meals, like those in overcrowded prisons and new detention camps, should be offered. Maybe the Thursday tradition of pea soup with pork also could be reconsidered.

But now was not the right time to raise that issue. Perhaps the problem would resolve itself when all of Sweden became pork-free forever, he thought gloomily. The situation on the various fronts looked far from positive.

"Yeah, this should... taste... good..." he mumbled, returning to his seat.

"One thing we know that the enemy knows is where both Zone 1 and Zone 2 are located," Alfred Baksi continued before handing over to Army Chief Brännström.

"We can see that the enemy is moving north from Jönköping, along the western shore of Lake Vättern, presumably targeting Zone 1, but we have high hopes of stopping them," began the Army Chief. "They're moving in civilian cars, which we can easily blow up. We can also see that they're expanding their territory around Lake Mälaren, now controlling the entire area from Västerås—Eskilstuna to the west of Örebro. They're attempting a squeeze to encircle us as they continue the European Highway 18 all the way to Lake Vänern by Kristinehamn, thereby cutting off our northern retreat route. However, they will likely be met, and most likely stopped, by our infantry units positioned around Karlskoga and in Hallsberg, where we'll soon, by train, have access to twenty Leopard tanks. Unfortunately, we've received information that a Panama-flagged cargo ship has sneaked in via Lake Mälaren and has offloaded around thirty armored vehicles in the town of Köping. Twelve of these vehicles are state-of-the-art American Abrams battle tanks of the M1A2 model, equipped with what's called TUSK armament."

Most of those present were familiar with the American Abrams tanks, knowing they were highly formidable and equipped with world-class armament. Only a handful knew that TUSK was the acronym for Tank Urban Survival Kit, an armored net around the tank that causes armor-piercing weapons to explode prematurely. However, none of the uninformed wanted to reveal their lack of knowledge.

"Unfortunately, we must admit that our German Leopards are obsolete and can't compete with the Abrams tanks, which boast superior targeting systems, guided missiles, and firing range. Our anti-tank units in the region currently have a stock of twelve Bofors anti-tank robots, fifty-nine units of which are deployed from specialized vehicles. Furthermore, we possess hundreds of handheld armor shot m/86, so there's a chance we can hold off the Abrams tanks without air support. But, sadly, we're in a tough spot," he remarked absentmindedly, casting a long glance at Flight Colonel Wennergren.

"We've sold thousands of the 86s to various countries, so there's no shortage of real combat data, but the reports are somewhat contradictory. We're uncertain of their true effectiveness against the TUSK-equipped Abrams. We believe the 86 would need to shoot half a dozen hits, with the first shot targeting the Abrams tracks diagonally from the front or directly from the side. However, the armaments on the Abrams were nasty, so the missile crews would not survive for long. Being an anti-tank missile soldier requires not just nerves of steel. The shooters should have a death wish, too, as it often involves suicide missions. An additional advantage of model 86 is that it can be fired inside closed rooms, making it perfect for urban environments," continued Army Chief Brännström.

"How the hell did we let enemy ships into Lake Mälaren?" exclaimed the prime minister angrily. "Bergström, wasn't it you who said the navy would easily block all significant harbors? But now we have the enemy and his indestructible Abram tanks about to unload in Mälaren."

Bertil Wiklund, the head of MUST, came to Bergström's defense before Bergström could react.

"The intrusion happened on the fourth day of the war, July twenty-first. According to the information we've obtained, this ship entered Lake Mälaren via the Södertälje Canal on July sixteen, the day before the outbreak of the war. It then anchored just outside Kungsör, citing engine problems, and declined assistance, saying spare parts were on the way. No one thought anything of it, and the ship lay there undisturbed until July twenty-first when it docked in Köping. Köping incidentally is Sweden's largest lake port; by then, it was in the hands of the *Holy Warriors*, and the rest is history."

Gyllenstierna signaled for Brännström to continue.

"We have 4,000 troops from the rapid reaction force stationed in Linköping and Motala. We estimate we can use the 1,800 in Motala by relocating them north to join the troops in Hallsberg or by boat across Lake Vättern to Karlsborg. We'll keep them in Motala as reserves until we see where they're needed. It's not certain that we'll even need them to defend Zone 1. We have many other concerns, such as our capital, Stockholm, where the situation looks pretty bleak," concluded Brännström, turning his head toward Major Gunhild Svartenbrandt, responsible for operations in Stockholm and its suburbs.

"By the way, I forgot the 2,200 from the National Task Force stationed in Linköping. We believe they're well-positioned there to ensure the aircraft factory in Malmslätt doesn't fall into Muslim hands. They can also fight to prevent the Muslims from moving westward from Norrköping."

Major Svartenbrandt lit up a map of the "zero eight" area – the old area code for regional phone calls to Stockholm, as it was still called. She stood by the screen and began pointing with her ballpoint pen as she spoke.

"Today, we're a week into the war, and we can see some stabilization, although the situation is chaotic and confusing, to say the least. The enemy is still gaining ground almost everywhere, although we've managed to deflect operational combat groups. Still, they're not yet fully operational. Hats off to the National Task Force, the first to mobilize," she said, smiling at the force's commander, Björn Väster, seated on Brännström's left. "I don't know how we would've managed the first days without you."

Väster looked pleased and confident without commenting further. He was dressed in a black general's uniform, which he had helped design, with epaulets, narrow stripes, and gold buttons. The golden lightning bolt, the symbol of the National Task Force, gleamed on both sides of his collar. *Generalissimo* Väster, as he referred to himself in the third person—an old habit—had gotten off to a good start in the war, and he purred like a cat as he sat comfortably leaning back, rocking on his chair with his hands clasped behind his neck. *Generalissimo* Väster felt that his time was approaching, and the war might activate a total and final power takeover.

"In a nutshell, we control the northern suburbs, including the European Highway 4 and the Arlanda Airport, and the European Highway 18 up to Norrtälje," continued Svartenbrandt. "The enemy controls Uppsala and its surroundings. The Islamists have full control over the western suburbs and even Bromma Airport, which is a bit worrying considering potential reinforcements. We're hell-bent on retaking Bromma Airport and are preparing a broad-front attack to commence at dawn, as early as tonight. As for the more central areas, the enemy controls Kungsholmen, Gamla

Stan, Reimersholme, Långholmen, and the Essinge Islands. Östermalm and Djurgården are also in enemy hands."

"Slow down so the rest of us can keep up. Not everyone here is a die-hard *zero-eighter*," the minister of agriculture said in his distinctive Finnish-Swedish accent.

"Intense fighting is ongoing in Stockholm's inner city at Kungsholmen and the northern parts of Vasastan. A major concern for us is the suicide bombers undermining morale and causing general panic. About twenty suicide bombers have managed to detonate themselves so far, and we can't see an end to this mess. I hear it's even worse in Gothenburg. We're on the verge of losing our capital, and I can only see one solution that could turn the tide: deploying the entire Gotland battle group and the Gotland Battalion, which we can arrange in three to four days."

"Would we leave the whole island of Gotland completely defenseless?" objected the minister of education.

"Exactly," responded Svartenbrandt. "Just like what happened for twelve years when politicians were crazy enough to leave the island completely unguarded until we remilitarized Gotland in 2017. Luckily, nothing happened in those twelve years. Leaving just thirty infantrymen to keep the Muslims at bay, should they attempt anything, should be enough. I don't think they have many resources on Gotland. Not much interest either."

"The idea is solid," concluded Brännström. Here, we're talking about at least 450 well-trained and well-equipped soldiers. Of course, we should deploy them for the battle in our own capital. It could tip the scales in our favor and decide the entire outcome—not just for Stockholm but the whole war."

"But if the Russians make a move, Gotland would be completely defenseless," the education minister persisted. "We know the Russians have coveted Gotland since medieval times, when the Danes occupied the island."

"Vladimir Putin had twelve years to do something and didn't," noted Navy Chief Bergström. "And back then, you politicians had almost disbanded the entire navy, so we had nothing to counter, yet nothing happened. I'm in favor," he said, raising his hand.

"Me too," said the prime minister, surprising everyone by raising her hand since she usually voted against the military.

"I find us in agreement," summarized Gyllenstierna. "Let's get Svartenbrandt to bring in the troops from Gotland as soon as possible, and we'll surely give them Muslims a run for their money!"

At that moment, Gyllenstierna seemed to forget that he himself was a Muslim, albeit a blue and yellow one.

Chapter 15

Doomsday in Luleå

July 30, 2032, around lunchtime

Rain drizzled slowly on the backs of the people of Luleå as tens of thousands of them kneeled for Friday prayers, with their foreheads pressed to the damp asphalt of the streets. Their Muslim overlords had promised prayer mats for all, but none had been provided.

Around two weeks earlier, veils had been distributed a couple of days after the occupation began. Women's heads were covered with black fabric, and once the deliveries arrived, they would wear full black burqas. Men were forbidden to shave and began to resemble how Muslim men were supposed to look. Those who defied the shaving ban were beaten with batons by the morality police or publicly whipped at special whipping posts erected on the city's main street. Some were shot without further explanation.

Those who defied the tobacco or alcohol bans were hung from lampposts, their decaying bodies swaying as a warning to others. After a few days of birds pecking out their eyes, the bodies were usually taken down to avoid the risk of disease spreading. Bodies dangled in long rows at entrances and along main roads. No one would doubt who was in power or what happened to those who defied it. Not even children were spared. Many teenagers, and even children as young as ten, hung from lampposts for being caught with their snuff tobacco under their lips.

All workplaces and schools were closed on this cloudy Friday, as they would remain closed on Fridays for all eternity, the new day of rest. The people of Luleå had been ordered to gather in the city center, at their designated spots, by noon at the latest. Those who did not obey faced severe punishment, which could mean execution, so most people chose to comply.The neighborhoods around the city center were deserted, except for Muslim morality police patrolling every residential area, checking that no one was hiding in apartments and houses. The Muslim morality police were guided and assisted by a few hundred Luleå residents who had quickly and astutely realized which way the wind was blowing and had begged to convert to serve their new masters. Everyone who voluntarily sought Islam was welcomed with open arms to encourage others to do the same. Instead of beatings and punching, they received friendly smiles. The choice seemed simple; at least, it was a very practical first step.

Conversion was an easy and safe way to avoid punishment and many other problems. All that was needed was to recite the Muslim declaration of faith, the *shahadah,* or at least claim to have done so. No witnesses or special documents were needed. Just reciting that simple sentence made one a Muslim. Then, of course, it was necessary to dress and behave like a Muslim as best as one could. The new masters were lenient with the little mistakes that newbies always make as long as you tried your best and showed progress in your new role.

Everyone was to attend, absolutely everyone. Yet, hundreds of Luleå residents risked their lives by hiding in their homes instead of showing up downtown. Some had consumed the last drops of alcohol they had stashed away, realizing those drops would be the very last for a long time, as the Swedish alcohol retailer Systembolaget had been blown up and all drinking establishments were dry. Fermenting alcohol or possessing a distillation apparatus was punished by public beheading. Beheadings were preceded by a hundred lashes administered by Muslim executioners, who had been secretly trained in the basement of the Al-Hakim Mosque on the island of Hertsön, outside of Luleå. Some executioners were even "native" Luleå locals who had lived there for generations.

Sometimes, a lone gunshot echoed through the air as someone had their head shot off. It happened when someone dared to glance up and assess the situation despite being instructed to remain in prayer, with their forehead on the ground and their backside in the air. Or, as it was cynically put, with their forehead to the devil and their behind to God.

After twenty minutes of praying, the *Holy Warriors* began kicking with their military boots and poking the bodies of the infidels with the barrels of their rifles, signaling them to rise again. "Up-up-up, and quickly! *Jalla-jalla-jalla!*" Those not quick enough were beaten with batons. The newly converted locals, already in the service of the Muslims, seemed especially eager to use the batons to show loyalty to their new masters and thus avoid putting themselves in danger. Strange situations arose when fair-skinned Luleå residents, dressed in ankle-length dressings like *thawbs* and *keffiyehs* on their heads, beat neighbors and former friends who couldn't believe their eyes. Friends and acquaintances with whom they had shared a drink just a few weeks ago now violently attacked them.

On the large TV screens, the Luleå residents could see the well-known Imam, Abd al Haqq Bielat, appear. For decades, he had been allowed to spread his claims that Islam was the religion of peace and love in the local media. The imam's message was that Muslims fully respected Christians and Jews as people of the book. Not once had the imam's statements been publicly questioned to avoid offending the Muslims, but now the people of Luleå were too late to realize the true worth of the imam's words. After twenty-five years in Sweden, the imam spoke perfect Swedish. However, he still began with a few sentences in Arabic while smiling and waving to his terrified and paralyzed audience on the main street. He reveled in his power. Having the power over life and death gave him an almost divine feeling. "*Allahu akbar*! Dear beloved residents of Luleå! Today is the greatest day of your life. Finally, the day has come when the all-seeing and all-knowing Allah brings light, wisdom, love, and the utmost purity to your minds and hearts. Enjoy this day and remember it for the rest of your lives as the most beautiful and wonderful day! In less than an hour, you will all be reborn as Muslims when we recite our Muslim creed together, which is all that's needed to start your journey to becoming a good Muslim. Soon, you will experience the first day of your new lives, but first, let us inform you and attend to some other matters. Please look up at the screens to see what is happening!"

The screens split into four panels showing the Cathedral, Church of Örnäs, Church of Mjölkudden, and the Mission Church. Ten seconds later, a loud bang echoed across Luleå as three of the churches were simultaneously blown to bits. Many Luleå residents were injured or even killed by flying debris and stones, but the Muslims, who had taken shelter in time, were unharmed. It was the unbelievers who suffered, entirely in accordance with the Prophet's will and command."God is great!" continued the imam. "In His infinite wisdom, Allah has decided to preserve and transform the Church of Mjölkudden into a mosque originally designed with a minaret. On the grounds of the three destroyed devil's lairs, new grand mosques will be built, funded by our wealthy friends in Saudi Arabia. Fridays are now the day of rest, and anyone caught defying Muhammad's commands will be punished. Friday prayers are mandatory, and until the mosques are built, we will gather at improvised locations indicated on bulletin boards where you live. On Saturdays and Sundays, we work as usual. Consumption of pork is forbidden. The large pig farm in Alvik has been burned down, and I can guarantee that not a single pig, including the owners, escaped the flames. For many years, they have spread immense amounts of filth that has poisoned people's souls and bodies. Pet dogs are forbidden and will not be allowed. Dogs should be euthanized immediately, and those who do not obey this command will face severe punishment. All toilet paper, as well as dog food, has been cleared from stores and burned. Intimate hygiene should be maintained using water and the left hand. Everything else is *haram*. It's also important to always exit the restroom with the right foot first – yes, you have much to learn, but we are all beginners! But I will gladly guide you on the right path as your good father. Free Qurans in Swedish will be distributed to all families, but only for a transitional period before Arabic Qurans are distributed. Al-Hakim Mosque is now initiating an intensive educational program called 'With Arabic Towards Paradise,' also known as WATP, aiming all Luleå residents to read the Quran in its beautiful original language within three years. Since the equality law was passed in 2025, the municipality has provided all services and information in Swedish and Arabic. Still, it will be only in Arabic in two years, as Swedish will disappear, so it's best to devote your time and energy to studying. Good teachers will lead schools and daycare centers from Al-Hakim Mosque and fully transition to Arabic at the start of the fall term in three weeks. It's a great privilege for you Luleå residents to be included in the vast and growing Muslim-Arab cultural sphere. Soon, you can converse with your brothers and sisters in twenty-five Arabic-speaking countries and, of course, with all Arabs spreading like wildfire across the world. Muslim doctors will have clinics in every neighborhood to provide all men with the privilege of free circumcision.We must purge the worst sinners before building our wonderful new world together. I regret that we must be somewhat harsh, but that's what our great Prophet has decreed. It's the same with adults as with children who don't understand what *halal* is and what *haram* is. They must be beaten into obedience for their own good. Otherwise, they are eternally damned to hell. *Inshallah!* A mosque can never be built on a corrupt foundation. You are all impure and have lived in sin your entire lives. Allah is indeed strict but wonderful and merciful to all who convert to become good Muslims. You can be cleansed of all your sins. For Allah's grace, it's never too late to improve and purify oneself. In accordance with the Prophet's wise command, we will now decisively remove the most impure of the impure, the cancerous human offspring that must be cut away. We begin with the filthy dogs that engage in sex with other unbelieving dogs of the same sex."

For years, Al-Hakim Mosque has been compiling databases of those openly living as LGBTQ+ people, using the Swedish Association for Sexuality Education register as a base, along with those noted to visit the gay café in the district of Skurholmen regularly. The database included 146 people, of whom only forty-five had been captured. The rest realized what would happen to them and remained hidden."Luleå's nine-story former city hall, known as the 'Marble Palace', was displayed on the large screens. The screen was split into two parts; one half showed the entire wall of the building from street level, and the other showed the street from above through a camera placed on the roof. The first bound victim was brought to the roof edge, wearing a black blindfold, and escorted by a *Holy Warrior* on each side. Without hesitating for a second, they pushed the victim over the edge. Microphones cleverly installed on several floors transmitted the horrifying scream and the dull thud when the body hit the ground. The scene was repeated forty-five times. By the time the last body was pushed off, the bodies of the previous victims had reached up to the first floor.

"*Allahu akbar*," the imam continued. "Now, we will cleanse the city of those who have led and encouraged your sins from their high horses. Many of the city's leaders have much to atone for. Here are the first thirty-eight people who will get a taste of the sword."

The imam smiled as he spoke the last words and pointed to the screens, which now showed a gallows placed on the main street opposite the City Hotel. One by one, the tied-up leaders were brought forward, but when it came to beheading, the victims were not blindfolded.

The group consisted of politicians, journalists, editors, and managers within the county administrative board and the municipality. But here, you could also see the bishop, two female priests, well-known entrepreneurs, and surprisingly, four school principals, a local hockey star, and a black female basketball star.

First to the gallows was the Chairman of the Municipal Board, Niklas Nordträsk, who ironically had paved the way for Muslim establishment in Luleå and ensured that the taxpayers' money was used for the mosque construction. Nordträsk was often referred to as "the North Bothnian warlord of the Muslims," having dedicated a significant part of his political career to supporting Muslim expansion in his hometown.

What Nordträsk didn't know was that Muslims detest traitors more than anything else. Since the time of Muhammad, it has always been the collaborators of Muslims who are executed first. The aversion to defectors also explains why very few Muslims ever leave the group, as it is synonymous with receiving a death sentence. On his way to the scaffold, Nordträsk twisted and turned his head in a desperate attempt to make eye contact with a high-ranking Muslim who might save him. Finally, he made eye contact with the city's second imam, who looked amused and nodded at Nordträsk mockingly."Help me now, Mohamed!" Nordträsk shouted desperately. "We're old friends! You just visited me at my summer house a couple of weeks ago. Don't you remember? It must be a mistake. It's ME, Niklas! Can't you see?"

The deputy imam could only offer a slight wave as a farewell. It seemed Nordträsk couldn't believe that what was about to happen would happen. Not to him. That was until he felt four strong hands pushing him down onto the scaffold, and he sensed the motion of the falling sword.

The procedure was repeated thirty-eight times. The victim was laid face down on the wooden bench while a *Holy Warrior* held and pulled the victim's hair tightly, stretching the exposed neck, after which the executioner's sword fell.

A little commotion arose when the bald and large-built fire chief was to be decapitated. He screamed and thrashed about, tossing his big head back and forth before he could finally be subdued with a few hard blows from a cudgel to the back of the head. Most heads required two blows to be completely removed, but a handful fell to the ground with a single blow, including the fire chief's, despite his unusually thick and muscular neck.

"There, we've sent the worst sinners to hell," the imam stated calmly. "They will burn and suffer for eternity. Now, it's finally time, finally time for all of you to begin your lives as good Muslims. We will recite the *Shahadah*, the Islamic declaration of faith, as it is written in the Quran's 37th, 47th, and 48th chapters. I'll recite it first in Arabic, and you should listen: *La ilaha illallah. Muhammad rasul Allah.* Now, repeat after me. It's just one sentence. Speak loudly and clearly so your companions can hear every word. Anyone who refuses or merely moves their lips will be immediately sent to hell with a bullet through the head. Get ready! There is no God but Allah, and Muhammad is his messenger."The crowd obediently repeated the entire sentence, which sounded like a powerful murmur from the heavens over the cityscape.

A score of shots were fired shortly thereafter for those choosing a quick and painless death over surrender to the Muslims. The imam smiled broadly and genuinely pleased himself for the first time. He even gave a slight bow of his head, thanking his audience. The imam thought proudly that not even the Prophet had saved so many souls at the same time. Upwards of fifty thousand souls had been saved. And who could ever believe that the Prophet's teachings would spread almost to the North Pole?

Allah would surely thank him for this great deed when that day came. His place in paradise was secured many times over. Tonight, he would sleep better than ever before.

"Congratulations! A hearty congratulations! Now, we are all Muslims, and from now on, you will be met with an entirely different respect than when you lived in sin as unbelieving dogs. I truly hope we will not see any more bodies hanging from the lampposts. Those hanging there will be taken down today. We will keep only the scaffold in front of the City Hotel and hope it will be sufficient, although many lashings will likely be administered. This is the happiest day of my life! My heart rejoices at receiving so many new souls all at once! Now, you are free to go home and do as you wish. Go home, enjoy the peace of Friday, and take good care of your families! But remember to always, in every moment, live as it befits good Muslims. Otherwise, you don't deserve your respect and freedom. And Allah sees and knows it all! Allah is merciful to the believers but ruthless to those who defy Him! I look forward to seeing all of you at Friday prayers in a week. Then, I will introduce you to Islam's inherent love and mercy. Thank you for coming! Have a truly wonderful Friday evening!"

The shocked residents of Luleå looked around in surprise, glancing at each other in wonder before quickly and silently distancing themselves as fast as they could while keeping their lives intact. Was this nightmare over? Were they truly free now?

Perhaps it would be possible to live a normal life under the new rulers as long as one minded one's business and attended Friday prayers.

Chapter 16

Exile Government in Helsinki

August 3, 2032

The outbreak of war on July 17 gave rise to unprecedented chaos and confusion in the Swedish capital. On the first day of the war, tens of thousands of frightened Stockholmers streamed out of the city, eager to escape the violence, often without a clear idea of where they were headed. Many believed they would be safer in the countryside, and as events would prove, they were right.

Particularly anxious to leave were those in positions of power, especially politicians. Rumors, somewhat exaggerated, spread that thousands of leading Swedes had been murdered in their homes on the first night of the war, with thousands more on death lists. Since the Muslim occupiers quickly seized control of central Stockholm and the southern district called Södermalm, most refugee streams headed northward. Explosions, ongoing gunfire, and smoke from burning buildings in the eastern parts of the city spoke volumes. It was imperative to flee while it was still possible.

Those who realized they might be on the death list chose the main road connection, Roslagsvägen, leading out north from Stockholm towards the town of Norrtälje, intending to reach safety in Finland by boat. One of them was Sweden's Minister of Social Affairs, Annika Strandberg. Despite the heavily congested roads, she managed to cross the bridge over the strait of Stocksund before Swedish engineer soldiers blew it up. Foreseeing as she was, she had packed her small backpack with food from the refrigerator and put on her running shoes before leaving her home near Fridhemsplan on Kungsholmen. She was forced to abandon her newly purchased electric car on Sankt Eriksgatan after waiting hours without moving an inch. The sound and smoke from a couple of detonating grenades the next block over facilitated the decision to leave the expensive car to its fate. Annika Strandberg was in good shape thanks to being in the final stages of a year-long training period for the Stockholm Half Marathon, so she set off northward on light feet, confident that they could carry her far. What worried her was her personal safety. It had been many years since women could move freely—without male escorts and where there weren't people constantly moving—and now she was heading into the countryside. No woman would go out in the forest alone to pick mushrooms in this new environment or use the jogging trails, for that matter. But considering the tens of thousands of ordinary people on the move, she expected, like one in a school of fish, to seek protection by blending into the crowd.

Roslagsvägen was crowded, and the line of stationary cars stretched for miles. Strandberg walked faster than almost everyone else, only occasionally pausing to drink water from lakes and streams while also taking the opportunity to eat something. Being charitable, she generously shared from her backpack with those in greater need, of whom there were many. Unfortunately, that meant she was out of food faster than anticipated.

The weather was quite pleasant, with variable clouds and dry conditions. Her destination was the harbor of Kapellskär, just under sixty miles to the north. She planned to take the ferry to the Finnish island of Åland and the capital, Mariehamn, to find refuge in Finland. She realized she probably shared that plan with many others, so she hurried on, not wanting to have thousands of others ahead of her when she reached Kapellskär. The line of stationary cars with engines off seemed endless. Many vehicles were empty, obviously abandoned by owners who had given up and continued their trip walking. The smell of smoke from the burning and bombed city stung her nose, even though she had walked twenty miles from Stockholm. When she turned around and looked back, she saw a gigantic cloud of black smoke over the burning and bombed city, and the cloud only grew larger as time went on.

Just before the village of Brottby, she caught up with two well-known trade unionists, men whom she vaguely recognized, and joined them. The two union men's escape plan was identical to her own, to the safety of Mariehamn via the ferry from Kapellskär. The two large and overweight men were indeed a bit too old to defend her against potential attackers, but when night fell, it would still be safe with male escorts. The journey became significantly slower, but it was offset by time passing faster when she had someone to talk to.

When they reached Brottby, the road was blocked by a crowd that funneled into a stop. The fleeing trio noticed that hundreds of people were sitting on the road and the roadside eating, and they soon found the reason for the celebration. In the middle of the road were large piles of groceries to help themselves to. Two middle-aged men on motorcycles drove back and forth between the site and the grocery store in Brottby, where they had broken the glass in the entrance door to help the stranded pedestrians.

They grabbed a few cheeses, some cans of tuna and sardines, and a plastic bag of thin white bread, the only bread they could find. After twenty-two hours of hiking, Strandberg and her exhausted companions reached the ferry terminal in Kapellskär, only to find, along with hundreds of others, that no ferry was in sight. A handwritten sign explained that ferry services had been suspended indefinitely for security reasons. In reality, the Swedish Armed Forces had already requisitioned the ferry in Visby harbor, which later would prove useful as the transport vessel of the Gotland Battle Group to the mainland.

Most people who learned that the ferry connection no longer existed spontaneously thought of continuing north along the coast of Roslagen, but the long Norrtälje Bay blocked the road. To continue north, they first had to walk fifteen miles west to Norrtälje, where they could turn north. Everyone was tired, and the situation was dire. There was no food supply in Kapellskär. The only alternative seemed to be Norrtälje, where they could hope for organized food distribution or help from volunteers.

But fate intervened and gave them a better option. Outside the pier lay a smaller, German-flagged sailboat, and Annika Strandberg could see that the boat's home port was Kiel. The Germans dared not dock at the pier for fear that desperate Swedish refugees would hijack the boat.

They had anchored and lay adrift at a safe distance, with about a hundred feet of water between them and the pier. Annika Strandberg attempted to reach out to them.

"I am a minister of the Swedish government. I am in danger of being killed. Please help us!"

The German couple shook their heads and gestured helplessly. They had already been asked at least fifty times, and they didn't think the woman looked like a member of the Swedish government if it even mattered. Then suddenly, one of the union men came to life and surprised everyone by addressing the couple in the boat in perfect, completely at-ease German.

"Kommst du aus Kiel? Es ist meine Heimatstadt."

The German on the sailboat looked as if he had been struck by lightning. He stared speechlessly at the union man for a few seconds.

"Und Herrgott! Kann das wahr sein? Du musst der Schwede sein!"

"Natürlich bin ich wie alle anderen Schweden hier."

As it often does, the world again proved to be a small place. The union man's grandmother was German, and he had spent a few summer weeks in Kiel every year during his upbringing. There, he often played soccer with the boys in the neighborhood, and the man on the boat turned out to be one of them. The union man couldn't recall who the man was, but it didn't matter. He did, however, faintly remember that half a century earlier, he used to be called "the Swede" by his German playmates.

The man on the boat immediately cast off the small dinghy and rowed to the dock. The dinghy was so small that they had to cross in two trips, but soon, the exhausted refugees could stretch out on the bunks in the cramped cabin.

"Is your grandmother still alive?" wondered the German named Sven.

"No, unfortunately, she passed away a few years ago."

"That's sad to hear. Elsa was a fine woman. I remember she used to bring out orange juice and buns when we played ball. Now, I might have the opportunity to repay the generosity. Where do you want to go?"

The Germans promised to take them to Mariehamn, but first, they would sail to the picturesque archipelago village of Grisslehamn to meet up with their friends, who had also sailed from Kiel. The last thing that happened before mobile phone service disappeared was that they set a time via text to meet at the Havsbaden Hotel, where the other couple had checked in to treat themselves to a comfortable bed on land.

Two days later, an armada of thirty-eight recreational boats of various types and sizes, including two German-flagged sailboats, set sail from Grisslehamn with the destination of Mariehamn and Åland. The twenty-mile crossing over the Åland Sea was easily navigated in the summer weather. On July 22, the entire armada docked at the pier in Mariehamn – in the freedom of Finland. Eighty years earlier, refugee traffic across the Baltic Sea had gone in the opposite direction, as hundreds of Balts had made their way to Gotland in rowboats in a much riskier crossing, escaping from the war.

As a Minister, Strandberg became a prioritized passenger, and together with the two men from the union, she secured a seat on the first flight to Helsinki, where the Finnish authorities cared for them well. Helsinki became a popular destination for Swedish refugees, with the bar at the Scandic Park Hotel serving as a common meeting point. The Finnish government viewed with some concern that Helsinki seemed to be evolving into the capital of the Swedish exiles. The hospitality carried obligations toward the Swedes. These obligations could potentially disrupt the ever-present question of relations with Moscow, which was currently more sensitive than it had been since the end of the Cold War.

As a gesture of assistance, the Finnish authorities had booked the entire hotel, including the conference facility, for the Swedish refugees. Various groups of Swedes held meetings almost around the clock, unaware that everything said was being recorded and analyzed by the Finnish security police. Unbeknownst to the Swedes, Moscow continuously received extensive information about the discussions from infiltrators and spies.

Sweden lacked a government because the prime minister, as well as other ministers, had been murdered. Twelve Swedes, holding leading positions in politics, trade union movement, and society, eight Swedish Social Democrats, formed an exile government in Helsinki to represent Sweden in international relations. The decision was crucial if Sweden were to obtain international support. Social Minister Annika Strandberg, the only minister present, was appointed prime minister and head of government by the group. On August 3, seventeen days after the outbreak of war, it was time for the exiled government to make itself known to the world through a press conference on Sveaborg, the historical 18th-century fortress outside of Helsinki, where the exile government had been relocated for security reasons.

Sweden's Social Minister, Annika Strandberg, looked into the TV cameras with her most serious expression, trying to give the impression that she knew what she was doing. Her scattered gaze unsuccessfully revealed the opposite.

"So now you have formed an exile government here in Helsinki," noted the reporter from leading Finnish daily, Hufvudstadsbladet. And here, Carl Olof Cronstedt surrendered Sveaborg in 1808 without a fight, which led to Sweden losing Finland, its eastern half, to Russia. But what legitimacy does this so-called government have? And who are all the other names in this so-called government? I don't recognize a single one of them."

"We are twelve people, all with leadership backgrounds. I have taken on the role of prime minister because I am the only government member alive. The others are mainly union and municipal leaders. We are the only Swedish government that exists now; therefore, we are legitimate."Die Welt's experienced reporter, covering the Nordics, stood up with a raised hand and took the floor without being asked.

"You are known for being very positive about the Islamization of Sweden, what you Swedes have been calling the 'multicultural society.' You have often appeared wearing a veil together with Muslim representatives, and you have many times tweeted and written things like Islam is the religion of peace and love. How do you now view your previous statements?"

"Yes, well, perhaps one shouldn't always interpret everything so literally, and we have indeed received assurances from imams and other Muslim leaders many times that they are working for peace and harmony in a democratic spirit. Cooperation has been strengthened by the close collaboration the Muslim organizations have had with my party—the Social Democrats. All statements must be seen in their context and the prevailing spirit of the times."

"But isn't it quite naive to believe that Muslims, who have pursued a policy of conquest for fourteen hundred years, would change in our time?"

"No, I don't think so. What has happened in Sweden is a result of the policies of an extreme organization, which, unfortunately, has affected our country. The majority of Muslims are, of course, good and peaceful."

"But isn't that the problem in itself?" interjected the reporter from another Finnish newspaper, Helsingin Sanomat. "How do you know which Muslims are good and which are bad? There are all shades on the grayscale. It seems that it is always the militant and aggressive Muslims who eventually call the shots. And the core of Islam is precisely war, conquest, and forcibly converting or annihilating all others. Everything is in the Quran, which they consider God's word. Islam is much more than a religion; rather, it is a political ideology of violence and extremism. Had any of the Swedish politicians ever read the Quran before deciding to let millions of Muslims enter your country?"

"That's hard to say," Strandberg replied, wiping a few beads of sweat from her forehead. You can only hope for the best and continue the work in good democratic order. I haven't read the Quran. Isn't it quite thick and difficult to read? I don't know what significance these old writings have today. Is there anyone who cares about them seriously?"

The twenty reporters present burst into loud laughter, which soon turned into a quiet murmur.

"But now it is a fact that Sweden is at war," objected the reporter from Latvian television. "Maybe different methods other than democratic integration work need to be used? And the question of equality may not be at the top of the agenda right now, or at least shouldn't be. What does the prime minister say?"

"All we can do now is appeal for international help since Sweden's defense has proven not to work, which we must clearly blame Sweden's incompetent military leadership for. We have recently had a visit from Russia's Ambassador to Helsinki, Boris Chigorin, here in Sveaborg, and he was very interested in discussing military support efforts from the Russian side. The discussions will continue, and I have received an invitation to meet with President Putin at his summer residence in Yalta next week."

"But isn't there a great risk associated with appealing for Russian military aid?" wondered the reporter from Die Welt, who had stood up again. "Having a meeting in Crimea sends strange signals, considering what happened there in 2014 and 2022. Wouldn't it be more reasonable to appeal for German or French military aid?"

"Yes, but what are we to do when the whole of Western Europe is shaking at its foundations, and no one else is interested in helping us?" Strandberg asked rhetorically. "The USA has withdrawn all its military and declared that we Europeans must fend for ourselves. Germany and France seem to have had enough of their own problems, as does Britain. We must accept any conceivable help we can get. Otherwise, Sweden will be turned into a Muslim Country."

"But isn't that what you wanted?" said the reporter from Hufvudstadsbladet, without hiding his mockery.

The room was again filled with loud and mocking laughter.

"We now urge the world to recognize us as the legitimate government of Sweden. Feel free to write that down in your media!" Strandberg concluded.

The press conference was over.

Russian TV channels broadcasted selected parts of the press conference that same evening. The news that Sweden was appealing for Russian military aid was highlighted as the most important, followed by the announcement that Russia was the first to recognize the new Swedish government.

As a follow-up to the press conference coverage, an interview with Russia's Ambassador to Finland, Boris Chigorin, was broadcast, commenting on the altered security situation in the Baltic Sea region.

"Russia has every reason to be on its guard and to review its legitimate security interests," Chigorin stated. "The ongoing war in Sweden turns the entire security balance upside down. We cannot risk wasting centuries of Russian efforts in the Baltic Sea region. The Russian government is currently discussing appropriate measures."

Two days later, after seeing the Russian broadcast, the Chinese and North Korean leaders sent word of recognition of the Swedish Exile Government.

Chapter 17

Recruitment of new suicide bombers

August 10, 2032

It's in the bustling shopping mall named "The Fiver" where the Moroccans in Gothenburg gather. This is also where much of the drug trade takes place. Mostly prime cannabis from their homeland, sold under the name "Moroccan." The brown smoke heroin, "brown sugar," however, comes from Afghanistan and Iran, as well as the white, refined heroin. It's like regular sugar. The brown one is milder and preferable, but the white one has a stronger kick.

Inside "The Fiver," it's warm and cozy; for most Moroccans, the mall is like their second home, a constant in their lives, the place they always return to. Nearly eight hundred Moroccan men consider Gothenburg to be their home base. Many have spent most of their adult lives on the streets of Gothenburg, but only a few were children when they arrived. Despite that, Swedish media kept referring to the whole group as children.

The influx of new Moroccans had long ceased because Sweden was no longer seen as an attractive destination. During Sweden's economic crisis, benefits were cut and eventually disappeared altogether. All privileges were withdrawn, and the goodwill and generosity of the Swedes vanished. Life in Sweden wasn't better than anywhere else in Europe. Moreover, winters were long and cold, and occasionally, nights had to be spent outdoors since public transportation was no longer free for Moroccans.

For a few years now, the Moroccans had to support themselves. Some of them were fortunate enough to be lovers of older women who no longer had the allure to afford younger lovers for free. Taxpayers no longer funded the so-called "batik witches'" love lives, but their Moroccan lovers were still seen as cheap to maintain and didn't require much cash. Usually, food and a place to sleep were enough. Some of the women kept multiple lovers, which was rarely a problem for the Moroccans, who were more than willing to offer threesomes, free weed, or whatever their batik witch desired.

Most Moroccans supported themselves by giving blow jobs to Gothenburg gay men for a few hundred kronor each. Some of the Moroccans dolled themselves up, dressed as women, and offered themselves on various forums as professionally trained masseurs specializing in Tantric massage, Nuru massage, and prostate stimulation. This transformation act significantly expanded the market, as most massage customers were heterosexual men and even the occasional woman. Offering sexual services was safer than drug dealing, which could lead to problems with both the Police and violent competitors. Sometimes, the Moroccan sex workers had a connection with a wealthy Gothenburg person, which provided opportunities for gifts and extra cash if they managed to deliver passionately.

The most comfortable way to make a living was to have regular customers, preferably as many as possible. Still, customers had an annoying tendency to constantly want to try new mouths in hopes of finding the perfect one. Such customers were passed around like chain letters among the Moroccans, and those who brought in customers within the network could, in return, receive new customers as thanks for their help. Some were lucky enough to have politicians or police chiefs on their client list, which could lead to unforeseen benefits.

Certainly, the occasional purse snatching and the odd clipped gold necklace contributed to the Moroccans' livelihood, but such occurrences had become much rarer. Swedish women had learned and rarely wore their pearls and diamonds when out and about in town if they ventured out into the streets anymore. Since the Morality Police took control of the streets, it was no longer allowed for women to appear without traditional Muslim attire, which effectively concealed any jewelry. Nowadays, it wasn't that common to catch a naive Swede off guard at an ATM, like they used to on weekends when there were more drunk Swedes out and about.

Even home burglaries had become a dwindling industry, as Swedes had learned not to leave cash and valuables lying around their homes. Everything had worsened since 2014, when the first Moroccans discovered Gothenburg.

Of course, most Moroccan men preferred women, but the obstacles to having sex with men were non-existent, as almost all Moroccans had homosexual experiences from their upbringing. Perhaps the constant smoking and intake of other drugs also contributed to the obstacles being loose and eventually disappearing altogether. Getting ahold of a willing girl without marrying her was impossible back home in Morocco, and what girls would want to marry street boys anyway?

It was the same in all Muslim countries, which paradoxically were always officially homophobic, with death penalties, floggings, or lengthy prison sentences for homosexual acts. But in practice, it didn't apply to ordinary men, and not even real gays, as long as they were discreet.

In Muslim countries, trans people are usually appointed as official scapegoats and forced to shoulder all the world's sins and, like Jesus, be vicariously suffering for everyone else. Trans people stand out and are suitable to use as sacrificial lambs in the abhorrent and murderous spectacle called morality in Muslim countries. It is usually the transsexuals who are executed or given draconian punishments for homosexual acts.

This day, however, was not like other days. With persuasion and coercion, the *Holy Warriors* gathered four to five hundred Moroccans in a big park named Brunnsparken. Their Muslim brothers had lured them there, hoping they would find work and earn good money.

Everyone looked curiously but somewhat distrustfully at the stylish and charismatic man in uniform who grabbed the microphone and welcomed them in official Arabic. But suddenly, something happened that made them drop their jaws in sheer amazement.

The man at the podium, who introduced himself as the supreme commander of the Muslim invasion, unexpectedly transitioned from formal Arabic to Moroccan street slang. It was pure magic. How could such a refined and esteemed man suddenly speak just like them? He must have been sent directly by Allah. It must be Allah speaking directly, through him. If they didn't all know that Muhammad, once and for all, had declared himself the last prophet ever, they might have guessed that a new prophet stood before them.

But the man before them was no prophet. He had just run out of suicide bombers and was now going to replenish the stock.

"Therefore, you are all called to fight in *jihad*. The Swedes are infidel dogs, and you know what Allah, through the great Prophet, has determined that we should do with them? When you reach paradise, seventy-two virgins will await you to welcome you to eternal happiness and pleasure, where nothing is forbidden. In Allah's wonderful paradise – you do what you want with these divinely beautiful virgins. There is exquisite food, sweet fruits, and the finest of drinks in abundance. As martyrs, Allah ensures that you always have the best of the best. Nothing will ever be lacking for you. And already here on earth, in sinful Gothenburg, you will be richly rewarded before you have the great joy of coming to paradise as martyrs. I know that deep in your hearts, you can hardly wait for that day to come finally!"

The recruitment campaign resulted in 155 new suicide bombers enlisting to be used throughout Sweden, wherever they could do the most damage. Bomb belts are easy to produce. Some candidates were rejected because they were considered too unreliable. Some of those who appeared healthy and strong were recruited as *Holy Warriors*.

There are few things as anxiety-inducing as suicide bombers. The creeping discomfort of not being able to trust anyone for a single second and the world could explode into an inferno of dead bodies at any moment. That can break even the most stable psyches.

The worst situations are when two or more suicide bombers are used in tandem. First, a devastating explosion covers the area with lifeless or screaming people who have lost body parts, slowly drawn into eternal darkness while they bleed to death. Then, another blast, when the rescue team and volunteers come to the rescue, and perhaps even another blast when new rescuers arrive. No one who has experienced this hell ever becomes themselves again.

This is a good day. Now it shall be crowned with the greatest pleasures Allah has given us humans, thought Ahmed, as he, accompanied by the two most beautiful boys he could find, strolled towards Hotel Europa, where the presidential suite awaited.

Now, he would once again relive the blissful moments of youth when, as a boy, he bestowed pleasure upon another boy. The boys back home in Casablanca used to close their eyes and dream that it was that flirtatious cousin they secretly loved who enveloped them with their soft lips or maybe that voluptuous aunt with the lovely bosom. But Ahmed was different and always struggled, during the blissful moments, not to reveal his secret. He never closed his eyes. He enjoyed observing the situation as it was. Then, the giver would shamefully close his eyes until the act ended.

Ahmed didn't know that one of Mahmoud's informants discreetly filmed his brief walk with the boys. Mahmoud, Ahmed's right-hand man, had long suspected his superior's weakness and intuitively felt that something inappropriate was going on secretly when Ahmed deviated from his clandestine meetings that no one was informed about.

Mahmoud was not the kind of man to let such an opportunity slip by. Besides, he didn't like that Ahmed smoked—they had imposed a tobacco ban in the caliphate of Sweden, and a good Muslim lives by the rules. Truly living by the book is the core of preaching, like the Prophet. After all, should we, the Muslims, be led by a man who spits out the seeds when he eats grapes? *Aw kayf*, what kind of man is that?

Mahmoud thought it was probably the grape seeds that first aroused his suspicions. He watched the short film while opening another package of honey cakes. He struggled to open the plastic packaging, his eyes fixed on what was happening on the screen.

"*Haiwan*! Do they have to make the packages burglar-proof?!" he cursed himself until he managed to bite a hole in the plastic with his back teeth. *Sharmoota!*"

It was as if he could think better when he nibbled on the wonderful, crispy honey cakes.

No, there was no longer any doubt. Ahmed engaged in *haram*; the Prophet would never have accepted that. And that music he listened to with headphones and closed eyes—*The Mahavishnu Orchestra*—apparently, music by polytheists! He just had to wait for the right moment when he would end the misconduct – in the name of the Prophet. That time would come.

Chapter 18

Meeting in the Muslim Staff

August 7, 2032

The staff celebrated Ahmed's forty-fifth birthday with an extraordinary dinner of Moroccan delicacies, which Hassan and his kitchen staff had been working on all day. An exquisite aromatic tagine of fish and seafood was on the table, accompanied by Couscous and Harissa. The pastilla of the day was based on garlic-braised calf liver, baked in a Berber-style pastry garnished with toasted almonds. Alongside the coriander-spiced Hariran, dried dates and figs were served, as the birthday tradition dictates.

"Unbelievable, Hassan," praised Ahmed. "I never expected to enjoy a real seafood tagine, served in a proper tagine dish, during a war. My grandmother's family was Berber, known for making the best food in Morocco. At home, we ate tagine at least twice a week, always in many variations."

"Absolutely delicious," agreed the Jordanian colonel. "Almost half of Jordan's population is Bedouin, and their cuisine clearly resembles the Berbers'. I can attest that they make the best food. Nothing beats a real *Mansaf* made on a goat, cooked in a pit over flaming coals! *Wallah*!"

"Yet, there are five hundred miles between Jordan and Morocco," the colonel continued. "It's truly remarkable that their cuisine shares so many similarities. I have many Bedouins in my family, and I can attest that much of their culinary art surpasses that of the Arabs."

"Yes, yes, yes. *Mansaf* is famous all over the world," the Chechen general concurred.

After they had concluded the meal, with coffee spiced with cinnamon and a touch of ginger or apple mint tea for those who preferred it, Hassan took the floor. Everyone joined in a unified tribute song to their admired and almost divinely talented leader: "Have a good year, beautiful one, have a good year, beautiful one..."

General Mohamed from Damascus had by far the most experience in real battles. When General Mohamed spoke, the others always listened attentively. They knew he spoke from his own experiences, not just what he had learned at the military academy.

The battles in Syria had been raging for over a decade, and skirmishes could still flare up unexpectedly. It seemed impossible to root out ISIS entirely. Mohamed knew everything there was to know about urban warfare—and then some.

"Today, I think we should not only celebrate Ahmed, but also celebrate that it has been a month since we invaded the Swedes. A month of success! We have every reason to be very pleased with the progress so far, even though the Swedes appear to have mustered up more resources than we could have imagined. Perhaps they are not as foolish and cowardly as we assumed. It's not just a matter of putting out our boots. We must fight, too! What has surprised me is the looting of the weapon depots, which we did not anticipate. It seems we are now fighting against several groups of free forces not controlled from Zone 1. It is starting to resemble the situation in Syria during the worst years. You never know what to expect, as nothing is governed by a higher logic, but I'm used to quick and improvised warfare, so it's not a problem. The Swedes have established a base in Flottsbro to drive a wedge between Skärholmen and Botkyrka, which have long been one hundred percent Muslim population."

General Mohamed zoomed in on the map and placed his rugged finger on Flottsbro, on the eastern shore of Albysjön, an idyllic lake south of Stockholm.

According to information from our infiltrators, the free army south of Stockholm is growing constantly, now totaling perhaps ten thousand lightly armed and untrained soldiers. This Swedish amateur army is led by Uno Svensson, who reportedly works as a carpenter. It doesn't seem like there's much cause for concern, but we should remain vigilant. They have likely acquired light weapons to arm around twenty thousand men, so we have something to watch out for, especially as they are likely to establish contact with our archenemies, the Christian Syrians in Södertälje. The Syrians are highly motivated to fight against us, of course, but they barely have any weapons. We anticipate that the Swedes in Flottsbro will arm the Syrians, as the Swedes have a surplus of weapons and logically prefer to gain more allied soldiers. Trust me, we will soon fight both Syrians and Swedes in Botkyrka. Botkyrka is strategically important for our securing control over Stockholm. *Inshallah*! I will request to return shortly with an update on the situation in Botkyrka."

General Mohamed grabbed the remote control and zoomed in on the Norrbotten coast.

"Up north, on the southern side of the Lule River, an army of free soldiers has gathered in a place called Unbyn, a village between Luleå and Boden. It's probably three to four thousand amateur soldiers in touch with the Swedish infantry and ranger soldiers north of Luleå. According to our information, they have emptied three large weapons depots, which should mean that they have an abundance of weapons. Frankly, I have difficulty seeing how we can hold Luleå and Boden, given the significant losses we suffered initially. But maybe it doesn't matter so much. We should focus on our core areas instead."

General Mohamed glanced questioningly at Ahmed, who nodded without commenting, signaling General Mohamed to continue his presentation. General Mohamed grabbed the remote control again and zoomed in on the West Coast.

"I saved the best for last. We now hold the entire West Coast, from Trelleborg, via Malmö – Landskrona – Helsingborg – Halmstad – Falkenberg – Varberg – Mölndal – Göteborg, all the way to our troop concentration in Vänersborg – Trollhättan – Uddevalla. It has been unexpectedly easy. The Swedes have barely resisted at all, and the feeble attempts they've made have been quickly crushed by our *Holy Warriors*. Now, the Swedes know that anyone who offers any form of resistance is immediately executed, along with all their relatives. Their bodies are left to dangle on lampposts until they rot. To ensure the Swedes don't forget the rules, we have been bombing their homes and apartments if they show any sign of resistance. This act is a good reminder for their neighbors! The West Coast is ours, and I see no immediate threats to our control over the area. Now we enter phase two of Operation Perfect Storm, which means we will establish a corridor connecting our forces on the West Coast with those advancing westward from Örebro."

General Mohamed pointed at the map displayed on the screen and paused to make sure everyone was paying attention.

Instead of heading south towards Zone 1, as the Swedes expect, we will surprise them by advancing north of Lake Vänern. Let them sit there in Zone 1. Why should we waste all our resources on them? Just let them sit there while we occupy the country. They will give up voluntarily once we have secured control over all territory south of the two great lakes. *Inshallah!* We will follow the European Highway 18 via Karlstad, which is already under our control. Then, we will continue south via Åmål and Säffle until we unite our troops at the southern tip of Lake Vänern. This way, we will cut Sweden into two parts, with the southern part becoming the caliphate of *Alzuwid*, as we've discussed. The fate of the northern part of Sweden is something the future will decide. There are mostly forests and wilderness there, and perhaps the Prophet didn't intend to extend his rule all the way up to the North Pole. What's there to do anyway? Eventually, they will voluntarily join *Alzuwid*, if not for anything else but economic reasons, as we block the Baltic Sea. Allah has a plan for everything, and I believe even the North Pole is part of the plan – and in the not-too-distant future, the Moon and Mars will also be inhabited by Muslims," he added philosophically, eliciting encouraging cheers and small applause. "The entire solar system!"

Ahmed interjected with a comment.

"When we have established a contiguous corridor dividing Sweden into two parts, I will go out to the world's media and proclaim the Muslim state of *Alzuwid*, with *Makat Almukarama* as its capital. So, we'll take the opportunity to give Stockholm a new name while declaring the new state. But first, we must have full control over Stockholm! We will, of course, be immediately recognized by at least the twenty to twenty-five states where our Muslim brothers reign. We believe we will also be recognized quickly by France, the United Kingdom, and perhaps Germany, which cannot resist the pressure from their indigenous Muslims. Then follow the remaining states in Western Europe and a dozen African countries where we have good relations. It will take two to three years before the whole world recognizes us as legitimate rulers, but we have all the time in the world! And we know that whoever has military control is eventually recognized as the legitimate government, so everything will work out in the long run."

General Mohamed continued:

"On the eastern front, the situation is different. Swedish military units have established themselves with good resources north of Stockholm. This means we should approach Stockholm from Eskilstuna, south of Lake Mälaren. Then, we will follow the European Highway 18 eastward from Eskilstuna, and I expect to proceed without major resistance from Strängnäs and Mariefred until we reach Södertälje. However, there may be local pockets of resistance, both from military troops and free soldiers, which must be restrained, and will slow down our advance. I assess that we will arrive at Södertälje no later than September first. We expect to suspend fighting for a few weeks east of Södertälje because our troops will need rest by then. This will give us time to reorganize ourselves for the march towards Stockholm and receive reinforcements from existing troops from Norrköping, where we have full control."

General Mohamed paused briefly to flip through his notes before resuming his presentation.

"As I mentioned, I will now return to Botkyrka, the strategically important area between Södertälje and Stockholm. We can see that the Swedes aren't sitting still and mustering greater resources than anticipated. From their base in Flottsbro, their civilian forces have had the time to organize resistance, which unfortunately includes Södertälje. We will face significant opposition, and I believe we will be stuck for a few weeks, perhaps even months, before reaching the southern parts of Stockholm, where we can join our own units. My experiences from the battles in Damascus and Homs tell me this will be a tough nut to crack. Urban combat is truly something special, but it's something we master better than anyone else. The situation in central Stockholm changes daily, so we cannot predict what awaits us there. But one thing is certain: we must secure control over Stockholm to break the Swedish resistance."

Ahmed interjected again.

"Once we have secured control over Stockholm, it will be time for us in leadership to permanently move to Stockholm. As you know, we chose to initially establish ourselves in Gothenburg, expecting it to be easy to take control of the West Coast, and we were right. But we have decided to set up our headquarters in the Royal Palace in Stockholm, which expresses deep symbolism. Sweden has been governed from this strategic location for a thousand years, controlling the connection between inner Lake Mälaren and the Baltic Sea. Additionally, the Swedes are unlikely to bomb their palace if they manage to muster resources for such an act. We hear their artillery remains stuck in Boden; one wonders what they were thinking."

They shook their heads and laughed loudly at the Swedes' idiocy.

"Why didn't they store the artillery on the moon instead? Hahaha!"

"How can you know so much about the Swedes?" wondered the Chechen colonel. "You seem to know every detail of their history."

In response, Ahmed glanced at the Chechen colonel with a patronizing smile and continued.

"We expect the Swedes will be unwilling to destroy their historical buildings, which carry significant meaning. For that reason, we will blow up and remove virtually everything. We will break their resistance and dissolve their identity by depriving the Swedes of their national symbols. Much has already been done through the long-term work initiated by a Swedish immigrant who served as minister of culture in the days—may she rest in peace!"

"But how on earth do you know a person like her?" the Chechen colonel wondered, fascinated.

"I met her for the first time in 2019 when the Muslim Brotherhood invited her as a speaker. She's my type, even though she's black, a very strong and multifaceted woman, I must say. Since then, we've been in regular contact, and we bumped into each other by pure chance in Brussels in 2025. The Swedes never discovered that she's been on our payroll since 2019. It's unbelievable how naive the Swedes are."

"So, what happened to her?" the Saudi asked.

"She was murdered by a Swedish nationalist a couple of days after we invaded—a few shots in her back from close range. Swedish police arrested the shooter, and his whereabouts are unclear. Perhaps he will be hailed as a Swedish national hero."

"Oh, but how come the Swedes allowed her to work and destroy their culture for so many years?"

"Yes, that's something I'll never understand," Ahmed replied. "In Sweden, there's been a peculiar atmosphere where politicians benefited from distancing themselves from their countrymen and culture. A large part of the Swede's money has been sent abroad to support their enemies. Try to comprehend that if you can. The money has often been secretly tied to the sale of Swedish weapons. The peace-loving Swedes have built up a world-class arms industry and exported huge quantities of weapons to our own countries. Sweden is the world's largest per capita arms exporter. They even surpass the Jews in occupied Palestine. Is this a love for peace or a guise?"

"But how can this be possible?" wondered the Saudi. "How? I can't comprehend."

"In Sweden, somehow, it's been considered more prestigious to be an internationalist than a nationalist. Swedishness has been viewed as old-fashioned and narrow-minded. Especially by the left-leaning, which is cosmopolitan, akin to liberalism, but oddly enough, within certain conservative circles. They had a conservative Prime Minister, Fredrik Reinfeldt was his name, who traveled around vilifying his own culture in his speeches. He outright said he thought Swedes were barbarians! It may seem unbelievable, but that's how it is."

"The female leaders in Sweden – just the fact that they are female leaders, by the way – often pretend to be virtuous Muslims by posing in hijab, and now they'll get the chance to become Muslims for real! But I wonder if they've thought through what that entails for them. They're used to dominating their men and taking up significant space in public life, but that's not how good Muslim women behave. And we know that women want the security of letting strong men decide for them. One of them was named Mona Sahlin," Ahmed continued. "A socialist who almost became prime minister, who used to show up in hijab and say that Swedish culture was so low-standing that it wasn't even worth calling culture, can you believe that?"

"In our countries, such politicians would be immediately killed by the audience!" Mahmoud remarked.

"Yes, and that's what such politicians deserve," the Chechen colonel stated. "It's blatant treason. They should be skinned alive before being thrown into the fire."

"It's very difficult to understand the West, especially what they call liberalism and democracy. They talk about individual freedom all the time. I've spent years studying their system, but I'm not sure I've truly grasped the core of it yet. It's as if they want to punish themselves. I believe it's ultimately about pure decadence and a lack of morals and ethics. That's why they are in such great need of our leadership to cleanse themselves by living under Sharia," said Ahmed.

"Yes, we shall help the Swedes and show them the right path," said the Saudi. "It's Allah's will that we should educate them with our insights and teach them to become good Muslims as we ourselves are. But it seems like it's a long road ahead. Perhaps it will take generations. I have a question," the Saudi continued. "I can't understand how you know and remember precisely everything you've read over so many years," asked the Saudi.

"Haha, I've explained this to you before. For me, it's the opposite. I can never forget anything I've read, even though I wish I could. I can visualize every thousands of pages I've read about Sweden, from newspapers, books, and reports. It's like I can recall them from when I read them yesterday. Switch them on and off, so to speak. I know everything about Sweden's short history. I can give you the names of all Swedes who've been in their parliament over the last thirty years," said Ahmed.

"Thank you, thank you, but that's enough. You've been given a great gift from Allah; perhaps it was the same gift the Prophet received. But the Prophet was the last of the prophets, so you're probably not a new prophet after all," said the Saudi. "Although one might think so!"

"Allah may have changed his mind," interjected General Mohamed. "Muhammad was, after all, only Allah's messenger. We who have studied the Quran know that there are many contradictions but that everything still has its logical explanation because Allah sometimes changes his mind. No one can question Allah's will! Perhaps Allah decided to send a new messenger to earth. You can never know."

"No, you can't," replied Ahmed. "But I'm not your new prophet. I'm just an ordinary person who has been given an extraordinary brain, which might even resemble the Prophet's. Muhammed remembered everything he ever saw and heard, and his words came directly from Allah. But my words only come from myself, and I have weaknesses like everyone else. Or what do you say about it, Mahmoud? You know me well and have been my trusted friend for many years. We have always been a hundred percent loyal to each other, haven't we?"

Mahmoud jerked back, momentarily losing both his eloquence and composure. From the corner of his eye, he noticed Hassan, Ahmed's loyal aide, studying him intently. The film thought Mahmoud, Ahmed knows

I'm watching him. Now I'm done for! Damn, it must be Hassan who's caught wind of something.

"I say you are our leader here and now and that your fantastic brain works in the name of Islam," Mahmoud stammered out.

"Thank you, Mahmoud, my friend, *habibi*. I knew I could always count on you! Let's return to reality now and continue!" Ahmed responded.

Mahmoud sensed the others observing him discreetly, without directly staring at him. They sensed that something significant had transpired between Ahmed and Mahmoud that wasn't good, but they couldn't understand what it was about.

In the corner of his eye, Mahmoud saw a hint of a smile on Hassan's face before he turned away and returned to clearing the food. Mahmoud nervously fumbled in his pocket and pulled out a honey cake with sesame seeds, which he casually started nibbling on to appear distracted and unaffected.

Ahmed resumed speaking.

"Old Town of Stockholm and the areas around Slussen and Norrström will have Muslim architecture with monumental buildings far surpass the existing ones. The Sager Palace, the prime minister's residence, will be the first building to be demolished, apart from the churches. And, eventually, the Royal Palace, but it will serve as our headquarters for a while. I have devised these plans in collaboration with our architects, which I will show you in detail once we are in the palace. Everything has been meticulously prepared and considered.

Makat Almukarama will become the most beautiful city in the world! No one can overlook that Allah has been extremely generous and has beautiful nature in this area surrounded by water, and we will fully exploit that. Inshallah! *Makat Almukarama* will become a pilgrimage site to the delight of Muslims worldwide. Old Town will be completely demolished and transformed into the world's largest mosque area that will rival Mecca's grandeur. We will begin construction next spring where the Stockholm Cathedral currently stands. All the plans are ready. The name will be decided on by the Sacred Committee of the Muslim Brotherhood, of which I am a member. The island Riddarholmen will become a commercial center and meeting place for Muslims worldwide, with a traditional bazaar, many Arabic restaurants, and tea houses. And a gigantic *Hamam*, housed in a state-of-the-art glass and white marble conference center. Exquisite, blonde, fair-skinned girls will abound in the men's section, where there will be a hundred private rooms for recreation and contemplation in the company of girls."

The audience burst into laughter and nodded eagerly.

"*Jamil! Shukran!*" exclaimed the Chechen in a spontaneous outburst.

"We can hardly contain ourselves! Hahaha! Hahaha!" The Chechen laughed until he was short of breath, and his face turned red.

"It's not that we lack beautiful blonde women, as it is now, but they really need to be trained in the art of massage," said the Jordanian. The ideal would be Swedish blondes with fingers like a Thai woman!"

"*Hahahascchhhhaaaah-ha! Sccchhhaaahasccchaaha!*" Mahmoud joined in with a loud and somewhat exaggerated burst of laughter.

The guttural grunting and snorting from Mahmoud's nose and mouth resembled the grunting of a pig in labor, causing everyone to fall silent and turn their gaze toward his hunched-over body, which lay face down on the table, shaking with convulsions."

"*Wallah!*" Mahmoud concluded in an attempt to pull himself together. He sat straight, wiped his eyes with his knuckles, and returned to reality.

Ahmed was the only one not laughing.

"The island of Skeppsholmen will be transformed into a cultural center for Islamic culture, named the Gamal Abdel Nasser Institute. Something in the style of the Arab Institute in Paris, but bigger! The attractions on Djurgården will be transformed, but the amusement park Gröna Lund will remain as it is, though the alcohol bars will, of course, be closed and converted into prayer rooms. At the outdoor museum, Skansen, the old wooden buildings have already been burned down to make way for the exhibition of Muslim artifacts and traditional Muslim art. Swedish girls will be taught carpet weaving to produce high-quality prayer mats. At Skansen, which will be renamed *Dijlat al Khair,* visitors can observe the girls' diligent work and even have the chance to try their hand at this noble art. The Nordic Museum will be removed for a newly built military academy with global Muslim geopolitics as its main theme. The playground, Junibacken, will be renamed "One Thousand and One Nights" and feature appropriate fairy tale characters from the Arab fairy tales."

Ahmed waved his hands and paused for a few seconds before continuing.

"*Makat Almukarama* will become an enticing attraction for Muslims worldwide. We expect millions of visitors every year. Here, good Muslims can truly enjoy life. But life has an end before it begins anew for those who will be admitted to paradise.

Therefore, we have already begun transforming the Woodland Cemetery into a Muslim burial ground. The Jewish section has already been plowed away and sanitized with burnt lime. To be safe, we have also had all contaminated Jewish soil excavated, removed, and replaced with halal soil. The same will soon happen to the Christian section. *Jawad Kadhimain* is the new name of the cemetery."

It was midnight and time to adjourn the meeting for much-needed sleep.

"Tomorrow, we will serve meze, with influences from Turkish-Greek cuisine," Hassan concluded, bowing lightly and gracefully to his principals. As he turned to leave, he could feel Mahmoud's gaze burning into his back."

Chapter 19

Prince Carl Philip is Crowned King

September 9, 2032, Zone 1

The news of Queen Victoria's passing cast a somber mood in the underground chambers of Zone 1. The Malaysian government's press release stated, "Sweden's Queen, Victoria Bernadotte, passed away suddenly on September 4, 2032, in her suite at the Mandarin Oriental in Kuala Lumpur, where she had been staying since the attack on Sweden on July 17."

The cause of death was cited as heart failure due to depression and self-starvation. Despite the swift intervention of cardiac specialists, her life could not be saved. Malaysia's government expressed compassion in the communication, acknowledging the chaotic situation in Sweden, which made it difficult to convey condolences directly.

The Queen's passing came at a particularly distraught time, given Sweden's dire situation, especially with Mahmoud's death squads having murdered the majority of Swedish leadership. Swedish governance was needed, but uncertainties arose with the Queen's children being minors.

The day after the Queen's passing, Gyllenstierna initiated a meeting with the newly appointed Prime Minister, Anna-Lena Beckstedt, who had previously served as the Minister of Justice and was thus expected to provide clarity.

"I've considered the situation," began Beckstedt, "and I've already been in touch with Prince Daniel, which I'll elaborate on shortly. Since 1980, Sweden has adopted full cognatic primogeniture, meaning the monarch's oldest heir inherits the throne regardless of gender."

"Yes, I see. I wasn't familiar with that term, but I understand its implications," replied Gyllenstierna.

"In the first paragraph of the succession order, it is explicitly stated that older siblings and their descendants take precedence over younger siblings and their descendants," Beckstedt explained.

Gyllenstierna nodded in agreement. As I suspected, this must mean that Princess Estelle will ascend to the throne, thought Gyllenstierna.

"Direct line of descent, then!" remarked Gyllenstierna.

"Exactly," said Beckstedt. "Estelle is twenty years old, and according to the law, she can assume the role of Head of State. But, in my opinion, having a twenty-year-old on the throne is still inappropriate when Sweden needs all forms of unified leadership. One option could be for Prince Daniel to ensure that his children renounce their claims to the throne. I've already spoken with Daniel, and he's determined to shield his children from the responsibilities of monarchy at this time. Daniel is a wise man who understands that Sweden desperately needs strong leadership. So, the children will renounce their claims."

"In that case, I assume the ball falls to Prince Carl Philip," said Gyllenstierna. "It's very interesting, especially since the prince is known as a true Swedish patriot and has a good reputation in the military."

"Exactly, and I've already prepared him for the possibility. He accepts without any reservation," Beckstedt confirmed.

"Fantastic work, Anna-Lena!" praised Gyllenstierna.

Two days later, Princess Madeleine, Victoria's younger sister, gave a widely publicized interview in The New York Times, where she unequivocally renounced all claims to the Swedish throne, both for herself and her children: "I have lived in New York my entire adult life and feel more American than Swedish. I have nothing left in Sweden, especially since my beloved sister Victoria tragically passed away. Victoria was an outstanding role model to whom I cannot compare myself. All I want is to live and age peacefully with my husband and children and perhaps one day have the joy of experiencing my grandchildren. No one stands to gain from harming me. Therefore, I appeal to be left alone for the rest of my life."

At the oval conference table in Zone 1, pea soup and pancakes with jam, accompanied by overly whipped cream bordering on butter, were served. The meeting participants took their seats with the plates in front of them.

No one could help raise their eyebrows when they realized who today's guest was. Unfazed by everyone's stares, Prince Carl Philip immediately began spooning the pea soup with a hearty appetite. Once everyone had settled into their seats, Gyllenstierna spoke up.

"As you know, our country is without a head of state since the poisoning of our beloved Queen Victoria. You have been informed that Queen Victoria's children have renounced their places in the succession order. This means that Prince Carl Philip now stands next in line to the throne. Let us warmly welcome Prince Carl Philip with a big round of applause. We are eager to hear from you!"

Everyone rose to their feet and applauded vigorously for thirty seconds while the prince remained seated. Everyone anticipated what was next on the agenda, after which Prime Minister Beckstedt took the floor.

"Welcome, we all wish you, Prince Carl Philip! Sweden's interim government – the participants in this meeting – will now decide to crown Prince Carl Philip Bernadotte as the King of Sweden. Those who approve this proposal should raise their hands."

All hands went up quickly without the slightest delay.

"A vote count is unnecessary, as all present support the proposal. Prince Carl Philip Bernadotte is now elected as the King of Sweden by acclamation. Let it be recorded! May I ask the Prince, or should I perhaps already say the King, to stand up and deliver his royal oath?"

The fifty-four-year-old prince rose quickly, with the ease of a teenager, and strode resolutely to the podium. The spectators scrutinized the future King before them, who was still in his prime despite the salt-and-pepper hair and beard, which showed that he was experienced and able.

Prince Carl Philip was not as elegantly attired as his father, Carl XVI Gustaf, when he took his royal oath in the Royal Palace's council chamber fifty-nine years earlier. A tailcoat was not available in Zone 1, but the prince had been lent a handsome, white ceremonial uniform that was conveniently on hand. Not a single medal dangled from his chest. It would be a simple coronation, eighty meters below the surface and without TV cameras, but everything was documented on video for posterity.

"Hello, everyone! It's a great honor to stand here before you," the prince began in a subdued tone. "It's been less than an hour since I've arrived in Zone 1. I hope you'll forgive me for being a bit hungry, but it took thirty-eight hours – without food – to get here, and we were nearly ambushed by the enemy many times. We were chased, but I managed to outdrive them, so here we are."

The prime minister handed him a paper, from which the future king began to read aloud:

"As my beloved sister, Queen Victoria, has passed away, I shall succeed her as the king of our country. My regnal name shall be Carl VII Philip, and I have the royal title of King of Sweden. My motto shall be: For a free Sweden – to the last drop of blood."

Much like his father, the future king wasn't quite comfortable in the role of communicator and representative of Sweden. Like his father, King Carl XVI Gustaf, the prince sometimes said he wasn't made for offices and halls but thrived best outdoors. Outdoors, the prince could indulge in hunting, motorsports, and outdoor activities, giving him freedom. Freedom from the demanding and suffocating role fate had assigned him as a prince.

Dyslexia had made the long journey through school tiresome and boring, and it sometimes became all too clear that he wasn't a theoretical genius. But like his father, he possessed a strong sense of duty, high work capacity, and genuine humility despite his position. With a nice physique and good social skills, he had the ability to pull himself together and stand up when needed. In short, he was an impressive individual who inspired trust.

"Now, let's proceed to the royal oath. Please repeat the words I'm about to read, sentence by sentence," said Prime Minister Beckstedt. "This will take about four minutes."

"We, Carl Philip, King of Sweden ... in accordance with the Instrument of Government of 1809 ... and accordance with current laws ... King of Sweden... so help me God, to life and soul."

The new King of Sweden then sat down and signed his recently recited royal oath. Sweden now had its ninth Bernadotte on the throne in 223 years.

As soon as the pen scratched the paper, the Royal Anthem spontaneously burst out, accompanied by dynamic applause from those present. The song seemed to have never been sung with such emotion and power as in this moment. When the song died, a loud cheer erupted for the new King, piercingly echoing in the underground chamber where they were gathered.

"Thank you, thank you so much!" said the king. "We are at war now, and I want to clarify one thing clearly. I want you to call me Carl or Kalle, but don't waste energy speaking pompous language. I've done a long military service in the navy, and everyone there knows I was just one of the guys and worked under the same conditions as everyone else," he said, gazing towards Navy Chief Fred Bergström.

"Yes, I can certainly attest to that," said Bergström, "since I was Kalle's supervisor. The king graduated with top marks and the highest commendations possible. And as the captain of a patrol boat, it wasn't just about being one of the guys but also about exercising very concrete leadership, isn't that right, Your Majesty?" Berggren added, winking.

The king nodded in agreement and continued:

"Right now, I'm most interested in those pancakes, with cream and ... Queen's jam ..."

Suddenly, tears welled up in the king's eyes.

"Poor Vickan, she was the best big sister one could wish for. And what a wonderful sense of humor she had!"

Gyllenstierna stood up and summarized the meeting.

"Yes, there is much to mourn, not least the beloved Queen Victoria, cherished by the Swedish people. But today, above all, let us rejoice that Sweden has a new king. A new head of state to rally around, who will help lead the Swedish people toward a future free from foreign occupiers and civil war. We will now go out on all available channels, primarily the radio, and announce that Sweden has a new Head of State and that King Carl Philip VII will address the Swedish people in a radio speech tonight at 8:00 p.m."

"Let's just hope that the so-called exile government in Helsinki doesn't go out in the world media and denounce the coronation," remarked SÄPO Chief Bianca Popovic. "It would weaken the message to the Swedish people."

"Those clowns are soon obsolete," said Gyllenstierna. "No country, except for Russia, China, and North Korea, has recognized them as legitimate governments. The Finns don't know what to do with them, so they've put them on voluntary house arrest in Sveaborg. There, they can sit and pass the time however they like. We are the government here and no one else!"

Chapter 20

King Carl Philip addresses the Swedish people

September 9, 2032, 8 p.m.

As the clock struck 8 p.m., tension rose in the radio room in Zone 1 while the new king leaned back in his chair, preparing for his important speech to the Swedish people. The king appeared to meditate with closed eyes. The question of microphone placement was discussed.

"No, I want to stand up when I speak," said King Carl Philip.

"But wouldn't it be easier to read the script if you're sitting down?" asked Gyllenstierna.

"No, I don't read well if I have to speak simultaneously. I'll use my own tricks to remember what's in the script. If I get stuck, you can point out where we are in the speech so I can get back on track. Okay?"

The king requested to speak without an audience, meaning only Gyllenstierna, the prime minister, and Navy Chief Bergström were present. Bergström's presence served mainly as a coach and moral support since he had a calming and strengthening effect on the king.

Gyllenstierna announced the broadcast, stating that Prince Carl Philip Bernadotte had been chosen as the King of Sweden due to Queen Victoria's passing. King Carl Philip VII would now deliver his first address to the Swedish people.

"Dear Swedes. Dear Swedish citizens of all ethnicities. At noon today, eight hours ago, I, Carl Philip Bernadotte, was chosen as the King of Sweden by Sweden's legitimate government in a unanimous decision. My regnal name is Carl Philip VII. My motto is: 'For Sweden – to the last drop of blood.' It is a great honor for me now to address the entire Swedish population, which I do from a secret location, but I assure you that I am in our beloved country. We have been at war since July seventeen. We have been unjustly subjected to a cowardly and unprovoked attack by a foreign invader, not a country, but an organization called the Muslim Brotherhood."

Carl Philip Bernadotte was not known as a particularly good speaker. His voice was initially tense, somewhat unclear, and hesitant, not hitting the right tone. But after a few sentences, the voice became firm and strong. The king closed his eyes and swayed his head sideways slightly, back and forth, as he spoke into the hanging microphone.

The three listeners glanced at each other. Gyllenstierna pointed to the script that the king deviated from after the opening sentences. The prime minister shook her head and rolled her eyes while Bergström studied the king's facial expressions and movements.

This was not the young Carl Philip he had come to know thirty-five years ago. The ambitious, hardworking, yet insecure pupil had transformed into a powerful man who knew what he wanted. Now, he stood before them in a trance, with closed eyes and his right fist clenched in the air, like a Bolshevik salute from another era.

"I stand here dressed in the field uniform I shall wear until victory is won. I, King Carl Philip, will fight by your side – no matter what hardships await. And I know full well that all of you will fight, to the end, by my side."

The voice had become rough and almost hissing, with a slight whistling sound from the lower respiratory system that pierced through.

"We shall defeat the enemy in our cities. We shall annihilate the enemy and drive these inhumane and cowardly villains out of every village and every corner of our country. *We* shall tear down and blow up their mosques until only piles of rubble remain! *We* shall chase them out of our country without mercy. They shall see who they are dealing with, and they will regret ever touching foot on our land!"

The king had transformed into a roaring lion, leaving the script behind.

The prime minister pointed meaningfully at Gyllenstierna and the king, urging him to stop. Gyllenstierna stepped forward and patted the king on the shoulder, causing him to turn his head and fall silent momentarily as if shaking himself out of a trance. Then he continued with a low, whispering voice:

"But dear Swedes. Dear Swedes of all ethnicities and religions, listen to this very, very carefully now. The enemy is those who fight on the invaders' side – and only them. We must remember that hundreds of thousands of good Muslims are loyal Swedes, just like ourselves. I urge all Swedes not to harass our Swedish Muslims. I urge all Swedes to protect them, by all means, if they are unjustly subjected to attacks or harassment. We shall fight to defeat the enemy, but the enemy is not civilians and unarmed people. The enemy bears a weapon. Spare the civilians and use your strength against the real enemy! For Sweden – to the last drop of blood, is our new motto. For Sweden – to the last drop of blood! Never forget that I, King Carl Philip, will fight by your side every second until victory is achieved! Any message of our surrender is false! We fight together until the enemy surrenders or the last drop of blood has flowed from our bodies. We will never give up! Never, ever. Sweden belongs to us Swedes. Sweden for the Swedes!"

Gyllenstierna pressed the off button as the exhausted king sank into a chair. The last sentences had been delivered with a roar that no one believed Carl Philip capable of.

"Great, absolutely great!" exclaimed Bergström, shaking his head as if what he had just witnessed couldn't be true.

"Yes," replied Gyllenstierna. "This turned out much, much better than our script, fantastic!"

The prime minister stood up and left the room silently while Gyllenstierna and Bergström hugged the king.

Chapter 21

Sweden under military rule

September 15, 2032, Zone 1

The trio of Zone 1 politicians comprising the state, agriculture, and education ministers sat waiting on one side of the table as Gyllenstierna sat opposite them, smiling friendly. Despite his inviting demeanor, the three politicians wore stern expressions, choosing not to reciprocate Gyllenstierna's smile. Noticing the prime minister crossed arms, Gyllenstierna broke the silence.

"Well, you wanted to meet me about a pressing issue, but I hope we, as agreeable government colleagues, can find a solution," Gyllenstierna diplomatically began. "Let's hear it."

"I'll get straight to the point," replied Prime Minister Beckstedt. "We've become increasingly concerned about the legitimacy of our actions here in Zone 1. Especially since Foreign Minister Margot Wallfors seems to have risen from the dead and emerged as the new leader of the exile government in Helsinki."

"Yes, it's fortunate she could rehabilitate so quickly despite her injuries. But, yes, it was quite surprising for all of us."

"The concern is that Foreign Minister Wallfors is first in line of succession after our deceased prime minister, who is several steps ahead of me. This means I am not Sweden's legitimate prime minister, and everything we've done is legally flawed, not to mention could be considered treason. That scares me. We don't know the consequences after the war ends, which applies to all of us in our so-called government here in Zone 1."

"Yes, there are certain things to consider," Gyllenstierna replied.

"I've informed Margot that she should urgently come here and take on the role of prime minister and head of government," Beckstedt continued. "But she has already rejected the proposal. She says the situation is too dangerous, considering the Islamists are gaining more ground every day, and she's more useful alive than as a martyr. Margot won't come here."

"That's understandable, considering we lost both Mariestad and Karlsborg. Yesterday, I ordered preparations for evacuation to Zone 2, so maybe that's where Foreign Minister Wallfors will go instead. Brännström and Väster are currently transferring fifteen hundred soldiers from the task force by boat across Lake Vättern from Motala to Aspa Bruk, where we're establishing a new defense line. If Aspa Bruk falls, we'll evacuate to Zone 2.

If necessary, I assess that we'll have plenty of time for an orderly evacuation. We, the government, will take helicopters, which will be much safer.

"I hear what you're saying, but regardless of whether Zone 1 survives or not, I'm no longer the prime minister, which means we have an illegitimate government. All the decisions we've made are baseless. Sweden has no king, only a prince claiming to be king. The only legitimate government is the exile government in Helsinki, with Margot Wallfors as Prime Minister. The three of us, as political representatives, have decided to join the exile government in Helsinki. We now request secure transport to Gävle, which has not yet fallen."

"Then we'll have two competing governments, which would be very bad for Sweden. The exiled government lacks the means to enact any policy. We in Zone 1 have all the military resources and know how to use them. I seriously urge you three to reconsider your decision and stay with us. For the sake of our country's salvation."

"That's out of the question, as Margot Wallfors is undoubtedly our legitimate Prime Minister," interjected the agriculture minister.

"Margot Wallfors is primarily responsible for Sweden being at war. Margot Wallfors has ensured that billions of Swedish taxpayer dollars have been used to feed Muslim terrorist organizations, thus partially financing the Muslim Brotherhood's attacks on us. We have strong indications that Swedish taxpayers' money has ended up in the pockets of the Muslim Brotherhood and its affiliated organizations like ISIS and Al-Qaeda. Not to mention all the support for extremist-controlled Muslim organizations here in Sweden. They have been sailing under false flags and pretending to carry out integration and gender equality projects. Atrocious!"

"Wallfors is a good representative of the Swedish Social Democrats, just like myself, and a good representative of the Swedish model. And what about you, Gyllenstierna, or should I call you by your real name, Öztürk – don't you think we know it? Whose side are you really on?"

"I overheard you speaking Arabic over the radio link," the young minister of education said.

"Who were you talking to, if I may ask? Was it perhaps with the Islamist leader Ahmed Ben Barka?"

"I don't speak Arabic at all, so I'll pass on that question," replied Gyllenstierna, his face blushing. "As the Minister of Education, you should be able to distinguish between Turkish and Arabic. I speak Turkish, of course, which is my parents' mother tongue, and a bit of Kurdish because one of our branches of the family is Kurdish. I guess you heard me talking to my dad the other day. He has diabetes, and we can't get any medicine for him, so he asked if I could get some. Which I couldn't. Things are dire for all of us."

"What about Ali Baksi then?" wondered the minister of agriculture. "He also speaks a lot of gibberish on the radio link and the phone, and God knows who he's talking to. I feel uncomfortable with a lot of Muslims here in Zone 1. Who knows who they're really working for? It's the same everywhere in all organizations in Sweden."

"Now you need to stop with your pathetic conspiracy theories," snapped Gyllenstierna. "I was born in Sweden, and I am just as Swedish as you are! And pissed off now! It's you who have opened the country to uncontrolled Muslim and African mass immigration, not me and Ali. We have been consistent opponents of your totally insane policies."

"At least you don't look like Swedes when someone looks at you," retorted the Minister of Agriculture.

"Do you really imagine that I would work for the Muslim Brotherhood just because I have black hair and because my parents have Turkish descent? They have been Swedish citizens for fifty-five years. They are secular Muslims and hate Islamic extremism. Much more than the minister of education has shown during his political career, which has mostly been about creating a joke of a multicultural society."

"I have always stood up for multiculturalism and international solidarity," replied the minister of education, "and I still do."

"But you know what?" said Gyllenstierna. "The word multicultural is just a euphemism for Muslims. What you three have worked for throughout your political careers is a Muslim Sweden, but you're good at disguising your intentions. Or maybe you're so stupid that you don't understand what you're doing when you help promote Muslim extremists, even using taxpayer money? Personally, I have consistently opposed the Islamization of Sweden, just like Alfred Baksi. We know what Islamization entails and how incredibly dangerous it is once it takes hold. Look at what happened to Lebanon and now to Sweden!"

"Don't blame us politicians for Sweden being invaded," snapped the prime minister.

"In this country, there isn't a single politician who knows or has learned anything from history," replied Gyllenstierna. "The parliament is filled with uneducated, ignorant, opportunistic scum who deceive and misinform the Swedish people. Politicians are short-term opportunists led by the media, with the state and the Bonnier family at the forefront. It's you who have betrayed Sweden, not me and Ali!"

"But I bet you sit there and celebrate *Ramadan* and *Eid* with your families!" said the prime minister. "How Swedish is that? Sweden is multicultural, and people have multiple loyalties, some of which collide. You will never know which loyalty weighs heaviest when it comes down to it. Regardless, we have decided to leave Zone 1, and nothing can change that."

"Of course, we celebrate *Eid* and *Ramadan*," replied Gyllenstierna. "Those are our traditions, just like you celebrate Christmas and Easter. But you don't accuse Brännström of treason because he's a real Swede in your eyes. Have you considered that he has black hair and dark eyes? But Brännström's hair is straight, so he's not a 'real' blackhead in your eyes. But Ali's and mine's hair is curly, so we're blackheads. How many generations does one have to live in Sweden to be a real Swede?"

"It's not about time," said the minister of agriculture. "It's about embracing Swedish traditions."

"Those of you who point fingers at others and call them Nazis and racists are the real racists," said Gyllenstierna. "We with immigrant backgrounds have a sensitive radar for that. Leftists only see races and colors. You call it identity politics. Our experience is that those you call Nazis are often quite free from racism. Most of the time, they are decent people who see others for who they are and what they actually do, without a Marxist filter in front of their eyes."

"So, you're saying our parties are racist?" said the Minister of Education. "Really? You're joking!"

"The Social Democrats and the Center Party have the darkest history, with a past in both Nazism and eugenics. Sweden was the first in the world to establish a so-called eugenic institute with the premise that Swedes stood at the top of the evolutionary ladder. The Center Party believed that the Swedish people should reproduce according to the same principles as animal breeding. And here you are, bashing all the Sweden supporters. You don't want what's best for Sweden. You disgust me!"

"We're leaving now," said the prime minister. "After all, we're just your puppets. You, Ali, and Brännström decide everything, and we three function only as your political alibis. And we absolutely refuse to be in the same room as that Nazi Väster!"

"Out of consideration for the country's security, I can't help you with either transport or escort. Sweden must be defended, and only Zone 1 can do that. And by the way, Väster is an outstanding organizer who has built up the task force to what it is today. Without Väster's efforts, the enemy might have already taken over Zone 1. Besides, I believe Väster is a good democrat, which unfortunately, I can't say about you three or the parties you represent. All that Nazi talk is just lies fabricated by the media to deceive voters into voting for you and your party."

"Then we'll go on our own at our own risk," hissed Education Minister Gustav so intensely and hatefully that he turned red.

"Unfortunately, you can't do that," said Gyllenstierna. "I'm responsible for the politicians' security, and out of concern for your safety, I can't allow you to leave Zone 1 only to fall into the enemy's clutches. It's not just about your personal safety. You would fail miserably if you were to be captured and interrogated. We can't risk that. This is about the security of the territory now, sadly!"

"So now we're under house arrest here in Zone 1?" wondered the prime minister.

"No, you're in Zone 1 for the country's security and for your own personal safety, for which I'm also responsible."

"Gyllenstierna, don't for a moment think we'll continue to be your alibis! What you're doing now is a coup d'état and the imposition of military rule. You seem to fancy yourself as some Axel Oxenstierna, who once organized and modernized our country. But you, Ali, and Brännström will face impeachment under martial law. You risk execution, don't you understand that?"

"We will worry about that later after the war. I, Ali, Brännström, and all the other military personnel here in Zone 1 only follow our innermost conviction of what is right, and that is to defend Sweden. We need to focus on defending our country and reclaiming the territory controlled by the enemy."

"By your Muslim friends, you mean," the Minister of Agriculture snarled.

"The meeting is adjourned," declared Gyllenstierna. "You decide whether you want to attend the evening meeting and, indeed, any future meetings. Provided you don't waste valuable time by hurling baseless accusations of treason at your government colleagues."

"We ABSOLUTELY won't!" snapped the prime minister. "No more meetings for us! But it'll be a real pleasure to testify about the coup and to send you and your thugs to prison!"

"You add no value anyway," said Gyllenstierna, who was already on his way out of the room. Halfway through the doorway, he stopped and turned around.

"I'm now putting you under round-the-clock surveillance for the sake of the country's security. You will be subject to restrictions regarding contacts with the outside world. Everything must henceforth be approved and done under the supervision of Bianca Popovic's security personnel. Good night."

Gyllenstierna slammed the door shut and hurried off to the next meeting, which was a teleconference involving Zone 1's military leadership and a dozen local military leaders across the country. The Defense Force's landline network is the most robust and reliable communication link available and virtually impossible to knock out. The system is eighty years old and has been continuously modernized. Its structure consists of buried copper wire, built like a fishing net spanning across Sweden. Telephony can be conducted across all nodes, and if one node goes down, the system automatically chooses another path, making it impossible to stop the traffic. Moreover, unlike radio communications, the enemy cannot intercept the network; at least, that was the misconception that Sweden's military leadership lived under. What they didn't know was that for years, Muslims had infiltrated FRA and had full access to the defense's encryption keys. Muslim mathematicians recorded and deciphered all traffic on the defense's telephone network quickly. As well as by Russian mathematicians for decades. With mini-submarines help, the Russians had already installed half a dozen listening devices on cables lying on the seabed, including in Horsfjärden near the naval base in Berga.

Perhaps he was something of the Axel Oxenstierna of the twenty-first century, Gyllenstierna thought contentedly as he hurried through the corridors. The thought of having himself inscribed in the history books appealed to him. And truth be told, it was quite nice that the politicians had jumped ship. Without their participation, he could now work more efficiently in the leadership group, whether they were a legitimate government or not. Whoever holds the military power holds the real power – and the one who holds the military power was Gyllenstierna himself."

Chapter 22

Staff meeting at Flottsbro Manor

September 21, 2032

The camp in Flottsbro in Botkyrka municipality resembled an improvised refugee camp, of which there were hundreds all over Sweden. Caravans and tents of various types and colors stood side by side, spontaneously thrown out on whatever turf was available when erected. The largest tents were the faded green military ones from the 1980s, housing around twenty people each. Many people had to make do with small, nylon tents from low-price outlets, scavenged to support the defenders of Sweden. However, one key difference set Flottsbro apart from typical refugee camps: it was a military camp with over eight thousand freely operating, Sweden-friendly soldiers.

The cheap nylon tents offered little shelter from the heavy autumn rains and the impending winter cold. Soldiers, shivering in their cheap Chinese sleeping bags during the already chilly September nights, watched enviously as the smoke from the stoves of the military tents slowly rose into the sky.

In the military tents, soldiers slept in underwear, and boots were forbidden at night. Anyone who accidentally touched the hot stove in the tent's center wouldn't feel the heat until it was too late. A burning boot with a melting rubber sole could cause severe burns. However, the less fortunate soldiers would gladly endure the risk of burns.

A few hundred soldiers were fortunate enough to be housed in the camp's cottage village, which consisted of fifty-five winter-insulated cabins and caravans. These would have been warm and comfortable if there had been electricity for the radiators. Instead, the cabins and caravans were minimally heated by the bodies sleeping in them and by makeshift fireplaces using kerosene fuel.

The Flottsbro camp was located on the eastern side of the narrow strip of land separating Lake Tullinge and its northern extension, Lake Alby, essentially a bay of Lake Mälaren. The camp had expanded so much that no flat surface was left vacant in the hilly terrain. Instead, the expansion continued at Häggsta, barely a mile north along Lake Alby's eastern shore, where open grasslands awaited new tenants. The most attractive area was the vast and beautifully situated Saint Botvid's Muslim cemetery, which offered decent wind protection due to its sheltered location.

In the middle of the Muslim cemetery, squeezed between tombstones and stands for watering cans and small planting spades, Dragan had placed his command tent, which served as the headquarters for the "Yugos.", a nickname for Swedes with roots in former Yugoslavia. The fact that the Yugos command tent was placed on a recently dug family grave didn't bother Dragan Milosevic. It hadn't even crossed his mind that they were sleeping just a few feet above bodies in various stages of decay. He had seen far too much to care about trivial matters like dead bodies. "The earth belongs to the living," he used to say. "Everything is about winning and surviving!"

This little area, named Häggsta, had spontaneously and unplanned become what was commonly called the "Yugos camp", as most conversations there were in Serbian and Croatian. However, Slovenian and Macedonian were also quite common. Many Yugos could understand expressions in most Balkan languages, but Swedish was usually the most common language when different ethnicities met in Häggsta. Albanian was less common, except in the corner where the Albanians had cleared away tombstones, piling them up to make room for their tents.

The Yugos camp in Häggsta housed eighteen hundred combat-ready soldiers. The camp grew daily as new volunteers arrived by car, sometimes towing a welcome caravan. On the Swedish side, the regular nor the free troops had combat experience anywhere comparable to that in Häggsta.

Despite thirty-seven years since the Balkan Wars, many Yugo soldiers in Häggsta had significant combat experience. One of them was Dragan, now fifty-nine years old but still in excellent shape, with his muscular body as fiercely murderous as in his youth. When peace came to Balkan in 1995, Dragan was twenty-two years old. By then, he had braved five years of combat and had risen to lieutenant in the Serbian army under his famous namesake, Slobodan Milosevic.Dragan's military career began with the free troops during the Balkan War. As an active member of the soccer team Red Star's infamous supporter club, *Delije*. The club was owned and led by Serbian nationalist Željko "Arkan" Ražnatović, it was natural for Dragan to join the *Srpska Dobrovoljačka Garda*, the Serbian Volunteer Guard, known as Arkan's Tigers. Fighting under the powerful and revered Željko Ražnatović provided ample opportunities to conduct a war of extermination against Muslims.

Dragan was one of the leading figures under Bosnian Serb General Ratko Mladić during the massacres of Muslims in Srebrenica on July 11, 1995. He was visibly proud to have been a driving force behind the largest massacre in Europe since World War II. He often boasted that he personally killed over thirty Muslims with his bare hands, sometimes with the help of his army knife. Counting all those he and his unit murdered through surprise attacks on small Muslim villages in the Bosnian countryside, the number was significantly higher. "Surely up to a thousand," Dragan often said, though he exaggerated greatly.

Dragan's stories usually ended with him drawing his outstretched fingers across his throat, which left no room for misinterpretation. In Dragan's opinion, all Muslims in Europe should

disappear from the face of the earth, especially those who had made it to Sweden. "They have no place here! First, we take the Muslims in Sweden, then those in Bosnia-Herzegovina!"

On the open grasslands on the eastern side of Lake Tullinge at the outdoor bathing place Stendalsbadet, the Syrians from Södertälje had built a rapidly growing camp housing twelve hundred Syrian soldiers. The Orthodox Christian Syrians burned with historic hatred for Muslims, who had been their tormentors since the seventh century when Muhammad's followers occupied their land. If the Yugos were eager to attack the Muslims in Botkyrka, it was nothing compared to the white-hot hatred and contempt that burned in the Syrians' minds. "Not a single Muslim bastard should survive! Not one!"

The Syrians' leader, Jacob, was jovial, energetic, and constantly smiling. His easy-going, carefree demeanor made it easy to overlook that he was a seriously practicing Orthodox Christian willing to do anything in Jesus' name. Jacob was one of the leaders who drove out Muslims in the Södertälje immigrant-dense suburbs of Ronna and Hovsjö twenty-five years earlier. This was one reasons he was now accepted as the Syrians' military leader. Another reason was that he had been the congregation's priest at Saint George's Church in the suburb of Norsborg for many years before they were driven out by Muslims.

One group that particularly suffered in the current Swedish war was the Kurds, caught between other, more powerful groups as they have always been throughout history. On the one hand, the Kurds were historically despised by both Arabs and Turks. On the other hand, most Kurds were practicing Muslims, making them deeply mistrusted by the Swedes. As Sweden's Islamization increased, more Kurds chose to return to their homelands, fighting to build the Kurdish state.

The Swedish Kurds generally chose to fight on the Swedish side against their Muslim brothers. A free and independent Sweden was preferable to an Arab-dominated Muslim Sweden, and fighting Arabs was part of the Kurdish DNA. Since Kurdish Muslims couldn't possibly fight for either the Yugos or the Syrians, it was natural for the Kurds to fall under Swedish leadership. And the Swedes traditionally tolerated almost anything as long as everyone minded their business. The Kurds were given strict instructions to conduct their prayer sessions discreetly, away from Swedish eye shots.

Many of the Kurds were naturally warlike and battle-hardened from conflicts in their homelands, making them valued soldiers by the Swedish leadership. The Kurdish contingent was led by a short, stocky, bull-necked man named Abdullah, who had dark, bristly features but always introduced himself as Abbe. Abdullah had roots in Halabja, where, as a child in 1988, he narrowly escaped Saddam Hussein's infamous gas attack, sadly without his parents and siblings.

The Swedes' leader, Uno Svensson, had established his headquarters in Flottsbro Manor, which had become the heart of the free Swedes' operations south of Stockholm. The location was ideal, with the elongated lakes Alby and Tullinge serving as protective buffers to the west. The lakes were connected by the short Flottsbro Canal, which was wide enough to offer protection against a surprise attack from Botkyrka to the west and made the narrow isthmus between the lakes easy to guard with just a few machine gun teams.

The Swedes knew that the Muslims hadn't allocated substantial military resources to the suburb of Botkyrka, where they had ruled unchallenged for decades before the war broke out. Of Sweden's 284 Muslim enclaves or No-Go zones as they were often called, Botkyrka was perhaps the most heavily Islamized. Botkyrka's inhabitants had long lived under Sharia law, strictly enforced by ruthless imams. The last of the Syrians, Kurds, and Christian Yugos were driven out of Botkyrka as early as 2023, and since then, there has been no trace of opposition.

North and south of Flottsbro, along the eastern shores of the lakes, were the camps of the Yugos and Syrians situated, providing protective buffers. There was no fear of an attack from the east, as Swedish-friendly free troops controlled the vast area south of greater Stockholm. Around the small mountain of Tornberget, in the elevated forest landscape of Hanveden in central Södertörn, another base for the free forces had sprung up. The three-hundred-foot Tornberget provided a clear view of a large enough area to prevent surprise attacks. The Tornberget base was so inaccessible that even tracked military vehicles couldn't reach it. Soldiers operating from Tornberget moved exclusively on foot, carrying only light weaponry they could on their backs. Tornberget soldiers operated independently but coordinated as best they could with the forces at Flottsbro, sometimes communicating by radio. When the enemy jammed the radios, couriers ran with written messages between the bases, only about six miles apart.

The dense coniferous forests, rugged terrain, wetlands, and countless waterways, ponds, and lakes of Södertörn were perfect for Swedish guerrilla fighters, often recreational hunters accustomed to moving through woods and fields. The invading Muslims, used to fighting in arid desert areas, dared not venture there.

The forest was something they feared. Fierce wolves and other unknown beasts howled in the dark woods, waiting to sink their teeth into them. At least, that was how the dense northern forests were described in the Arabic folktales they had heard as children. Perhaps that was why most Muslim fighters felt panic as soon as darkness began to fall in the forest. The Swedish-born *Holy Warriors* were no more familiar with the area than their Muslim friends from desert countries, rarely straying more than a few hundred feet from the nearest subway station. Nordic nature was decidedly not for Muslims. Sweden's forests belonged to the Swedes and Swedes alone.

Before the first bridge at the isthmus, Fittjanäset, was built in 1669, the road between Stockholm and Södertälje ran right through the Flottsbro camp. The first bridge at Fittjanäset was built over the narrow passage between the two round peninsulas, among whom the locals nicknamed "Muhammed's Balls."

The floating pontoon bridge over the stream between Lake of Alby and Lake of Tullinge gave Flottsbro its name. Over this bridge, the remains of the heroic King Gustav II Adolf, who fell in the battle against the Catholics in Lützen in 1632, were transported home. When Gustav II Adolf's daughter, Queen Christina, betrayed her country, her father, and her entire clan by converting to Catholicism and emigrating to Rome, her path crossed over the same bridge that had carried her father's body in the opposite direction twenty years earlier.

The top of the three hundred feet-high ski slope, Flottsbrobacken, right next to the headquarters, offered a perfect vantage point for observing enemy movements in Botkyrka through binoculars.

The geographical location of the Flottsbro base was ideal from a defense perspective and also historically significant. Many battles and skirmishes had occurred in Flottsbro over the years, and history seemed poised to repeat itself.

"You can imagine what will happen if we unleash the Yugos in Botkyrka," said Filip to Uno Svensson, the leader of the Swedes. "I don't know if that's something we can stand behind, really. There might be a time after the war, too. The leaders of the Balkan Wars were captured and put on trial in the international court in The Hague, where they rotted until they died. Not something I would look forward to. Plus, it's about pure humanitarianism."

"Humanitarianism, bah!" Uno snorted. "Aren't you done with that crap yet? We need the Yugos' combat expertise. They're our best fighters, and you know that. Especially in urban warfare, where we have almost no experience. Without the Yugos, there is no guarantee we can take Botkyrka."

"I understand that, but still. And what about the Syrians? If the Yugos are murderous toward the Muslims, it's nothing compared to the Syrians."

"Yes, I know. Letting those 'kebab warriors' loose in Botkyrka is like letting a pack of wolves into a sheepfold. They're completely insane! Nevertheless, they fight for Sweden; we should be grateful for that. I wouldn't want to have them against us!"

"Seriously, you should stop calling them 'kebab warriors', that's derogatory. If they hear you, you'll lose their loyalty. Besides, they fight for the blue and yellow team, which should earn them some respect from you."

"Yeah, you're right. They don't like being called 'darkies,' but that's what they are—really good darkies."

Uno's clumsy language was uncharacteristic of the man Filip had known as a summer house neighbor for over fifteen years. Clearly, Uno was off-balance, perhaps nearing his breaking point, leading Filip to refrain from further reprimands. Filip just shook his head at his young comrade's thoughtless audacity and continued:

"When are you planning to launch the attack?"

"When the time is right. We need more time to drill with weapons. Remember, most of our soldiers have barely handled a military weapon before. They have no clue how to conduct themselves or move in combat. And military commands? Forget it."

"When do you think?"

"We're in a good position here for the moment. At Flottsbro, we're secure and have everything we need to prepare for the final attack. The front to the north, up in the southern suburbs, seems to have calmed down for a while, so we're not in a rush. Plus, the constant harassment from the Tornberget base will keep the Muslims occupied. It's better to attack Botkyrka when the circumstances are in our favor. I think we need up to a month."

"How do you plan to keep the Yugos and Syrians calm for an entire month?"

"I have a good dialogue with Dragan and Jacob, and they're involved in the staff meetings, so I hope they feel like part of the leadership. They understand the value of coordinating our resources and at least accept being subordinate to me at the moment. But who knows how I can control them? I can hardly do anything about it if they decide otherwise."

"All the more reason not to give them a reason to act differently! What do you think about Dragan's latest proposition?" Filip asked. "He's very persistent, and maybe it's best we do something together before he goes off alone."

"I think we should go ahead with it. If we push all the way to the European Highway 4 at Vårby and blow up the bridge, we separate Botkyrka and Skärholmen. Botkyrka will be completely cut off in all directions and unable to receive reinforcements while we can build up our strength in peace. Plus, we'll starve them out, so they're nice and tender when we finally move into the area."

"The plan is good, but we have to expect the Muslims to attack from Skärholmen."

"Yes, that's likely, but if we blow up both the E4 bridge at Vårby and the bridge at 'Muhammed's Balls'—Highway 259—we'll have achieved our goal of isolating Botkyrka," Uno said. "I've already asked 'The Russian' to detail the advance with Dragan," Uno added. "The idea is to advance with one division of Swedes and one of Yugos, a total of four hundred soldiers. The Swedes will take Vårby, and the Yugos will take 'Muhammed's Balls.' The Syrians will wait their turn. It's too complicated to coordinate three units for such a small goal. Maybe we can bring along some of their experts on explosives. They're quite advanced with pyrotechnics and have their own gear."

"The most important thing is to surprise the enemy," Filip said.

"Exactly! That's why only 'The Russian' and Dragan know the plan, plus you and me. Four people should be able to keep a secret. No one else will know anything until we give instructions half an hour before departure. We'll move in cars and buses along Highway 259, and if we reach the targets in fifteen minutes and blow the bridges before the enemy realizes what's happening, we'll have achieved our objective. Then, we'll decide whether to hold our positions or retreat to the bases. There's really no need to stay once the bridges are blown. We might also send a boat unit via the Lake of Alby, but we haven't finalized that part yet," continued Uno. "Don't forget, we Swedes have been seafaring people since ancient times," he added, trying to sound as thoughtful and wise as Filip always did.

"Yeah, 'The Russian.' Sometimes I wonder who he really is," said Filip. "His identity doesn't match reality. He claims he's Russian and grew up in Krasnodar, down by the Black Sea, but yesterday, one of our guys, whose mother is from Krasnodar, told me that 'The Russian' doesn't have the dialect from that area. He was absolutely certain."

"That's strange! Why would he lie about his background? He's proven to be a good strategist and leader, and no one hates the Muslims more than he does."

"Yeah, I know, and I really like him personally. He's very good. But that guy yesterday, who speaks fluent Russian, believes 'The Russian' must have lived in Moscow for a long time. And what's worse, he's sure he has traces of a Chechen accent that he's trying to hide. Apparently, Chechens can never quite pronounce certain Russian words properly, no matter how long they've lived in Russia."

"If he's Chechen, then he's a Muslim. Holy hell, do we have an infiltrator in authority?"

"I'm not saying that's the case, but I'm saying we should be cautious with the guy. It could be as simple as him being one hundred percent loyal but him hiding his Chechen identity because he thinks we wouldn't accept him otherwise."

"The first thing that comes to mind is that he has been involved in all our failed attacks, where the enemy ambushed us. Could it be that he's caused the loss of a couple hundred of our guys and girls? I get chills just thinking about it. You know those attacks where the enemy suddenly showed up out of nowhere with resources they shouldn't have had on hand. Like the last one, south of Huddinge. Suddenly, grenades rained down on us, and our retreat routes were cut off."

"I've thought about that too. After the Huddinge disaster, I had a strong feeling the enemy was tipped off in advance. So what do we do now?" asked Filip.

"Next time, 'The Russian' won't know the exact details when we blow the bridges. We'll give him false locations and times and see if the enemy responds to that information. It's a trap! And if the enemy sets up at those spots... then we know who 'The Russian' is really fighting for."

"Sounds smart, let's do it. Another security issue is that sleazy profiteer who calls himself Björne Kork. He seems to move freely back and forth across the front line with his pig truck without any problems. How does he manage that?"

"He claims he's playing a double game, fooling the Muslims into thinking he's their agent while he's working for us. We've benefited from his food deliveries," said Uno. "His vouchers turn into real food, even when he gets advance payments. And the Muslims don't want the pigs anyway, which allows Kork to claim he's doing a social service by using what would otherwise go to waste."

"Maybe, but we've had to pay exorbitant prices, too, just like the civilians. That filthy profiteer Kork is getting rich exploiting the desperation of starving families, and the more desperate they are, the more they must pay. Consider how much he makes on a single shipment of pigs, with two levels in the truck, probably two to three hundred pigs in one load. But this is the worst part," continued Filip, "Kork is a social butterfly who talks to everyone, potentially leaking classified information. A couple of weeks ago, when I was looking for 'The Russian' at headquarters, I found Kork and 'The Russian' in a hush-hush conversation. When I opened the door, Kork quickly stuffed a letter into his pocket, which I assumed was payment for his food deliveries, but maybe it was something entirely different!"

"Do you think Kork is selling intelligence to the Muslims?" asked Uno.

"I wouldn't be surprised at all! The guy lacks any form of morality. He'd sell his own mother if he got a good price. I heard he forces starving civilians to pay with their cars, watches, and jewelry. And with sex, of course. His favorite is making the women perform oral sex on him while their husbands watch. He supposedly has a whole parking lot full of cars at the old mill of Gladö," said Filip. "And thousands of wristwatches. He plans to sell everything after the war. They say he's hidden away twenty pounds of gold jewelry."

"Yeah, he's extremely slimy and greedy, but we still need his deliveries. We'll keep him under surveillance, and I suggest we search him the next time he leaves the camp. It's a wonder how he can pass through Muslim checkpoints with a truck full of pigs. That's not something I'd try!"

"I think he's giving as much information about us to the Muslims as vice versa."

Before Uno could respond, there was a hard knock on the door, which was opened by Uno's assistant.

"We have another newcomer. You said you wanted to check all new arrivals," said the deputy, nodding toward a young blonde man standing beside him before turning away and leaving.

Uno and Filip scrutinized the young man from head to toe with assessing glances without getting up, as their newly arrived guest remained standing.

"Who are you?" Uno asked coldly. "And why have you come here?"

"My name is Max, and I'm here to join you."

"Where are you from?" Filip inquired. "Do you have an ID?"

Max pulled out his passport and driver's license from his inner pocket and handed them to Uno's extended hand.

"I'm from Djursholm, outside of Stockholm. It took me almost two days to get here through enemy lines. I'm hungry. Do you have anything to eat?"

"Maximilian Moritz Wilhelm Douglas Winston Adlerswärd," read Uno in astonishment before bursting into laughter. "Is that really your name? You've got to be kidding," he chuckled. "Hahaha, I'm Uno Greger Svensson, which suits me perfectly!"

"Yeah, just call me Max."

"Who names their son something like that?" Uno said, fixing Max with a sharp look. "I bet your dad's some kind of noble something."

"Yes, he is a count. Impressive that you picked up on that. But I'm just Max, and I want to join the Free Forces and fight for Sweden."

"What can you do?" Uno asked skeptically. "And don't call me 'sir,' it annoys me! Do you know you could die here?"

"I'm a trained assault diver and a coastal ranger. I've been in the military for four years and graduated top of my class in both programs. But I absolutely don't want to be an officer. I want to do my own thing. I should also mention that I won the Ironman in Hawaii in 2028 and 2029, as well as the World Championship in Triathlon."

The room fell silent until Filip broke the silence.

"Wow! Bravo, Max, we need people like you! Glad you made it here!"

"Assault diver," Uno repeated thoughtfully, studying Max intently. "Sit down, kid. You might get the chance to do something great very soon. Filip, can you order some food for our hungry young man? Max, could you plant explosives underwater and blow up some bridge pillars?"

"We've trained for that, and it's not particularly difficult. But I need diving equipment, explosives, and a support boat. Do we have those?"

"Yes, we've pulled all that from military stockpiles, and we have hundreds of boats. There are even a couple of those underwater sleds. The only thing we've been lacking is someone with the expertise, but now we have you!"

"With an underwater sled, I can approach almost two miles away from a support boat. If I load the sled with explosives and tow a carrier sled, I can do it in one trip, but if necessary, I'll make multiple trips. Working at night, you usually remain undisturbed."

"Great, Max!" said Uno. "You'll stay here at Flottsbrogården with us in the command. We'll devise a thorough plan that no one else will know about until we go live. Just remember, never mention to anyone that you're an assault diver or that we're planning something. You're a coastal ranger and nothing else. This camp leaks like a sieve. Assume that everything you say reaches the enemy. Do you understand? Especially watch out for a big guy with a beard called 'The Russian' and a chubby little peddler named Kork."

"Peddler," Max repeated thoughtfully. "Sounds like something from the old king's time," he continued, not realizing he sounded just like his aristocratic father.

"Understood," Max said loudly after thinking for a few seconds and dug into the steaming sausage stew with rice that had been placed on the table. "Got any ketchup?"

Chapter 23

Battalion Viking Lagerbäck Battalion

September 29, 2032

The dissolution of the Nordic Council in 2031 was the logical consequence of the Nordic countries drifting apart in global politics despite their intertwined histories. This divergence was driven by geopolitical forces that these small nations neither could nor wanted to resist.

The immediate cause of the Council's dissolution was the Nordic neighbors' imposition of visa requirements for Swedish citizens, ending seventy-nine years of passport-free travel. They had had enough of the Muslim terrorist attacks, which were consistently traced back to Sweden, and to them, strict border controls were necessary to avoid suffering the same fate as Sweden.

Sweden's neighboring countries could not risk the uncontrolled influx of Muslim immigrants in Sweden spreading across their own borders. This was, in fact, part of the Muslim Brotherhood's strategy. Over the last fifty years, the demographic changes in Sweden had reached a point where its Nordic neighbors no longer felt an ethnic or linguistic kinship with Swedes. This was the real reason behind the dissolution of the Nordic Council.

The demographic shift also meant that Swedes no longer looked like their Nordic neighbors. It was becoming increasingly clear that the fundamental values that upheld the Nordic identity were no longer shared. Democracy, freedom of speech, gender equality, and equality before the law existed only on paper in Sweden. The rise of Islam as the dominant religion, after a thousand years of Christianity, further fueled the desire to dismantle the Nordic Council.

Sweden's flag change in 2030, replacing the cross with three vertical fields, also contributed to a feeling of diminished unity with its Nordic neighbors.

If a Nordic identity still existed, it proved to be of little value after the outbreak of war on July 17, 2032. Three days after the war began, Norway was the first to declare that it would remain strictly neutral and would not allow any transport of materials or people related to the Swedish conflict to pass through its territory.

Two days later, on July 22, Denmark and Finland followed suit with their own declarations of strict neutrality. The Finnish declaration included a conciliatory note stating that Finland would provide humanitarian aid to the Swedish people and offer refuge to Swedish refugees, except Muslims.

The independent-minded Icelanders took their usual distinct path, announcing to the world that they would "contribute to the Swedish people's struggle for freedom and national independence based on Nordic values in every conceivable way and with all available means." The world's oldest democracy, through wise policies, had not allowed itself to be infiltrated by Muslim columnists and had managed to preserve the ancient democratic and sound values that always characterized the country. The Icelanders were not prepared to sell out their freedom at any price, and their politicians stood firmly by the belief that tribal Islam had no place in their land.

The Icelandic author Skallagrim Sigurðsson's grand rally in the gorge of Tingvalla, under the slogan "Sweden's Cause is Ours," became the catalyst for Icelanders' deep engagement in the Swedish war. The location was well-chosen since Tingvalla is the birthplace of modern democracy. The Icelanders came to view the Swedes' desperate struggle as a fight for their own democracy and national independence.

It was in Tingvalla that the seed for "Battalion Viking" was sown. Sigurðsson's rally sparked a recruitment campaign for Icelandic volunteer soldiers to fight alongside the Swedes. At the Tingvalla rally, a list of thirty-four volunteers was established, and within a couple of months, the number grew to nearly four hundred. By the fall of 2027, there wasn't one single Icelander not familiar with the slogan: "Sweden's Cause is Ours."

A total of 342 Icelandic men and women came to Sweden to fight. These Icelanders formed the backbone of Battalion Viking, supplemented by volunteers from Norway, Finland, and the Baltic states. At its peak, Battalion Viking, also called the Lagerbäck Battalion, included 774 combat soldiers. Some of the Icelandic and Norwegian volunteers had backgrounds as soccer players. Some even had personal experiences with the legendary Swedish soccer coach Lars Lagerbäck, who had been the Coach of the national teams of Iceland, Sweden, and Norway.

"Lars taught us that a strong and well-organized defense is the foundation for winning matches," they joked. "Why didn't the Swedes listen to 'Lasse'?"

"But if the morale is high and everyone works together, it's possible to turn games around—even when they have a losing start!"

Battalion Viking was not considered a fit for Sweden's regular army, which operated under principles that didn't align with those of volunteer fighters. The battalion was equipped with weapons purchased on the global market, funded by collections and donations from wealthy Icelanders, and with the help of the Norwegian friend of Sweden and hotel magnate Petter Storfjord. Due to the battalion's different armaments from regular troops, concerns were raised about potential logistical issues.

On September 29, the interim government that had been solely governing Sweden since the politicians were removed from the leadership group—Gyllenstierna, Brännström, and Baksi—decided to place Battalion Viking under the command of the National Task Force, led by Björn Väster.

The National Task Force's great successes in the first months of the war demonstrated that its organization was more effective and flexible than the militarys. General Väster approached the new assignment with his usual energy, quickly putting his own stamp on Battalion Viking. The battalion was frequently deployed in areas requiring special forces, a euphemism for the true mission: the preemptive ethnic cleansing of entire communities and smaller towns where the war had not yet erupted.

Since the occupants had taken control of nearly all major cities, it became the highest priority for the Swedes to secure control over the countryside to have any chance of organizing counterattacks. General Väster operated those special forces with complete autonomy, while the ruling triumvirate turned a blind eye to the activities.

Battalion Viking complemented the National Task Force's black uniforms with a Thor's hammer in gold sewn at the top of the left arm. The legend of the black-clad soldiers with Thor's hammer spread like wildfire across the country. The mere sight of the black uniforms with the gold hammer was often enough for Muslims to evacuate their residential areas without resistance.

Those who did not quickly heed the warning were mercilessly gunned down on the spot. Once Battalion Viking perfected their methods, a sweep of a large residential area could be completed in a couple of hours.

A few days before a clearing operation, leaflets and information in the relevant languages—usually Arabic, Somali, Tigrinya, Dari, or Pashto—were distributed and posted. Residents were informed that they needed to evacuate the area by a certain date and time. Those who did not comply did so at their own risk, and any resistance would be considered acts of war against the Swedes.

At the designated time, riflemen surrounded the area while buses were brought in. The buses were filled with those who complied, typically around ninety-nine percent, after which Viking soldiers went from apartment to apartment, swiftly dealing with those who did not heed the warning. The bus transport went to a nearby residential area that had been converted to a detention camp, fenced with barbed wire, and guarded by watchtowers.

In the camps, the evacuees were crowded into the sparsely heated apartments as best they could. In cases where a residential area was converted to a camp instead of being emptied of residents, the area was surrounded without warning, because the intention was for the residents to remain within the barbed wire just like the evacuees.

The detention camps were seen as temporary. Due to the difficulty of feeding all the people, mass deportations using passenger ferries converted into floating prisons were planned to begin immediately after victory was secured. This was the ruling triumvirate's secret post-war plan, and General Väster was tasked with organizing these deportations.

In most smaller towns, Battalion Viking was unnecessary because hundreds of local militias spontaneously formed across the country, handling the necessary ethnic cleansing on their own. These militia groups were typically led by a retired military or police officer who had already proven themselves as leaders of the local Civil Guard. Sometimes it was a younger leader from the Home Guard. In very small communities, the most respected hunter often took command naturally, as everyone was accustomed to during their moose hunts.

The weaponry and uniforms of the militias varied. In the best cases, they acquired military weapons from nearby depots. Still, sometimes, their armaments consisted only of hunting rifles and a few automatic guns from the Home Guard. Sweden's five hundred thousand hunters played a crucial role in helping the Swedes secure control over the countryside. Occasionally, the ethnic cleansing operations spiraled out of control, leading to systematic killing, especially when local jihadists resisted and angered the Swedes. The worst disasters during these operations occurred in the small towns of Vingåker and Katrineholm on October 2, 2027, where nearly all Muslims were killed and dumped in the old Askö mine. The mine shaft served as a mass grave for up to a thousand bodies, though the exact number was never determined.

As the war dragged on and internal organization improved, the independent militia groups became increasingly significant. They conducted guerrilla warfare against the occupiers, sabotaging and sudden attacks where the enemy least expected it. With superior local knowledge, the militias could strike unexpectedly, retreat, and disappear before the enemy could counterattack. The occupiers developed an almost panicked fear of entering the forests, making life easier for the militias, whose bases were always deep within the woods.

Collaboration between militia groups across municipal borders became increasingly common. By the end of 2032, the largest militias could count a few thousand lightly but adequately armed soldiers. Most militias sought spontaneous cooperation with the defense leadership and were willing to subordinate themselves when appropriate.

After the General Staff's evacuation to Zone 2, the defense leadership actively and successfully worked to lead and organize the independent militia groups. However, some militia groups refused to subordinate themselves to the defense leadership and developed their own agendas, which were not always aligned with Sweden's interests. At times, it seemed as though the militia leaders were ruling over small principalities to enrich themselves, with no intention of ever relinquishing power. Unfortunately, Internal conflicts within these militias and purges of dissenting countrymen weakened the resistance in several areas and counteracted Sweden's interests.

During the fall of 2032, clashes and skirmishes between local militia groups occurred across the country, escalating into open conflicts by the end of the year. These battles were often about who had the right to collect taxes in their respective areas. When two or more militias claimed the same taxation rights, negotiations would typically begin, with the largest militia demanding the others join and subordinate themselves. When negotiations broke down, fighting would quickly ensue.

Chapter 24

Operation Eunuch

September 29, 2032

From their stronghold at Bromma Airport, the Muslims advanced unopposed across the bridges of Nockeby and Drottningholm, seizing control of the strategically important Lake Mälaren Islands: Lovön, Färingsö, and Ekerö. En route, they destroyed the main building of Drottningholm Palace, which had recently been the residence of Queen Victoria and her consort, Prince Daniel. The significant Chinese Pavilion was obliterated with a few quick shots from their armored vehicles.

After destroying the Swedish national treasures at Drottningholm, the main force continued along Ekerö Road. A company of 120 *Holy Warriors,* reinforced with fifteen Muslim elite soldiers and eight armored vehicles, veered right onto Rörby Road, where the National Defence Radio Establishment, FRA, was located.

When the Muslim force reached the FRA, they found – contrary to expectations – that the entire compound had been hastily abandoned and left completely undefended. Without having to fire a single shot, the Muslims were able to blow up the very heart of Sweden's signals intelligence operations.

In practice, the Muslims only controlled the main roads of the Mälaren Islands, as local militia units hid in the forests, continually harassing the occupiers with guerrilla tactics. On Ekerö, they only controlled the east of the island's narrow middle, from the line of Älvnäs to Träkvista. The western part of the island and Munsö, part of Ekerö, were held by a militia group called the 'Berserkers.'

The Berserkers numbered around seventy men and women. In militia terms, they were heavily armed because, on the twelfth day of the war, July 29, they succeeded in forcing and looting the army's storage depot outside Närsta. The Berserkers had access to all kinds of hand-held weapons and two units of the Bofors Pansarvärnsrobot 59. The powerful anti-tank robot had dual warheads and could be fired from special vehicles.

Through radio communication and couriers traveling by small boats at night, the Flottsbro headquarters maintained close contact with the Berserkers. Coordinating their operations would significantly increase their effectiveness. The Berserkers' leader, Lars Söderström, often called "Lasse Söder," personally visited Flottsbro almost weekly. With local knowledge, it was easy during nighttime to move stealthily and remain undetected by using a small boat between the Mälaren Islands.

Occasionally, small boats were spotted and fired upon by *Holy Warriors*, positioned to monitor the waterways with night-vision scopes. But the *Holy Warriors* were generally poor marksmen, and aiming in the dark was even more challenging for them. It was sufficiently safe as long as they stayed a quarter of a mile from the Muslim-controlled shores. The boats' electric motors were silent except for the faint hum of the propellers, which a slight breeze could easily mask.

The leaders of the two independent groups, Uno Svensson and Lasse Söder, worked together in utmost secrecy to create a bold plan to sever the connection between the Muslims' positions in Botkyrka and Skärholmen. The plan involved blowing up the bridge on European Highway 4 at Vårby and County Road 259 at Fittja over the peninsulas known as Muhammad's Balls. Appropriately, the operation was named "Eunuch" since the "balls" now should be cut off.

The bridge connections were well-guarded by a company of *Holy Warriors*, reinforced by a couple of platoons of elite soldiers on both sides. The strategic importance of the connection between Botkyrka and Skärholmen was undeniable for Muslims. For the Swedes, it was crucial to sever this link in preparation for the attack on the strategically located Botkyrka, which would prevent the Muslims from receiving reinforcements from the north. Group leaders Uno Svensson and Lasse Söder knew that taking the bridges by conventional assault would be challenging. The well-entrenched defenders would undoubtedly inflict heavy artillery on the attackers, resulting in many casualties. Even if they managed to reach the bridges, the Muslims had blocked County Road 259 further on at Masmo subway station with concrete barriers and heavier weapons. The path would be almost impossible.

Their solution combined covert operations and an unexpected surprise attack from the lake. Thanks to Max's skills as a combat diver, over a couple of long and dark nights, six hundred pounds of explosives were attached four feet below the waterline to the six bridge pillars at Muhammad's Balls. Max worked alone with his underwater sled, which carried the heavy explosive packages from a support boat hidden behind a small promontory half a mile from the bridge pillars. Once the remote detonator was installed, it was just a matter of pressing the button when the time was right.

The bridge connection on European Highway 4 at Vårby was too big a project and too far from the Swedish territory at Flottsbro for Max to approach underwater. It involved dual lanes in both directions, with massive bridge pillars requiring five to six times more explosives than the bridges at Muhammad's Balls.

Lasse Söder came up with the solution. From their positions on the promontory at Träkvista, they observed the Muslims occasionally operating a car ferry between Ekerö and the ferry dock at Slagsta. The ferry transported vehicles, troops, and supplies. The Slagsta ferry dock was only a quarter of a mile from the bridges at Vårby that needed to be destroyed, which inspired Lasse Söder's idea.

Lasse Söder had long contemplated a bold plan to storm the ferry dock on Ekerö with just ten to fifteen soldiers and disable the ferry, but the plan had yet to be executed. Söder believed that their retreat would be cut off by the Muslims, making it a suicide mission. Sneaking from Träkvista along the small roads and through the dense forest to the ferry dock under the cover of darkness was one thing, but how would they return to their territory in western Ekerö once the Muslims were alerted?

A brilliant plan began to take shape. Instead of destroying the ferry, they would hijack it, eliminating the need for a retreat. Söder decided to do exactly what the occupiers wouldn't expect: advance from Träkvista along Jungfrusundsvägen to the ferry dock in broad daylight. All previous guerilla operations had been carried out at night, so a daytime assault would be completely unexpected.

Reconnaissance revealed that the occupiers had set up a checkpoint halfway to the ferry dock, where Jungfrusundsvägen intersects with a smaller north-south road. The checkpoint was guarded by half a dozen *Holy Warriors* positioned behind a machine gun in the middle of the road, shielded by some stone blocks.

At 3:15 a.m. on September 29, twenty Berserkers left their base in Träkvista, cautiously moving forward in small groups along the minor roads. At the end of Ledungsvägen, where the forest begins, eight of them turned north towards the checkpoint on Jungfrusundsvägen. It was only a quarter of a mile through the forest, where they would wait under camouflage nets until it was time.

The remaining twelve Berserkers, led by Lasse Söder, continued through the forest towards the ferry dock, which lay just over half a mile ahead. Around 4:30 a.m., they stopped in a small depression at the forest's edge, less than a quarter of a mile from the ferry. They pulled camouflage nets over themselves and made futile attempts to get some sleep. They could see the ferry from the ridge above their position at sunrise.

Shortly after 11:00 a.m., activity increased among the *Holy Warriors* manning the checkpoint on the road Jungfrusundsvägen. They saw a military vehicle approaching from the west and assumed it was one of their own. The hidden Berserkers in the forest above could hear orders shouted in Arabic and saw a couple of *Holy Warriors* position themselves at the machine gun, ready for action. At that moment, the eight Berserkers rose from their hiding spots and jogged, crouched and silent, towards the backs of the *Holy Warriors*. Since the *Holy Warriors* were fully focused on the approaching vehicle, they didn't notice the threat behind them until it was too late. A few sweeping bursts from the automatic rifles was all it took.

The eight Berserkers quickly moved the stones out of the way, allowing two tracked vehicles, each carrying a Bofors anti-tank missile unit, to pass. The vehicles paused briefly to pick up four Berserkers each before proceeding towards the ferry dock, about half a mile away. As they approached, despite the noise from the tracked vehicles, they could hear gunfire from the other group of Berserkers launching their attack. Upon arrival, the vehicles found the Berserkers engaged in a fierce firefight with the defenders, entrenched in and around a small house fortified with a waist-high wall of sandbags. The first tracked vehicle stopped two hundred feet from the house, and after a few seconds, blasted a shot which blew the house apart, killing the defenders.

With the path clear, they quickly boarded the ferry, bringing along their vehicles, personnel, and the bodies of three fallen Berserkers. Within two minutes, the ferry left the dock. After a six-minute journey across the dark waters of Lake Mälaren, the ferry approached the dock Slagsta Brygga. Everything seemed normal. A couple of *Holy Warriors* sat smoking on a bench on the landing, lounging with their legs stretched out and assault rifles on the table in front of them. A few civilians moved around the shore without any apparent stress. There was no special guard at the ferry dock in the middle of Muslim-controlled territory between Skärholmen and Botkyrka. They hadn't received any alarm from their comrades on Ekerö.

From the top of Flottsbro hill, Uno, Filip, and Max carefully observed the ferry's movements.

"Be ready, Max," Uno said.

As the ferry neared the dock Slagsta Brygga, Max pressed the remote detonator, triggering an explosion that reduced the support pillars of Muhammed's Balls to rubble and caused the roadways to collapse into the water. The explosion left the bridge completely unusable.

The idea was that the explosion at Muhammed's Balls would make the defenders rush to that location, thinking the Swedes were launching an attack. The plan worked, and many of the defenders at the E4 bridges moved quickly toward the supposed attackers. To intensify the effect, Uno installed some grenade launchers on Flottsbro hill, which began

pouring grenades into the defenders. It seemed like a massive assault, causing the defense at the E4 bridges to thin out as most soldiers left their positions to respond to the attack a quarter of a mile south, below Masmo subway station.

Instead of docking at Slagsta Brygga, the ferry unexpectedly moved into the bay at the marina. Before anyone realized what was happening, the ferry had navigated a thousand feet to the narrow channel connecting Lake Mälaren and Lake Albysjön, by the E4 bridge.

The first Bofors missiles were launched at the visible bridge pillars at five hundred feet. The ferry stopped 250 feet from the bridges, and missile after missile was fired with perfect accuracy.

The remaining defenders at the bridge finally reacted, now showering the ferry with bullets, but the regular booms from the missile launches continued undeterred. The missile operators were protected inside their vehicles, which could withstand much more than machine guns and assault rifle fires.

Once the bridges were completely demolished, the ferry slowly moved out of the bay, heading back toward the waiting Berserkers at Träkvista on Ekerö. However, just as the ferry reached the bay's mouth, parallel to the ferry dock, it was hit by two grenades, losing its steering and veering uncontrollably to starboard. The seventeen surviving Berserkers were powerless as the ferry drifted and eventually ran aground a few feet from the shore below Vårby Gård subway station, where forty enemy soldiers awaited, bombarding them with heavy fire from elevated positions. The Berserkers fought desperately against overwhelming odds until their assault rifles fell silent one by one. After ten minutes of intense combat, a half-dozen grenades ended the fight, and silence fell again. One of the last Berserkers to fall was their brave leader, Lasse Söder.

Chapter 25

Stockholm under seizure

September 27, 2032

From the very first day of the war, Östermalm, City, Gamla Stan, and Södermalm fell under Muslim control and had remained so ever since. As a result, these areas of the city's buildings were relatively intact. In contrast, parts of the city like Vasastan, Kungsholmen, Birkastan, Sundbyberg, Solna, Sollentuna, Kista, Husby, Bergshamra, and nearby northern suburbs were turned into battlefields, with widespread destruction of their infrastructure as a result.

In Södermalm and Enskede, situated just south of Södermalm, the invading forces received significant assistance from *Holy Warriors* and Swedish leftist activists residing in the area. Many of these leftist activists worked in the media, making them effective propagandists. Hundreds of these opinion leaders received payments from organizations linked to Muslim extremism, though few beneficiaries acknowledged this. These 'side hustles' provided a welcome supplement income on top of their regular salaries, usually funded by Swedish taxpayers. This allowed many journalists to maintain a comfortable lifestyle, including desirable apartments, international travel, and frequent visits to the trendiest restaurants and bars in Södermalm. On the other hand, exclusive cars and clothes were not part of their image. Instead, they dressed in a proletarian style and used bicycles as transport between their assignments, all to display a sustainable lifestyle. Environmental polluters were deeply despised, and the highest status was manifested by connecting a children's cart to their bicycles.

Most of those on the Muslim payroll had been working for them for many years, some as far back as thirty years. Their job was to implement ideas in the Swedes' psyche that would justify the Islamization of Sweden and pave the way for the Muslims' eventual takeover.

They succeeded far beyond their Muslim employers' expectations. The state-owned television and the Bonnier media house held the minds of the Swedes in a firm grip. For most Swedes, state-owned television news was the undisputable truth, aside from daily newspapers Dagens Nyheter, Svenska Dagbladet, Göteborgsposten, and Sydsvenskan, which ranked even higher.

It was unclear what these leftist activists truly wanted beyond making money, expressing Marxist views, and supporting reduced carbon dioxide emissions. Constantly exaggerated articles about the so-called greenhouse effect created climate anxiety, causing Swedes to overlook Islamization.

The "supposedly" quickly escalating climate change was the external enemy needed to divert attention from the real threat, the Muslim infiltration.

Perhaps the leftist activists themselves didn't even know what they wanted. However, they continually promoted a multicultural society, which was merely a euphemism for Islamization. The more Islamized an area was, the more multicultural it was claimed to be. Fully developed multiculturalism in practice was equal to Muslim monoculture. Free media and journalism have no place in a Muslim society, a fact they seemed oblivious to. The same applied to feminists and the LGBTQ movement. And what about the Jewish population, who had such a strong influence in the media? How did they justify aiding their Muslim enemies?

It became evident to everyone living in the occupied area that the leftist activists had betrayed their country. In the middle of Medborgarplatsen, where a former prime minister once proclaimed that Muslims from all over the world were welcome to Sweden, a scaffold was erected, where the heads of the left-wing activists were the first to roll. Other leftist activists' bodies swayed in the wind, hanging from the lampposts.

In 2014, Sweden's Prime Minister Stefan Löfven proclaimed to the world, "My Europe builds no walls," a sentiment that now appeared tragically ironic as the country's naive and self-destructive policies were rewritten. If the leftist activists still had their wits about them and knew their history, they would have realized it was just a replay of Iran in 1979, when the communists helped the Muslims seize power by overthrowing the pro-Western shah. As always in Muslim takeovers, the Muslim allies were seen as potential threats that needed elimination. The Prophet's utter disdain for traitors and defectors only fueled the Muslims' uncompromising brutality.

Even though the Swedish traitors aided the Muslims, they were still traitors in the eyes of the Muslims. They were nothing more than pests to be eradicated, precisely what happened on Medborgarplatsen.

In history, Muslim takeovers typically follow a pattern. Islam aims for all people to submit to Allah's will, not to exterminate everyone else, as many believe. After the first phase, where all conceivable opposition is eradicated, and the public is frightened into total obedience and silence, a more constructive second phase follows. During this second phase, a conciliatory hand is extended to the public, inviting them to convert and join the Muslim community. Conversion can be done independently by reciting the Muslim creed, a single short sentence: "There is no god but Allah, and Muhammad is his messenger," repeated three times.

There are no registries or documents to confirm conversion, and no imam needs to give approval. All that is required is to dress and live as a good Muslim. The outward attributes are crucial and decisive. Men must grow beards, women must cover themselves, and men should wear small droll caps on their heads. Alcohol and pork are strictly forbidden, as are pet dogs. Attendance at Friday prayers in the mosque is mandatory, as are five daily prayer sessions. Living as a good Muslim is enough to be considered a good Muslim. Although Allah always knows what people think, He does not punish sinful thoughts as long as one respects the many ceremonial and ritual aspects of Islam. It is the practical actions that count, not the way of thinking.

Islam focuses on the external, unlike Christianity, which demands sincerity and inner truth. This difference explains why Muslims do not hesitate to deceive infidels. Muslims view Christians as naive. "When the Christian turns the other cheek, we Muslims strike with full force." To deceive a Christian by lying is considered a victory by the Muslim.

Those who insist on not living as Muslims are required to pay *jizya*, a special tax for unbelievers. These agnostics are considered second-class citizens and face discrimination in every possible way, both in the legal system and in daily life. Muslims always have precedence. In court, the testimony of a Muslim man has the same value as two non-Muslim men's testimonies and equal to that of four non-Muslim women. When a Muslim and a Christian meet on the sidewalk, the Christian must step aside. If Muslims find a restaurant fully booked, non-Muslim guests must immediately vacate their tables. Failure to comply grants Muslims the right to punish and, if they wish, kill the infidels. A Muslim always has the right to kill a non-believer without needing to justify their actions afterward.

In the long run, this unjust system compels nearly everyone to convert to Islam, which is the system's primary goal. The aim is not to terrorize non-believers but to encourage them to convert. The core and ultimate goal of Islam is to enlighten all people about the true faith, to spread the mission until the whole world is Muslim. This allows everyone to obey the *Sharia* laws decreed by Allah and conveyed through His infallible messenger, Muhammad.

To ensure Muslim growth and dominance, Muslim women are always forbidden from marrying non-Muslims. Muslim men, however, are encouraged to marry non-Muslim women, provided the woman converts to Islam. This system ensures that the proportion of Muslims steadily increases at the expense of other groups.

Signs of the second, more peaceful phase were already appearing in Södermalm. More and more Swedish men and women had begun wearing the Muslim attire distributed freely by the occupiers. Many residents of

Södermalm saw it as a 'happening,' a festive masquerade, as they roamed the streets, secretly grinning at each other's new outfits. Cool idea, with multiculturalism! It felt new and fresh somehow. Inspiring, even. Now the bourgeoisie had something to think about; 'hahaha!'. To hell with the lame Swedish traditions. There were so many new and exciting to learn and embrace.

Unfortunately, alcohol was forbidden, but Muslims sold hashish and other drugs at reasonable prices, so it evened out. One challenge was that good Muslims must observe extreme cleanliness regarding personal hygiene, clothing, and orderliness of their homes, but hey, you had to work on that.

Another issue was that the old working-class district of Södermalm, and more recently Enskede, had steadily become gentrified. Since the sexual revolution of the 1960s, this area attracted homosexuals from all over Northern Europe, especially gays from Finland and the Baltic states, as well as gay Swedes, of course. Södermalm and Enskede housed thousands of homosexuals, but the most important thing for the Muslims was that sexual orientation could be concealed behind Muslim attire. A couple of hundred known homosexuals had been pushed off the roof from the twenty-six-story-high skyscraper called 'Skrapan', but these executions now appeared to be over. As long as one was discreet about their orientation, no one cared. The explanation was that homosexual relations between Muslim men are an old and widely practiced tradition. Homosexual acts are not a particularly severe sin as long as one does not live openly as a homosexual.

For women, the official problem of lesbianism was non-existent, as they were always covered behind large pieces of cloth and should know their place in all situations. The major concern for women was that their general mobility and freedom were increasingly restricted, with new rules and restrictions announced by the imams in Zayed's mosque during Friday prayers. Every woman had to be under the control of a designated man, and if she did not obey, it was the man's duty to beat her into submission. Men who failed to keep their women in line risked severe punishment themselves through caning.

Zayed's Mosque, sometimes called the Great Mosque of Stockholm, is conveniently located at Medborgarplatsen. Here, mosque visitors could hardly avoid witnessing the public punishments, which were most frequent right after Friday prayers. The women, exiting through their designated back door, were always herded into the square to ensure they didn't miss the didactic beheadings and floggings.

A large sign was prominently displayed at the top of the scaffold, declaring in Arabic and Swedish: "Seize them and slay them wherever you find them. For against such, we have given you clear authority." Quran 4:89.

The death penalty by stoning women who committed adultery had recently been introduced but had not yet been practiced. A special pit was being prepared right before the stairs to Medborgarhuset. It was clear the occupiers planned to provide the residents of Södermalm with a new form of entertainment they had never imagined witnessing.

Östermalmstorg – the big square on Östermalm – had also been transformed into a public place for execution. Besides the frequently used scaffold in front of the entrance to the market hall, a sooty metal cage had been placed in the center of the square. A sign hung on it, declaring in both Arabic and Swedish the 56th verse of the fourth sura of the Quran: "Those who disbelieve our signs, we will surely burn them in fire. As often as their skins are roasted through, we will exchange them for other skins that they may taste the punishment." The bottom of the cage was covered in a thick layer of ash and burnt bone fragments. Next to the cage was a stack of birch logs, organized in eight rows, sending a clear message to the residents of Östermalm.

Conditions were very different in other parts of the city, such as City, Vasastan, Birkastan, Hagastan, Kungsholmen, and nearby areas like Bromma, Solna, and Sundbyberg. Street fighting had raged for weeks and occasionally flared up, but it had become clear that the invading forces were in the final stages of securing control over these areas. The repeated battles over Bromma Airport were particularly intense, turning the runway into a cratered moonscape. Eventually, the occupiers secured the airport, and now Swedes, through high-altitude drone cameras, could watch hour by hour as asphalt machines and steamrollers worked furiously, causing concern about potential Muslim reinforcements arriving by air.

After ten weeks of bitter fighting, it seemed all parties needed a pause to recharge. Occasionally, grenades exploded, and sporadic bursts of automatic gunfire could be heard. The buildings in the war-torn areas suffered significant damage. Explosions from grenade launchers, anti-tank weapons, and suicide bombers had caused many roofs to collapse, and several buildings partially standing. Intense shelling from tanks and armored vehicles had turned many into rubble. Other buildings were dynamited by the occupiers, including all the churches, now lying in ruins, awaiting the construction of new mosques.

Prominent landmarks like the Opera House, Dramatic Theatre, Concert Hall, Central Station, Stockholm Waterfront, the police headquarters on Kungsholmen, the Clarion Hotel at Norra Bantorget, Wennergren Center, both Tors Towers, the Cedergren Tower in Stocksund, Victoria Tower, Kista Science Tower, and the brand new 110-story skyscraper, which had not even been named, were shot to pieces, and reduced to dusty piles of stones and bare steel skeletons. However, the City Hall remained completely intact, as the Muslims intended to use that building for purposes that would be revealed later. The plaster on the facades was partially shot off and fallen, and where it still clung, it was perforated by hundreds of thousands of bullet holes from automatic rifles and machine guns.

A crucial reason the Swedes still held the front line around Stockholm, which curved in an arc over Stäket, Rotebro, and Stocksundet, was that the Gotland Battle Group and the Gotland Battalion, to the Muslims' surprise, had landed in Kapellskär and joined from the north with Leopard tanks and mobile artillery pieces. Additionally, parts of the National Task Force reinforced the regular troops with 850 soldiers transferred from Linköping. The Swedes put up a fight and held their ground far more than the Muslim command had expected. However, the capital was in Muslim hands, and things looked bleak for the Swedes further west.

The bridges at Stäket and Stocksund were blown up by Swedish engineer units on the fourth and fifth days of the war, respectively. When the Stocksund Bridge was demolished by boat-borne engineer soldiers, 260 elite Muslim soldiers were traveling north along Roslagsvägen. When they encountered the well-rested and well-equipped Gotland Battalion, the already exhausted soldiers were decisively defeated and decimated until the last eighty-four saw fit to wave the white flag and surrender. They were temporarily housed at Kastellet on the small island outside Vaxholm, where they were treated properly in accordance with the Third Geneva Convention.

In the south, the free troops under Uno Svensson blew up the bridges on the E4 at Vårby and at County Road 289 at Fittja. The Tranebergsbron, which was Stockholm's western exit, had been destroyed by mortar fire. The road north along the E4 was blocked by Swedish regular troops who had taken positions in Norrviken, between Rotebro and Sollentuna.

Stockholm was cut off in all directions except towards Värmdö, which was still a dead end towards the Baltic Sea. At the destroyed bridges, Swedes and Muslims stood on opposite sides, except for the Tranebergsbron, where the Muslims controlled the areas on both sides of the strait of Traneberg. The military situation around Stockholm had temporarily stabilized with closed positions.

Further west, things looked worse for the Swedes. Muslim forces advanced along the European Highway 18 north of Lake Vänern, appearing poised to split the country in two with a corridor stretching from Södertälje westward, through Örebro and Karlstad down to Gothenburg. The Muslims' Abram tanks repeatedly broke through the Swedish defensive positions and had already reached Åmål. Only a transport stretch of fifty miles remained before they would connect with the Muslim base in

Vänersborg. The decisive blow that would split Sweden in half was on the verge of completion."

Chapter 26

Putin's Speech

October 1, 2032

When Russian television announces changes to its programming for a Presidential address by President Putin, both the Russian people and foreign ministries worldwide know that something significant is about to be announced. Putin's appearances are typically limited to around three times a year, signaling to many Russians, Belarusians, Ukrainians, Balts, Finns, Georgians, Turks, Kazakhs, Uzbeks, Afghans, Mongolians, and Chinese that it's a good idea to tune in. In Sweden, there was usually a moderate interest in Putin's speeches, but this time, Sweden itself was the topic.

President Vladimir Putin began with a historical overview and a brief summary of the security policy situation in the Baltic Sea region. Geopolitics was Putin's favorite subject, and he was exceptionally knowledgeable. He proved himself a skilled strategist and negotiator—a classic, successful, and cynical power player.

"Due to the war in Sweden, our forces have been put on the highest alert, prepared to repel any attack on Russia. We stand strong and fear no one. All Russian citizens can feel safe and confident in our military leaders. Additional naval units have been relocated from the Mediterranean and the Black Sea to the Baltic Sea.

This is a significant consolidation of forces to ensure Russia's security and act as a moderating and balancing presence in the region where our country has operated for hundreds of years. Historically, Russia has always felt constrained in the Baltic, where our country is the largest. Sweden has traditionally acted like the Baltic Sea belongs to them, but that is not the case. Since the humiliating defeat of the Swedes at Poltava in 1709, they have had to adapt to the will of the Russian bear. The Swedish exile government in Helsinki—Sweden's legitimate government—has come to us for help through our old friend, Prime Minister Margot Wallfors.

The Swedes have been our friends for a long time. We Russians are loyal and reliable, and we do not abandon a friend in need. Therefore, as a Russian, I am proud to announce that we have responded to the Swedes' plea this afternoon by landing significant combat forces by sea and air on the island of Gotland to protect its population and general Swedish interests. Gotland is a strategic location for Russia to help stabilize the situation in Sweden and the Baltic region.

The construction of the Baltic's largest naval base will begin shortly. Other infrastructure, such as airfields, missile bases, and ports, will be expanded or newly constructed as soon as possible. The nearly sixty thousand Gotlanders are now unconditionally offered protection by the Russian military, which they gratefully accept. They are now given guidance, at the expense of the Russian state, to temporarily relocate to safe and modern housing near *Starosvedske,* the 'Old Swedish Village.' This is where Catherine the Great, 241 years ago, generously sheltered the Swedes who, at the time, lived under the harshest conditions on the Estonian island of Dagö. When the situation permits, the Gotlanders can return to their island. No one can say when the situation will stabilize enough for a repatriation of the island. Should the repatriation be delayed, they will all be offered Russian citizenship with our well-known Russian generosity, including good pensions and free healthcare. I, Vladimir Putin, guarantee that our Swedish friends will be well cared for. Thank you all for your attention. Good evening!"

Putin appeared visibly satisfied and smiled at the camera, his lips tightly pressed together as always, but his wolf-like eyes remained as cold as ever. Surprisingly fresh for his eighty years of age, there was no indication that he would cease to be Russia's president anytime soon.

Nor was there any indication that the Russians intended to return Gotland to the Swedes or that the Gotlanders would ever have the opportunity to return to their island home.

After centuries of naval power struggles, the balance of power in the Baltic had tipped in Russia's favor in just a few hours. Swedish ships navigating the Baltic would now and forever do so at Russia's mercy.

Chapter 27

The Defense Headquarters evacuates

October 1, 2032

The situation deteriorated rapidly. Reports indicated that the occupying forces, advancing westward via the northern route around Lake Vänern, had reached the town of Vänersborg, where they had joined the Muslim forces already stationed there. Sweden was effectively divided into two parts, with the command center located south of the corridor and established by the occupiers across the country. It appeared it was only a matter of time before the southern part of Sweden would entirely fall into the occupiers' hands.

Gyllenstierna's calm voice echoed through the loudspeakers in all corners of Zone 1.

"We will begin the evacuation at 4 p.m. Only a small bag of personal belongings is allowed, with a maximum weight of two pounds. Everything we need will be available upon arrival at Zone 2. Additional luggage will arrive later. Stay in your rooms and be prepared. You will be picked up from where you are. The last group will be evacuated around 8 p.m. but expect some uncertainties in the schedule."

The three helicopters, which would soon shuttle back and forth, had already been rolled out from their hangars and were ready for take-off on their platforms hidden under camouflage nets. In the little village of Grythyttan, six buses awaited to transport the two hundred people from Zone 1 to Zone 2.

The first helicopter, which took off on time, carried the leadership trio Gyllenstierna, Brännström, Baksi, King Carl Philip, Björn Väster, the highest commanders of the navy and air force, and the heads of the intelligence agencies MUST, FRA, and SÄPO. The individuals most critical to national security were flown out first. In the final departures, kitchen staff and service personnel were evacuated. Conversation was allowed once the helicopter took off and everyone adjusted their headphones and microphones.

"A really tough day," began Air Force Colonel Wennergren. "For the first time in history, the Russians are on Gotland, and how the hell are we ever going to get them off that island?"

"We should have kept the Gotland battle group there," said Navy Chief Bergström. "God may forgive us, but the people of Gotland never will! Gotland is lost just like when we lost Dagö."

"Gotland is something we'll have to think about once the war is over," remarked SÄPO Chief Bianca Popovic. "Who knows what the global political situation will look like then? Western Europe is in shambles."

"For now, I think we should focus on the Muslims who are tightening their grip on Sweden," said Brännström, always focused on what was essential and possible to achieve. "We can't control the Russians anyway," he continued. "I wouldn't be surprised if they have more than Gotland on their radar, but we'll find out soon enough. In any case, the Gotlanders have played a crucial role in Stockholm. I would make the same decision again."

"I agree with Brännström," said Gyllenstierna. "One advantage of evacuating is releasing the entire force guarding Zone 1 for other missions. We're talking about eight hundred soldiers moving north to breach the enemy's line."

"Yes, and everything indicates they will succeed," said Brännström. "It appears that enemy's defense line is too long and scattered for them to hold it together. Ideally, I'd like to send them south to retake Jönköping, but it's too risky right now if they get cut off down there, between Lake Vättern and Lake Vänern."

"Speaking of the Russians, I just received information that the Americans intercepted a conversation yesterday suggesting that the Russians plan to begin bombing the occupiers," said Rudolf Enbom, head of the FRA.

"That would be more than welcome," said MUST Chief Bertil Wiklund. "So maybe the bloody Russians will do something good for the first time in history."

"I can't wait for them to start," said Alfred Baksi. "It looks like we need outside help if we're going to turn the tide and win this war. Even Russian bombs can be good bombs. When do they start?"

"There is no information on that yet," said Enbom. "The Americans interpreted the conversation as a planning stage, so the Russians themselves probably don't even know."

The helicopter went down for landing at the bus terminal in Grythyttan.

"By the way," said Baksi, "I received information this morning that Israel's Ambassador, Deborah Dayan, is offering us 180 military advisors and instructors who are experts in urban warfare. I have temporarily accepted," Baksi continued, glancing at Brännström.

"Very interesting. We'll definitely accept, and I want them here as soon as possible," said Brännström, glancing at Gyllenstierna, who nodded. "As many as possible, with as many weapons as possible! Tell our Israeli friends I want half of that crew at Arlanda Airport and the other half at Växjö Airport."

The engine was turned off, and the rotor blades slowed down before coming to a complete stop.

"It will take us three and a half hours to get there, and you will hardly notice that you're no longer in Zone 1," said Gyllenstierna. "Our headquarters in Noppikoski are incredibly similar to the other one."

Chapter 28

The declaration of the caliphate Alzuwid

October 4, 2032

It was a monumental day for Ahmed Ben Barka and Muslims worldwide. The world was about to gain its twenty-sixth Muslim state, an event broadcast live across the other twenty-five countries already existing. Many Muslim news channels had flown their reporters into Bromma Airport a few days ahead. Around ten newspapers, many digital media operations, and media from France, Belgium, and India were on site.

The press conference was held in the Blue Hall of the Stockholm City Hall, where Nobel banquets were previously hosted, but would never be held again since no more Nobel Prizes would be awarded. This is because the Muslims considered the Nobel Prize a form of post-colonial oppression that glorified the white race and Jews, awarding a minuscule number of Muslim Nobel laureates throughout history.

To ensure the Blue Hall didn't appear empty, four hundred *Holy Warriors*, dressed in traditional Muslim attire, were ordered to take seats in the audience. The leader of the Muslim Brotherhood, Muhammed Badie, who was also Ahmed's superior, took the podium and recited the Brotherhood's motto in Arabic:

"Allah is our goal. The Prophet is our leader. The Quran is our law. *Jihad* is our way, and dying for the glory of Allah is our highest aspiration!"

A long and intense applause echoed through the Blue Hall.

"At last, the teachings of the Prophet have reached the barbarians in the North. Now, the light shall grace the infidel Swedes. They will now experience the great joy of knowing Allah's wisdom and mercy."

A map illuminated the large screen, showing Sweden as south from a straight line drawn from a point north of Uppsala straight west to the Norwegian border, north of Arvika.

"Hereby, I declare the Muslim state of *Alzuwid*, with *Makat Almukarama*, historically known as Stockholm, as our capital!"

A dozen flags were unfurled from the upper floor and hung from the railings. The new Swedish national flag featured a crescent moon and a yellow star set against the green background of Islam.

The applause and cheers seemed endless but eventually quieted as the Brotherhood's leader spoke again:

"Through diplomatic channels, we know that most countries worldwide will soon recognize the new state of *Alzuwid* and its new legitimate leader. A new era dawns for Europe. From *Alzuwid*, the teachings of the Prophet will spread, first across all of Scandinavia and then further south until all of Europe is part of our Muslim community. Next to witness the light are the decadent Norwegians, who are truly yearning for our guidance! *Alzuwid's* first president is Ahmed Ben Barka, who has successfully led the country's liberation. President Ben Barka will now share his vision for transforming *Alzuwid* and detail how *Makat Almukarama* will swiftly rise from its current primitive state to become a shining jewel, a Muslim pilgrimage site to rival even Mecca."

By the end of the day, all twenty-five Muslim states, plus a handful of African countries, had issued official recognitions of the new state as legitimate. In the following days, recognitions came from France, Belgium, the Philippines, and several small Oceatic states.

By contrast, the major powers—the USA, China, Russia, and India—issued statements declaring the attempt to establish a new state in northern Europe was illegitimate. They stated they had no intention of accepting the new state's borders or leadership. However, both the USA and China clarified that no military actions were planned and that Europe's fate must be handled by the Europeans themselves.

Chapter 29

Night reconnaissance

October 12, 2032

Reconnaissance soldiers are the most elite of all soldiers, the best of the best. They receive specialized training in intelligence gathering behind enemy lines, providing information on enemy units and activities. This intelligence leads to decisions on how other units should be deployed.

To become a reconnaissance soldier in the ranger battalions, one needs to be at the very top of their physical and mental capacity, combined with an iron will, to undergo training that sometimes exceeds even that of elite athletes. Most of the training involves running, as infiltration behind enemy lines is often the most efficient on foot. A reconnaissance soldier must be able to cover thirty miles a day through pathless terrain and possess exceptional navigation skills, often chosen for their natural, internal compass that always appears to guide them the right way. Their pack gear contains only the essentials to maximize mobility. Sometimes, reconnaissance soldiers on missions don't even carry an automatic rifle; instead, high-powered binoculars and a camera with a telephoto lens are usually part of their basic equipment. In addition, most of these elite soldiers have specialized training in disciplines such as parachuting, diving, sharpshooting, or communications.

Since reconnaissance soldiers sometimes need to stay behind enemy lines longer than planned, they are also trained in the art of foraging in nature, which can be quite challenging in the winter in northern Sweden. Even under these harsh conditions, a soldier's endurance can be extended by weeks.

The mission ahead for Kiruna native Pelle Nyberg and Småland native Carl-Johan Öving from the army's ranger battalion in Arvidsjaur seemed relatively easy. After paddling solo kayaks for nearly a mile between the small isles of Brändön and Granön, they were to conduct a reconnaissance covering a roughly fifteen-mile round trip in relatively easy terrain. The area consisted mostly of conifer forests and slightly hilly terrain in a network of forest roads that hadn't been overgrown because of recent logging operations.

"This is something any sixteen-year-old scout could handle," Nyberg declared confidently, the defiant miner's son that he was. "It will be pure enjoyment to take in the beautiful coastal landscape and breathe fresh air in peace and quiet!"

"Yes, unless the Muslims have scouts with night vision binoculars on Granön who spot us when we paddle across. Then we might be in trouble. Apart from that, there could possibly be a little challenge with the shorelines both north and south of the Hertsö lake, at least judging by the satellite images. But it probably shouldn't be anything major." said Öving, like the soft-spoken and thoughtful Småland farm boy he was.

"We might want to bring some wire to set snares as we go, maybe get a couple of black grouse to take home?" the ever-optimistic Nyberg suggested without expecting an answer. "I'm getting tired of army rations."

"Yeah, that wouldn't be a bad idea," Öving agreed half-heartedly, as food was mostly fuel for him. In Öving's world, energy bars were far more interesting than braised grouse breasts.

The Muslims had established a base in Bensbyn, where two hundred *Holy Warriors* were stationed. They blocked the entry into Luleå via Bensbyvägen, across the narrow strait Sinksundet. Before the attacking ranger units could overcome the resistance, the Muslims would have time to blow up the bridge over Sinksundet, which was guarded by a company of *Holy Warriors* with machine guns and anti-tank weapons.

The intersection of European Highway 4 and Haparandavägen had been turned into a fortified stronghold. At least one hundred were heavily armed and entrenched with the Muslim elite soldiers, backed by twice as many *Holy Warriors*, half a dozen tanks, twice as many lighter armored vehicles, and a handful of howitzers.

The entire Highway 97 between Luleå and Boden was in the hands of the Muslims. Gammelstad, like the intersection of European Highway 4 and Haparandavägen, had been turned into a fortress since the Swedes had no access to combat aircraft, artillery, or armor. There were over 700 Muslim soldiers in Gammelstad.

Given their numerical inferiority and lack of heavy weapons, the ranger units' only option was field battles. They had established their main base in Persön, about seven miles north of the Muslim strongholds in Rutvik and Bensbyn. Field battles also required infantry troops with heavier weapons and more soldiers than the mobile and flexible ranger units.

A side maneuver was planned to avoid field battles—over water and through the forest, precisely where the Muslims wouldn't expect an attack. The question was whether the approach to Luleå should be made south or north of lake Hertsöträsket, or as a combination of both, and possibly neither. That was a mission for reconnaissance soldiers Nyberg and Öving to decide.

Nyberg would scout the southern side, while Öving would cover the north. They would traverse the path to Hertsöträsket, which, despite the name, is not a swamp but a two-mile-long lake whose outline is reminiscent of the Kingdom of Sweden. Most importantly, they would die if their presence was revealed to the enemy.

Pelle Nyberg and Carl-Johan Öving left the base in Persön in an old Audi at four in the morning. While it was still dark, they would drive with lights off all the way to Brändö Lodge, which advertised its rental kayaks and canoes. The plan was to borrow a couple of single kayaks for the crossing to Granön, just two miles south of the lodge.

During the day, they planned to carry the kayaks to Brändön's southernmost point, from where they would cross to Granön the next night at 2 a.m. Plan B was to use a rowboat, which was likely to be found by the dozens in the surrounding neighborhood.

They arrived at the darkened lodge, just as dawn was breaking in the east. They noticed stacks of firewood everywhere, by every single one of the camping cabins, which, to their surprise, appeared to be inhabited. Even the large main building was surrounded by piles of wood.

It turned out that Brändön Lodge was sheltering ninety-four residents of Luleå who had managed to escape the relentless regime of the Muslim occupation of their town. There was no electricity, so they started producing lanterns from old gasoline drum metal. The lanterns were fueled with seal oil, extracted by boiling the seals' thick blubber layer.

The lodge's managers, also the owners, had much to share. So far, the residents had fed themselves reasonably well, thanks to fishing and moose hunting. They ate the occasional stray reindeer that wandered to the coast, some roe deer, and forest birds they now trapped using snares or baited with piles of blueberries surrounded by trap fishing nets, as they had run out of ammunition. Recently, a female bear had discovered their nets and the easy pickings so they stopped using the traps.

They grew some of their own local almond potatoes on the nearby fields and could buy or trade for more potatoes from the farmers in Persön and Börjelslandet. They had traded a fairly new Volkswagen Transporter for two dairy cows from a farmer in Sundom, so now they were making their own cheese, flavored with caraway seeds that grew wild on Brändön.

Flour was scarce, but they could trade some seal meat and oil they harvested for unthreshed barley and oats from the Persö farmers.

An antique hand threshing machine found at the small homestead museum in the village was used as a model for newly manufactured flails, which were used for threshing in the same way as they did in the Stone Ages.

Since threshing with flails was laborious and time-consuming, they planned to build a small windmill using an old millstone that now served as a step outside one of the village's traditional bakehouses. They showed the new visitors a detailed and neat pencil drawing made by a mechanical engineer from the technical university, who lived in one of the camping cabins and was literally constructing all the movable parts.

Fortunately, the seal population in the Gulf of Bothnia had reached record levels in recent years. It consisted mostly of ringed seals but also some gray seals, which they could shoot in nearly unlimited numbers, provided they had fuel for the boat engines and bullets for the rifles. And that was precisely the problem, the lodge owner explained to the two reconnaissance soldiers.

"We don't know how we're going to survive if this drags on for years," said Östen Johansson worriedly. "We have twenty-six bullets left, and it usually takes three or four per seal, maybe fewer for moose, but we're soon going to deplete the whole population of moose here on Brändön. We've started digging pit traps, but that's mainly for the few reindeer who are dumb enough to be herded into them. Everything here on Brändön is quickly heading back to the Stone Ages, you know!"

"Unfortunately, we can't give away our personal weapons, as you can understand, but we'll see if we can figure something out to help you out when we finish our mission," said Pelle Nyberg, looking at Öving, who nodded in agreement.

"The best long-term help we can give you is to defeat and drive out the Muslims from Norrbotten," said Öving. "And we expect to do that quite soon!"

"Yes, please! said Johansson. "You can take the kayaks as long as you need but please return them. Please keep us in mind. We have dozens of children to feed and care for. And absolutely no one is trading their ammunition, no matter what they're offered. I tried trading a large seal for ten bullets or two gallons of gasoline, but it was impossible. No one gives up their remaining fuel, and electric motors are out of the question. Our next project is to trade for a horse, and then we'll need to start raising pigs and chickens to survive long-term. I might be able to trade some seals for piglets."

Fortunately, the kayaks were light and even though they were an amateur model, and they carried them without any problems on their heads for the two miles to the strait they would take that night. Then they returned to Brändön Lodge, where they were treated to a tasty seal ragu with almond potatoes. They could scoop roe from large bowls on the table as an appetizer and snack. The vendace had faithfully returned in millions this fall, and under normal circumstances, very exclusive vendace roe was now a staple food at Brändön Lodge. The vendace was salted and stored in whatever containers were available. However, the salt shortage was becoming a significant concern. Salting a few hundred pounds of vendace that year had comprised half of their remaining stockpile.

At 1:30 a.m., Nyberg and Öving placed a box of four hundred army chocolate bars on the hosts' dining table and headed out into the darkness. They carried light packs, each with a double paddle, small backpacks with provisions, wire, a camera, knives, pistols, and small binoculars in holsters for easy access. Their AK 5D rifles were slung over their shoulders, stocks folded. They carefully scanned the shore of Granön with night vision goggles but saw no signs of activity, as expected. There was a waning crescent moon, but the cloud cover allowed only a faint light to penetrate, which they noted with gratitude.

They were almost invisible in their dark camouflage uniforms, with blackened faces and gloves. Though their kayaks were bright red plastic, they had attached spruce branches to the sides, breaking up the outline in case someone swept the water with night vision goggles. Homemade stealth kayaks.

The water was almost still, and they felt a light breeze from the Gulf of Bothnia. This breeze would be enough to mask the faint sounds of their paddles as they gently dipped them in and out of the water, perfect conditions.

Carefully, they pushed the kayaks into the water and settled in, then paddled silently but powerfully toward Granön, Nyberg leading and Öving following a hundred feet behind. Keeping some distance between them was a routine they followed by instinct. They chose the path between the small islands in the middle of the strait because it offered protection in case they came under fire.

The opposite shore was completely still as they cautiously pulled the kayaks up and hid them in the reeds. Without exchanging a word, they set off with silent, light steps, moving briskly like jogging, Nyberg first and Öving a hundred feet behind. "Like the Sami walk," Nyberg often said. He had often noted that no one, not even himself, moved faster in this terrain than the Sami people.

Nyberg liked to think that he had war in his blood, making him a particularly good soldier. His grandfather made magnetic bombs at a small factory Nybergs Mekaniska Verkstad in Kiruna during World War II. These bombs were attached to ship hulls and delivered to resistance movements in both Norway and Denmark. At least two German ships were sunk in the harbor by what the Germans called the *Nüberg-bombe*, a hidden threat that deeply worried them. Their detailed but unexecuted plan to occupy Kiruna included blowing up Nyberg's Mekaniska Verkstad and capturing and executing Grandfather Nyberg himself. Nyberg's father fought as a UN soldier in the Congo in 1961, where he was wounded in battle with the Congolese army, *Force Publique*, which had rebelled against the Belgians. His father had narrowly avoided being the twentieth Swedish soldier to die in that conflict.

They had chosen a route across the center of Granön, where they believed the risk of encountering Muslim scouts was minimal. Any scouts would likely be patrolling the coastlines. After three miles of fast walking on small roads and logging tracks made by forestry machines, Nyberg stopped to check his GPS. Öving stopped about three hundred feet behind him and did the same.

No problems—they were exactly where they expected to be, where Granön transitions into Mulön, part of the mainland. Here, they needed to be extra cautious, as Mulön was connected to the Muslims' base in Bensbyn via the narrow Likskär Bridge. The bridge was almost certainly guarded, and they suspected there could be a post on Mulön near the bridge or possibly further inland.

They kept to the eastern part of Mulön, a quarter of a mile from the coast as planned, which meant they never got closer than a quarter to Likskär Bridge. Keeping up their brisk pace, they quickly crossed several clearings in various stages of regrowth, crouching low. The moon was still hidden behind the clouds, so it would take a lot for human eyes to spot the two shadowy figures moving silently, at least to human ears, through the forest.

When they reached the midpoint where Mulön transitions into Hertsön, about a quarter of a mile east of the small marina in Hagaviken, there was a sudden crash in the bushes. They heard the sound of running, heavy, fleeing steps. Instinctively, they threw themselves to the ground with their fingers on the triggers, three hundred feet apart. The adrenaline hit instantly and intensely, putting them on high alert within two seconds. Were they revealed? Had they stumbled upon a Muslim post?

They lay still for two minutes, scanning intensely from ground level in breathless tension, but nothing else happened. Nyberg cautiously lifted his head and observed for another two minutes through his night vision goggles before slowly rising, step by step, low and crouched with his finger on the trigger, moving toward the small clearing where the sounds had come from. Öving stayed behind to cover him in case the enemy opened fire.

After a hundred feet, Nyberg reached the clearing but couldn't see anything unusual. He turned on his headlamp at the lowest setting, which barely provided more than a guiding light, and crawled around the clearing, inspecting the ground. It revealed three depressions where the grass was pressed down: one large and two smaller. Evidently, an unexpected visitor had disturbed a moose cow with two calves from their night's rest.

Nyberg signaled to Öving, and they resumed their rapid march, carefully crossing the little beach route, Hagavikens Strandväg, which they knew was guarded, near Hertsö Centrum, where the massive al-Hakim Mosque stood. They were now just half a mile from the northern end of the lake Hertsöträsket, where Nyberg would follow the eastern shore to the southern end while Öving would scout the northern end.

When they reached the northern tip of Hertsöträsket, Nyberg headed south along the lake without looking back while Öving stopped to survey the surroundings with his night vision goggles thoroughly. It was only a quarter of a mile to the power line leading to Hertsö Centrum, which they had chosen as a potential route for the operation.

Öving cautiously approached and managed to cross the five-hundred-foot-wide swampy area without getting wet, created by the nonexistent and almost stagnant inflow to the lake. He was concerned about the deep and visible footprints he left behind but had no choice. Soon, he was on dry, solid ground again.

When he was about four hundred feet from the power line path, he suddenly saw a faint light flare up for a few seconds, seemingly from a spot under the power lines. He decided to take a look. Silently, he took his thick fleece socks from his pocket and rolled them over his boots, just as he did when stalking roe deer on the rocky fields back home in Småland. After years of stalking, he had developed a way to move so silently that even the sharpest and craftiest old roebucks didn't notice him until it was too late. Consequently, he had probably the most impressive collection of rose antlers in Småland, displayed at his mother's cottage.

As he cautiously approached the power line path, he smelled a faint smell of cigarette smoke, which was exactly what he expected, but he couldn't see any people. He snuck out

in the middle of the power line path, sought shelter among the densely growing small birches, and scouted where the smoking sentinel should be. Suddenly, the cigarette glow appeared two hundred feet away from him, as if it had previously been hidden behind the soldier's body.

The lone sentry was sitting and smoking on a stool at the far side of the power line. But why wasn't there a second guard as usual? "Well, he's already breaking the rules by smoking, so you can't expect normal behavior from these *Holy Warriors*," Öving was thinking for himself. "I'll have to sneak up and eliminate him first when we launch the attack, so he doesn't have time to raise the alarm," Öving was contemplating again.

Suddenly, he heard a cough and clearing of the throat, followed by someone blowing their nose loudly, just a few feet from the bush where he was hiding. This sent Öving's adrenaline into overdrive, spreading that almost intoxicating sensation through his body. Apparently, he had sneaked past a guard thirty feet behind him without noticing him. The guard had likely been asleep at his post until he started coughing.

Without warning, the clouds parted, and the moonlight suddenly bathed the power line path in light. Given the loud nose-blowing, Öving was sure he hadn't been detected yet, but how was he supposed to cross the open area back to the forest edge now that it was illuminated? He had no choice but to stay put and wait for the moon to be covered by clouds again, though it seemed unlikely. The bright moonlight at least allowed him to watch the guard from between the bushes where he lay hidden, flat on the ground.

After just a few minutes, the guard dozed off again, leaning forward on the stool with his head resting in his hands. Öving waited another two minutes before carefully taking out the wire snare, hoping he wouldn't have to use it. He eased the flap of his pistol holster and checked that his army knife was in place, just in case. Crouching low and silent, he sneaked across the open area back toward the forest edge. When he was only twenty feet from the guard, he suddenly lifted his head and turned in Öving's direction.

Öving took a few quick steps and leaped, agile as a panther, onto the drowsy guard, who didn't have time to react. The stool toppled backward, and the guard couldn't defend himself. Öving landed on top of him, slipped the snare over his neck, and tightened it until his knuckles turned white before the guard could resist. A faint, half-choked cry, unnoticed by the other guard two hundred feet away, was all he managed to utter before the wire cut off his air supply for good. After what felt like an eternity of kicking and flailing, the guard's body went limp. Öving secured the snare tightly, ensuring no air could pass through.

Öving lifted the body slightly and realized it was significantly heavier than his lean, hundred-and-fifty-pound frame. Reconnaissance soldiers are generally small and light, as mobility is crucial, and Öving was no exception.

He removed the guard's heavy magazine-filled jacket, boots, and belt with other gear to lighten the load. Despite being lightweight, Öving was surprisingly strong after years of working out. He knelt down and, with some effort, hoisted the lifeless body over his shoulder in a classic fireman's grip, staggering off into the forest. He knew he could only manage a couple hundred feet at most and recalled a small tarn, which rather was more of a large waterhole, he had passed just before the power line street.

He swore silently to himself as he struggled like an animal to carry the two-hundred-pound body. The guy wasn't taller than him, but he was solidly built and quite overweight. He could feel the bloated, fat belly against his right shoulder. There was a popular Max hamburger restaurant opposite the al-Hakim Mosque that didn't offer bacon with the burgers, and the guy was likely a regular, Öving mused as he struggled under his heavy load. He found himself silently grinning, lugging a corpse over his shoulder and wondered how he could lose focus so completely and drift off given the precarious situation he was in.

When he reached the edge of the small pond, with his leg muscles burning, he let the body fall into the water. He immediately snuck back to the spot where he had strangled the guard. A change of guard could happen any minute, so there was no time to waste. He quickly gathered all of his equipment, slung the guard's AK-47 over his shoulder, and stuffed the magazines into his cargo pockets. He silently walked back to the pond where he had left the body.

The warrior's equipment, except for the assault rifle, magazines, and half-full canteen, hit the water a couple of feet out, and he ensured everything sank to the bottom. The clothes sank as expected, thanks to pockets filled with stones, but he kept the scarf in his pocket. He put on the warrior's boots, which were a few sizes too big, and then tied his own boots together and hung them around his neck.

Finally, he covered the body with moss and spruce branches, making it impossible to be discovered by human eyes. Luckily, Muslims rarely used dogs, as dogs were considered *haram*, just like pigs.

Now that he had done what he could to erase his tracks, he began the return to Brändön. When he reached the swamp, he visibly placed the warrior's canteen on a stump. He made sure to step heavily in his own previous footprints, reversing the direction and leaving the tracks of the warrior's boots.

After a hundred feet, he wedged the warrior's scarf between the branches at the top of a small juniper bush. If anyone followed the tracks in daylight, they would inevitably find the canteen and the scarf.

Soon, the Muslims would realize a guard was missing, and Öving couldn't predict what conclusions they would draw. Maybe they would think the warrior had deserted or simply walked into the forest to shoot himself. Suicide was not uncommon among traumatized soldiers with frayed nerves. Muslims' fear of venturing into the forest would likely mean they wouldn't search too thoroughly. But if they did search, they would undoubtedly reach the swamp and find the tracks showing the warrior had left voluntarily and disappeared into the forest on the other side. That should work, Öving thought, and increased his pace once he reached solid ground.

After a quarter of a mile, he switched back to his own boots and shoved the Muslim warrior's boots deep into a badger den. An hour later, he was back at the strait between Granön and Brändön and found both kayaks still hidden in the reeds. Nyberg soon emerged from his hiding spot and pointed questioningly at Öving's Kalashnikov, which Öving answered with a small smile.

They pushed the kayaks into the water, and soon they would be back on Brändön. They hadn't exchanged a single word since they left Brändön Lodge three hours earlier, but they knew there would soon be plenty of time to discuss their respective observations.

The host couple at the Lodge received the Muslim warrior's eighty bullets and his AK-47 with enormous gratitude. A few weeks later, a female bear, charging to attack two eight-year-olds playing, was quickly shot down with a short burst from the assault rifle's barrel. A story neither soldier would ever live to hear about.

Chapter 30

The battle of Luleå

October 15, 2032

Hugo's 3,500 "free soldiers" were an impressive army in numbers. Still, the lack of military expertise and communication equipment made coordination poor, and most operations had to be improvised on the spot.

In military terms, the free soldiers were comparable to the enemy's *Holy Warriors* but were generally better marksmen because most Swedes were recreational hunters.

The combat effectiveness of the 3,500 soldiers was nowhere near the power of the 850 ranger soldiers who had been ferried overnight across the strait from Brändön to Granön to begin the six-mile-long march through the forest toward Hertsön. From there, they would advance on to central Luleå from the east. The ranger soldiers were comparable to the Muslims' imported elite soldiers but better trained and extremely motivated, fueled by a burning desire to defend Sweden and annihilate the invaders. The Muslim elite soldiers were well-trained, but mercenaries were soldiers who fought for their pay, against any opponent, and for whom fighting was just a job done reluctantly.

The width of the Lule River posed a difficult barrier for the free army since both the new and old Gäddvik Bridges had been destroyed by the Muslims. The Bergnäs Bridge had been blown up on the third day of the war, July 20th.

Going directly towards Luleå by boat down the river was not an option, as Hugo's reconnaissance soldiers had confirmed that the Muslims had set up a heavily armed post on the island of Granden. This post effectively blocked the river at the strait of Gäddvik, where it was narrowest. The river was only about two hundred feet wide on either side of Granden, which meant any boat attempting to pass thru would be shot to pieces before it made any headway thru the gap. Hugo's soldiers were based in the small villages Unbyn and Avan, where they had been forcibly situated in their farms just as during both world wars. The free soldiers were placed on the southern side of the river, and only boats could take them across.

"We Swedes have been a seafaring people for thousands of years," Hugo proclaimed as he rallied the soldiers. They would attempt to cross at Lövudden, where they had gathered seventy-six small boats. Hugo had calculated that the boats must make four trips to get the entire army across. "Let us, like our ancestors, the Vikings, go into battle with courage, determination, and a conviction that will frighten our enemies into surrender!"

There was a constant shortage of fuel, but Hugo's soldiers had found the occasional gasoline barrel hidden in barns, and in some garages, they had found several rows of plastic jugs. The fuel was confiscated in exchange for handwritten receipts signed by the highest-ranking officer nearby. The recipients were assured they would get their gallons back after the war, but the value of those gallons then would likely be a fraction of their current worth. The affected gasoline owners grimaced but had no choice but to comply and appear cheerful. Many didn't even bother to keep their receipts.

Hugo and his staff had decided that half of the entire troop should embark at Storsand, near Gammelstad, where long sandy beaches awaited. These long beaches were similar to Operation Dragoon in 1944 when the Allies landed on the famous beaches outside Saint-Tropez. This association with sandy beaches was why the operation was eventually codenamed Operation Dragoon during planning. Initially, the staff used the name Operation Overlord, but it was changed because it was deemed too revealing about the operation's nature if the name reached the wrong ears, which it often did one way or another.

From Storsand, the plan was to move through the Storheden commercial area and then follow Highway 97, Bodenvägen, the remaining four miles to the center. The idea was to drive a wedge between the Muslim troops in Gammelstad and those in Luleå. The staff anticipated that the enemy troops in Gammelstad would move toward Luleå once they realized it was a major attack. The soldiers landing in Storsand would stop the enemy on Highway 97, thus relieving the ranger soldiers advancing on Luleå from the east. Meanwhile, the other half of the free soldiers, landing at Furunäsudden in northern Gäddvik, would have a clear march toward Luleå by following the European Highway 4 one mile north before turning east and following the shore past Notviken and Mjölkudden.

Operation Dragoon was a grand plan, but as it happens in war, many plans tend to go wrong due to unforeseen events. The hiccup that day was when Hugo's reconnaissance soldiers stopped at the landing site instead of continuing inland to gather more intelligence on the enemy's activities. Perhaps the lack of communication equipment led to this unnecessary and devastating blunder, as the communication radios used during moose hunts didn't work over such a long distance. As soon as the seventy-six boats from Lövudden were a quarter of a mile from shore, they were spotted by Muslim scouts in Gammelstad, who were sweeping the water's surface with their night-vision goggles. This triggered an alarm at the Muslim base, unbeknownst to the Swedes. Within ten minutes, nearly 750

Muslim soldiers were mobilized, with 400 of them ordered to board trucks and buses while the remaining 350 were held in reserve.

Meanwhile, the small invasion boats had reached their destinations at Storsand and Furunäsudden and were returning to Lövudden to pick up more soldiers.

The Muslim trucks and buses headed toward Storsand, noting the landing just one mile from their base in Gammelstad. They did not allocate any soldiers to counter the landing at Furunäsudden, which they deemed far enough from their base and Luleå.

The landing at Furunäsudden would have to be dealt with later, potentially by the reserves, depending on how things developed.

Before the boats with the second wave of free soldiers reached Storsand, the Muslims took positions in the forest above the beach. They awaited the incoming boats without engaging the previously landed soldiers, who had been ordered to wait on the beach until all soldiers had crossed. Just as the last of the thirty-eight small boats drove straight onto the sandy beach and the soldiers began disembarking, all hell broke loose. Violent gunfire and grenade bombardments rained down on the landed soldiers. Operation Dragoon had unexpectedly transformed into Operation Overlord, as Storsand turned into a bloody Omaha Beach. Soldiers fell like bowling pins as the enemy fired from their positions in the sparse pine forest atop the lower sand shoreline.

After ten minutes of intense gunfire, 393 Swedish free soldiers lay dead or wounded on the sand, while the remaining 480 managed to advance a bit into the forest, where they could find cover and engage the enemy more evenly. The battle raged all day, with the Muslims' grenade launchers continuously reducing the number of attacking Swedes. In the afternoon, the fifty-nine surviving free soldiers tried to surrender, but the Muslims had strict orders not to take any prisoners. The site would later become a beautiful memorial grove for the Swedish free soldiers who gave their lives for their country.

At Furunäsudden, things went better, and the landing proceeded as planned, without resistance. Consequently, all boats were redirected there after the battle at Storsand broke out. At Furunäsudden, 2,600 soldiers landed and began moving in groups along the European Highway 4.

Near Karlshäll, close to where the amiable and popular *Oberleutnant* Walter Sindel had overseen the large German warehouse during World War II—a well-known landmark that had been burned down a year earlier—the first group encountered resistance from about fifty Muslim elite soldiers and *Holy Warriors*. They had positioned themselves on both sides of the

European Highway 4, blocking the road. More groups of Swedish soldiers were approaching and managed to flank the enemy from both sides, giving them no chance. After twenty-five minutes, the enemy was defeated, and the Swedish soldiers resumed their march toward Luleå. Some groups that had bypassed the battlefield were already a few miles ahead.

Meanwhile, 850 ranger soldiers halted at the northern tip of the lake Hertsöträsk after a seven-mile forced march through the forest from Granön, where they had landed overnight. Reconnaissance soldiers Carl-Johan Öving and Pelle Nyberg, familiar with the terrain from their mission three days earlier, moved a quarter of a mile ahead of the troops to ensure they wouldn't encounter any surprises, like ambushes or unexpected troop concentrations.

A steady breeze blew from the sea, making the branches sway. Öving didn't bother rolling his fleece socks over his boots this time. Human ears are almost deaf compared to the hypersensitive ears of roe deer, which perk up at the slightest hint of danger. Human noses are so hopelessly inferior and insensitive that Öving didn't even need to consider it, though he automatically noted the wind direction and his own course relative to it.

Öving crept slowly through the forest toward where he had observed two guard posts during his night mission, having had to kill and hide one of them. Nyberg followed two hundred feet behind, ready to cover his comrade if anything happened.

When they were six hundred feet from the power line where the Muslim guards had been during his last visit, Öving passed the small pond where he had sunk the dead guard's belongings and covered his body with moss and branches. The body remained hidden under the brush, indicating that the Muslims hadn't found it.

Öving's plan was to eliminate the two guards expected to be on duty without them raising an alarm. This would allow the main force to march along the power line path to Hertsö center quickly. From there, the main force would have a clear path to central Luleå. Öving held his favorite weapon, a small .22 Long Rifle, in his right hand as he cautiously advanced to a point at the edge of the power line path, where he could see the guards if they were in the same place.

His favorite weapon, an old and worn Husqvarna 1640 with an Aimpoint red dot scope and a Stalon Whisper W110 suppressor had taken down almost all of his "big game" back home in Småland in recent years. With talent, the shot had to be placed right in the skull, a challenge for any master marksman, but Öving loved challenges. No "spoiled meat" either; Öving was a true thrifty Smålander.

Bingo! The guards were sitting on their stools in the exact same place as before. From his position in the middle of the guards, it was only a hundred feet between each one of them. Öving knelt down, hidden among the bushes, and took support against a sturdy birch tree. He aimed the red dot at the right guard's temple. The shot went off with a quiet "poppfffss," similar to the sound of an air rifle, causing the guard's head to slump and his body to fall off the stool slowly.

Öving quickly swung his rifle to the left and noticed the other guard had turned towards his comrade. He had likely caught the low sound of the shot without realizing it was a gunshot since the wind was blowing in his direction. The sound could have been mistaken for a human sneeze, so the guard probably thought his colleague had caught a cold. Öving quickly aimed the red dot at the guard's nose and fired another "poppfffss," causing him to fall forward just as he stood up to check on his comrade.

Nyberg, who had observed the events from his position on a small hill behind Öving, pressed the button on his radio.

"It's all clear. Come on."

"Roger that. We're moving to the target onward. Over."

"Roger. Out."

Öving sped along the power line path, with Nyberg close behind, soon followed by 850 rangers on the same trail. Four minutes later, Öving and Nyberg reached Hertsövägen, from where they could see it: the northernmost mosque in the world, the massive al-Hakim Mosque, with its missile-like minarets rising high above Hertsö center. Three minutes later, the first rangers arrived, led by their platoon leaders, continuing in groups onto Hertsövägen without stopping. Öving and Nyberg had completed their scouting mission and joined the last platoon as regular infantry soldiers.

Hertsövägen was clear, and the main forces marched quickly toward Örnäset without encountering resistance, while three platoons, including a special pyrotechnic platoon, veered off towards the al-Hakim Mosque. They met a half-dozen lightly armed *Holy Warriors* who were easily defeated in a few minutes. However, one ranger was severely injured by a burst of gunfire that hit both his thighs, causing him to bleed and die within minutes.

The octogen-based HMX bombs were placed within minutes at strategic points inside and outside the mosque and around the minarets at waist height. The powerful detonation caused most of the mosque walls to collapse, leading to the large dome crumbling into a cloud of dust created by falling debris. The four minarets were reduced to what looked like feet-high stumps of fallen trees.

Meanwhile, the first ranger platoons reached the roundabout at Svartövägen. One platoon veered off to clear and secure the Islamic Association building on Krongårdsringen, waiting for the special explosives platoon to arrive. There was no resistance, but in passing, they shot the dozen or so Muslims who happened to be in the association's building at what was clearly the wrong time. The rangers met no resistance and continued their advance along Hertsövägen, into Malmudden, where they could see central Luleå.

While the situation was unexpectedly calm for the rangers, the opposite was true for the part of the free soldiers approaching Luleå from the west along Highway 97. As anticipated, the Muslims sent their remaining reserves from their base in Gammelstad to defend Luleå. A mixed force of four hundred *Holy Warriors* and a hundred elite soldiers attacked the Swedes from the rear, triggering an intense battle. The Swedes held their ground on both sides of the road with light anti-tank weapons and machine guns, effectively blocking the Muslims' armored vehicles.

The seven hundred Swedish soldiers following the shoreline had already reached Mjölkudden. From there, they could see the North Harbor and the hangar-like building known as the "House of Culture," which served as the Muslims' headquarters.

Simultaneously, the Muslims in Gammelstad received an unpleasant surprise. 250 rangers had managed to advance twelve miles through the forest west of the European Highway 4 from their base in Persön. The Muslim base had only forty *Holy Warriors* left behind to guard it.

The rangers spread out in a semicircle around the base, subjecting it to an intense barrage of machine guns, grenade launchers, and automatic rifles, advancing bit by bit until they were inside the base. The remaining sixteen *Holy Warriors* surrendered and were taken as prisoners.

Two hundred rangers then moved along Highway ninety-seven towards Notviken, where the free army was engaged in combat with the Muslims. After about an hour, the rangers reached the battlefield, and the Muslims found themselves trapped in a formation maneuver they couldn't escape. After four hours of fighting, the remaining 150 Muslims surrendered.

The rangers advancing from Hertsön had an easy journey, encountering no resistance. This was because ninety percent of the Muslims' forces were stationed in their bases in Rutvik, Bensbyn, and Gammelstad, where they believed they were blocking all routes into Luleå, since the bridges over the Lule River had been destroyed.

The remaining ten percent of the Muslim troops, consisting of three hundred *Holy Warriors*, were stationed at the Cape of Gültzau as a reserve. They were expecting an attack by boats from Bergnäset, which never happened.

In the city center, on the main island, the Muslims relied solely on the constantly patrolling moral police equipped with AK-47s. The rangers were now inside central Luleå, moving west along Storgatan and Sandviksgatan. They encountered sporadic gunfire from the moral police, who retreated while firing wildly and inaccurately. Groups of free soldiers following the shoreline from Storheden simultaneously began to reach the city center in a disordered but uncomplicated advance over the causeway connecting Mjölkudden with central Luleå.

About a hundred soldiers attacked the Muslims' headquarters in Kulturens Hus. Meeting little resistance, they easily mowed down the guards and entered the building, mercilessly shooting all twenty-four people inside. At North Harbor, the advancing Swedes encountered a couple of hundred *Holy Warriors* from the base at Gültzauudden, who had taken positions and were shooting wildly without aim, getting nowhere.

Meanwhile, large groups of rangers poured into the city through the park, Hermelinsparken, flanking the defending Muslims and trapping them without any chance of escape. After half an hour of gunfire, the remaining 120 *Holy Warriors* surrendered and were taken captive. The last of the Muslim occupiers retreated to the far end of the Cape Gültzau, fighting to the last man. They were systematically eliminated one by one by the rangers.

At 2:15 p.m. on October 15, 2027, the last fleeing Muslim was killed by a well-aimed shot to the back from five hundred feet away by Pelle Nyberg's AK 5 rifle. Luleå was liberated without the city being reduced to ruins, but hundreds of Luleå residents had been executed by the Muslim occupiers. No one knew how many. The people of Luleå could breathe a sigh of relief and regain hope for the future after a three-month-long Muslim nightmare. However, they could not foresee facing a far worse catastrophe that would unfold just nineteen days after their liberation.

Chapter 31

A sausage stuffer's dilemma

October 15, 2032

Benno Ronkanen never imagined he would become a sausage salesman, but that was precisely what happened. He had been one of Sweden's most celebrated and high-profile newspaper columnists for nearly a decade. The highest-paid, with the highest level of fame, enjoying all the perks that came with the job. Benno's sharp and exact jabs had brought down numerous powerful figures and even more insignificant little hotshots. Being mentioned in Benno's Friday column was a bad premonition for those targeted by his sharp pen.

Benno's greatest triumphs came when his victims fell into the classic trap of entangling themselves in their own lies, unaware that Benno had even more incriminating information. He had a habit of releasing information bit by bit, and as cunning as he was, he never showed his hand until it was time for the final "execution." This final punch always came with the delightful insults and witty barbs that had become Benno's signature. The "execution" usually resulted in the victim losing their job, as no employer or client wanted to risk their reputation through "guilt by association." This was high-level entertainment for Benno as well as for his animated readers.

But one day, the rug was suddenly pulled out from under him, and Benno found himself forced to take his own bitter medicine. A handful of women working in the media and culture sphere simultaneously posted on social media, accusing Benno of sexual assault during his wild partying years. The shitstorm—Benno's initial term for it—escalated beyond description. This was the mob of all mobs, and Benno Ronkanen found himself splashed across the front pages for weeks, accompanied by one shocking accusation after another. His former journalist friends joined in, reveling in the salacious details of Benno's private life based on statements from anonymous women. Pure fabrications, Benno thought. Jealousy. Pettiness. Pure evil. It was a nightmare.

Benno's assignments disappeared overnight, and his old colleagues were suddenly gone. None of those he once thought were his friends would say hi to him anymore when he passed them on the street. In Södermalm bars, he had to sit alone and drink. Even the bar owners, who had collected millions of kronor from Benno and his thirsty journalist friends over the years, began greeting him coldly as if his presence tainted the air.

Benno thought it was all incredibly unfair. For the past seven or eight years, he had lived as a responsible and mostly monogamous family man, so why should he be blamed for things that happened in the past? Benno usually took the kids to daycare and school. How many parent-teacher conferences had he attended? How many times had he organized events at his boys' karate club? He hadn't touched drugs since his first son was born, except for alcohol. Sure, he drank a bit, but no worse than anyone else.

Benno tried to remember and reflect on his old partying days, which spanned half a decade, to analyze his behavior seriously. How many girls had he actually slept with? Was it a hundred? Seventy-five? He had no idea.

Of the five jealous and insignificant women who had ruined his life, he couldn't even recall meeting two of them. He hadn't even heard of them. Maybe they were girls he had barely spoken to before they ended up in his bedroom, the kind who easily went home with the great Ronkanen. On some nights he had found plenty of such quick flings in taxi queues, and those encounters certainly didn't stick in his memory. Sure, he had slept with the other three at least once, but being labeled a rapist was definitely not the truth. Besides, he had seen them at the journalists' club, the Gothenburg Book Fair, and some film premieres, and they had all behaved normally and returned his greetings. Why didn't they report it to the police when it happened if they had felt violated? Making vague accusations a decade later shouldn't have been enough to bring him down, but that's exactly what happened.

The word rape also means violence, and as far as he could remember, he had never used violence. Violence wasn't his style; if anything, he considered himself somewhat submissive. He liked women who took the initiative. Okay, maybe he had been a bit more aggressive with some inexperienced girl who didn't seem to understand why she was in Benno's famous bedroom. It was almost always young girls. Young women around twenty or twenty-five with dreams of becoming journalists, musicians, or actresses. Girls with low self-esteem who idolized men with star status. The hottest targets for these girls were musicians, Benno had noted. If he could get a famous musician to join him at the bar, his own stock soared like a rocket. Hockey and soccer players were also popular with the girls, not least because of their strong and appealing physique. Hockey players were said to be the best "fuck machines," but Benno did his best to uphold the reputation of the "cultural men." Sports stars were usually richer than cultural men, but they were rarely out at bars, so Benno had to settle for letting the girls shake hands with some of the retired sports stars he knew.

Benno believed that the five sly cultural women who had orchestrated the well-planned smear campaign were merely groupies who used their bodies to mingle with prominent men expected to open the right doors. Benno himself had been a coveted trophy, something these women could boast about to their friends. Should he be held accountable just because many women sought success through sexual means? Not at all, in his opinion. Everyone involved knew the rules of the game. They flirted in bars, indulged in a little line of cocaine or two, and laughed with like-minded people until it was time to go home, in pairs or threes, and have sex into the early hours. After all, sex was the whole point. To be completely honest with himself, Benno had spiked drinks with amphetamines three or four times. The beauty of spiked drinks was that the woman usually didn't realize she was drugged. She just felt unusually free and uninhibited, ready to do things she normally wouldn't. Perhaps he had drugged some of the five women who brought him down without them realizing it until much later. But it was never about rape, Benno thought. He certainly wasn't a rapist. The only thing he truly regretted was that he was often so drunk and high that he went on autopilot, missing the finer nuances of making love he later learned to appreciate. Not even the memories remained, except as vague fragments.

Benno's life as a journalist was irrevocably over. There was no mercy for a publicly accused sex offender, true or not—at least not for men. Now, Benno's life was about sausage casings, stuffing, and smoking. Sausage, sausage, and more sausage. Production, packaging, marketing, and selling sausage. Just as Benno could never have imagined becoming a sausage vendor, he could never have imagined actually loving it.

But it bothered him that commercial ventures had such low status in his circles. In his circles, it was admirable and prestigious to become wealthy by writing music, painting, making films, or writing books. But someone who got rich selling sausage was just a greedy capitalist. However, getting rich by running restaurants and wine bars or baking sourdough bread was considered much better. Pubs and pizzerias were borderline cases. The distinctions were subtle and not always easy to understand for the uninitiated.

Benno had occasionally thought he might be more suited to being an entrepreneur than a journalist. An experienced and successful businessperson who had become his mentor often said Benno had all the typical entrepreneurial qualities: a quick intellect, boundless energy, a cheerful disposition, personal integrity, and a lack of self-conciousness. Well, he certainly had no inhibitions, Benno thought with self-irony. At least, that's what the media had published. And strangely enough, he woke up happy every morning, even when the smear campaign was at its worst. It was almost as if he were mentally invulnerable. Regardless of the situation, he kept going like a robot, switching gears when necessary without giving it much thought. Maybe he really was a psychopath, he wondered with a hint of uncertainty.

The business had grown from promising to brilliant in just two years. Ronkanen's Södermalm Sausage quickly became a well-known brand, and the product line expanded. Benno's mentor, who had bought twenty-five percent of the shares, constantly harped on diversifying the business.

To convey the right retro artisanal feel behind the sausages, a stylized image of eighteenth-century houses in Vitabergsparken was used as a background, with the company name written in blood-red letters. Below the company name, the specific sausage type was written in cursive, eco-friendly green letters.

The bestseller was the wild boar sausage, which had a quite peppery flavor due to fresh chili peppers added to the mix right before smoking. Something sensational happened when the sweet red chili combined with the slightly tangy wild boar fat. The combination of these ingredients made taste buds tingle and sent sensations all the way to the ears. Some customers claimed they felt the impulses through their necks down their backs. Ronkanen's wild boar sausage was the perfect snack in Södermalm pubs, which proudly boasted local products.

The sausage money poured in at an increasing rate, and Benno reinvested everything into machinery and automation. In a few years, the sausage-making transitioned from artisanal to small industrial with three full-time employees. For image reasons, the factory was located in the old Slaughterhouse area near the Globe arena, south of Södermalm, which was now mostly residential. Despite the shift to industrial production, the taste did not suffer. It was all about using the finest meat and ensuring the spices were fresh, even if they were expensive.

Benno's favorite ingredients, shallots and garlic, were used in such quantities that he considered entering the greenhouse business to grow them instead of buying from the Netherlands and Southern Europe. Perhaps his business would evolve into an entire conglomerate, he thought, enjoying all the money flowing into the accounts of the great capital owner, Benno Ronkanen. But on July 17, 2027, the rug was suddenly pulled out from under him for the second time, and Benno was down for the count again.

The outbreak of war quickly caused Benno's business to collapse. Everything changed overnight. The payment system no longer worked, but even if it had, most of his retailers had stopped ordering sausages for other reasons. A couple of months after the outbreak of war, Ronkanen's Södermalm Sausage was insolvent and would have gone bankrupt if normal societal functions were still operating, but they were not. Benno adapted to the situation by ceasing to pay his interest and principal payments and payments to suppliers who could no longer be used. Benno's business became local again, as it had been initially. Both customers and suppliers were now exclusively in the vicinity. Benno scraped by, but there was no longer any point in accounting and bookkeeping since no one asked for such things. Benno's transactions were now directly with his own wallet and on a much smaller scale, but he still earned enough to support himself and his family.

During the early days of the war in July, Benno realized which way the wind was blowing. He removed and erased all traces of pork from the marketing. Ingredient declarations were removed because eighty percent of the product line was pork-based. Benno knew enough about Islam to realize that it was not wise to challenge the new rulers' will.

On the same day that the *Alzuwid* Caliphate was proclaimed in the City Hall, October 4, Benno made the painful decision to cease all pork handling. The hardest part was removing the popular wild boar sausage that generated most of the profit. Benno's mentor had harped on the eighty-twenty rule, which meant twenty percent of the product line generated eighty percent of the revenue. Essentially, only the wild boar sausage made money and was his livelihood. The wild boar sausage was so popular that he could almost double the price per pound compared to other sausages.

The other sausages existed mostly to give the company a serious image that supported the sale of wild boar sausage. But Benno had seen people beheaded for lesser offenses than handling pork, so he bit the bullet and developed new products like turkey, chicken, and ostrich sausage instead. Benno's long-term goal was to halal-certify the entire product line, which required all his meat suppliers to have halal certificates. The ultimate goal was to get the products into dedicated halal stores where the Muslim leaders shopped. This would bring him closer to those in power, which the advantages could help in the long term.

Nowadays, Benno wore a full-length kaftan and a small white crocheted topi on his head. He already had a bushy beard before the occupation, and he believed the beard might have saved him during the first weeks when he hadn't yet removed traces of pork from the factory. Benno's appearance seemed to appeal to the new rulers, and being as flexible and adaptable as he was, he had no intention of giving them a reason to punish him. He just kept working and tried to stay under the Muslims' radar as best he could.

A few weeks later, Benno realized that his old customer base was not particularly attracted to turkey, chicken, and ostrich sausages. Orders had virtually ceased, and in his desperation, Benno hatched an idea. Necessity is the mother of invention, he thought as he made up his mind. The wild boar sausage with red chili had to be back in the lineup, but it must be done discreetly. Benno realized that he had previously not understood that he had only been lucky when he created the flavorful hit that boosted the business. His customers used to say the sausage was so good they couldn't stop eating it, and Benno agreed with them. The wild boar sausage was the best sausage he had ever tasted. The flavor was sensational.

But from now on, the wild boar sausage would be called venison sausage and delivered with winks to the customers. Since his customers were accomplices, as pork consumers, he didn't need to worry about being exposed. And wild boar is probably not as bad as domestic pork, Benno thought. Maybe it was even fully acceptable, but he didn't intend to ask.

Benno was now alone in the small factory in the Slaughterhouse area. One Thursday afternoon, while he was busy cleaning the sausage stuffer, he was visited by two enforcers from the newly established Muslim tax authority. They came several times a month to collect the *jizya*, and Benno had prepared a white envelope with the money. Benno bowed humbly and handed the envelope to the enforcer who handled the conversation and introduced himself as Muhammad. Muhammad, who looked like he had a background in East Africa, spoke fluent suburb staccato-Swedish, and Benno guessed he was born in Sweden.

"Please accept my *jizya*," Benno said.

"Thank you, it's good that you're compliant," Muhammad replied. "We're a bit hungry today and were wondering if you might have some halal sausage to offer."

"Of course, no problem," Benno replied, noticing that the other tax enforcer had already started looking through the powerless refrigerators without waiting for Benno's response.

The two tax enforcers took their time and carefully tasted the various sausages.

"This one is really, really good," Muhammad said. "What's in it?"

"It's a smoked sausage based on venison, red chili, garlic, and vinegar," Benno replied. "I sell it under the name venison sausage."

"Is it certified *halal*?" the enforcer asked while munching on another venison sausage.

"It's halal-slaughtered venison, but I haven't gotten the halal certificate yet," Benno replied. "Everything is halal; it's just formalities before I can advertise that we only sell halal products."

"It looks suspiciously similar to the wild boar sausage you used to sell. We've looked at your old website. It's not wild boar meat, is it? Because if it is, you're dead."

"No, no, no, absolutely not! I am a serious convert and only eat halal products now. All parts of the machines that encounter the sausage have been replaced, and nothing but halal has ever been encountered. Take as much sausage as you want home to your families and friends."

"Okay, thanks. Just to be sure, I'll send a venison sausage for a lab test to ensure there's no trace of wild boar. It'll take a couple of weeks to get the results."

"No problem, you can be one hundred percent confident that my sausages only contain halal."

"Let's hope that's the case. Is it okay if we take some bags of this venison sausage that's so incredibly good? I'm thinking of giving a couple of bags to the imam and the highest Muslim council to get in good standing with those in power. You know, favors and returns."

"Of course, of course," Benno agreed, feeling sweat beads form on his forehead. "Take as much as you want!"

"By the way, you should change your logo, too," Muhammad said. "Those old wooden houses in Vitabergsparken will be burned down in a few days. You must have heard the imam announce it at Friday prayers. Everything reminiscent of old Sweden must go, and your logo must go, too."

"Yes, I just haven't had time.

"Do you think it's okay to use Zayed's Mosque as the background image instead?"

"It's okay once you've got the halal certification. Until then, run without a logo, got it?"

"Of course, of course!"

Benno waved off the tax collectors with his most pleasant smile, but as soon as they closed the door behind them, he collapsed onto a chair, leaning forward with his head in his hands.

"Damn!" he shouted, his voice echoing in the small factory. "Damn, hell, shit!"

Benno realized he was as smoked as his sausages. It was time to run and leave the occupation zone quickly. He left the factory just as it was, without tidying up, and jogged across the Skansbron bridge towards his home at Nytorget Square. On the way, he remembered that he should have disposed of the hidden wild boar fat. But he was too terrified by the thought of ending up dangling from the gallows at Medborgarplatsen to risk going back. He had decided to leave and wouldn't stay a minute longer than necessary.

Chapter 32

Discussions at Flottsbrogården

October 15, 2032

Uno glanced at the date window on his old, scratched Certina watch. His cellphone was useless, with many radio towers and central hubs destroyed. Today was Filip's 65th birthday, Uno thought, and he pondered whether it was appropriate to offer best wishes given the current circumstances.

That means it's been exactly ten years since I first met Filip at that meeting in the cottage association on Värmdö, Uno recalled. He remembered how everyone cheered for the newly turned fifty-five-year-old, who wore a straw hat with a flat crown that looked like it was from the 1800s author Strindberg's days, which it was. With the straw hat on his head, it was impossible not to see Filip's resemblance to the great national poet, except that Filip was eight inches taller than the icon had been. Uno fondly remembered how they had sat for hours, talking over a few glasses of wine, and how a soul connection quickly formed between them despite their different backgrounds and lives. It was their differences that added excitement to their relationship. Filip was twenty-four years older, and Uno was barely an adult, though he had already been running his construction company for eight years. The following week, he spent a day and a half nailing together Filip's new little prefabricated house, and he remembered how astonished Filip had been at how quickly it was done. In Filip's world, the project would have taken several weeks.

Uno occasionally thought about that housewarming party at Filip's new six-room apartment at Mosebacke Square on Södermalm in Stockholm. The nice champagne toasts on the terrace, with the fantastic panorama of parts of the city like Old Town and Östermalm. All the intellectual guests discussed their latest book projects, film, theater, media, all things he knew and cared nothing about. They seemed so worldly and well-traveled, talking about restaurants and hotels in New York and Paris as if those places were just around the corner. He understood that his own charter trips to Thailand and Tenerife wouldn't be of interest, so instead, he chose to be a listener that evening.

He wore his best blazer with a neatly tied tie, but Filip's guests seemed to mingle in simple, sloppy clothes. An inattentive eye might have thought they were poor. Uno's intuition told him that the other guests spent much more time and money on their outfits than he did. He thought of the word "chic," which he wasn't sure of the meaning of. Maybe this was how you dressed chic? Or was it just their style?

Particularly amusing was the all-knowing, ever-present "National Oracle," who arrived in full hunting gear—with muddy boots and dried bloodstains on his hunting vest. Uno, an avid hunter himself, found it strange because it was clear that the National Oracle had freshly showered beneath the dirty hunting clothes. He definitely didn't show up at the party straight from hunting.

The witty and amusing National Oracle ranted all evening while his drunkenness increased alarmingly. There was a certain aura around him. Despite his increasingly incoherent babbling, he was constantly surrounded by a small gaggle of admirers who politely helped him find the words when he lost them. It was like being in another world. What did Uno offer in this fancy, intellectual world, having barely read a book? He recognized some of them from TV and columns in the tabloids. These were people he barely believed existed in real life because they were so far away from his own reality. That smug, short-statured, left-wing columnist holding court with a few admirers around him. A big-game hunter, too. An obscene one, who used to pose sitting on elephants and giraffes that his hunting guides had tracked and pointed out. Apparently, he pulled the trigger all by himself.

The long, thin woman with round glasses who had written many books asked Uno what his profession was. When Uno explained that he was a builder, she reacted as if he had said something inappropriate and immediately turned her attention away. This didn't surprise Uno; he knew he was quite unremarkable.

Most peculiar, however, was the guy with the strange first name. He wandered around in a white tuxedo jacket hidden behind his dark sunglasses, with a silk scarf neatly tied high around his neck. Uno recognized him as one of those who gave out the Nobel Prize in Literature. The prize-giver was obviously friends with that flamboyant Frenchman who unabashedly groped all the women, and no one seemed to find it odd, not even their husbands.

Another odd character was Benno Ronkanen, the cultural columnist from the tabloid Aftonposten. He was obviously high as a kite and just grinned foolishly when Uno tried to speak with him.

However, the overly arrogant TV celebrity Robert, known as "The Ass," who had made a fortune by harassing and persecuting good, decent Swedes, elicited a much stronger reaction from Uno. Uno felt the adrenaline rise when he heard Robert's forced and provocative staccato voice coming from a fat, sagging face that most resembled a pig's snout. It took all of Uno's self-control to avoid planting a solid carpenter's punch squarely on The Ass's pig snout face.

No, that world was not his. But his already considerable admiration for Filip grew even more when he realized what an exalted position Filip held in that distant, elite world. His admiration for Filip's intelligence and vast knowledge was almost boundless. He had never met anyone like Filip before or since, and he felt lucky to have such a friend.

Filip was an inexhaustible source of wisdom and fact, which was why Uno had engaged him as his personal advisor in the war against the Muslims. An advisor who understood politics and society and who could explain and interpret what was happening on a broader scale. He noted that Filip had an uncanny ability to foresee political events long in advance, even on the international stage. Filip claimed to have a crystal ball he would look into to see the future, and it certainly seemed like he was telling the truth about that. But he had never shown Uno the ball.

What Uno found most peculiar, and perhaps most appealing about Filip, was that he would often say that Uno was the smarter of the two and seemed to genuinely mean it.

"I promise you would score significantly higher than me on an IQ test," Filip had said multiple times. "Far higher than I would. I'm just a product of growing up in an academic family where I coasted through all the schools and social circles. You know, both mom and dad wrote books quite successfully, and with that came many other social perks."

When Filip looked at himself in the mirror, he saw a somewhat absent-minded academic who could only articulate life and the world in words he typed on his computer. Practical tasks like upgrading his phone were daunting with all the new features, while Uno would handle new gadgets effortlessly. When Filip looked at Uno, he saw a great talent who absorbed facts faster than anyone he had seen and was extremely organized in all contexts. A person who could build houses, a person to admire. A person who had complete control over the actions of the Swedes, the Yugos, and the Syrians in the war against the Muslims. A man of action with an inherent, never-ending creativity that was the foundation of all their operations. A person who always appeared to be the natural leader without ever demanding to be so. Except at intellectual parties in Södermalm, of course.

Once the birthday congratulations were over, they sat down with a few glasses of homemade liquor, the only thing available, to philosophize about life, as they had done together so many times before. A "Flottsbro Special" with lukewarm cola might not have been the best drink, but it sufficed. As always, Filip's thoughts drove the conversation, while Uno absorbed the wisdom with fascination.

"In hindsight, I just can't understand what we were doing. For decades, we were useful idiots for the Muslims without realizing it. Not until 2028 or 2029, something like that, did I begin to see what was happening, and many of my friends probably also asleep until the outbreak of war."

"If they've even woken up now," said Uno.

"It probably doesn't matter if they're awake or not when their heads roll at the scaffold. I think it was that naive and insidious idea of multiculturalism that made everyone... eh... lose their heads, excuse my dark humor. It sounds so idyllic: rich and tolerant multiculturalism, but it's based on everyone respecting each other. It sounds especially good if you're an anti-racist, homosexual, or feminist, or all three at once, which is often the case. I'm gay myself, as you know. And of course, anti-racist. It's no wonder LGBTQ people dream of a society where they are not seen as different and where everyone respects each other."

"And Muslims hardly do that," said Uno.

"Muslims never respect non-Muslims and never will. Not to mention gays. Islam is all about Muslims being a chosen elite whose divine duty is to either convert or eliminate everyone else. Allah has given them the mission and the authority to kill anyone, anytime. It's not just a right; it's an obligation for all Muslims! Just as Muslim men have a duty to ensure that women are discriminated against and remain subordinate to men."

"In a way, Muslims are much like Jews," said Uno.

"Yes, there are many similarities, but there are crucial differences. Even though Jews also see themselves as the chosen people, they haven't been given a divine mission to wipe out everyone else."

"Yes, and Jews have left all that behind, just like we Christians," said Uno. "Christians and Jews stopped taking the scriptures literally a very long time ago."

"Islam, on the other hand, can never be reformed," said Filip. "Since Muhammad declared himself the last prophet, the Quran can never be questioned. Anyone who tries to is to be killed immediately because questioning the scripture is, by definition, the act of false prophets. Heretics. The Quran is God's pure word to Muslims, where no comma can be doubted."

"I've heard the Quran is full of evil and calls to kill infidels," said Uno.

"Yes, I can confirm that. I've read the Quran very carefully, as you know, twice, just to be sure. It's not very long. Besides being boring, as it constantly repeats the same nonsense about God creating the sun, moon, and stars over and over, it's filled with commands to kill infidels and to wage jihad to spread Islam. And not just to kill them, but to torture them as well."

"How? Does it say anything specific?" Uno asked.

"Yes, indeed. The hands and feet of infidels are to be cut off crosswise. They are to be crucified, chained, roasted in fire, and beheaded wherever they are found. Those who flee are to be hunted down without mercy."

"Doesn't seem to be much room for inclusion there, does it?"

"Unfortunately, the tolerance for dissent is zero, to put it mathematically. Islam is simply not compatible with any ideology."

"That explains why Muslims don't fit into Western society," said Uno.

"Yes, exactly. Islam doesn't fit into Eastern societies either or anywhere else. It's them or us – in an eternal struggle. We can never coexist."

"One wonders what our idiot politicians were thinking when they decided that Sweden would be enriched by mass immigration of Muslims."

"A historical mistake. We were like a closed little club living in our own bubble. We in the media and all the politicians, except the nationalists who understood what was happening. The ones we called Nazis and fascists were the only ones who really got it. Somehow, we in the media and politics managed to convince ourselves that the Muslims who had been at war with us for fourteen hundred years would finally see how great we Swedes are and change and start loving us, just in our generation."

"Pretty speculative to bet everything on such odds that are clearly against us," said Uno.

"Speculative, naive, short-sightedly opportunistic, and totally out of touch with reality, and I was one of the biggest sinners," said Filip. "I don't know how many columns I wrote about Islam being misunderstood and actually a good ideology. I can't even count how many dissenters I publicly branded as Nazis or at least far-right extremists."

"Just for standing up for Sweden?"

"Yes, just for standing up for our freedom, democracy, and not least for equality. I'm ashamed and will continue to be ashamed until the day I die. It's something I will have to live with for the rest of my life."

"What the hell were you all thinking? The discussions on construction sites where I've spent my entire life aren't exactly intellectual. Yet everyone was completely clear about what was happening. How can people who don't even read newspapers know better than you who have all the knowledge and write the newspapers?"

"That's a good question. But as you know, women were burned at the stake as witches. Astronomers who realized the Earth wasn't the center of the universe were also burned. It's fundamentally the same ideologies. Mass hysteria seems to hit people harder the more books they've read. Just look at communism, for example. With rational arguments, communists have killed hundreds of millions of people. The murders have always been led by pseudo-intellectual madmen who managed to impress the masses with their so-called wisdom. A stack of thick books that most people can't be bothered to read seems enough to fool people. Just look at the Bible and the Quran, which few practitioners have actually managed to read."

"That's wisdom we can probably do without. But tomorrow is another day. Happy 65th birthday again, and good night."

"Good night to you, too!"

Chapter 33

The Russian is held accountable

October 23, 2032

The evidence was irrefutable. When Uno's security chief thoroughly searched "the Russian's" bedroom, they found detailed sketches of the defense positions held by the Swedes, Yugos, and Syrians. They also found hand-drawn maps with arrows and notes on potential march routes, attacks, and minor operations that were planned and discussed. There were also diagrams listing the numbers and types of various weapons they had in their possession.

All the material was found in an envelope identical to one Filip had previously seen "the Russian" handing over to the ruthless profiteer Björne Kork, who had since disappeared without a trace. However, Kork had managed to issue about ten bacon vouchers for advance payments of various kinds before he fled, so he had made off with the money. It was impossible to know if he would return or if he had somehow been informed that "the Russian" had been captured and imprisoned.

"Think of how many good soldiers we've lost just because of one damn spy," said Uno bitterly. "It must be around fifty. Fine men and women. Young. Swedes. And the responsibility is entirely mine. I'm grateful I don't have to look their parents in the eye. How could I have been so naive to trust someone we knew nothing about? It was me who brought him into the staff."

"Yes, it's absolutely terrible. So tragic. And how many more spies are in the camp?" wondered Filip. "We have to assume that we are constantly infiltrated."

"We need to keep this information within our small group—you, me, and Max—and only inform key personnel as last minute as possible before we act."

"Yes, that's best. Unfortunately, this includes Jacob and Dragan. I'm sure both are loyal, but we must assume their staff is also infiltrated," Filip concluded.

"Of course. There's a mix of Christians, secular Christians, secular half- and quarter-Muslims, and so on among their compatriots. So how can we fully trust anyone?"

"You ordered the general assembly for 2 p.m., right? It's 1:50 now."

"Correct! Are you going to watch?"

"No, I'd rather not. Do what you must, but I don't need to see it. Do you really have to do it yourself?"

"It would be convenient to let someone else do it, but I think it's an important signal not to pass off the dirty work, especially when it's my fault. It's important for the troops to see that the staff is prepared to face the consequences of their own decisions. Hopefully, it increases their respect and trust in our leadership."

"I can't handle that, but good luck anyway, or whatever one is supposed to say..."

Over twelve hundred soldiers assembled, braving the freezing drizzle on the field. A soldier from each platoon, officer, and commander had been ordered to assemble in all three camps. No soldier in the camps could avoid finding out what happened that day.

"The Russian's" bald head was bowed, his hands bound behind his back with a black plastic zip tie. On either side of him stood a Yugo soldier, holding him up with a firm grip under his arms. Without their support, "the Russian" would have collapsed, exhausted as he was after three days of interrogation and beatings, and without any food. Uno had let the Yugo experts handle the interrogation, and as expected, they had extracted all the information "the Russian" had.

Uno gave a short speech explaining the reason for their gathering in the rain:

"Everyone should know what happens to traitors. Spies, turncoats, and deserters will get what is coming to them. No mercy will be given. Let this be a warning and a reminder to stay vigilant about your comrades' actions. Never trust anyone. Keep your information to yourself, and never share what you know unnecessarily, not even with your best friend. This is what happens to traitors!" Uno shouted as he pulled up his Glock 88D from the inside of his belt.

The single shot went through the spine at the top of the kneeling Russian's exposed neck, fired from an inch. Uno put the pistol back inside his belt and slowly left the scene.

At Flottsbrogården, Filip was waiting with a bottle of Flottsbro Special.

"Here, take a few good swigs."

Uno gratefully grabbed the bottle and took a few large gulps.

"Now I know how executioners feel," Uno said thoughtfully. "And it's not a good feeling. But it was necessary, and in war, nothing can stand in the way of victory, especially not the sentimental feelings of us in charge."

Chapter 34

The Beginning of the Kebab War

October 19, 2032

Winter arrived unusually early in the war-torn fall of 2032, almost breaking weather records. It seems like a rule that every wartime winter is exceptionally cold, as if nature punishes sinful humans, making their existence even more unbearable. The bitterly cold winters during World War II were a decisive factor, as the Germans, unlike the Soviet armies, were ill-prepared for winter warfare regarding weapons, clothing, or winter-hardened soldiers.

Though it was only October, the frozen ground was already covered by an inch-thick layer of fresh snow, gradually thickening as more snowflakes fell. It was a few degrees below freezing, dark, and cold, but the adrenaline-fueled soldiers felt none. Their feet should have been ice-cold in their boots, but they weren't.

The tension was palpable. The assembled soldiers knew this wasn't one of their usual drills, with annoying nocturnal assemblies or false alarms when the Muslims conducted feigned attacks to exhaust and disturb their sleep. Something significant was about to happen, but for security reasons, the soldiers were only informed of the mission five minutes before departure. Finally, after weeks of rumors, it was time to launch an attack on the Muslims' positions in Botkyrka, south of Stockholm.

At 3:30 a.m., Uno Svensson signaled the march to the first two hundred of the six hundred Swedish soldiers standing in formation at the Flottsbro camp for nearly an hour, with strict orders not to talk or smoke. In tense silence, they crept towards the eastern shore of Alby Lake, where the boats awaited. There were twenty small civilian boats of various sizes and makes. Their commander led each group to their assigned boat.

The first group's half-mile journey across Alby Lake was estimated to take about four minutes. The boats moved at limited speed to ensure they all landed on the western shore simultaneously. The crossing would be done in three waves since the twenty civilian boats could only carry two hundred soldiers at a time. Once the first group landed, the boats would shuttle back at maximum speed to quickly bring reinforcements. It was estimated to take about twenty minutes to ship over all six hundred soldiers, assuming no boats were hit.

It was unlikely that the first group would reach enemy territory unnoticed. Still, by spreading the boats three hundred feet apart, the enemy could barely fire on more than a few before the others landed and secured the beachhead for the remaining four hundred soldiers.

Assuming the enemy had not been tipped off about the impending attack, which was hard to know. There could be more infiltrators in Flottsbro than "the Russian."

When the scattered armada of small boats was about five hundred feet from shore, hell broke loose in the form of machine gun fire, immediately returned from the boats. The shooting came from a small hill on the western shore, where the Muslims had placed a few machine guns, now sweeping deadly fire over the water, covering the entire lake. The pitch darkness of the completely blacked-out surroundings made it difficult for the gunners to identify targets, which landed a few seconds later, and the soldiers quickly disembarked and vanished into the darkness.

The machine gun fire from the hill caused devastating losses to four boats in the middle, with no Swedish survivors in the cold water, while the other sixteen boats veered towards the lake's ends, eight to each end, to avoid the gunfire as much as possible.

The eighty soldiers at the north end landed at Muhammed's Balls and immediately attacked the small group of *Holy Warriors* guarding the narrow railway bridge, intentionally left standing after the large road bridges were blown up by Max. Given the weak defense, no one clearly expected an attack over the narrow railway bridge.

At the same time, Dragan Milosevic gave his final orders and instructions to the Yugo troops on the other side of the railway bridge, motivating his eager soldiers.

"We all know what happened on the Field of Blackbirds in 1389, *Kosovo Polje*, and now the time has come to exact our revenge! Death to the Muslims!"

As the machine gun fire began on the boats, the first Yugo soldiers, who had crept up from their camp in Häggsta, sprinted the five hundred feet across the railway bridge, which quickly filled with more and more of the eight hundred Yugo soldiers in the attack.

The single-track railway bridge was so narrow that it wasn't possible to run two abreast, forcing the Yugos to attack Fittja in a single-file column, leading to devastating consequences. Many were mowed down by enemy positions that awoke surprisingly quickly. When the first Yugos began shooting down from the railway bridge, it took only a minute before the defenders' weapons at the bridgehead fell silent, allowing the Yugos to pour into Fittja. But precious minutes were lost.

When the chaos subsided, only 470 of the eight hundred Yugoslavs survived the four hundred feet across the bridge. 330 Yugo soldiers floated in the bloody water below the railway bridge. It was a disastrous start to the attack, with casualties ten times higher than expected.

At the same time, at the southern end of Alby Lake, the eighty Swedish soldiers who had landed attacked the defenders guarding the narrow Flottsbro Canal connecting Alby Lake and Tullinge Lake. Entrenched soldiers on both sides fought fiercely. The Swedes from the other side of the canal also heavily fired upon the defenders.

Swedish soldiers were shipped across the canal in small boats south of the canal's small bulge called Katthavet, suffering devastating losses that claimed about half the soldiers before they even crossed. Despite continuing heavy losses, the shipping persisted stubbornly in shuttle service.

When the second group of soldiers was shipped across Alby Lake in the sixteen remaining boats directed by Uno to the southern end of the lake, the overwhelming force became too strong for the defending Muslims. The remaining forty-three defenders surrendered to the Swedes despite the tempting virgins awaiting them in paradise.

Swedish soldiers were now ferried across the narrow canal without being fired upon, and after a few hours, five thousand Swedes were on enemy territory, slowly moving north towards Alby. Even for the Swedes, initial losses were much greater than feared, with 269 already fallen around the Flottsbro Canal and in the boats on the lake. But with the crossing of five thousand soldiers, the battle was practically over before it started.

Seven hundred Syrians were approaching from the south. 350 of them followed the European Highway 4, north by foot, while the other half followed St. Botvid's Road on the narrow strip of land between Lake Aspen and Lake Born to attack Norsborg and Alby from the west.

Following the European Highway 4, the group was effectively stopped on the barely three-hundred-foot-wide strip of land between Northern and Southern Aspen, remaining there throughout the battle of Botkyrka. It proved impossible to breach the well-fortified Muslim positions.

The Syrians following St. Botvid's Road had greater success. After four hours of intense fighting, they broke through the Muslim defense with a flanking maneuver that surprised the defenders. The road from the west to Norsborg was now open, but in Norsborg, hundreds of well-entrenched *Holy Warriors* awaited, supported by smaller units of elite soldiers who would fight to the last breath. They knew well what awaited them if captured by the Syrians.

It was 10 a.m., and daylight had long since replaced the darkness. The fighting had temporarily subsided. Botkyrka was cut off in all directions, and it was only a matter of time before the remaining Muslim soldiers, estimated to be fewer than a thousand, would be defeated or surrendered.

Uno ordered Dragan and Jacob via radio to halt their troops, rest, and regroup for the final attack. There was no rush. The enemy was surrounded and unable to bring in reinforcements. Time was running out for Botkyrka's defenders, like inexorably flowing sand in an hourglass. The exhausted Swedes, Yugos, and Syrians set up camp to gather strength while the defenders regrouped to strengthen their positions. Only sporadic shots and explosions were heard occasionally.

"Perhaps it's best to try to get the Muslims to surrender without needless loss of life," Uno thought, standing with Filip, Max, and some officers from the Yugos and Syrian staffs on top of the hill of Flottsbro, tensely watching the developments. It was still cold in the air, but at least it had stopped snowing, and the snow on the ground probably wouldn't last long.

"The question is whether we should let time pass and simply starve them out," said Filip. "We've suffered terrible losses so far, especially the Yugos. We should keep our cool and carefully consider the next step. As for the Muslims' losses, I don't care the least bit anymore. They deserve only to die!"

"No, who the hell cares about them," Uno replied. "But I was also thinking about more bloodless solutions. We should try to start negotiations with their leader in Botkyrka, who is said to be named Zulema."

"That is a good idea," Filip replied. "If there aren't any fights this afternoon, we should start with a broadcast on the radio. We have their frequencies, and we've already listened to Zulema's Arabic rants. If they respond well, we can send a negotiator with a white flag, or they can send someone to us."

"They should send someone to us. We set the conditions here and need to be very clear about that. If you give Muslims an inch, they'll take a mile."

"I suggest we give them a forty-eight-hour ultimatum," Filip said. "Either they surrender unconditionally, or we annihilate them without mercy."

"That sounds reasonable," Uno said, smiling suddenly. "But what happened to your humanitarian principles, my dear brother?"

Filip froze as Uno's question hit a sensitive nerve. Often, Filip lay awake at night, pondering what war did to people's minds in general and what this war had done to his own brain. To "annihilate everyone without mercy" was as far from his former humanitarian principles as one could get. How could he say something like that so casually, as if he were talking about buying a couple of liters of milk?

It was as if the war, slowly and imperceptibly, severed, and poisoned people's minds, bit by bit, minute by minute, without them realizing what was happening to them. Like farmers who don't smell the manure constantly surrounding them while everyone else reacts with disgust. Is that how it's going to be after the war? Will those who haven't been part of it, who haven't had their minds poisoned by hate, react with disgust against those who have? Against us, against me? Against those who fought and defended everyone else?

He had seen too many good Swedes transform into cynical and hateful murderers in just a few weeks and was shocked at the realization of what instincts and destructive forces lay dormant within almost every person, including himself, under the thin veneer called civilization and humanity. Humanity, for that matter, were humans really any better than warring ape tribes, just a bit more advanced in their methods? Ultimately, it seemed that all existence was about groups fighting for survival and defending their territories, with occasional breaks for peace when one group was annihilated or temporarily torn apart. How could it be any other way?

Everything else seemed like naive dreams, judging by what was happening before his eyes, something he had never thought possible in a country like Sweden, one of the world's most homogeneous and stable countries for hundreds of years, until the day the nation's low-IQ and history-ignorant prime minister opened the gates to Muslim mass immigration. People seemed driven by instincts and forces beyond their conscious control, with sexual drive often emerging victorious in the internal struggle.

Filip had closely observed how respect for human life and empathy for others' suffering evaporated in moments when life turned into a struggle for survival.

"How could normal, empathetic Swedish men rape, abuse, and even kill Muslim women without caring at all about the victims' suffering," he wondered. Perhaps they enjoyed the suffering while committing their vile acts. Is this humanity's true state? Have we just tasted paradise briefly in small, insignificant parentheses of peace and democracy?

Was the good life in Södermalm, Stockholm, just a dream, a vain illusion existing only in his mind? Sometimes, he seriously wondered if he was going mad. Strange and frightening thoughts and dreams had haunted him over the past weeks, and they scared him. Everything seemed out of his control, like a self-driving car speeding away—beyond the control of computers—and he felt increasingly like a stranger when he looked at himself in the mirror. An obscure stranger. Who was that tall, slender, slightly hunched man with the piercing gaze in the unshaven and lined face who thought he had the answers to all existential questions?

The strangest thing was that he had started to feel a growing hatred toward all those rainbow people populating Söder despite being gay himself. How would Freud explain that? Self-loathing?

And the forbidden feeling of Jew hatred that poisoned his thoughts, where did that come from? He had, after all, many good and wonderful Jewish friends in the cultural scene, most of whom had been killed by the Muslims. He admired the intellectual, cosmopolitan Jewish culture. He strongly supported Israel, which wasn't exactly popular among the other cultural Marxists in Södermalm, not even among the Jewish cultural Marxists themselves. They were often the most vocal critics of Israel, with their ideological high priest being the spy-convicted upper-class Marxist and big game hunter, who barely managed to conceal his Jew hatred in his popular and widely read columns. Ultimately, Filip concluded that he hated everything and everyone deep down, which stemmed from his growing hatred for life, at least for humanity.

But for some reason, he didn't hate Uno, who seemed to be the same Uno as before the war. For Uno, there didn't seem to be much difference between leading moose hunters and soldiers as long as one worked purposefully, efficiently, and competently to take down the targets. For Uno, it was just about playing the ball into the goal, regardless of which match was being played. Uno simply wanted to succeed and be successful at what he did without wasting energy on moral or philosophical dilemmas. Filip wished he had such an untroubled attitude, but he wasn't built that way.

More and more often, Filip had begun to consider borrowing Uno's pistol and ending his life with a straight bullet. The feeling of hopelessness and meaninglessness, so familiar from his tumultuous teenage years when he was a tall but weak and insecure closeted gay called "the giraffe," had suddenly resurfaced—now even stronger than before. To his dismay, the giraffe had awakened from the dead in a forced and highly unwanted reincarnation and started to roam around eating leaves from the treetops again—and he hated every spot on that ugly monstrosity of an animal.

At least the buildings and cozy squares in Södermalm are still there, he thought in a moment of reassurance. But are the people still there, or have they all turned into psychotic monsters? Will I ever again be able to sit and enjoy the atmosphere over a beer at cafés with smiling people, where submissive latte dads, seemingly unaware of the mental oppression they live under, help triumphant mom lesbians with their strollers up the stairs? He thought I will write a book about this when peace comes. It's a very interesting subject to delve into, if there's ever peace again. But how will we ever restore Sweden to a peaceful and loving place?

"And what about the looming war crimes tribunal in The Hague?" Uno continued, unaware of how deeply his words cut into Filip.

"Ah, I couldn't care less about my former principles now," replied Filip. "The Hague has been under Muslim control for a couple of months, so the prison there feels a bit out of reach, to say the least. A bigger concern is the women taken as sex slaves in the Muslim brothel in Hallunda. If we attack, they'll likely kill them before we can reach them, and we're talking about thirty to forty innocent women."

"Maybe a little rescue operation before we attack?" Uno suggested. "We have those female rangers—Jolanta Grembowska and Ina Sjöstrand—who keep pushing to rescue the enslaved women. They have a plan worked out with Max."

"We can't exactly conduct a rescue operation while negotiating a surrender, so the negotiations will have to wait," Filip said.

"Let's meet with Max and the girls tonight," said Uno, raising his binoculars as new explosions sounded from Alby's direction. "We'll see how it goes. Max, 8 p.m. at headquarters, does that work?"

"Of course. I'll make sure Jolanta and Ina are there," Max replied.

At precisely 8 p.m., the small group convened: Uno, Filip, Max, Jolanta, and Ina. Dragan and Jacob would normally be present, but they were recovering with their soldiers after a grueling day in the field.

"I know how much you all would rather be out there in the action," Uno began. "But I can't risk my best soldiers on routine operations. We need the best for special missions, so take it as a compliment that you're here."

"It's okay," Jolanta said. "I hope we're going to discuss rescuing those sex slaves now!"

"Yes, we are," Uno replied, "but not exactly in the way you three planned. It's too risky and unlikely that you'd come back. But I believe my plan could work during the chaos of our main attack."

"Interesting," said Max.

"Instead of parachuting into Hallunda Square, which I think would be suicide, I have another idea from one of our soldiers who works as a service technician for Svenska Kraftnät – the public authority responsible for Sweden's transmission system. You see, there's a cable tunnel that the Muslims probably don't know about, running parallel to the subway tunnel they've blocked off."

"Exciting," said Jolanta.

Ina, as usual, remained silent and just listened. She never spoke more than necessary.

"I plan for the three of you to enter the cable tunnel, followed by a squad of six soldiers once we've taken the Alby subway station. We plan to move toward Alby Center with the Swedes at an early stage. You'll follow the tunnel almost to Hallunda subway station, where the cable tunnel veers toward Hallunda Square. There's a hatch at ground level in the square's southwest corner, less than three hundred feet from the local community house, where the women are held. It's dark, and you should be able to sneak to the community house undetected. The local community house is deep in their territory, and there's no reason to believe it's guarded by more than a couple of their fighters. My idea is for two of you to free the women while one covers the retreat," Uno explained. "The challenge is getting thirty women down a twenty feet ladder into the cable tunnel. It will take at least three or four minutes to get them all down, but the squad should be able to hold off any attackers. To secure the retreat, we'll send eighty soldiers via the road Tre Källors Väg to reach Hallunda Square before you arrive with the women," Uno continued.

"Sounds like a good plan," said Max.

"The key is to free the women before the soldiers start advancing along Tre Källors Väg," said Uno. "We have to assume the Muslims will kill them if they feel they're losing control of Hallunda."

"When do we go?" Jolanta asked eagerly.

"When we launch the assault on Botkyrka. The soldiers are currently recovering. I think they need a couple of days."

The rest period lasted three days before the attackers were ready to launch their offensive against the defenders in Botkyrka.

Chapter 35

Benno Ronkanen joins the free army

October 19, 2032

Since the terrifying incident four days earlier, when two Muslim tax collectors visited Benno Ronkanen at his small sausage factory, he had been hiding in his apartment by Nytorget square most of the time. Knowing that the feared Imam and his entire council had eaten wild boar sausage made Benno tremble. The lab results regarding the sausage's contents could return any day soon, and he wouldn't even dare to think about the consequences if it was revealed that the Muslim leaders had feasted on pork.

They wouldn't let him off with a quick beheading or hanging. Most likely, he would be slowly whipped to death. Benno knew that floggings were often prolonged over time, with a few lashes each day for especially severe crimes to maximize the victim's suffering. In the worst-case scenario, he would be whipped every day for months until he finally succumbed.

Now, Benno was waiting for the right moment. He observed the street from his third-floor window. There had been unusually high activity over the past few days for unknown reasons. He guessed that some Swedish freedom fighter had struck and perhaps managed to kill a leading Muslim. This had happened a few times and usually resulted in the beheading of fifty Swedes as retaliation. From his window, Benno noticed that the morality police were frisking and harassing an unusually high number of people, so he decided to stay in his apartment until things calmed down. But now it was time.

Benno cautiously opened the door to Nytorgsgatan and peered out. The street was mostly deserted despite it being early afternoon. Wearing his long kaftan and crocheted cap, he drew no attention as he strolled south along the streets with his small brown Burberry briefcase slung over his shoulder. He had dyed his beard and eyebrows black by carefully massaging in black shoe polish. He chose the street Renstiernas Gata and continued Katarina Bangata, knowing there were no permanent street posts. He took a small path through the big park of Stora Blecktornsparken and followed the quay towards the bridge Skansbron, where he would cross over to the quarters of Hammarby.

When he reached the stairs to Skansbron, he spotted a checkpoint manned by four *Holy Warriors* with Kalashnikovs. As expected, Benno continued leisurely up to the checkpoint, where he was addressed in Arabic and waved over.

"I don't speak Arabic," Benno said, taking out an envelope that he had handed to the nearest Warrior and his driver's license.

"Okay, we speak Swedish too," replied the *Warrior* who had taken the envelope. "I'm from Fisksätra," he continued.

The warrior studied the driver's license carefully while Benno studied the *Warrior's* expression just as closely. Benno guessed that he had roots in Syria or Iraq, as he spoke fluent Arabic and looked Middle Eastern. Benno watched as his attention turned to the stiff, cardboard-like envelope he curiously opened to examine its contents.

Inside the envelope was a letter, printed on high-quality designer paper with embossed Muslim symbols and gold stamps, containing a short text in Arabic followed by the same text in Swedish. As a journalist and PR consultant, Benno had the skills and contacts to produce any printed material in an hour. He had designed the letter and the envelope on his computer, with the Arabic text provided by an old friend who had a PhD in Arabic from Stockholm University. The printing had been done at a small advertising agency in a basement on Skånegatan, which he had collaborated with for many years.

The *Warrior* read the text aloud in Swedish.

"Benno Ronkanen is on a mission from the highest Muslim council at the Zayed Mosque. He will reach our base at the Swedish Exhibition and Congress Center to contact the enemy for a secret and urgent assignment. Ronkanen must be assisted in every way to complete his mission. Anyone who hinders Ronkanen in his task will be punished without mercy."

Both texts were signed by the highest imam at the Zayed Mosque, dated October 19, 2032.

The warrior showed the letter to his comrades, who nodded thoughtfully.

"Okay, you can pass. Do you need an escort to the exhibition center?"

"Yes, that might be a good idea if there are more checkpoints," Benno replied.

"Unfortunately, we don't have a vehicle, so we'll have to walk."

"That's fine. It's only three or four miles."

The *Warrior* in command signaled another warrior to accompany Benno.

After passing two more checkpoints, efficiently handled by the Arabic-speaking escort warrior, they stood at the gate to Parking D at the

Swedish Exhibition and Congress Center after about an hour. Benno's escort gave the guard a brief explanation in Arabic and then asked him to present his envelope with the letter. This time, Benno took the letter out of the envelope and held it up for the guard, who quickly glanced at it. The guard pointed to one of the other guarding warriors: "You escort this man to the commander's headquarters and inform them that he is here on a mission from the 'Highest Muslim Council,' understood?"

Benno waved a friendly goodbye to his escort and soon found himself comfortably seated in a leather armchair outside the commander's office. After a few minutes, a uniformed female secretary came and showed him into the commander's office. The commander had already read and made a copy of the recommendation letter.

"So, how do you plan to contact the enemy?" the commander asked, eyeing Benno suspiciously.

"Unless you have a better suggestion, I thought I would carry a white flag and slowly walk across the front line in broad daylight with your soldiers covering me. I don't think the Swedes will shoot if I come unarmed with a white flag."

"Actually, I'd like to check a few things first. I will send a courier to the Zayed Mosque to get answers to some questions. There are no phone connections, and the radio is jammed, so it's impossible to get any clear information that way."

"Oh. How long will that take?" Benno asked.

"The courier rides a motorcycle, so it will only take a few minutes to get there. The question is how long it will take to contact the council. If we're lucky, everything will be done in an hour."

Benno felt sweat starting to bead on his forehead.

"I can under no circumstances allow any delay," said Benno. "Every minute is precious."

"If it's so urgent, why didn't the council arrange transport and escort?" the commander asked.

"I had an escort," Benno replied. "There were no available vehicles, and as you know, fuel is scarce."

"So, I should sit here for hours?" Benno continued, feigning agitation. "If this mission fails because of you, you'll personally face the consequences."

"What is the mission?" the commander asked sharply.

"Excuse me, but that's none of your concern. As you can see in the letter, the mission is secret. You're committing a breach of duty by even asking. In wartime, unnecessary information is neither shared nor sought, and you should know that!"

The commander regarded Benno with a disapproving look.

"Why did you dye your beard?" he asked, examining Benno's driver's license again. "It's obvious the dye smudged onto your skin."

Benno looked back calmly, pausing for a few seconds before responding. He lifted the intricately designed letter and tapped it with his finger on the hard, parchment-like paper as he spoke.

"Okay, you're making a personal choice here, just so you know. Either you sit here wasting my time with trivialities or do your duty and help me with the mission. I'll report exactly what happens to the council. You'll either be rewarded with a gold star or executed for insubordination and sabotaging the council's mission. Make your choice but make it quickly!"

Benno ended his tirade by slamming his fist on the desk as hard as he could, glaring fiercely at the commander.

After a few seconds of hesitation, the commander opened the door to the adjoining room where his secretary was sitting. Benno could hear him giving instructions in long, rapid-fire Arabic, realizing that his fate was being decided at that moment, but unable to understand the words.

The commander returned, accompanied by his uniformed secretary, with a neutral expression.

"Fatima will escort you to the front-line commander who will care for you. Don't hesitate to communicate any requests. You won't need to show the letter again. Good luck!"

On his way out, Benno observed that the exhibition center's entire A and B halls were filled with hundreds of soldiers. The C hall, on the other hand, was full of equipment and crates. The Stockholm Exhibition and Congress Center had been transformed into a substantial military base. Benno wondered why no Swedish JAS firefighter planes had attacked the base yet. A few missiles would cause maximum damage here.

Outside, Benno noticed about forty combat vehicles in the parking lot, spread out as much as possible to maximize the distance between them.

The fighting had been quiet for a while, except for occasional shelling and sniper shots from both sides. The road of Älvsjövägen was no man's land. About three hundred feet on the other side of the road were the Swedish positions, defended by free soldiers under the command of the staff in Flottsbro.

Benno held up the pole, so the white sheet was visible above the roadside, standing in the ditch. To be safe, he stayed there for a couple of minutes, waving the flag back and forth so the soldiers on the other side of Älvsjövägen couldn't miss it. Taking slow, deliberate steps, he left the ditch and appeared fully visible on the road. No shots yet, at least, he thought.

Benno continued onto the deserted road and began crossing it toward the Swedish positions. When he reached the middle of the road, a voice suddenly echoed through a megaphone.

"Stop right where you are, or we'll shoot you dead!"

Benno halted and dropped the white flag on the asphalt, cupping his hands around his mouth.

"I'm Swedish! Don't shoot!"

"What do you want?"

Benno waved both arms above his head to make it clear he was unarmed. His whole body was tense, expecting to be torn apart by bullets at any moment.

"I have an important message for you!"

"Who are you, wearing that ridiculous clown costume?"

The megaphone voice spoke with an unmistakable dialect from one of the southern Stockholm suburbs, lazily and nonchalantly, showing no urgency despite the situation. This worried Benno, who was fighting for his life.

"I'm Benno Ronkanen!"

"You said you were Swedish?"

"I'm Benno Ronkanen, the journalist from Aftonposten who raped so many women!" he yelled, not realizing the absurdity of the situation.

"Oh, so you're that bastard!" the megaphone replied.

There were a few seconds of silence before the soldier with the megaphone found his voice again. Benno suddenly realized he might not have introduced himself in the best way. He began to fear he wouldn't be welcome on the Swedish side.

"Take off that clown costume until you're down to your underwear. We've had enough of suicide bombers, and something tells me you're not here of your own free will."

Benno took off his white kaftan and dropped it demonstratively on the street with an outstretched arm. Underneath, he wore a fleece sweater, which he also discarded. Finally, he removed the baggy white pants and stood still in the middle of the road in his underwear.

"Okay, 'Ronk-anen, Wank-anen', or whatever your name is. Once you've removed your shoes and dropped your fancy briefcase, you can come over, but leave that clown outfit there!" The megaphone's lazy and nonchalant voice boomed. "Something tells me you might get a few shots in the back soon!"

Benno walked resolutely across the road and down into the ditch on the other side, out of sight from the Muslim side. He continued barefoot across the icy, muddy field until he reached a trench where two soldiers had dug in and built a small wall with sandbags.

"Hi, I'm Benno Ronkanen!" he said almost hysterically, extending his hand.

Benno's survival system had released so much adrenaline that his body could no longer perceive trivialities, like the icy wind on his bare skin. He didn't even feel cold in his feet. It felt like he could walk around naked for hours without freezing.

In response, the soldier stood up and handed Benno one of the army's green jackets.

"I never thought you'd get out of that alive," said the young soldier. "It's your lucky day! Now let's go to the lieutenant and see if your luck continues."

In Flottsbro, after a short ride, it was time to be scrutinized by another commander, this time named Uno Svensson. Uno's gaze swept over Benno's frame, which had slimmed down due to the war's meager rations, making him look reasonably well-trimmed.

"So, you're that journalist," Uno remarked thoughtfully. "Do you have any military training?"

"Maybe more than you think," Benno replied. "My authoritarian father tried to straighten out his hash-smoking slacker son by forcing him to do military service in Finland, where we're from, and that's a bit different than in Sweden."

"Okay, what was your rank and branch?"

"I'm a sergeant in Finland's legendary 12th Infantry Regiment, known as IR12, and trained as an anti-tank soldier. My job is to destroy as many Russian tanks as possible before I die."

"That's life sometimes. Full of death," Uno replied pensively. "Especially for anti-tank soldiers."

"The officers harassed us to the point where many considered suicide. I was never called anything but *'Ruotsin homo,'* – 'the Swedish fag', at least when they yelled at me, which was most of the time. I've never forgiven my father for what I endured."

"Yeah, the Finns are tough on their conscripts, no doubt."

"Inhumanly tough! They made it very clear that I was being trained for a suicide mission and that no one would miss a damn Swedish fag anyway."

"So now you're here to fight for Sweden?"

"Yes, absolutely, to the death! Strangely enough, I love this country despite everything that's happened to me in public. Even though Sweden has turned into a criminal and poor shithole since our family moved here, it's still better than the alternative I've experienced for a few months at Södermalm. Damn!"

"You're a bit old to fight. Could you organize and train anti-tank units?"

"Yeah, I think I could, even though it's been a while since I was in Finland. What equipment do you have?" Benno asked.

"We have several Robot 56 Bill, manned by a gunner, loader, and group leader. And plenty of the modern portable anti-tank missile Robot 57, which you probably know about. Finland has bought a lot of them."

"The 56 is more powerful," Benno said, "but the advantage of the 57 is that it's easier to handle and can be fired indoors."

"Seems like you're well-informed," Uno praised.

Suddenly, they were interrupted by a few knocks on the door, which opened to reveal Filip standing in the doorway, observing the newest addition to the free army.

"Well, if it isn't Filip!" Benno said in astonishment, rising from his chair.

"No one less than Benno Ronkanen himself, I see!" Filip said, beaming.

They hugged each other as the good friends they were. Filip was one of the few journalists who had questioned the media frenzy against Benno and the validity of the rape accusations he faced, which Benno had noted with gratitude.

"You look like a full-on Muslim," Filip said. "Have you converted?"

"Not for much longer," Benno replied. "But I had to pretend to be a convert for a few months to stay alive. Can someone get me a razor? I'm ready to re-convert to Christianity!"

"Don't forget your ridiculous hat!" Filip said with a grin.

Realizing he still had his crocheted topi on his head, Benno tore it off, threw it on the floor, and stomped on it angrily.

Chapter 36

Crisis meeting in the Treasury

October 20, 2032

Since relocating from Gothenburg, the Muslim leadership held staff meetings in the Treasury of Stockholm Palace. The Treasury was considered the best location, situated in the basement and protected by thick stone walls.

The Treasury no longer looked like a treasury. The treasures had been removed, with the gold melted down and the precious stones sold off. Sweden's national treasures were to be disposed of once and for all. The Treasury was just a meeting room with an oval table in the center, accommodating eighteen people. The only reminder of the room's past was the large, beautifully gilded mirror fixed to the wall, stretching from floor to ceiling.

"*Iinahum sakhif qurun*, damn bastards!" Mahmoud said irritably, pounding his fist on the table. "We'll give them a hell of a fight like they've never seen!"

"No prisoners," said the Chechen colonel. "We'll gouge out the eyes of every infidel dog we capture. Just like we've always done with the Russians, we'll cut off their dicks and stuff them in their mouths. It terrified Russian soldiers in the Caucasus for hundreds of years and recently in Afghanistan and Chechnya. They should know they're fighting an enemy whose brutality knows no bounds and have nightmares about being captured!"

"Yes, they'll pay a high price for Botkyrka," agreed the Syrian general responsible for the Muslims' defense of Botkyrka. "But now that the Swedes have managed to ship thousands of soldiers to our side of the Flottsbro Canal, we must admit that Botkyrka will be lost. The question is what orders we give our warriors in the end."

"Their Yugo and Syrian forces are willing to sacrifice comparable to ours. They keep moving forward and take the losses," continued the colonel. "They're tough opponents, even if they don't act like competent, experienced professional soldiers."

Ahmed listened with an amused smile despite the critical situation for their own troops, who were surrounded with no chance of breaking out.

"We'll set up our defense line in Vårby and Skärholmen instead," Ahmed said. "We've controlled Huddinge for a long time, so there's no risk of being unable to defend Stockholm from southern attacks. Reinforcements are already on their way to Vårby. We'll give our warriors the chance to become martyrs, meet Allah, and enjoy a blissful existence in paradise forever. My order is to fight to the last man and eliminate as many infidels as possible. It's also a form of psychological warfare to let them know the tremendous sacrifices ahead. This will weaken the Swedes' will to fight and make them realize that unconditional surrender is their best option."

The Syrian general pondered for a moment and turned to Ahmed.

"We have about nine hundred *Warriors* left to defend us, fifty of whom are elite soldiers. We shouldn't meet the enemy on the ground since they're superior in numbers. I'll order our *Warriors* to spread out as much as possible and position themselves on the upper floors of high-rises throughout Botkyrka to gain maximum oversight and good firing angles, making it difficult for the enemy to advance. Additionally, we'll turn every basement into bunkers with sandbags in front of the windows to fire at the enemy at ground level. If they want to capture Botkyrka, they'll have to pulverize nearly every building, and they don't have an air force or artillery, so it will be an almost impossible task that will keep them occupied for weeks, maybe longer. Then there's the question of what we do with our non-combatants. The elderly, women, and children," he concluded.

"They'll be our human shields," Ahmed replied. "The Swedes will hesitate when they see thousands of civilians in and around the buildings where our warriors are entrenched. We're talking about maybe fifty thousand civilians, and if I know the Swedes, they'll spare them. They call this humanity."

"That's likely true," Mahmod said, "but the question is how the Syrians and Yugos will react. I suspect at least the Syrians will let the machine guns rip, considering their history. They likely have several Yazidi soldiers burning for revenge after what ISIS did to them in Syria."

"Let their machine guns rip," Ahmed said unconcernedly, spreading his hands. "Even massacres of Muslims strangely weaken the Swedes' will to fight, though it should be the opposite. I understand their peculiar reasoning and know how their weak minds work. Our non-combatants will, in their own way, give their lives for the prophet's jihad and enjoy martyrdom just like the warriors. Only Allah knows how it will turn out, *inshallah*!"

Ahmed stood up.

"Let us perform our *salah* together today and pray to Allah to let our people in Botkyrka become martyrs. It's time for *maghrib*, the evening prayer, and I've asked Hassan to prepare the washroom to perform our ablutions properly, as befitting good Muslims. Let us perform our *wudu* extra carefully today to meet Allah with purer minds and bodies than ever. Then we will go to the prayer room, specially decorated today, where our imam will read some well-chosen *hadiths* and lead us in communal prayer. *Bismillahi ar-Rahman ar-Rahim*, in the name of God, the Most Gracious, the Most Merciful!"

"*Bismillahi ar-Rahman ar-Rahim*," everyone responded in unison, standing up.

Chapter 37

The grim end of the Kebab War

October 23, 2032

The encircled Muslims in northern Botkyrka prepared for their final battle, following the orders of their leaders. Today's five prayer sessions lasted longer than usual, and Allah received many more wishes than usual, but fortunately, Allah's capacity and wisdom are limitless. Many of the wishes were about reuniting with loved ones in paradise, especially children lost, or parents lost when the supplicants themselves were children.

The fervent, plaintive, and heartfelt calls to prayer, delivered by raspy, life-worn voices from the minarets, formed a constant background sound. The calls to prayer conveyed verses from the Quran about jihad, the holy war, and the rewards in paradise awaiting all martyrs. Other proclamations included recitations from the most militant hadiths and those about love, goodness, and peace of mind.

Islam answers all of humanity's questions and more with simple and easily understandable responses, in contrast to Christianity, which often leaves much for the questioners to ponder.

As Allah's chosen warriors, they were granted the privilege of becoming martyrs in jihad, and most accepted their fate without complaint; many even rejoiced at being chosen. The more infidels they sent to hell, the greater the reward they would receive when they met Allah in paradise. The thought of escaping the hardships of earth and war, to be rewarded instead with seventy-two virgins in a place where the grass is always green, and the sky is always blue, was alluring. They would enjoy eternal happiness in paradise, crossed by streams of the purest water. Many of the *Holy Warriors* eagerly anticipated meeting the enemy. Joyfully and with smiles on their faces, they would do what Allah expected of them: kill as many infidels as possible before they themselves left earthly life as martyrs.

There was no lack of willingness to sacrifice among the *Holy Warriors*, as history had shown, and it could make any opponent waver, lose confidence, and surrender sooner than they should, or even unnecessarily, against an inferior enemy. Perhaps a miracle would occur in Botkyrka despite an enemy with superior resources and many more soldiers. Just like in the days of the caliphs, the Prophet's successors, whose conquests by *Holy Warriors,* spread Islam at a speed no one had thought possible, which historians still find hard to explain.

The nearly nine hundred Muslim warriors spread out in Alby, Fittja, and Hallunda-Norsborg high-rises. Machine guns were mounted in basement windows behind walls of sandbags. On the top floors, riflemen took positions with machine guns, AK-47s, and grenades to shower the enemy from their elevated vantage points. The infidel dogs would face an inferno of bullets and explosions. They would not gain an inch of ground without sacrifices.

Women, children, and the elderly had to fend for themselves as best they could. Most huddled anxiously in their apartments, awaiting the inevitable. The anxiety and frustration grew worse for those who had to rely on others' efforts. Only Allah knew what would happen; everything was written in the great book and predetermined. Everyone had to accept their fate. Perhaps there will be a tomorrow, *inshallah*. Perhaps not. Only Allah knows, but Allah has a purpose for everything that happens. Trust in Allah's infinite wisdom! Fear not!

The Swedes, Yugos, and Syrians gathering for the final decisive attack worshipped a different God if they worshipped at all. Few of them hoped for anyone other than themselves to defeat the enemy, but in both the Syrians' and Yugos camps, they still sang "Te Deum" repeatedly. It couldn't be ruled out that divine intervention would decide the battle in their favor.

Only the Kurdish contingent, part of the Swedish army, prepared similarly to the enemy, with many long prayer sessions, their foreheads to the devil, and their asses to God, as the Swedish soldiers rudely said. But the Kurds performed their prayers discreetly, away from the Swedes. Even though the Swedish soldiers held a deep disdain for anything related to Islam, they respected their Kurdish comrades for their martial dedication and extensive combat experience, which the Swedes largely lacked. The Kurds were capable and effective fighters who knew how to inflict maximum damage to the enemy without exposing themselves to unnecessary risks. Protecting their own lives was not cowardice on the Kurds' part. They knew from bitter experience in battles in Syria and Iraq against Arabs and Turks that dead soldiers were of no use. This set them apart significantly from their overly sacrificial co-religionists in Botkyrka, who now awaited the infidels' assault from a military perspective.

"We will attack the murderous bastards with the greatest force and determination, but with great patience," repeated Abdullah, the powerful Kurdish leader, to his eager soldiers, fixing them with his piercing gaze. "It is important that we don't rush. We have all the time in the world, and we shouldn't sacrifice our lives unnecessarily. For every Kurd who gives their life, at least twenty Arabs and Turks must die!"

Since the Battle of Botkyrka—what the Swedish soldiers called the Kebab War—began four days ago with violent clashes and many casualties, there had been a relative calm. The wounded were tended to with the meager resources available. The bodies of the fallen were cleared away and buried to prevent epidemics. It was as if all the combatants were gathering strength for the decisive battle everyone knew was coming. The past four days had been marked by sporadic gunfire and brief periods of bombardment whenever someone launched the mortars, which were always promptly answered by the opposing side.

At dawn on Saturday, October 23, the relative calm ended when Uno Svensson ordered the Swedish units to advance north and take Alby. The Alby Mosque was the first strategic target, as its destruction was believed to have a demoralizing effect on the defenders. The overarching goal was to annihilate the enemy once and for all and bring Botkyrka under Swedish control by day's end. Simultaneously, 350 Syrians following the road called Saint Botvid's väg and west of Norsborg-Hallunda were given marching orders. But for some reason, Uno Svensson couldn't understand why the Syrians remained in their positions. The other Syrians, half the force, were stuck where they were on the European Highway 4, unable to dislodge the Muslims from the narrow three hundred feet-wide isthmus between the lakes North and South Aspen. Two hundred left the stalemate to join the force west of Norsborg-Hallunda. They were deemed expendable as it was considered unlikely that the Muslims at the European Highway 4 would launch an attack.

The Yugos were ordered to hold their positions on the western side of Muhammed's Balls, in a rather tight spot partially under the railway bridge. They had suffered terrible losses during the crossing on the narrow railway bridge four days earlier, and neither Uno Svensson nor the Yugo leader Dragan Milosevic, who shared his soldiers' hardships in the field without any special privileges, thought it wise for the Yugos to assault the heavily defended Fittja in what would resemble another suicide mission. Uno and Dragan agreed that the severely decimated Yugo battalion would wait until the Swedes approached from the south along Lake Alby. The Swedes had also suffered heavy losses, but nothing close to the inferno of death the Yugos had endured. Most importantly, the Swedes had a superior number of fresh and rested soldiers—five thousand strong.

From the top of the hill of Flottsbro, the operations command and a couple of people from the Yugos staff in Häggsta could follow the events through binoculars from a front-row seat. For some reason, the representatives from the Syrian staff didn't show up, but no one thought much of it. They had probably been forced to make other priorities. The first Swedish units had already reached the hangar of Subtopia, the hangar-like multi-arena, by following the shore of Lake Alby across the open fields west of the lake.

Other Swedish units, including a platoon of pyrotechnic experts, advanced parallel through the residential areas northward towards the Alby Mosque. Thousands of Swedes filled in from behind. The large free army in Flottsbro displayed an impressive display of force.

"So far, so good," noted Filip. "The resistance seems surprisingly weak."

"As expected, based on our intelligence," said Uno. "Our scouts observed no fortifications along Lake Alby. They've taken positions in the high-rises, which will be a tough nut to crack and require heavy losses on our part."

"Probably a smart tactic not to waste their resources on a futile battle against a superior enemy in the open fields," said Filip. "They've turned every high-rise into a fortress. One option could be to besiege and starve them out, like in the medieval times when defenders were holed up in impregnable castles."

"But why the hell aren't the kebab warriors advancing? Jacob, what are you up to?" Uno muttered to himself, frustrated.

At the Alby Mosque, an intense firefight had broken out. Apparently, about fifty *Holy Warriors* had been waiting inside the mosque, rushing out with total disregard for their lives and catching the Swedes by surprise before they could take cover.

"What a circus going on down there," said Filip.

Uno forced a smile despite seeing many good Swedes fall before his eyes. He knew Filip was referring to Cirkus Cirkör, Sweden's only circus right next to the Alby Mosque. Sometimes, he didn't follow Filip's deep and subtle insights, but this time, he did.

"What is that?" Filip asked, pointing at a helicopter coming from the south, heading towards the battlefield, with something hanging underneath it. The helicopter was still far away but rapidly approaching. Uno managed to focus with his binoculars.

"There's something hanging in a net under the helicopter; it looks like barrels. Strange to see a transport helicopter here in the middle of the battle. Are they delivering supplies or weapons to the enemy?"

The helicopter approached, and it was clear that three barrels hung in a net underneath. At the same time, another helicopter appeared, carrying a net with barrels.

"What the hell does this mean?" Uno wondered aloud.

Uno soon got his answer from the sky in the form of a bright flash. The helicopter hovered four hundred feet above Norsborg-Hallunda. Once it was stationary, the net opened, and the three barrels plummeted, crashing onto the roof of one of the high-rises. The entire roof and one of the outer walls erupted in a massive fireball.

They stood there, breathless, watching. The helicopter headed back south, while the second one repeated the first's bombing trick, setting another high-rise ablaze, its roof and top floor engulfed in flames.

"I'm going to strangle that damn fool, Jacob!" Uno shouted angrily.

"It might be too late. This is the kind of thing that will put us before the International Criminal Tribunal in The Hague, rotting in prison for the rest of our lives. We won't escape responsibility for this; it's mostly civilians dying," said Filip.

"Then let's hope the Muslims hold The Hague until we're dead," Uno replied with a wry smile.

To their right, they saw the flash from the explosion as Alby Mosque turned into a pile of rubble, silencing the droning call to prayer. The dull thud reached them a second after they saw the flash, and they thought they could feel the shockwave shortly after, or perhaps it was just a gust of wind. The first Swedish soldiers were approaching the Yugo's positions, and they could see the Yugo soldiers leaving their positions and heading briskly towards Fittja Mosque. Undoubtedly, the Yugos were keen to be first on the scene.

At the same time, the two helicopters returned, almost in unison, with new loads of barrels. Further away, they saw the Syrians slowly leaving their positions to prepare for the advance. They encountered no gunfire. The Muslims waited for them in their fortifications in the high-rises.

The helicopters dropped their deadly gasoline bombs over Fittja this time, turning another high-rise into a giant torch. The second load of barrels missed its target, landing on the ground where a large area flared up in six-feet-high flames, engulfing a dozen people trying to flee the building when they realized the helicopters had chosen their building as the bomb target.

In Fittja Mosque, the Yugos bomb experts were surprised by a platoon of *Holy Warriors* hiding in the women's room, where menstruating women usually stay while the others perform their *qibla* prayers on all fours. The surprise was complete because everyone thought the mosque was secure after the defending holy warriors around and inside the mosque had been mowed down one by one. As the five explosives experts were setting their charges, they suddenly found themselves facing the Muslims' AK-47s and were taken hostage.

The Holy Warriors in the mosque turned out to be Swedes of Bosnian descent, harboring intense hatred towards the Christian Yugos, especially the Serbs, and particularly the Bosnian Serbs, who had slaughtered tens of thousands of innocent Muslims during the Balkan Wars over thirty years earlier, not to mention a thousand years of perceived grievances.

A heated discussion ensued about what to do with the defenseless explosives' experts, who had been bound with black plastic zip ties and were now lying face down on the floor at the back of the mosque, behind the pulpit. The Muslims had recognized at least some of the five captives as Bosnian Serbs because they had picked up the characteristic soft, slightly drawling Banja-Luka accent as the pyrotechnicians talked to each other.

Meanwhile, other Yugo soldiers had noticed the situation and started pushing into the mosque despite heavy gunfire from the Bosniaks inside the mosque.

The Bosniak officer, weathered and scarred, came to Bosnia in 1993 as a mujahideen fighter from Mashhad, Iran. After settling in the Muslim town of Jajce in Bosnia, he moved to Alby in 2031 to fight for the Muslim Brotherhood during the attack on Sweden. Without waiting for the other's opinions, the mujahideen officer decided. He drew his Tokarev pistol from the Crvena Zastava factory and approached the nearest of the lying captives. Finally, he had the chance to avenge the massacres of Bosniaks during the Balkan Wars. He aimed the gun at the back of the prisoner's head and fired.

"For *Srebrenica*!"

He took a step to the next man in line.

"For *Ahmići*!"

Then another step forward.

"For *Stupni Do*!"

When he reached the fourth of the five captives, he suddenly hesitated. Tugging at his impressive beard with his free left hand, he looked confused, unsure what to do next.

"Give them one for *Sarajevo* and *Vukovar*!" said a Montenegrin whose parents were part of Montenegro's Bosnian Muslim minority.

"For *Sarajevo*!" the officer rasped in his distinctly Persian accent and fired.

As he moved to the fifth and last captive, the prisoner lifted his head and said, "We weren't even in Vukovar!"

"For *Vukovar*!" the officer declared and ended the man's life with a shot to the crown of his head.

After completing the executions, realizing they stood no chance against the advancing Yugo soldiers, the officer turned the pistol to his own temple. "Long live *Alija Izetbegović*!" he shouted, but before he could pull the trigger, he was mowed down by the incoming Yugo soldiers who fired as they stormed in.

Luckily, there were more pyrotechnicians, and twenty minutes later, the Yugos could savor the sight of the collapsing mosque as the previously planted charges detonated.

The helicopter pilots continued their hard work, flying back and forth, and now no fewer than twenty high-rises were ablaze: ten in Alby, eight in Fittja, and two in in the Hallunda shopping center.

"Look, it's like candles on birthday cakes," said Uno.

"Yes, indeed," replied Filip, seeing the resemblance.

From a distance, the high-rises resembled flaming candles, their flames contrasting beautifully against the snow-covered ground, making everything look like a giant cream cake.

"It's actually beautiful," said Uno.

"Except there are no excited children waiting to blow out the candles," Filip responded.

Hundreds of Muslim soldiers and residents poured out of both the burning buildings and those yet to be bombed, creating total chaos. No one knew where to go, and there was no shelter. People ran around in full panic, like headless chickens, while the attackers' machine guns and automatic rifles chattered relentlessly, cutting down civilians, holy warriors, and elite soldiers alike.

"What a slaughter!" Uno said to Filip, watching the inferno from the top of the hill of Flottsbro through their binoculars. "The worst I've ever seen. I've never heard of anything like this."

"Maybe Dresden or Tokyo in the spring of 1945," Filip replied. "They used phosphorus bombs on a much larger scale, causing firestorms that consumed oxygen and suffocated and burned people to death by the tens of thousands. The Allies ended the war in the dirtiest way imaginable. It was counterproductive. The bombings of German cities strengthened the Germans' resolve and prolonged the war. And then the atomic bombs, just to show Stalin what they had..."

"I knew the Syrians and the Yugos would be ruthless. And the Kurds, of course, but I never thought our Swedish boys and girls would participate in the outright executions of defenseless people," said Uno.

"We might as well start mentally preparing for The Hague," Filip replied dejectedly. "No one will ever forgive us for this. We'll live the rest of our lives as mass-murdering monsters."

"But, that Englishman Harris, who was behind the ruthless bombings of the German civilian population at the end of World War II, never sat in prison," said Uno.

"No, and yet he killed tens of times more civilians than Milosevic and Mladic combined. Srebrenica and Vukovar were nothing compared to Dresden. And no American has ever been tried for Hiroshima and Nagasaki, the greatest crimes against humanity ever committed."

"So, we need to win the war and ensure that others are held accountable!"

"Yes, that's the only way. The victor writes the history, so let's focus on winning the war and nothing else."

"Yes, it's better to organize Nuremberg trials for others than to be judged there ourselves. There should have been a Nuremberg for the Allied war criminals too. Just think about what the Russians did when they flooded into Germany; words can't even describe it!"

"Not much has been written about the suffering of the German people during World War II, which can only be compared to the horrors that the Russians and Ukrainians endured."

"The victors always write history to suit themselves," Filip concluded.

The Syrians pushed forward in western Norsborg, closing in on Hallunda Center, where hundreds of Muslims were fleeing their burning homes in desperation. The Syrians showed no mercy, mowing down as many as they could, regardless of whether they were combatants or civilians.

From a basement window, an improvised white flag emerged, made from a sheet attached to a broomstick found in one of the storage rooms. The Syrian officer waved back to the flag bearers, gave a thumbs-up, and pointed to her assault rifle, signaling that the Muslims should surrender their weapons. After a few seconds, automatic rifles began to be tossed out of the basement window. The officer counted seven before descending the short concrete stairs and opening the door to the basement. Inside stood seven exhausted fighters with their hands on their heads. Their eyes widened as they saw the Syrian officer was a woman. She swept her AK-5 over the group without firing and motioned for them to turn and press their palms against the wall.

More Syrian soldiers, including another female soldier, entered and bound the fighters' wrists and ankles with several layers of wide silver tape. They turned the fighters to face the room so they could see the officer who began to speak. She looked each of the fighters in the eyes with a hateful expression and burning intensity.

"I am a Yazidi," she said loudly and clearly, "from Sinjar, where you killed all my relatives. Yazidis, like my comrade here," she continued, pointing to the other female soldier. "We are the people you Muslims have treated like animals for centuries, despite our belief in one God. You know what you've done to our people and our women in Syria, and now you will pay for it!"

"Let's just shoot them," said one of the Syrian soldiers. "That's enough."

"No, they won't get off that easily!"

The Muslims' eyes were wide with fear, some whimpering, sensing what was about to happen.

"Leave us women alone with these vile Muslim scum," the officer ordered, gesturing for the Syrian men to leave. She drew her army knife and held it between her teeth.

The other Syrian woman did the same. As the Syrian men exited, they saw the women kneel before one of the fighters, unbuckling his belt and starting to pull down his pants. As they climbed the stairs, they heard the fighters' anguished screams, so piercing and disturbing that they hurried their steps and covered their ears.

Unaware of what was happening above ground, a small team of nine people approached Hallunda Square through the Swedish Power net's cable tunnel. It was a comfortable walk beside the heavy but well-insulated power cables resting on sturdy aluminum ladders.

Jolanta went first, climbing the twenty feet to ground level using the wall-mounted ladder rungs, while the others waited. She turned the heavy arm that released the steel hatch and peeked out cautiously, surveying the square. It was deserted; no one wanted to expose themselves to snipers in the open areas. Both the fighters and civilians were apparently holed up in the apartments.

She pushed the hatch open, crouched, and stepped into the square, fully visible. Like the others, she wore the typical fighter uniform: a black jumpsuit and a cap. Ina and Max followed shortly after. Both had dyed their hair black to avoid standing out and wore sunglasses to mask their blue eyes. The six riflemen in their group were selected based on appearance. Five had features and coloring that could pass for Middle Eastern, and the sixth was a young Swede with Nigerian heritage. Two spoke passable Arabic and would act as officers if questioned. It was unlikely anyone would notice they were enemy soldiers unless too many questions were asked. If confronted by one or a few people, they planned to eliminate them discreetly with knives.

They would unlikely be confronted on the short walk to the People's House, but if they were, they felt confident they could handle it. It was only about a hundred meters to the People's House, where the enslaved women were held. As the group of nine began to move, they noticed a helicopter a couple of hundred meters above, heading toward a new target to set ablaze.

Outside the People's House entrance, not a single guard was in sight. Jolanta took the lead and opened the door, with Ina and Max close behind, while the six riflemen sat on the benches outside, trying to look as if they were waiting for an assignment.

Inside the lobby, a lone fighter sat on a chair with his AK-47 on the table before him. He looked up, bored. Another visitor looking to relieve some tension, he thought. How does he even have time for that now when we're under attack? There wasn't a single visitor in the brothel at the moment. Well, men always seem to find time for that, under any circumstances, he mused. And he was sure this one would have fun, considering he could choose freely among the women.

"*Nadil, kayf alhal,* hey, how are you?" Jolanta greeted in her newly acquired Arabic, walking briskly toward the fighter. He looked surprised when he realized the burly figure approaching was a woman. But what is a woman doing here? was his last thought before Ina shot him twice in the throat from just over three feet away with her silenced Glock, hidden behind Jolanta's broad back.

Jolanta and Ina sprinted up the stairs while Max stayed behind to cover the lobby. Max could see the riflemen sitting undisturbed on their benches through the window. It would take a significantly alert and strong force of fighters to emerge victorious in a firefight against this group of nine of Sweden's best soldiers.

According to their intelligence, the women were being held in a large conference room at the end of the corridor, marked with a taped-up A4 sheet labeled "Harem" in thick marker. Clients would choose their company here before moving to one of the smaller rooms furnished with beds.

Jolanta was the first to open the door and step in. Indeed, there were twenty to twenty-five young women, neatly dressed, from around the world, though about ten appeared typically Swedish. They sat in groups, talking, and looked genuinely surprised when they saw these weren't the usual customers. Some stood by the window, observing the ongoing battle, and didn't even notice the door open.

"You are free!" Jolanta shouted. "Come with us, quickly. Leave all your belongings. Run, run, run! Now!"

The women looked hesitant, but when Jolanta and Ina began gesturing toward the door and pulling a couple of women by the arm, they started to move quickly, running through the corridor and down the stairs to the lobby.

"There are ten more girls in the VIP room!" one of the Swedish women shouted, pointing to a door in the corridor.

"Okay, I'll get them," Jolanta said. "Ina, take this group ahead. There's bound to be a bottleneck at the tunnel!"

Ina led the fleeing women, and in less than a minute, they were at the hatch in Hallunda Square, accompanied by three riflemen. At the same time, the remaining three soldiers stayed at the entrance to the People's House to cover Jolanta's retreat.

The women, young and agile, quickly climbed down the ladder. The evacuation proceeded faster than expected. Each woman received a small flashlight from Ina upon descending and was sent along the tunnel to avoid blocking the way for those coming after. Everything went perfectly. Meanwhile, Jolanta was sprinting out of the People's House with ten women following. She first saw the three riflemen staring skyward, their mouths agape. When Jolanta looked up, she saw something falling from the sky just before she, the riflemen, and the ten women were killed by a violent explosion and engulfed in flames, giving the term "friendly fire" a whole new meaning.

The three riflemen guarding the tunnel entrance at Hallunda Square were almost knocked over by the shockwave from the simultaneous explosion of gasoline barrels and the downed helicopter. It took only a few seconds to realize they could do nothing for those hit and burned. The last of the three soldiers took the time to close the hatch from the inside before they headed off through the cable tunnel the same way they had come.

"Did you see that? The helicopter went down right by the People's House!" Filip exclaimed from his position on Flottsbro Hill.

"Damn, what bad luck," Uno replied. "It looked like the group that came out got caught, probably some of our own."

"No chance they survived that blast and the flames," Filip confirmed.

"But the first group made it into the tunnel without any problems, I saw that. Let's hope for the best. I want Ina, Jolanta, and Max back. They're our sharpest special forces."

The inferno before their eyes continued, accompanied by the dry rattle of automatic weapons and occasional explosions. At times, they let their binoculars hang by their necks, unable to take in any more violence.

The sky was black with smoke from burning buildings and exploding bombs. By afternoon, the gasoline bombings had ceased, and fewer people ran around in panic, explained by the many dead and those still alive finding shelter somewhere.

Toward evening, as dusk fell, the gunfire became more sporadic, finally ceasing as darkness enveloped Botkyrka's ruins. The night turned cold, dropping to below zero, and most of the wounded lying on the ground didn't survive the cold and blood loss.

Morning brought an eerie silence over northern Botkyrka. It was a cold day, with breath turning to vapor. Not even the birds seemed active, perhaps having fled during the fighting.

The next day, almost all the Muslims accepted the offer to surrender with their hands above their heads. The offer applied to combatants and civilians alike. The cold had sapped the Muslims' will to fight as they sat in freezing apartments. The war prisoners' first task was to load dead bodies onto trucks brought in for the purpose, and there was plenty to do.

The Battle of Botkyrka, known as the Kebab War, claimed around twenty-three thousand lives. The exact number will never be known. Bodies were dumped from trucks into deep, muddy mass graves dug by excavators in the nearby fields, Muslims and freedom fighters mixed together.

After two days of hard work, the streets and apartments were cleared of the dead. The surviving civilians were ordered, pending deportation, to cram into the undamaged houses in Norsborg–Hallunda, which were surrounded by a low barbed wire fence with guards every three hundred feet.

The 241 surviving fighters were interned at Hall Prison, which had been half-emptied after Uno Svensson granted the inmates freedom through a self-proclaimed general amnesty he claimed was decided by the government.

However, Uno's amnesty came with a condition. The inmates had to join the free forces as combat soldiers to gain freedom. The alternative was to remain interned with new cellmates, the fighters, an option chosen by the Muslim prisoners, who made up about half of the 450 inmates in the overcrowded prison. They wouldn't have had any other choice, anyway, as becoming Swedish soldiers was not an option for them. Not a single non-Muslim prisoner chose to stay at Hall Prison, which would have meant a death sentence.

The free army's total losses during the Kebab War amounted to 794 killed and a couple of hundred rendered unfit for combat due to various injuries. The thinning ranks needed replenishing, and the inmates from Hall were just what they needed, filling the ranks with 235 fresh soldiers, disproportionately many of whom were Kurds, Yugos, and Syrians. Many of the new soldiers were already familiar with handling automatic weapons. The inmates at Asptuna Prison, only one mile from Norsborg, also received Uno's amnesty offer, providing an additional seventy-three soldiers.

Chapter 38

Operation Deluge

October 31, 2032

"The Northern Caliphate is lost," Ahmed stated flatly. "Luleå is back under the control of the infidels. The new al-Hakim mosque, the northernmost in the world, has been blown to bits!"

"Very unfortunate. But we still partially hold Boden and the northern side of the Lule River and Highway 97 up to Gammelstad," Mahmoud countered. "I will provide you with a plan to retake Luleå. Those who allowed themselves to be captured don't deserve a place in God's kingdom. They deserve execution anyway. And in the name of the Prophet, we will slaughter the infidels who destroyed our beautiful mosque."

Mahmoud pointed at the screen displaying a map of Luleå and its surroundings while Ahmed watched disinterestedly. He had the map in his head; that was good enough.

Over the years, Mahmoud's bald spot had grown, making him look more like Mussolini with each passing day. Years of eating honey cakes had given his worn, crooked front teeth a dull, brownish tint. His potbelly seemed to be constantly expanding, unsurprisingly, given the food orgies the command indulged in, with Mahmoud and Ahmed being the leading gourmands. The two were true food enthusiasts, daily catered to by one of the Arab world's best chefs. Ahmed, however, maintained his slim and well-toned physique. It must be the honey cakes, Ahmed thought. I'll send him to a dentist when the war ends, so I don't have to endure his foul breath.

"How many fighters do we have left?" Ahmed asked.

"550 to 600, I'm not sure," Mahmoud replied. "But enough to make an attempt. We have about thirty armored vehicles that we can use as battering rams. We can surprise the infidels with a flanking maneuver through Rutvik and approach Luleå from the north. There's no defense there, and we could reach Porsön in an hour. Then it's a straight shot into central Luleå."

"What's the point? The infidels have mobilized around four thousand soldiers in the region. Perhaps fifteen hundred are well-trained rangers and infantry, unfortunately far more effective than our *Holy Warriors*. The rest are irregular soldiers with skills comparable to our own. Their rangers are mainly north of the Lule River, while their irregulars are on the southern side. We needed our experienced elite soldiers who died on the quays in Luleå's harbor. Willingness to sacrifice and enthusiasm are good, but competence and training weigh heavier. We must be realistic. The infidels' rangers are world-class; it's only a matter of time. They will reclaim all territory up there in this cold, godforsaken part of the world where we good Muslims have difficulty living anyway, so let them have their worthless land back. We have done what we needed. We took out the military air fleet of F21 and paralyzed their artillery at A9, even if we failed to completely disable the artillery. Now, only the power plants remain."

Mahmoud nodded, listening attentively to his chief's little sermon while dipping his freshly baked *aish* into the delicious Egyptian *fuul* they had been served by Hassan as a snack.

"Just like moms, so wonderfully good, you must try it! Yes, yes, you are right. The Northern Caliphate is lost. We anticipated this, but not that it would happen so quickly. We thought it would take years, not months. It's all because of those damned JAS planes from Vidsel that we failed to destroy."

"Very well. I now decide to initiate Operation Deluge," Ahmed said.

"What about our men? Shouldn't they get the chance to become martyrs? Isn't it too early for Operation Deluge?"

"They'll get their chance. They'll hold the line at Gammelstad and block European Highway 4 at Rutvik. As you know, the Bergnäs Bridge is blown, so the people of Luleå have no way to cross the river southward. The road north over Sinksundet will flood before anyone realizes what's happening. The narrow road will be clogged if they try to evacuate that way. There's no way out. The infidels are trapped in Luleå and will drown like rats!"

"Yes, you're right. If we wait, they will evacuate north along European Highway 4, which would be unnecessary. I'll immediately order our commander in Jokkmokk to execute Operation Deluge!"

"Good, but as you know, Operation Deluge isn't really about drowning the infidels, although it's a pleasant side effect," Ahmed said. "The main goal is to take out all fifteen power plants along the Lule Rivers, which together make up nearly half of Sweden's hydroelectric power. It's going to be a dark and cold winter in large parts of Sweden, especially in the capital!"

A few months before the invasion began, Muslim engineer-soldiers prepared the Suorva Dam for demolition by placing nearly a ton of explosives in the middle of the two-hundred-foot-high embankment, a massive mile-long barrier of blasted rock. Divers positioned large quantities of explosives below the waterline for maximum impact. The work proceeded undisturbed, as the remote facility was entirely unguarded, situated as far into the wilderness as a vehicle could go.

To avoid drawing attention from the few Sami and hikers, the operatives used the national energy company's service vehicles and wore overalls with the company's logo on the back. Any observers would assume it was routine maintenance or repairs. Leakage was a constant and concerning issue, downplayed by the company and authorities to prevent panic among residents of the Lule River Valley. The local Sami knew the problem, especially since some were employed by the energy company at the massive power plant in Porjus, further down the valley.

The drive from Porjus took just over an hour in one of company's vehicles. The energy company was infiltrated by many Muslim agents, some in high managerial positions, providing access to the company's equipment and resources. The two infiltrators now gazing at the enormous rock embankment that held back the waters were fully aware of the gravity of their impending actions.

The colossal stone wall before them made the famous pyramids of Giza seem like toys, thought Ali, a native of Cairo. In his youth, Ali had worked as a self-proclaimed guide for tourists foolish enough to pay for his nonexistent knowledge and rudimentary English, spoken with a heavy Arabic accent.

Many of the tourists were Swedes, who seemed more gullible than others, believing everything he said. Both the tourists he had met at the pyramids and those now living in Norrbotten, where he operated, seemed oddly truthful, except for the size of the fish they caught. But why did no Swedish tourists come here, where there was something truly magnificent to see, while they traveled all the way to Cairo to look at the small pyramids?

"*Allahu Akbar,*" they said in unison, closing their eyes as Ali pressed the button on the remote detonator.

With a dull thud, the explosives erupted, sending rocks and gravel flying hundreds of feet. At the same time, an underwater blast launched a massive cascade of water, soaking the backs of the two infiltrators as they took cover behind a boulder. When the echo of the explosion faded, an eerie silence ensued. At first, they thought they had failed—only a small hole, about a three feet wide, in the middle of the embankment. Had their pyrotechnic experts miscalculated?

But then the valley filled with the increasing roar of rushing water, and they saw the rocks being tossed around by the immense water pressure like weightless beach balls. The hole rapidly widened before their eyes as the two-hundred-foot-high wall of water gained momentum. The roar grew into a low-frequency, thunder-like rumble, shaking the ground beneath them. In thirty hours, six billion cubic meters of water would flow into the

Gulf of Bothnia, flooding and destroying every community, power plant, and bridge along its path to the sea.

"Let's go!" yelled the young man still holding the remote detonator, staring at it before flinging it away with a flick of his wrist. "Or we'll get a free ride all the way to Luleå!" he shouted as they jumped into the car, though his companion could hear nothing over the thunderous rumble.

A minute and a half later, the only road from Suorva was already under six feet of water. With the surging water close behind, they sped towards Porjus, continuing on to safety in Arvidsjaur, far from the soon-to-be-devastated Lule River Valley. Nothing in the world could stop the onrushing floodwaters.

Eight hours later, a similar scene unfolded at the one-mile-long and four-hundred-feet-high embankment damming the fifteen-mile-long Lake Tjaktjajaure, forming the Seitevare Dam.

The area was an engineer's dream for the power plant planners in the early 1960s. Even in their wildest fantasies, they could hardly have conceived a better site. The Black River, which, before the construction, drained Lake Tjaktjajaure, dropped seven hundred foot over a short distance. Here, kinetic energy was abundant, concentrated in a small, easily exploitable area, ripe for harvesting. While ordinary people stood in awe of nature's grandeur, feeling joy and gratitude for the chance to experience such splendor, the energy company's economists and engineers saw only flowing gold.

The Sami of Lule Valley sat unknowingly on immense wealth exploited by outsiders, just as other foreigners exploited the oil riches of the Arabian Peninsula. The Sami and the Arabs were nomads, following seasonal shifts, with their livelihoods tied to reindeer and camels, respectively. Every part of these valuable animals was utilized: meat, skin, bones—everything had a purpose. Despite the difference in temperature in their environments, the similarities between the cultures were undeniable.

The exploitation of Lapland and Arabia mirrored the colonization of North America and Australia, but a few centuries later. The nomadic peoples of Lapland and Arabia were at the mercy of foreign exploiters encroaching on their lands, just as the indigenous peoples of North America and Australia had been. They had no lawyers or PR consultants to advocate for them and lacked military resources to defend themselves.

However, the behavior of the exploiters differed significantly. In Arabia, the native population became incredibly wealthy, whereas the Sami were forcibly bought out for a pittance in a colossal government-backed robbery. Yet, the riches of flowing water are eternal, unlike oil and gas, which have an end. The few hundred Lule Sami could have become immeasurably wealthy for all time, but that didn't happen. Even a minuscule fraction, just one ten-thousandth of the revenue generated by the turbines, which functioned like gigantic, spinning cash registers, would have made them prosperous water sheikhs.

Before the water was diverted through tunnels to drive the enormous turbines, a series of spectacular waterfalls formed the sacred site of Passekårtje, the Holy Falls, where the Lule Sami had gathered to celebrate their festivals since time immemorial. But for seventy years, all that remained of Passekårtje's majestic natural wonder was a small trickle, said by local legend to be composed of the Sami's tears. The Black River, after a short descent from the mountains, merges into the Little Lule River, which joins the Big Lule River, or Stuor Julevädno in Lule Sami, at Vuollerim.

The thunderous explosion startled the two men from Jåhågasska Sami village, finishing their morning coffee, causing them to jump to their feet. What was happening? As far as they knew, no blasting was planned, and the energy company knew better than to create chaos in reindeer herding with unannounced explosions.

From their small campsite, a couple hundred feet up the slope towards the western shore of Tjaktjajaure, they could see a hole opening in the enormous stone wall that dammed the lake below them. Breathless and wide-eyed, they watched silently as the water regained its freedom and began filling the Black River's original channel. Billions of tons of water pressed on and demolished the barriers as the water's speed increased.

The water mass seemed to have longed for freedom, like a prisoner condemned to life. It rushed out through the freshly blasted hole in the prison wall, forming a giant jacuzzi, and celebrating its newfound liberty with violent eruptions and cascades.

"Look, Mihkkel, Passekårtje lives again! And more than ever before. Imagine if Mother Biret had seen this. She always said Passekårtje would live again!"

"Yes, I remember. She used to say those responsible for the destruction would one day get their punishment, and now it has come! But many still remember Passekårtje as it was—they will be so happy to hear this!"

"The people of Luleå will soon have to swim. I do feel sorry for them. Now, it will be their tears that flow."

"I don't know about that. Have you thought about Vattenfall's regional office in Luleå going underwater?"

"Yes, of course, but still... I feel sorry for the people living there. And we won't have electricity anymore, but we'll live like we used to. It worked well then, so it will work now too."

"Yes, we Sami survive in any situation, as we have for thousands of years. We have our reindeer and our houses; we'll just have to use wood for heating now. The Muslims won't come here. I'm not worried at all."

They climbed into the helicopter and put on their headsets in silence, as the rotor blades began to spin faster above their heads until they lifted off and resumed their conversation.

"We need to go to Jokkmokk and warn them because the phones aren't working anymore! But first, let's take a look at Passekårtje, with more water than it's ever had and never will again. Look, the whole valley is flooding!"

"Do you think they will rebuild the dam?"

"Not likely for a hundred years. There's war all over the country and the Swedes are losing. And what do the Arabs know about hydropower anyway?"

Chapter 39

The Deluge

November 1-2, 2032

In Vuollerim, the Big and Little Lule rivers join at Näset, about a mile north of the community. Once, Vuollerim was a Swedish version of Koblenz in Germany, where the mighty Rhine and Mosel rivers meet at the imposing Deutsches Eck monument, further out on the pointed promontory flanked by the two famous rivers.

No one had bothered to build monuments on the isthmus except the people who had inhabited it six thousand years earlier and whose remains can still be seen.

The majestic spectacle of the two Norrbotten rivers uniting has not been visible for seventy years due to the dams and power plants along the Little Lule River, which have tamed and chained the river to the point where its overgrown channel is periodically dry.

The alarming news reached the 692 residents of Vuollerim via radio just in time to evacuate. The unthinkable had happened. The local radio reported that the Suorva Dam had burst, and under the weight of billions of tons of rushing water, the massive Porjus Dam had also given way. The anxious residents of Vuollerim correctly deduced that the dams at the power stations in Ligga and Kuouka, located between Porjus and Vuollerim, would suffer the same fate.

To make matters worse, the reservoirs were full in preparation for the approaching winter. The timing couldn't have been worse. Each burst dam added more water, increasing the volume as it rushed toward the coast. Authorities had calculated the worst-case scenario of the Suorva Dam breaking, but no one anticipated the downstream dams falling like dominoes.

The locals were aware of the authorities' information and calculations. They knew that the water from the Suorva Dam was expected to raise the water level in their village by thirty feet, enough to flood nearly the entire village. What could they expect now, with water from four broken dams headed their way?

Nervously, they stood on small hills around the village, tens of feet above the area expected to flood. Authorities had repeatedly assured them that no tidal wave would form. The water would rise quickly from the river, but not so fast that people couldn't escape to higher ground. Cars and snowmobiles had already been moved to higher ground, loaded with as many household items, clothes, and food as they could carry. When it's urgent, people can accomplish more than they realize in a couple of hours.

Had the residents of Vuollerim known the full extent of the disaster, they would have fled higher up the hills. However, most wanted to watch their homes, which would soon be flooded or washed away. It was painful, but they wanted to witness it and record it on their phones for posterity. They could no longer make calls or browse the internet, but their phones still functioned as cameras.

Most men and women had instinctively grabbed their rifles and shotguns in the face of the impending danger. Now, the guns stood in long rows, leaning against the small, spindly pine trees. These firearms, next to their snowmobiles, were their dearest possessions. The large side pockets of their bulky, knee-length jackets bulged with heavy boxes of ammunition or loose cartridges that jingled metallically as they moved. What use would firearms be against the floodwaters? Knives hung from their belts, always handy, many with beautifully carved reindeer horn sheaths from their own reindeers. On their heads were the ubiquitous caps, mostly in dark colors, but some bright yellow or orange, essential for visibility to fellow hunters during moose hunting season.

Minutes remained before the floodwaters would inundate the village. Upon hearing the alarm, the most cautious and insightful had quickly gathered essential items and driven up the forest roads to await the disaster. In their cars, they could spend the night keeping warm with the engine idling while figuring out their next steps. Nighttime temperatures were around fifteen degrees, typical for the Arctic Circle in late autumn. Though not ideal, everyone could endure sleeping under the open sky if necessary.

Authorities had assured that the water would recede within 24 hours, so it seemed reasonable to stay close and see what remained of their homes to salvage whatever they could.

"It's coming!" shouted a stout woman, evidently equipped with the sharpest eyes. "God help us," she added in a higher pitch that broke before she finished the last word.

A low murmur spread as many dropped to their knees, clasping their hands, eyes lifted to the heavens, their lips uttering silent prayers for help, mercy, forgiveness, and grace—at least for the children.

"They said there wouldn't be a tidal wave, but that sure looks like one!"

The flood wave, leading the surge, was at least five to six feet high, though hard to judge as everything was obscured by white foam. The foaming wave had now passed Näset, and the villagers saw that part of the water was flowing up the Little Lule River against its natural direction.

From their elevated positions, they could see the Porsi Dam and the power plant where many of them worked. The dam lay just below the village, and they watched it rapidly fill to the brim. Water began spilling over the dam's wall, cascading down the valley. The water level rose quickly, flooding the shores at an accelerating pace. The high concrete wall of the dam held for now, a teen feet below the violent stream. Though they could no longer see it, they knew it was only a matter of time before it would give way and shatter under the immense pressure. No engineers could design something to withstand the overwhelming force creating the roaring inferno before their eyes.

The water continued to rise, but after four anxious hours, the rate of increase slowed significantly. It seemed the water was nearing its peak. Eventually, it would begin to recede.

The entire village was flooded. Some houses had collapsed and been swept away, but most remained, giving their desperate owners a glimmer of hope. Maybe the village could be rebuilt after all.

Just as the residents of Vuollerim breathed a sigh of relief, realizing that almost all of them had survived the unthinkable and started contemplating their next steps once the water receded, they were hit with another shock.

"Look, here comes the little river too!"

"Damn, damn, damn, it must be the Seitevare Dam!"

"That's even worse. Now we're getting all the lake Tjaktjajaure. The municipality estimated a fifty-feet rise for Seitevare. With Suorva, that adds up to over eighty feet, probably higher than this hill we're on."

"But you can't add water levels like that. Once the water reaches a certain height, it spills out onto the marshlands, and there are miles of marshes to flow into. You can't just stack the water levels on each other!"

"You're probably right. But for a moment, I thought our last moment had come."

Now Sweden's Koblenz lived up to its comparison with the famous German town. For the first time in seventy years, the waters from both rivers met in an unforgettable—though terrifying—spectacle. Cascades from the colliding torrents shot eighty feet into the air, filling the atmosphere with a dense mist that soaked their clothes as if pouring rain. The water began rising again, now much faster than before, but as expected, it spread out into the marshes, creating swift streams running in all directions. Näset transformed into an island before their eyes as the Little Lule River took a shortcut to its larger sibling by carving a new path right through the village, sweeping away house after house.

Soon, the water level surpassed the previous height. Chimneys were no longer visible. On the far side of the hill where they stood, a several-foot-deep lake formed, and they realized they were stranded on an island—with no way to escape.

After three hours, the water stopped rising. The marsh across the river had turned into a vast lake. Through binoculars, they saw moose and bears moving to higher ground. Above, buzzards, ravens, and owls circled, anticipating a feast on the tens of thousands of dead lemmings and voles floating below. If their diet felt monotonous, they could instead gorge on fish, which had been cast onto the marsh and floated lifelessly, belly up.

Many villagers sat on the ground, weeping with their heads in their hands, while others cursed as they frantically gathered branches and wood to light campfires. They desperately needed these to dry their clothes before the cold night descended.

Fortunately, the pockets of their bulky jackets were always filled with lighters, matches, and plenty of food, thanks to those who had been foresighted. They could see campfires already blazing on some nearby hills. They would survive the night and several more, if necessary, but what would they do afterward?

"What do we do when the water recedes? Winter is coming, and we have no houses left."

"If we had more fuel for the cars, we could drive to other river valleys for help, but I only have ten gallons left, and I have to save that."

"Same here. The gas is for emergencies. We won't get more fuel for a long time. But some of the highest houses are still standing. And the hunting cabins and teepees are intact. They're warm, and there's plenty of firewood. Some even have saunas."

"But there are hundreds of us. How can we all fit in? And how will we feed so many?"

"We have the barns by the meadow. We can insulate them with moss and peat, and it's easy to build fireplaces with stones, so they'll be warm enough. We can hunt reindeer for food, no matter who owns them. It's an emergency. And there's always moose and grouse. We'll have enough to survive until summer."

"Yeah, we'll manage somehow. We always have."

Less than a day later, the floodwaters reached the coast and began pouring into the Gulf of Bothnia near the southern part of Luleå's city center. The further downstream the communities were, the more water they received, as all fifteen hydroelectric dams had broken. Though being further down the river valley meant larger volumes of water, the extended warning time compensated for it.

The residents of Luleå had a whole day to act and didn't waste it. A few thousand people evacuated in boats, crossing to the river's southern side. Once across, they continued on foot along the European Highway 4, hoping to find help in Piteå despite the usually unwelcoming locals.

Those who tried to head north on the European Highway 4 were stopped by the *Holy Warriors* at Gammelstad and Rutvik. The *Holy Warriors* at Rutvik weren't necessary, as the floodwaters had found an ice age outlet to the sea through the glacial rift via Smedsbyn and Persön, cutting off all routes north. Luleå had become an island, at least for a day or two.

The floodwaters also reopened the old connection via Gammelstadsviken, just below the church village, where the port and ancient trading post from the Vendel era had been abandoned 379 years earlier due to land elevation. Instead, the new trading post, Luleå Sjöstad, was established on a peninsula further out on the mainland.

Gammelstadsviken, a shallow, muddy lake, became a navigable bay again, with fresh water flowing into the Gulf of Bothnia via the narrow strait Sinksundet.

A smaller flow into the sea formed via the normally sluggish Lulsund Canal, which now overflowed its banks, turning into a roaring rapid that flooded the bay of Skurholmsfjärden. The torrent submerged large parts of Skurholmen, Malmudden, and South Harbor. The Lule River now had four outlets into the Gulf of Bothnia, alleviating the main channel and reducing the disaster's impact.

A few thousand pragmatic Luleå residents headed to the marinas, where they sat in their boats on blocks under tarps for winter storage. Seated in their boats with their belongings, they experienced the earliest launch of their lives as the water lifted the boats off their blocks as if by an invisible hand. Once afloat, hundreds of boats rescued many people stranded by the rising water. Some landed on the island of Altappen. The same shore where their ancestors had fled into the water during the great sawmill fire of 1908 now saw their descendants wading in the opposite direction to seek refuge on land. They say history swings like a pendulum, and this was a strikingly concrete example. The old Master Builder's Villa, which had survived the sawmill fire, was already comfortably warm, as some Luleå residents had fled the God's Warriors and settled there months earlier.

Other boats went to the island Gråsjälören, close enough to South Harbor to wave to the *Holy Warriors*. Gråsjälören sheltered refugees who had escaped Muslim terror and lived in tents on the small island. They now helped the new boat refugees. Hindersön, Junkön, and the outer parts of Brändön were also islands populated by hundreds of Luleå residents who had fled. The refugees took shelter in any available summer cottages, regardless of ownership.

Most Luleå residents gathered on the nearby hills of Mjölkuddsberget, Skurholmsberget, and Ormberget. They safely watched the immense and slowly worsening disaster from these heights. According to the authorities' dam failure brochure, evacuees were allowed to bring their pets. The Luleå residents had clearly taken this to heart, judging by the hundreds of barking dogs, long rows of cages with cats, guinea pigs, parakeets, and even a few small aquariums with colorful fish that had been hauled up the hills.

After sixteen hours, the water reached its highest level, twenty feet above normal, submerging nearly all of Luleå and its surroundings. The coastal sea level temporarily rose by a few inches. The highest parts of Luleå's city center, on the island, remained dry. Thousands of eyes from the nearby hills observed that the ruins of the bombed cathedral were never engulfed by the water. Only 312 residents of Luleå perished in the flood, a significant disappointment for Ahmed, who had hoped for a hundred times that number. The opening of three ancient river outlets to the sea and the low-lying nature of Luleå's surroundings, which absorbed large amounts of water, kept the water level rise lower than theoretical estimates. Historically, Luleå had been destroyed by fire no less than four times and, like Jerusalem, had risen again after each devastation. It would do so once more.

The situation worsened further up the river valley, with water rising significantly higher in the narrower valley. The Edefors, Harads, and Bodträskfors communities were almost entirely washed away, but nearly all residents evacuated to higher ground.

Boden faced a particularly dire situation. According to the authorities' dam failure brochure, the water would rise thirty feet if the Suorva Dam broke, equivalent to reaching the fourth floor of the city hall in the center of town. The combined volume from fifteen broken dams meant that the water at its peak reached the sixth floor of the city hall. The *Holy Warriors*, who still controlled Boden, refused to allow evacuation, shooting anyone who approached the exits. As a result, 5,258 residents of Boden lost their lives.

The *Holy Warriors* in Boden, Gammelstad, and Rutvik eventually had to seek higher ground themselves. They splintered into smaller groups, becoming easy targets for the combat-ready hunter units stationed in the forests.

Those *Holy Warriors* who crossed to the south side of the river were quickly tracked down by Hugo's free troops and mercilessly eliminated. No prisoners were to be taken, according to an unspoken order. Any who were captured by more humane soldiers were later executed by others who felt no compassion for those who had murdered so many innocent Swedes.

The people of Norrbotten faced a harsh winter. Still, generous and efficient Finnish Baltic aid, coordinated from Helsinki, was already en route in long convoys of hundreds of trucks loaded with supplies, medicines, tents with heaters, and diesel generators.

In Finland, Estonia, and Latvia, supportive families opened their homes to thousands of Swedish war children who would stay indefinitely.

Norrbotten was liberated on November 2, 2032, now celebrated as "Norrbotten's National Day."

Chapter 40

The unknown fate of a shameless profiteer

November 18, 2032

"Well, well, if it isn't the infamous pig trader and spy, Björne Kork, in the flesh," remarked Ernst Höök, leader of the National Guard, as he leaned back in his chair, legs stretched out, scratching his chin, and squinting thoughtfully. "What should we do with such a little piglet?" Höök asked rhetorically, with loud voice as his eyes were scrutinizing the nervous, sweaty man standing before him with a swollen lip and a blackened left eye.

Clearly, those who had captured Kork had taken the opportunity to give him a well-deserved beating before handing him over to the guards. Kork had been recognized from a widely circulated description: "Kork resembles the former Prime Minister Fredrik Reinfeldt, but much shorter."

"You'll get millions," Kork replied, straining. "Dollars, I mean! You'll get twenty pounds of gold and gold jewelry with gemstones. No one else will know! I swear on my honor," pleaded Kork, realizing that his life hung by a thread that could be cut at any moment by the phlegmatic man lounging in the chair. Kork felt unsettled that the seemingly relaxed and nonchalantly friendly man could explode into a rage at any moment. From media and rumors, he knew well that Höök was often described as just that—choleric.

"Quite interesting," Höök responded, half-absentmindedly picking his nose. "But you know, seeing is believing. So, where's your little treasure trove?"

"In Gladö Kvarn. In a house I've rented from Gladö Equestrian Club for many years."

"Gladö Kvarn? Isn't that a bit too close to the Muslims' territory?"

"Yes, of course, but I'm counting on nobody finding the stuff, even if the area gets occupied. Besides, I have free passage to the Muslim area, no matter what."

"Yeah, you do, and that's exactly why you're here now!" Höök unexpectedly roared, standing up, towering over Kork, and grabbing his upper arm with his massive hand. "Now, we're going to Gladö Equestrian Club, but remember, I'll shoot you on the spot if there's no treasure!"

"There is! But promise me, I get to keep half. You'll get much more later; I swear you'll profit from letting me go."

Twenty minutes later, two Mercedes SUVs stopped on the gravel lot before the equestrian club. Höök was meticulous about his personal security and never moved without his private security detail, consisting of eight burly men in their thirties. All eight guards had blond hair and blue eyes, resembling young Dolph Lundgren clones. The SUVs were bulletproof and had reinforced undercarriages to protect against roadside bombs.

"Those are my cars," Kork said, pointing to a row of about fifty vehicles of various makes, parked with meticulous precision, each the same distance apart.

"Okay," said Höök, "but can you drive that many cars simultaneously? Do you even need that many?"

"I rent that house," Kork said, pointing to a smaller building a bit away from the others.

"You stay here," Höök instructed, pointing to the five blonde guards who had arrived in the second vehicle.

When they reached the bunker-like little house, they were greeted by a steel door with a massive combination lock as big as Höök's outstretched hand. None of them had ever seen such a large and heavy padlock. Kork entered the six-digit code, lifted the two-pound heavy padlock, and opened the steel door.

"It's empty, damn it," Höök hissed. "I told you what would happen if you tricked me into coming here! If you start babbling about someone having emptied, it..."

"Just wait and see," Kork interrupted, leading the way into the room.

The room was sparsely furnished with a worn, dirty little table, two roughly hewn chairs, and an old IKEA shelf against one side wall. Kork pushed the empty shelf aside, revealing a locked low steel door. Kork lifted a panel in the floor where the bookshelf had stood, retrieved a large hidden key, unlocked the door, and turned on the light.

"Move aside, I'm going first," ordered Höök, shoving Kork, who had to brace himself with his feet to avoid being knocked over.

Höök folded his large body and ducked to pass through the doorway and the ten downward steps, but once inside the two hundred square foot room, the ceiling was of normal height. The underground room was twice the size of the building above ground. The sight that greeted Höök was surreal.

The metal shelving system resembled any car workshop. Still, instead of tools and boxes of bolts and nuts, the shelves were packed with gray plastic bins full of wristwatches and dozens of overstuffed moving boxes bowing under the weight of thousands of gold jewelry pieces. Höök had an unpleasant flashback to Auschwitz-Birkenau, a place he regretted ever visiting, as he still had nightmares about the piles of thousands of shoes and eyeglasses that testified to the horrific scenes that had occurred there.

On the wall, car keys hung in a long, straight row on small nails, neatly labeled with identical white plastic tags with registration numbers written in black ink. The plastic tags were all facing the same direction, with the registration numbers outward. Not a single tag deviated from the pattern. Order and precision clearly reigned here.

In the corner of a shelf stood a stack of neatly arranged small gold bars. At the top of the shelf was a pink plastic bin that caught Höök's attention. When he lifted it down, he found it full of sex toys of all kinds. He picked up a beige dildo and pressed the button, causing it to vibrate with an unexpectedly annoying buzzing sound.

"This is just so damn sick," Höök said angrily, picking up a couple of gold bars and studying them closely. "Valcambi Suisse, 50 grams Fine Gold 999.9," he read aloud on one and tossed it back onto the pile. "Boliden, Rönnskär, 100 grams Fine Gold," he continued before letting that gold bar follow the same arc as the first.

"What did I tell you?" Kork asked rhetorically. "And now half of it is yours!"

"Shut up, you damn pig!" Höök snapped back. "I'm tempted to kill you right here and now, but you're not getting off that easy. Is it true that you forced the women to blow you while you took their jewelry?"

"Uh, not exactly like that, but some of them had to earn their keep, so to speak. Maybe you'd like some yourself; I can arrange it if you're interested. Fine and fresh, gorgeous girls. And willing too, no problem. What colors do you prefer? You can have several at once if you want. I know some who are genuinely bisexual."

Höök slapped Kork across the head with the back of his hand, knocking him to the floor, where he lay motionless.

"You promised!" Kork sobbed desperately. "We made a golden handshake."

When Höök stepped outside, he signaled to the small group of blonde Dolph Lundgren look-alikes with a shorthand wave.

"Get all the garbage that is down there! The gold and jewelry go into my car, and the watches go into the escort car. I think we can fit it all in. Then we head back to headquarters. You can each pick one watch, but remember, only one per person! There are gold Rolexes and diamond-studded Hublots. Fancier than I've ever seen in pictures. One watch each. Anyone caught taking more will be punished. There will be an inspection later, just so you know."

"The car keys can stay where they are until we find the car owners. They won't get any gas as long as the war continues anyway."

Forty minutes later, Höök's SUVs pulled up in front of the stone steps leading to headquarters, always guarded by four soldiers in yellow vests with automatic rifles slung over their shoulders.

"Bring in the gold and jewelry," Höök ordered. "We'll use that to increase our weapon arsenal. Dump the watches on the asphalt in front of the entrance. Ola, you get the bulldozer from the bus garage. The keys are in it."

The six-ton Caterpillar chugged and squeaked toward the small group before the entrance. Höök held Kork's neck firmly with his massive right hand.

"Understand how much money is lying there," Kork pleaded. "Don't do this! It's so unnecessary. Sell them instead and keep the money. I can help you."

"Watch closely now, you disgusting, greedy pig."

The Caterpillar slowly approached the hundred-square-foot area covered in exclusive gold, white gold, and platinum wristwatches. Kork was still convinced this was just a show, as no one could be so foolish as to destroy so much money.

The Caterpillar swung towards the piles of watches. Only three feet away now. The bodyguards watched as if hypnotized, but some almost imperceptibly shook their heads.

"No, no!" Kork screamed. "That's millions! In dollars! Stop, stop now!"

The Caterpillar slowly crushed the watches to scrap under its massive tracks with a low-frequency growl that made the ground vibrate. To ensure complete destruction, the bulldozer drove back and forth in different directions, leaving behind only twisted metal remnants, shattered glass, and scattered diamonds. Höök still held Kork's neck firmly, and when he let go, he saw tears streaming down Kork's cheeks.

"You thought you could take them to heaven, didn't you, you idiot! But let me tell you, burial shrouds don't have pockets. Maybe the undertaker will shove a few gold Rolexes up your ass when it's time for the crematorium."

The Caterpillar stopped and fell silent, as did the audience, as they witnessed the spectacle. Höök pointed at the guards in yellow vests.

"Clean up this mess and dump everything in the middle of Magelungen. Every fragment must go into the water, got it? I want this place spotless when I come back!"

"No problem, boss, we'll take care of it! We'll wash down the yard with the hose, so no one gets a flat tire. We'll send you a video of the dumping."

"Good. Now Kork and I are heading to Farsta for some fun."

Kork looked questioningly at Höök but got no response. Maybe it's the women tempting him, Kork thought, feeling a glimmer of hope. Even the toughest men have weak spots, and women are often one of them. This is my chance, he thought.

Soon, the two Mercedes SUVs left headquarters and headed towards Farsta Center which was controlled by the Tornberg base's free forces.

In Farsta, Kork attempted to say, "I know some long-legged Russian women," without getting a response. And a couple of busty black women from the Caribbean. They really know what they're doing. You should feel their lips. There's no silicone there, hehe!"

"Your nervous giggling is getting on my nerves," said Höök. "Just shut up!"

In Farsta, the fighting had spontaneously subsided a couple of weeks ago, and the front was frozen in the position that prevailed during the *Holy Warriors'* last attack, which was easily repelled. Only sporadic shots were fired when snipers got a bead on some unfortunate soul who was careless with their safety. The best shooters hit fatally every other time at a quarter of a mile if there was no wind.

Part of the front followed the street of Molkomsbacken, a quarter of a mile northwest of Farsta Center. The depressingly ugly and worn-out rental barracks east of Molkomsbacken, notorious for their shady clientele, were in the hands of the Tornberg soldiers. The Muslims controlled the fresher, more prestigious, and well-renovated high-rises on the other side of the street.

The city jeeps braked at the square of Farstaplan and turned onto the small pathway, sheltered behind the long rental barracks. Given that they were in bulletproof cars, they weren't particularly worried about snipers, even though it was broad daylight.

On the ground floor of the street Molkomsbacken 21, the Tornberg forces had their outermost outpost against the front. On the other side of the street, at Molkomsbacken 24, the Muslims had established their outermost outpost. Steel plates and piles of sandbags stacked outside covered the windows on the ground floor on both sides. The distance between the outposts was only a hundred feet, and sometimes, the soldiers would cheerfully wave at each other through a vent not covered by steel plates. Occasionally, there were middle fingers and fist shakes in the air, but they no longer shot at each other, as everyone seemed content with the status quo for the moment.

Ernst Höök had long since stopped introducing himself, as his distinctive face had circulated in the media for so many years that no one could fail to recognize him. As the leader of the National Guard, the Yellow Vests, he commanded the greatest respect, and no one dared to cross him, especially since he was known to use his old skills as a heavyweight boxer eagerly.

Höök greeted the doorman nonchalantly, "Hi, today we're offering some extra special entertainment."

The doorman cautiously returned the greeting and bowed submissively while holding the door open for Höök and his entourage, which consisted of a ghostly pale Kork and three bodyguards, while the others guarded the cars.

"Take off your clothes, you perverted ass," ordered Höök, looking at Kork, who hesitantly began to unbutton his down jacket. "I'm really too kind to give you a chance."

Kork clung to the hopeful last word and grasped at the last straw by obediently stripping until he stood in just his underwear in front of Höök.

"Take off your underwear and get on all fours like a pig," ordered Höök.

Kork actually looked like a pig, standing naked on all fours, with his ruddy, fat, flabby body, and the swollen belly hanging towards the ground like a pot-bellied pig.

"Grunt like a pig and do it well, or I'll kill you!" screamed Höök.

"Oink, oink, oink," responded Kork, snorting back and forth through his nose as best he could.

"Now you're going to crawl across the street to your Muslim friends. If we don't hear your grunts all the way, I'll shoot you. Remember, this is your only and last chance, so do it damn well!"

Höök opened the door.

"Remember, we can see and hear you all the way, so don't mess up!"

Kork began to crawl towards the door—and salvation—while grunting and oinking as loudly as he could.

"Wait, you should take a little parting gift to the Muslims," said Höök, taking out the dildo he had grabbed from Kork's treasure trove.

Höök pressed the button that started the vibrator and, with a powerful movement, shoved it into Kork's rear, causing him to scream in pain until he caught himself and started grunting loudly again.

"Crawl over to your friends now," concluded Höök, giving a light kick to Kork's fat buttock, which set him moving.

Kork slowly crawled on all fours over the icy asphalt. They could hear the buzzing of the constant buzz from the vibrator, interrupted now and then by his grunts and oinks.

Kork played his role with as much conviction as he could muster, even though he was convinced that Höök would shoot him. But no shots came, and he slowly approached Molkomsbacken 24, where the Muslims were. Maybe there was a chance. He continued along the house wall to round the corner, which would at least shield him from Höök's expected bullets, but what would happen then? The Swedes suddenly heard loud and upset voices speaking Arabic.

"*Ya nabi alkariam, ma hdha lashay'an*? Holy Prophet, what is this?"

"*Laqad 'ursil hwla' ghyr almuminin khnizirihim al'akthar 'iitharatan lilaishmizaz*! The infidels have sent their filthiest pig!"

"*'Iinaha aldiynamiat ladayh fi alhimar*? Is that dynamite in his ass?"

The last thing the Swedes saw of him was when a military boot gave Kork a hard kick from below towards his hanging belly, causing him to collapse and lie still. Then two pairs of hands emerged from behind the corner, grabbed Kork's arms, and dragged his body behind the corner, out of sight of the Swedes.

"I wish you a pleasant day, Mr. Kork," concluded Höök with a grin. "You probably have a lot to explain to your Muslim friends."

Chapter 41

The Russian navy suffers losses

December 2, 2032

The twenty-six crew members aboard the HMS Västerbotten, the latest A20 model submarine, lay silently in their bunks, where they had already spent over a day. Most tried to sleep to pass the time. The dim lighting was set to night mode to save battery power. The air was thick and hard to breathe because the air conditioning system had been reduced to emergency mode for energy conservation. They were very hungry, but they would have to wait for food.

For now, they were forbidden to leave their bunks. Fortunately, each bunk had a space with emergency rations, prepared for such situations. In the worst case, they would remain completely still on the seabed for up to three weeks before finally attempting to break out if the search for them hadn't ended. It's no wonder the Navy's recruiters conducted extensive and thorough psychological tests and analyses.

On the water's surface, the Russian anti-submarine ship Amiral Tjabanenko crept along at four knots, barely maintaining steerage, dragging its hydrophones and active sonars at various depths. A single dropped box of snuff could be enough for them to be detected and destroyed by depth charges, but that was not something the submarine crew intended to allow. Conversations were prohibited until further orders and whispers were not allowed. They waited and waited, silent as mice, hoping their hiding place and the hull's stealth capabilities would protect them from the repeated "pinging" that two pairs of Russian ears in headphones were intently listening for.

The situation was precarious. HMS Västerbotten lay in a natural crevice on the seabed opposite Slite Harbor, seven hundred feet west of the island of Asunden off the east coast of Gotland. Thanks to their deep position in the crevice, they were shadowed by the active sonar pulses that constantly swept through the water above them. Unless Amiral Tjabanenko happened to pass directly overhead, which was highly unlikely, they were completely invisible where they lay. But even if the unlikely happened, they still had a good chance of remaining undetected thanks to the hull's coating, which provided excellent stealth properties, making the submarine nearly invisible to hydrophones.

The crew was not worried that the Russians would find their hiding place. Swedish submarines had eluded all American attempts to locate them for years during dozens of extensive exercises that the Americans paid handsomely for. Even in motion, the submarines' air-independent Stirling engines emitted so little noise that they were normally undetectable.

The Americans had long been trying to address the security gap posed by Swedish submarines, but so far, they had failed. The crew hoped the Russians hadn't solved the problem either, but one could never be sure with the Russians, who sometimes made groundbreaking discoveries. There was something special about Russian mathematicians and physicists. They seemed able to think "out of the box," despite the reputation that central control from Moscow made this impossible.

They had clearly underestimated how fast the Russians went into action. It had only been a couple of months since they invaded Gotland, yet they had already begun building the naval base in Slite, which HMS Västerbotten was tasked with studying. The Russians' speed could only be explained by the fact that plans and blueprints had been ready long before the invasion.

It would later turn out that the Russians had designed the naval base as early as 2010 in connection with the construction of the North Stream 1 gas pipeline, where Slite was used as a base port by the Russians. North Stream 1 was blown up by the Americans in 2022. The Russians' dream of Gotland was ancient and no secret, which should have made politicians reconsider. Still, they were as naive about the Russians as they were about Muslims and everything else on the international stage. Short-term opportunism guided the politicians, as always. Politicians who think beyond the next election are nonexistent, at least in real democracies.

What was worse, the Russians had already made significant progress with the blockade that ran from the ancient Battery Mojner on the mainland of Gotland via the islands of Enholmen and Grunnet to the island of Asunden, which is not a real island as there is a narrow connection to the mainland of Gotland.

At Enholmen Fortress, the Russians had already revived the decommissioned container base built into the rock, where they were now replacing the outdated Swedish installations with their own. Once the Russians installed their hydrophones, magnetometers, and mines, no one could threaten the naval base in Slite from the sea. The location in Slite Harbor was perfect. But for now, it was wide open to a stealthy submarine.

On the island of Grunnet, the Swedes, via HMS Västerbotten's optronic mast, had observed and photographed hundreds of rolls of submarine nets, from which they concluded that the Russians intended to completely block both the strait between Asunden and Grunnet and the strait between Grunnet and Enholmen, leaving only the passage west of Enholmen navigable, the same passage that HMS Västerbotten had chosen when it sneaked into the bay. It was possible that the Russians had already blocked one of the passages between the islands. Still, the Swedish submarine crew did not know which one, as they hadn't had time to check before their presence was revealed by the fixed hydrophones that the Russians, to their surprise, had already managed to deploy.

From time to time, HMS Västerbotten raised its optronic mast above the edge of the crevice, still eighty feet below the surface, to locate the Amiral Tjabanenko, which was currently searching for them further inside the bay. Suddenly, the optronic mast detected something alarming.

"Submarine heading straight towards us, bearing 38 degrees, speed five knots! Distance: thirty Nautic miles. It will reach us in less than three minutes!"

Commander Fridolf Palmquist faced the most important decision of his life. He didn't hesitate for a moment, immediately putting the submarine into a state of maximum combat readiness and defensive preparedness, ensuring all equipment was ready for battle and all personnel were at their combat stations.

"Battle stations! Battle stations!"

This was the kind of situation they had trained for years, hundreds of times in simulators. But now, it was real, and they had to keep their heads cool. Fridolf closed his eyes and pressed his palms against them to shut out the world entirely while concentrating his thoughts as quickly as possible.

Navy Chief Fred Bergström ordered them to avoid Russian units, even if they were encountered in Swedish territorial waters—even though the Russians occupied Gotland. A war with Russia was the last thing Sweden needed right now.

Most indications were that the submarine was Russian and part of the search for them. Still, the approaching submarine could certainly be of another nationality, given how many were interested in the Russians' activities in Slite. Fridolf knew for sure it wasn't Swedish; he would have known.

Remaining in their position and continuing to hide was too risky, as HMS Västerbotten would be in serious trouble if discovered. It was an emergency, and now it was about saving the submarine and its crew at any cost, a mandate held by every captain of all naval vessels worldwide.

It took Fridolf seven seconds to make his decision. Now it was all about speed and taking advantage of the element of surprise.

"Rapid ascent thirty-two feet, bearing eighteen degrees. Release and activate all torpedoes!"

The compressed air system immediately began blowing water out of the ballast tanks, causing the submarine to rise from the seabed where it had been lying, first slowly and majestically, then with increasing speed.

The technical development of torpedoes had turned submarine warfare into something reminiscent of Wild West shootouts. The one who got off a reasonably aimed shot first usually won, as modern, homing torpedoes rarely missed their targets.

Fridolf's plan was to surprise the opponent and launch a couple of torpedoes on the way up as soon as they crested the edge of the crevice before the opponent could perceive the threat. The gunners locked their sights on the approaching submarine.

"One and two, FIRE!"

At the same time, the aft torpedoes' sights were locked on Amiral Tjabanenko, which was seven hundred Nautical miles further inside the bay, where the enemy was futilely searching for them.

"Seven and eight, FIRE!"

The detonations when the approaching submarine was blown to pieces at just five hundred feet were so powerful that HMS Västerbotten lurched violently, forcing the crew to press themselves against the floor as everything else was impossible. However, the hull's construction and material strength were so high that there was no risk of serious damage. A 20th-century Gotland-class submarine, still the most common in the Swedish Navy, would have risked breaking apart from the shockwave.

For the anti-submarine ship Amiral Tjabanenko, the outlook was bleak once the torpedoes were fired. Even with the most advanced electronic countermeasures available, stopping guided, ultra-fast torpedoes is extremely difficult. Amiral Tjabanenko, being quite old, wasn't equipped with the modern anti-torpedo torpedoes that contemporary Russian warships typically carried. However, there was still a primitive but effective way to protect themselves. By deploying a protective barrier of detonating depth charges, the attacking torpedoes could be damaged or thrown off course, causing them to lose their target.

The powerful detonations alarmed Amiral Tjabanenko's first officer, Boris Dmitrievich Pankin, who was in command. The captain, Commander Gurin, had indulged in too much Stolichnaya Gold and was currently sleeping off his inebriation.

That combat had begun near Asunden Island was obvious, but what exactly was happening?

Pankin knew he had only seconds to decide if ultra-fast torpedoes were heading their way.

"Depth charges, all starboard launchers! 250 feet, detonation depth sixteen feet. Continuous firing every five seconds!"

After launching the torpedoes at Amiral Tjabanenko, HMS Västerbotten surged underwater, heading for the same strait they had used to enter the bay. Near the strait, just east of Enholmen, lay the heavily armed destroyer Volgograd from the Project 956 Sarych-class, known in the West as the Sovremenny-class, blocking their escape route. Commander Fridolf Palmquist had no desire to engage with such an opponent.

"Three and four, fire!"

When the crew of the destroyer Volgograd saw the detonations from the hit submarine, they immediately realized they could very well be the next target for the torpedoes, so they ordered full speed ahead, which meant through the strait that HMS Västerbotten intended to escape through. Captain Petrov's quickly improvised plan was to circle Enholmen to get out of sight of the torpedoes' seekers and, if necessary, continue circling Enholmen at full speed to shake off the homing torpedoes while deploying slow-burning decoy flares from the stern. Even though Volgograd's top speed was an impressive thirty-eight knots, Captain Petrov knew it was far from enough to outrun the torpedoes.

As the destroyer accelerated, one of the torpedoes that had breached the barrage detonated in front of the anti-submarine ship Amiral Tjabanenko. The latest Swedish torpedoes are smart in that they don't head straight for the target when multiple is fired simultaneously. By taking an evasive turn, the seventh torpedo maneuvered around the barrage and struck Amiral Tjabanenko just behind the bow on the starboard side, six feet below the waterline. Within fifteen minutes, the anti-submarine ship Amiral Tjabanenko would rest on the bottom of the Baltic Sea after first pointing its stern straight up towards the sky in a final proud salute as thanks and farewell for half a century of service in the Russian navy.

Commander Palmquist ordered a port turn and chose the passage between Grunnen and Asunden to avoid the deadly destroyer. Just as they entered the passage, they felt the shockwave from the third torpedo, which had caught up with the fleeing destroyer and tore its stern to pieces.

"Now let's hope they haven't deployed the submarine nets, or we'll come to a sudden stop," Palmquist muttered to himself, then said loudly, "Head south, maintain submarine depth! Onward to Karlskrona."

Chapter 42

Meeting in Zone 2

December 4, 2032

As Gyllenstierna had said, Zone 2 was deceptively similar to Zone 1. Everything, including the room layout, furniture, and color scheme, was built according to the same template.

One difference, however, was that they were spared the dull yellow plastic plates from Zone 1. In Zone 2, they were instead pale green, which felt like a step in the right direction, even if the fried—or rather, burnt—potatoes served with the classic Swedish dish Biff à la Lindström were barely lukewarm. The watery lingonberry drink tasted just as usual.

Twelve concerned individuals sat around the oval table, fueling up before the conference formally began. It would be impossible to claim that the food was anything other than necessary energy.

"A war with Russia is not exactly what Sweden needs right now," said Navy Chief Fred Bergström, "but I am proud of our effort. What other options did Palmquist really have?"

"He did what he had to, and he did it brilliantly," Gyllenstierna noted.

"It looks like the Baltic Sea is turning into a Russian lake. Essentially, at least," said Bertil Wiklund. "Information obtained by MUST through direct contacts with military leaderships indicates that neither Finland nor Denmark will declare war on Russia despite the occupation of their islands. The politicians choose to pretend they believe the Russians' official explanation, that it is merely temporary operations to support Sweden in the war against the Muslims."

"Perhaps it's easier that way. They definitely don't have the resources for a war against Russia," stated FRA Chief Rudolf Enbom. "And even if they did, they know the Russians have activated their eight thousand nuclear bombs. In any case, we've intercepted radio traffic over the Baltic Sea and phone calls in Moscow, revealing that the entire population of both the islands of Åland and Bornholm will be evacuated shortly to be replaced by incoming Russians. It's roughly the same number as on Gotland for both islands combined. The Ålanders are being transported by ferry to Turku, where it will become the Finns' problem to take care of them. The Bornholmers are being transported to Copenhagen. It appears that the Gotlanders taken to Russia are now being dispersed across the country and will take over the homes left by the departing Russians," Enbom continued. "A simple swap, much to the delight of the incoming Russians upgrading their living standards, but much worse for the Gotlanders.

What's more alarming is that we have confirmed the circulating rumors," Enbom went on. "They will take the island of Öland too, but we don't know exactly when they plan to strike. There's no defense, and we have no resources to deploy."

"How many people actually live on Öland?" asked Baksi.

"I think it's just under thirty thousand," said Enbom. "You'll see that even the Ölanders will fit into the vast, vast Russia," he continued, shaking his head in resignation. "Damn, this is shaping up to be a worse catastrophe than when we lost Finland! Sweden's time as the leading power of the Baltic Sea is over for good!"

"Yes, if Mother Svea even remains, she'll shrink considerably. Maybe it will end with Sweden consisting of the Mälaren Valley, Dalarna, and all the way up north to the Finnish border – nothing more. Then we'll be a nation of three to four million people, the smallest of the Nordic countries, except for Iceland. Always, these damned Russians," said Wiklund.

"But maybe the Russians can help us defeat the Muslims," said Brännström. "We should focus on that. The rest will be a post-war issue. Western Europe is at war, and it will end with the map of Europe being completely redrawn, like after the treaties of Versailles and Westphalia, and it won't be Swedes drawing the lines on the maps."

"Let's hope it's not just Russians and Muslims holding the pens. If only that damn idiot Wallfors in the so-called exile government on Sveaborg could keep her mouth shut, much would be gained," said Bergström.

"There will surely be some Germans holding the pens too, and maybe even the Americans when the dust settles," said Gyllenstierna.

"I believe there will still be a Sweden in some form," said Air Force Chief Wennergren optimistically. "Let's assume there are maybe six to seven million people who identify as ethnic Swedes and want to continue speaking Swedish. Let's assume that one million Swedes die in the war. There will still be five to six million ethnic Swedes left. Populations of that size usually get their own nations when maps are redrawn, so I'm fairly optimistic about Mother Svea's survival in some form. Of course, we might become a republic in the Russian Federation. But I'd rather we became a German federal state if I had the choice."

"Then there's the question of what it means to identify as an ethnic Swede," said Baksi. "I, for example..."

Suddenly, the door opened abruptly, and the FRA chief's information secretary appeared, looking agitated.

"Sorry to interrupt the meeting, but I have information for Rudolf that can't wait."

A few minutes later, Rudolf Enbom returned, visibly shaken.

"Listen, everyone, to this critical information our American friends at the NSA have shared with us in the strictest confidence."

The room fell silent as Enbom took a deep breath and collected himself. He looked distressed, and his voice barely held steady as he began to speak.

"The submarine that Palmquist sank was American! Thirty-eight American crew members lost their lives."

"Oh my God!" exclaimed Gyllenstierna. "Are we at war with the USA now too?"

"It would have been better to do what Palme did in the bay of Horsfjärden in 1982 and just let the Yankees go," said Bergström.

"Yes, but back then, he knew it was the Americans," noted SÄPO Chief Popovic. "Of course, we would have done the same again if we had the chance. The USA has been the only friend Sweden could always rely on since 1945."

A loud discussion broke out. Would the USA be drawn into the war, and what would that mean?

"Brave little Sweden against the rest of the world," remarked Baksi ironically. "Sure, we need to face the reality, but without exaggeration, we can say that the situation is quite worrisome. Not even Hitler managed to fight the whole world."

"But Putin actually managed to hold the fort pretty well, which was a bitter surprise for all of us," said Gyllenstierna.

The Muslim experts and Swedish patriots invited to increase their understanding of the enemy's long-term plans were hastily rescheduled for the following day. Given the situation, none of the attendees could think about anything other than Sweden's critical situation. Was this the definitive end for Sweden as a nation? It was hard to see how the Kingdom of Sweden could be restored.

Chapter 43

Putin declares war on the Nordic caliphate Alzuwid

December 5, 2032

President Vladimir Putin looked as cold and composed as ever as he strode to the podium with determined steps. He stared straight at the television viewers before speaking, unusually reading directly from a script.

"Russian men and women! Ukrainians, Belarusians, Lithuanians, and all honorable citizens of our beloved Russian Federation. To all Russian citizens watching this from your TVs and computers far from the Kremlin, out in the Far East. I believe most of you have heard about the disgraceful attack on our peacefully patrolling Russian warships in the Baltic Sea three days ago, despite them being in international waters where they had every right to be. The ships were miles well beyond Sweden's territorial boundary. We Russians do not let ourselves be intimidated by a few brazen bandits who think they can flout international law. We Russians always stand up against all injustice. We have endured many wars and have always ultimately defeated our enemies, no matter their military strength. The Germans know this, the French know this, the Swedes, Finns, Poles, Turks, Chechens, Syrians, Georgians, and many others who made the mistake of attacking us know this."

Putin raised his finger in the air in a cautionary gesture. "Never, ever provoke the Russian bear! When the Russian bear roars and strikes with its powerful paws, it has the strength to crush any enemy."

It was rare for Putin to show anything other than his emotionless stone face, but this time, his emotions were visibly stirred, and it was clear he had now departed from his script.

"So, who are these brazen bandits who think they can provoke us Russians and get away with it as if nothing happened? These vile Muslims have flooded into Western Europe like a tidal wave and are now quarreling with the Russian bear. They will regret coming here and will be driven out of Europe forever!"

Putin stared into the cameras and paused for effect.

"Dear Russian patriots, we have no choice but to respond to the acts of war we have been subjected to. In close cooperation with Sweden's legitimate government and its Prime Minister Margot Wallfors, based on Sveaborg outside Helsinki—the fortress that surrendered to Russian forces over two hundred years ago—we will now begin operations on the Swedish mainland. Our armed forces are proud to answer the call of our Swedish friends for Russian assistance in their difficult situation. Dear

Russian patriots, Russia is now at war with the so-called Muslim Caliphate *Alzuwid*, which has cowardly and unjustly occupied the southern parts of Sweden, led by a self-proclaimed prophet named Ahmed Ben Barka. Our intelligence services have gathered information, and we now know that this Ben Barka is nothing more than the result of a meeting between Moroccan street scums, which explains his brazen lawlessness. This puffed-up street scum will soon be captured and brought before Russian justice to answer for taking the lives of 103 heroic Russian sailors.

"I have ordered our armed forces to maintain the highest readiness from the Baltic Sea to the Pacific Ocean. The aircraft carrier Admiral Kuznetsov is being relocated from the Mediterranean to the Baltic Sea to strengthen our combat capability further. Our Russian air force, which has taken off from the recently liberated Swedish island of Gotland, is now launching the first bombings of the so-called Caliphate *Alzuwid* to free the Swedish people from their Muslim tormentors. You will all receive continuous reports on our actions to aid our Swedish friends. Anything less than unconditional victory is unthinkable. We will triumph within a few weeks. Long live Russia, forever!"

Putin turned his back and left the studio. Russia was at war, but with whom?

Chapter 44

Russian bombings begin

December 6, 2032

The Russians had succeeded well with the stealth characteristics of their new, fifth-generation Sukhoi Su-57 attack aircraft. That became evident to the Swedes when, on the morning of December 6, six of them went to attack the Berga Naval Base south of Stockholm.

The twenty-four K-77M missiles they fired from eighty miles away transformed a significant portion of Sweden's largest naval base into heaps of rubble, concrete fragments, and twisted steel skeletons in less than ten minutes.

The attack on Berga Naval Base was followed by a barrage of eighteen Kalibr cruise missiles launched from the missile cruiser Pyotr Velikiy from one hundred miles.

Despite being outdated when purchased at great expense fifteen years earlier, the American-made Patriot system, with its technological roots in the 1980s, proved effective once it identified the enemy. This was largely due to its Israeli high-performance missiles. One Sukhoi Su-57 and thirteen of the eighteen cruise missiles were shot down over the Baltic Sea.

The Achilles' heel of the Patriot system is its limited coverage—only 120 degrees of the horizon in the enemy's direction—making it vulnerable to rear attacks. The Russians exploited this weakness by using Sukhoi Su-24 attack aircraft to destroy all Patriot launchers in less than half an hour after they revealed their positions through firing.

Similar scenes unfolded at the naval base in Karlskrona, with the difference being that the Kalibr missiles were launched from two Russian Akula-class submarines. Sweden's only air defense regiment, LV6 in Halmstad, was in the hands of the Muslims, and the three JAS Gripen E, the only combat-ready aircraft Sweden had, were parked in Finnish Kuopio, where they remained until the end of the war. The Finns dared not risk their neutrality by allowing Swedish warplanes to take off from their airfields.

When all six of Sweden's Patriot launchers were knocked out by attack aircraft striking from behind, the skies were clear for Russia's strategic bombers. These bombers could fly in at desired altitudes and optimal speeds, ensuring nearly one hundred percent accuracy regardless of the weather.

The heavy bombs from the strategic bombers TU-22M Backfire and TU-160 Blackjack, which flew over Berga and Karlskrona, pulverized entire areas around the bases. The bombardment turned access roads, masts, buried communication links, port facilities, and quays into unrecognizable stone piles, gravel, concrete fragments, and twisted steel. It was clear that the Russians were thorough in their mission to incapacitate the entire Swedish navy with a single decisive blow to its two main bases.

Although parts of the nuclear bomb-proof bunkers at Berga and Karlskrona remained intact, the capacity of the Swedish naval bases was reduced to about one-tenth of their former capability. Over the next few weeks, four-fifths of the nearly intact Swedish navy at sea gathered in Finnish ports, where it remained until the end of the war. The rest of the navy was stranded in Copenhagen and Oslo, where it was temporarily seized by the military in those countries. The Danes and Norwegians, like the Finns, were unwilling to be drawn into a war with Russia in a futile attempt to aid Sweden.

But it wasn't just the Swedish naval bases that were bombed. The Russians were also keen to secure air superiority over the Baltic Sea once and for all. They were well-informed about every detail of "STRIL", the Swedish air force's command and control system. After the Patriot systems were knocked out and Sweden was left defenseless, the Russians used their heavy bombers, TU-22M Backfire, to pulverize StriC Grizzly, the defense forces' command and control center located outside Bålsta, northwest of Stockholm. At least all the surface facilities were pulverized, and most of the underground electronics were disabled by electromagnetic pulses from the bombardment. StriC Grizzly consolidates information from all of Sweden's military radar installations, which were used to identify and track enemy aircraft. The air battle controllers in the nuclear bomb-proof center of StriC Grizzly also directed Swedish fighter units to their targets. Still, this task was no longer relevant since Sweden's air force had been eradicated.

Since the Muslims had destroyed the six-story underground STRIL facility in Hästveda outside Hässleholm several months earlier, Sweden was left completely without air surveillance. Sweden's all-seeing eye had lost its vision.

Chapter 45

Ethnic cleansing in Vivalla

December 7, 2032

The day after the Russian bombings of the Swedish naval bases in Berga and Karlskrona, it was business as usual for the National Task Force, which had gathered in Örebro in recent days to tackle a particularly tough operation. The Muslim enclave of Vivalla, one of the first to achieve independence from Sweden, was to be emptied of Muslims, meaning all residents. Ethnic cleansing, one might call it.

Despite the ongoing war, Örebro had otherwise enjoyed a deceptive calm for a long time. The Muslims were in Vivalla, the Swedes in the rest of the city, and neither side seemed willing to break the peace. The Muslim troops, advancing westward with their Abrams tanks, passed along the European Highway 18 without entering Örebro itself. The city remained largely intact, as it was before the outbreak of the war.

The residential area of Vivalla was built in 1970 as a typical housing-program area, except for the unusual lack of high-rise buildings. The area consists of 2,400 apartments housed in regularly placed, concentration camp-like two-story barracks, originally intended to accommodate about 7,000 residents but which came to house three times as many, possibly up to 30,000. No one knew the exact number of residents since the majority in Vivalla were illegal immigrants living in the shadow society. The last non-Muslims were driven out of the area in 2020, and since then, a Muslim monoculture under Sharia law prevailed.

No more than thirty percent of the children growing up in Vivalla completed elementary school, which ranked the area at the bottom of the education level, competing with other known socio-economically extreme Swedish suburbs like Norsborg, Alby, Tensta, Rosengård, and Hammarkullen.

To say the least, being born in Vivalla was not a good start in life, at least by Swedish standards. Hardly anyone from Vivalla made it through the long road of schooling to well-paid top jobs if they even dreamed of it. Contempt for knowledge and hatred towards the Swedish majority society guided future choices. Those who adapted to Swedish society were viewed with suspicion and were bullied out by the Muslim majority, living in their parallel society under Sharia law. The difference between being a despised conformist and a turncoat who must be eliminated, a so-called "house Muslim," could be very slight.

Turning away from Islam or the traditions of the homelands is life-threatening, and defectors can count themselves lucky if they only suffer social ostracism. Women knew their place and expressed wholehearted support for the oppressive rules, restrictions, and traditions, at least on the surface.

Better to cower silently behind the niqab or veil than to be designated as a legitimate rape victim or to be beaten to a pulp with the risk of losing one's life or as is often the case, a combination of sexual assault and severe physical abuse. When mothers raise, abuse, and strictly control their daughters in the Muslim tradition, it is primarily out of concern for the girls' future health and safety. Women who know their place and never question it are safe and constantly protected.

Instead of going to school and doing homework, young boys and teenagers are trained by older Vivalla residents in the art of burning cars, attacking emergency personnel, selling and transporting drugs, committing robberies and home burglaries, handling weapons, and behaving aggressively and cheekily towards the lowly, impure, and immoral Swedes.

On the ruins of the Vivalla Mosque, which was burned down by a confused Muslim in 2017, a new, larger, and grander mosque was built with money from the wealthy Gulf states. The new mosque opened in 2021, and now it was also to be burned down, at least if the head of the National Guard, former heavyweight boxer, and motorcycle club president Ernst Höök had his way.

For bigger operations, the National Guard (NG) typically supported the National Task Force (NI). The National Guard could muster significantly more helping hands and batons, which, in the case of NG, resembled extended baseball bats, swung by the yellow vests with a weight and force that broke arms, legs, knees, or whatever happened to be in their way.

Vivalla was one of these larger National Task Force (NI) operations. It would have been easier to simply encircle Vivalla, enclosing the Muslims with barbed wire and turning the entire area into a holding camp until its residents could be deported. But NI's chief, Björn Väster, was not one to cut corners. The task was to conduct ethnic cleansing throughout the area held by the Swedes.

"Precisely because Vivalla is a Muslim stronghold, it must be cleansed," Väster insisted, always personally present to lead major operations. "Let's not take the easy way out; let's do what needs to be done. We must completely empty this illegal enclave and hand it over to Swedes who have had their homes destroyed. Today, Vivalla will be returned to the Swedes," Höök declared. "Today, we will uproot the bottomless evil of Islam, once and for all, here in Vivalla. The Swedish banner—the real flag with the cross—will fly proudly over Vivalla before the day ends. The mosque, this den of the devil, will be burned down, just as they did themselves in 2017. That's apparently how they want it," he continued with a crooked smile.

No one believed the Muslims would leave Vivalla without a fight. Still, the hope was that resistance would be quickly crushed, as NI, this time, took the Muslims by surprise and executed the operations with the utmost speed and brutality. Typically, residents were informed a few days in advance to give them a chance to pack their bags and surrender voluntarily.

Around Vivalla, NI's twelve hundred available soldiers began to appear out of nowhere without warning. They had been spread across Örebro with orders not to show their uniforms until the time came. Simultaneously, a couple of thousand street fighters from the National Guard (NG) approached on foot, donning their yellow vests from their pockets only upon arrival. The local Örebro police also contributed forty officers in marked cars and vans, specially invited by Björn Väster.

Buses were driven up and parked as the area was surrounded by yellow vests and task force soldiers equipped with AK5 rifles.

Last, three hundred soldiers from Battalion Viking, the Lagerbäck Battalion, arrived in dark green troop transport vehicles. When the Lagerbäck warriors stepped out in their well-tailored, black, and shiny uniforms, with the golden Thor's hammer gleaming in the sun, spontaneous cheers and applause erupted from the residents of Örebro who had gathered to witness the spectacle. Even NG's street fighters and the police applauded. The Lagerbäck warriors had achieved idol status and they reveled in it.

The soldiers from Battalion Viking were tasked with the most dangerous job: going from apartment to apartment to flush out or shoot those who tried to hide. It was well known that women and gay men particularly idolized the soldiers of Battalion Viking. They simply found the young, well-groomed soldiers attractive and sexy in their tight black uniforms, contrasting with their fair skin and blonde hair. These Nordic archetypes often charmed the women with captivating smiles and long, flirtatious looks. They seemed straight out of 19th-century German fairy tales about heroic and noble Aryan superwarriors or righteous heroes with superpowers from American comic books.

Battalion Viking soldiers always entered the apartments in groups of four, always wearing bulletproof vests and Kevlar helmets with bulletproof visors down, making them difficult targets for gun-happy and combative Muslims. Two soldiers forced the door open while the other two took cover in case of a confrontation. Once inside, all four moved in a line, splitting up depending on the number of rooms in the apartment. The group of four was accompanied by ten task force soldiers stationed on the ground floor by the entrance, ready to intervene if necessary. The three hundred Lagerbäck warriors formed seventy-five teams that cleared 2,400 apartments, thirty-two apartments per team. If the teams maintained an average speed of five minutes per apartment, the entire operation would be over in four hours. Battalion Viking was meticulous about minutes and seconds.

The role of the yellow vests was to expedite the process by beating those who streamed into the courtyard, shouting and pushing them until they were on the buses. Achieving a psychological intimidation effect was crucial to making the typically combative Muslims submit without a fight.

The police's role was passive presence to indicate that the operation had the government's blessing. Somehow, the flashing blue lights of the cars and vans created a fitting backdrop for the spectacle now in full swing. Large crowds of Muslims marched in lines, escorted by yellow vests who pushed and lightly hit them with batons on the shoulders and backs while shouting instructions in harsh voices.

"*Jalla, jalla, jalla*! Hurry up before I smash your head in!"

"Get on the bus, you damn Muslim hag!"

"If you don't shape up, I'll smash your ugly face!"

Some of the marching Muslims received such severe beatings with the batons that they couldn't get on the buses on their own. Those unable to walk were either thrown onto the buses or shot on the spot and left lying on the ground. NG's chief, Ernst Höök, seemed to relish the situation as he stood there, bareheaded in his black leather coat, arms crossed, legs firmly planted, with an evil grin but a perversely gleeful and expectant expression. This was pure Christmas for Höök, who occasionally lent a hand by letting his granite fists speak in short bursts against soft bodies, which immediately crumpled as ribs cracked and spleens ruptured.

Beside Höök stood the considerably smaller Björn Väster in his gaudy uniform with a large, peaked cap on his head. He observed the scene with a neutral, attentive expression, always ready to issue orders if necessary. Always rational and efficiency-minded, he constantly thought about what could be improved and what details needed polishing. He often had the operations filmed to use the footage in his detailed debriefings, much like football coaches do.

From the apartment blocks, sporadic gunfire could be heard as some residents did not quickly obey the commands shouted by the Lagerbäck warriors as they stormed the apartments. Thousands of residents voluntarily entered the courtyards to avoid unnecessary risks in the cramped apartments. Once in the courtyards, they were escorted by yellow vests to the buses, which drove off as soon as they were deemed full, often with well over a hundred crammed passengers.

Occasionally, bursts of automatic fire echoed through the area, signaling to both spectators and participants that a Muslim had chosen to fight rather than surrender. The automatic fire usually ended quickly with a few dull thuds as grenades were thrown into the apartment where the shooter was holed up.

Operation Vivalla was a resounding success and would become the template for future cleansing of Muslim enclaves. The entire area, with up to thirty thousand Muslims, was cleared in three hours, fifty-three minutes, and twelve seconds, according to Väster's timing. It was a record speed, with the cost being only three dead yellow vests and a few lightly injured from both NI and Battalion Viking.

The number of Muslims killed was estimated to be between thirty and fifty. No one bothered to count them.

When the operation was completed, Ernst Höök put his massive right arm around Väster's shoulders and pulled him into a friendly embrace, real men to real men. Väster looked like a little teddy bear compared to Höök's imposing figure.

"Hey, Björn – this is how it's done, right?"

"Yeah, right," Väster replied, wriggling out of Höök's bear hug. "Now we have an almost perfect model for future operations, and I wonder if we shouldn't have a little party in the Muslim ghetto Gottsunda, in Uppsala soon."

"A brilliant idea, brother! Just give me a date, and I promise that we in the NG will be there to help in every way possible."

"Great, Ernst. I know I can always count on you. Uppsala is a bit special since I studied cultural geography and political science there. Now let's go and have a meal at the Castle Restaurant on the task force's dime!"

"Thanks, thanks. We certainly deserve it after a day like this," Höök concluded.

Chapter 46

Lucia celebration at the Defense Headquarters

December 13, 2032

The kitchen in Zone 2 went all in on this cold winter day, baking traditional Swedish saffron buns. The buns were served with the mandatory watery coffee in the usual pale green plastic mugs but without saffron, which was no longer available. The bakers used food coloring to make the buns look authentic, with soft, delicious raisins.

Some women in Zone 2 organized an impromptu Lucia procession, using white sheets and candles as their only props. They couldn't recruit any singing star boys because the potential participants backed out, saying they looked like the Ku Klux Klan in their white sheets and rolled paper cones on their heads. Without gold stars on the dunce caps, they claimed they weren't real star boys anyway and deserted the effort with gloomy determination.

The soothing, highly appreciated singing of the sweet female voices was balm for the listeners' tormented souls, and they savored every second. But reality soon intruded as the singing faded away, with Lucia and her attendants slowly and heavily treading through the corridors to bring joy to the others in the next meeting room.

Alfred Baksi was the first to stand up and turn on the fluorescent lights when the Lucia procession was over, bathing the underground room in cold, harsh industrial lighting. Cozy lighting wasn't a feature when Zone 1 and Zone 2 were built.

"As we assumed, the Russian bombings of Berga and Karlskrona were just the beginning. Now we see they are indeed targeting the enemy Putin declared war on, and it wasn't Sweden, but the *Alzuwid* Caliphate," Baksi began.

"Putin is a well-known Islamophobe, and he doesn't want them as neighbors in Northern Europe," said SÄPO chief Bianca Popovic. "He actually called us his Swedish friends again, which might mean something."

"With friends like Putin, who needs enemies? The bombings of our naval bases must be seen in the context of the occupation of Öland and the operations they have now started on the mainland. The Russians have apparently decided to take full control of the Baltic Sea once and for all," said Army Chief Brännström. "And let me remind you, they haven't wasted a single gram of gunpowder on the Muslims yet, but tons on us!"

"This is a far greater disaster than the so-called 'Horsfjärd Disaster' at the island of Märsgarn in 1941," said Navy Chief Fred Bergström, the most educated military historian. "Back then, we lost three smaller ships, but now both Berga and Karlskrona are out of use. This event will probably go down in history as the Naval Base Disaster."

"Yes, but now it's about much more than just a few naval bases," interrupted Gyllenstierna irritably.

The others noted with some concern that Gyllenstierna showed signs of exhaustion and imbalance for the first time. The always positive and polished Supreme Commander was, after all, made of flesh and blood.

"Now it's about the survival of the Swedish nation," Gyllenstierna continued in a high-pitched voice. "The Naval Base Disaster will be a mere footnote when the history of the Swedish War is written. The Russians are landing troops on a large scale along the entire east coast south of Stockholm: in Oxelösund, Valdemarsvik, Västervik, Kalmar, Karlshamn, and Ystad. They are so confident they are even using regular passenger ferries, at least the ferry from Klaipeda," Baksi continued. "Considering that Iosif Vissarionovich, their despicable ambassador to Sweden, assured us that Stockholm, Gothenburg, Malmö, and Luleå would be nuked if we so much as come near their ships, they have every reason to be confident."

"Unfortunately, yes," agreed MUST chief Bertil Wiklund. "One can never know if such a threat is sanctioned by Putin or if Vissarionovich is just spouting off, but I wouldn't recommend taking the risk. They seem to have gone completely mad since Palmquist sank their warfare ships. So, it's probably best to leave them alone, even if it's tempting. For safety's sake, they've given us exact routes and times, so we can't claim we sank something thinking it was someone else."

"Let's hope we have full control over our naval units' activities," said Air Force Chief Wennergren, looking at Bergström. "And that no one decides to act on their own. We don't need a new naval hero right now."

"I think we have this under control," said Bergström. "Unlike the situation on land," he continued, glancing at Brännström. "But I assume the Russians are aware of the confusion and that there are independent fighting units we can't control no matter how much we'd like to."

"Vissarionovich didn't mention our land operations at all. Perhaps they see the resistance as harmless," Baksi said. "There have been attempts to defend the ports in smaller coastal towns like Oxelösund, Västervik, on the east coast, and Ystad in Skåne, but in each case, the defense was easily swept away by their attack helicopters. Their new fifth-generation Mi-28N Nighthunter is not to be trifled with!"

"No, it's a lost cause for ground forces without air defense. A few helicopters can sweep away ground resistance as easily as swatting a fly. The Nighthunter's firepower is greater than the combined firepower of an entire infantry company," Wennergren observed. "And it's virtually impossible to take down a Nighthunter with machine guns; they're too well-armored."

"A hit with an anti-tank weapon would do it," said Brännström, "but the helicopters move too fast and fly too high for us to hit them. We might get a lucky shot, even though they have effective countermeasures. But they seem to have endless numbers of helicopters, so it doesn't change anything."

"Completely logical," said Wiklund. "I remember when they made a defense decision about a thousand new helicopters around 2014, and these are the ones we see now. According to our intelligence, the final delivery of the thousand helicopters was completed just last year. Meanwhile, Sweden's defense force was working on an order for eighteen Helikopter 14s, if you remember those endless delivery problems, which says a lot about the imbalance between our military forces. We are simply facing an overwhelming enemy that we might have been able to thwart if our air force were intact."

"Our air force is so strong that we barely need air defense, at least that's what we thought back then," said Baksi.

"We should never have bought that Patriot junk when there were much better European alternatives, with full 360-degree coverage at half the price," Gyllenstierna noted. "But the government made the decision, overruling the defense force, to ensure US support in the event of a crisis. We'll see what that's worth now that we've sunk their submarine," said Gyllenstierna as he stood up to introduce the day's guest speaker, who had been shown into the room by Baksi's adjutant.

"Welcome, Katerina Kutepova-Andersson, Sweden's and perhaps the world's most prominent analyst of Russian geopolitics and a distinguished Kremlinologist. I believe you all know her from courses and war games at Karlberg, or at least you know of her through the media. Katerina predicted the events in Ukraine in detail years before they happened, which is impressive. Katerina has war in her blood," said Gyllenstierna. "Her grandfather was the chief of staff during the Battle of Kursk in 1943 and was awarded the highest honor, Hero of the Soviet Union."

"Wow! Kursk is the largest tank battle in history," said military historian Bergström. "That's where Adolf was defeated, and many military historians now consider Kursk a more important turning point than Stalingrad. It was the first time the Germans deployed their fantastic Tiger tanks. No weapon in history has ever been so far ahead of its time, but there were too few of them, and when they were swarmed by thousands of Soviet T-34s, which were much smaller and primitive..."

"Thank you, Fred, but perhaps another time. Not only that," Gyllenstierna continued, "Katerina's grandmother was one of the 'Night Witches'. Some of you might remember them from the military history course at Karlberg Military Academy."

"The 588th Night Bomber Regiment," Bergström exclaimed in fascination. "I think I'm going to faint! Those female pilots..."

Bergström fell silent when Gyllenstierna gave him a sharp look and gestured invitingly toward the guest speaker.

"Yes, as you can imagine, my house is full of medals and orders from my heroic ancestors who fought for the Soviet Union and ultimately defeated the Germans," began Kutepova-Andersson. "I just don't know what to do with them. When I realized how low my pension would be here in Sweden, I started considering selling them on the Alibaba web shop. There are plenty of wealthy Chinese collectors who pay well!"

Although it had been thirty years since Katerina Kutepova-Andersson left her hometown of Voronezh in southern Russia, her accent was still so strong that some participants had difficulty not smirking at the lecturer.

"Now the whole world thinks the Russians are launching an attack on the Muslims in the *Alzuwid* Caliphate to save Sweden and drive the Muslims out of Scandinavia. But I am sorry... very, very sorry for Sweden. It is Sweden that is the target. Not all of Sweden, because Moscow doesn't care about the northern part. It's all about controlling the connection between the Baltic Sea and the Atlantic, a Russian dream since the time of Peter the Great. The Russian elite troops—those you know as Spetsnaz and VDV units, who have landed—will quickly advance westward to the current ceasefire line between the Swedes and the Muslims, which roughly follows the European Highway 4, but they will stop there."

Kutepova-Andersson paused momentarily, gazing over the reverently listening audience to see if anyone had any objections before continuing.

"It's not that Vladimir Putin doubts they could easily defeat the Muslims, which anyone can figure out without the slightest knowledge of military capacity. Even though the Muslims are being reinforced via the ports in Gothenburg, it doesn't fundamentally change anything. But Putin is a cunning devil who knows peace comes after war. The world would never accept a total Russian occupation of Sweden. Both the Chinese, Americans, and Indians would strongly oppose it, causing Russia significant political and economic costs and perhaps even risking military intervention from at least the US or China. By the way, the Chinese have already sent a small fleet, including an aircraft carrier, towards the Baltic Sea, but you probably already know that?"

"Yes, we've received intelligence on this from our American friends," said MUSTs Chief, Wiklund.

"We'll soon see what your American friends are worth," Kutepova-Andersson replied. "It might have been better to have Russian friends," she continued with a cryptic smile.

Kutepova-Andersson took a small sip of her cold coffee and prepared to continue.

"Russia doesn't want to stand alone and isolated against a front of the world's three superpowers. Putin wants to gain control over the connection to the Atlantic at the lowest political, military, and economic cost possible. He achieves all this without spilling military resources by allowing the Muslims to remain in an occupied Swedish area. This justifies a long-term Russian presence in Sweden to ensure balance and ceasefire. By letting the Muslims stay, the Russians achieve exactly what they want at the lowest price. It's highly likely that the Russians have already informed Ahmed Ben Barka and his team of their plans, and the Muslims are not foolish enough to initiate hostilities against Russia. One thing I can't say for certain is how the Russians view western Skåne, which is strategically important for controlling the Öresund and is part of the Muslim-occupied zone. Now, let's move on to questions and discussions."

The silence in the room was profound as the audience pondered what had been said. This was not what the conference participants had expected. What more was there to discuss when the game was already lost? The word "capitulation" began to cross the minds of the listeners for the first time, but the mood lifted slightly when Kutepova-Andersson continued:

"Perhaps I should have said that Moscow definitely wants to maintain a Swedish state in the region. I wouldn't be surprised if the Russians liberate Stockholm for you, as Moscow has no interest in your capital now that they control the major islands in the Baltic Sea. If I were to give any advice, I would initiate direct negotiations with Moscow and appeal for help to liberate Stockholm. Having Russian troops liberate Stockholm gives Putin the credibility he needs and something impressive to show both at home and on the international stage while masking Russia's true intentions. But promise me one thing first: shut down that ridiculous so-called exile government in Helsinki, which Putin constantly uses to create confusion and uncertainty on the international stage. That Margot Wallfors must be eliminated as soon as possible!"

Chapter 47

Operation Ayatollah

December 22, 2032

It was the winter solstice on December 22, 2032, the shortest day of the year.

"It looks really good," said Ina Sjöstrand. "Light westerly wind, one to two miles per hour. I'll jump from two thousand feet. Then, it's easy to glide down to the roof. Today's the day!"

"It certainly looks like the weather gods are with us today," noted Filip. "What do you think, Max?"

"Every day is good for me, as long as it's dark—and it will be. And it won't be too rough on the sea. We're good to go!"

"Everything is set to proceed. The Cessna will take off at 7:15 p.m.," said Uno, "once we get the signal that the meeting has started. Unless they cancel the meeting, all signs point to it happening as planned at 6 p.m. Our infiltrator reported that their Master Chef Hassan is preparing an elaborate dinner for fifteen people, which those gluttons surely won't want to miss. The number of place settings suggests a larger meeting than usual—so much the better!"

"Let's make sure it's their last dinner on this earth," said Filip. "They'll be thrilled to meet all those virgins waiting for them in paradise!"

"We'll leave Smådalarö with the RIB boat at 3 p.m.," said Max, checking his watch. "It's tempting to take the shortcut through the strait of Skurusundet, but that would be to defy fate considering how narrow it is. Instead, we'll take the long way around the whole island of Värmdön and stay in the main shipping lane towards the city. The electric motors are virtually silent, and any sound is drowned out by the wind and waves. The boat is low, only three feet above the water, so they won't see us on radar, which I doubt they even have. My very own stealth variant," he chuckled contentedly. "Then we'll anchor the support boat in the bay of Waldemarsviken between Beckholmen and Waldemars Udde. Stockholm is completely dark. No one will see us in the darkness. The boat, the engine, and all the equipment are painted black, and winter fog will be on the water since it's below freezing. We'll be dressed in black with black hats and blackened faces. Visibility is minimal. Someone would have to shine a light directly on us to spot us. And if they do, they might not react to an apparently empty little rubber boat anchored there. If they do, we'll abort and head to Vaxholm, where our regular troops will probably offer us a cup of coffee," Max continued with a smile. "Then we'll try again another day with a modified plan. Because this is an incredibly good plan that must be executed!"

"I won't jump until I get the signal that you're in place with the underwater sled," said Ina, looking at Max. "Otherwise, I have no escape route. That plan B through the secret medieval tunnels is risky, but better than nothing. If something goes wrong, at least I'll get a chance to visit a museum."

As the Cessna approached the bay of Riddarfjärden in central Stockholm, they could see explosions flare up in the city. The troops in neighboring Stocksund complied with the order to fire some grenades for exactly five minutes, effectively masking the hum of the electric Cessna's propeller if anyone noticed it.

Soon, they saw the flames from the occupiers' mortar fire as they routinely returned fire. By the time the grenade exchange ceased, the Cessna would return to the base at the defunct military airfield in Tullinge, which once housed the flight regiment F18.

At 6:32 p.m., the pilot nodded at Ina and gave a thumbs-up.

"Max is in position. So are we. Good luck!"

"Thanks. See you tomorrow," Ina replied, jumping into the darkness and immediately pulling the parachute's ripcord.

The grenade explosions fell silent, and she could only hear the wind she generated with the parachute. Everything was dark in Old Town and the city center, but a few lights were on in parts of Södermalm and Östermalm in the otherwise completely blacked-out capital.

Thanks to her night vision goggles, she could clearly see the roof of the Royal Palace, where she would soon land.

On the way down, she focused as best she could on the quay at Logårdstrappan, where Max was waiting underwater, but she saw no sign of Max, which she didn't expect anyway.

She noticed that entrepreneurial tycoon Jan Stenbeck's traditional Christmas tree, which usually was erected on the quay of Skeppsbrokajen near Max, was conspicuously absent. The tree had been there every Christmas since she was a child, and its absence felt like a deeply personal loss.

The landing went smoothly, and she looked around while routinely folding the parachute to prevent it from blowing away—no signs of detection. Thanks to the high-altitude drone photos, she knew no guards were on the roof—a sign of overconfidence. They felt secure in the castle's basement, far from the front lines and protected from bomb attacks under layers of thick stone vaults. Had Ina been responsible for the Muslim command's security, there would have been scouts with night vision goggles and snipers on the roof around the clock. She knew better than anyone that what everyone believed to be impossible was indeed possible under the right circumstances—like tonight.

She carefully peeked over the edge of the roof into the inner courtyard and noted the glow of cigarettes from two groups of guards standing diagonally opposite each other in two of the corners. She could hear their low conversations in Arabic, amplified by the acoustics of the enclosed courtyard. One of them seemed to be telling a funny story, as the others watched him and chuckled.

When she looked over the edge towards the areas of Logården and Skeppsbron, she discovered she was directly above a group of eight soldiers shivering by the wall. There was quite a bit of ground-level security. Lucky for me, I'll be escaping through the secret tunnel beneath them, she thought.

As expected, the hatch was unlocked since it had no lock, and she quickly found herself in the narrow spiral staircase that led down to the basement vaults, connecting to the secret underground passages that had existed since the Middle Ages and the previous royal castle named Three Crowns.

It was unlikely the occupiers had bothered to explore the castle's hidden secrets. Perhaps they didn't even know that all castles had secret escape routes and hidden rooms. The spiral staircase hadn't been used for a long time, as she could tell from the thick dust that showed her footprints. Thanks to that amusing history professor from the National Heritage Board, they could explore the castle in detail on the screen. Every nook and cranny had been filmed with a 360-degree camera and stored in 3D format, allowing Ina to practice both the attack and the escape countless times with VR goggles. Everything was like in the VR environment, except everything had a greenish tint through her night vision goggles. If lost, she could use the handheld device to navigate using the 3D images. She felt completely calm, even exhilarated, like a ten-year-old exploring an attic for a secret club meeting.

At the end of the spiral staircase, she found herself in an underground vault with two simple wooden doors that looked very old. She noted the oversized hinges were hand forged. Behind the right door, she knew, was the long passage that now ended inside the Medieval Museum on the little islet of Helgeandsholmen.

Generations of beautiful girls have passed through here for nearly a millennium, she thought with a smile, recalling the history professor's colorful stories about the kings' private lives. And many handsome boys, too, especially during Gustav V's time, the professor had noted. Gustav V was the great-great-grandfather of the current King Carl Philip, popularly known as 'V-Gurra', often portrayed with his tennis racket. Besides being a tennis player, he was homosexual, which led many to suspect that the uninterrupted Bernadotte lineage might have had a break, Ina had recently learned from the professor.

Soon, she would open the door to the Helgeand Passage, take a left after two hundred feet, and follow the corridor behind the large wall mirror in the Treasury. The cleverly mounted mirror, reaching the floor, could be slid aside with minimal effort. Behind the mirror, tonight's targets were currently at a conference. They were about to have a surprise that would make them choke on their Arabic delicacies before being sent to hell, Ina thought. But first, she would ensure that the passage under Skeppsbron, leading to Logårdstrappan where Max waited, was intact and that the hatch at the end could be opened. She carefully opened the door, and the whole world exploded into a chaotic inferno. It took several seconds before she understood what was happening.

The beast came out of nowhere, galloping with a deep, lion-like growl. Before Ina could even register what was happening, she was on her back with the frenzied, muscular Rottweiler on top of her. The beast's 140 pounds against Ina's ninety-five was an uneven fight. The dog's head was nearly twice the size of Ina's, and its powerful jaws bit and tore violently at her left forearm, which she desperately tried to shield herself with. She instinctively knew the dog intended to kill her, and she briefly thought what a sad way this was to end her days. Somewhere, she had read that Muslims never had dogs, but apparently, not everything you read is true.

With her free hand, she managed with great effort to reach the knife she always carried behind her right calf. The beast was tearing at her left arm so fiercely it felt like it could detach from her body at any moment. She swung the knife with all her might towards the dog's neck in a stroke that would have slashed open any human throat, but the beast's thick fur and powerful neck muscles meant the razor-sharp knife only caused superficial wounds.

The knife strike made the dog flinch, still holding Ina's arm in its jaws, and Ina was thrown three feet into the air, landing on her knees thanks to her agility and natural coordination. Desperately, she buried the knife repeatedly into the dog's neck until it finally let go, roaring like a bull in heat, then gurgling like a clogged drain as blood spurted everywhere. Ina stayed on her knees until the dog, after a few seconds, lay on its side as the gurgling gradually subsided.

Ina was in shock and remained kneeling, expressionless, while her heart pounded like a hammer. Slowly, she regained her senses and looked, still wearing her night vision goggles, at her left arm, which was so battered it would never be the same. The jacket's strong and tough, lightly armored nylon fabric had protected her, so the bleeding was limited to where the dog's four fangs had pierced the fabric. The skeletal damage was worse. Her forearm was broken in two places, and it would later be found that the bones had severe crush injuries caused by the immense pressure of the dog's jaws. Ina was so pumped with adrenaline that she felt no pain, but she knew it would soon come, and it would be unbearable. She pulled out her specially prepared pill case and swallowed two pills. It was the first time she found a use for it.

Only now did she consider whether any guards had reacted and were coming to shoot or capture her, and in her current state, she was not in a condition to fight. But it was as silent as a tomb. The dog's last breaths had ceased, and the only sounds she could hear were her own breathing and the powerful heartbeat that began to slow both in strength and frequency.

She slowly stood up and looked at her left arm, which dangled helplessly. It was time to abort and try to escape through the tunnel to Max and the waiting underwater sled. No matter how much she wanted to, she couldn't complete her mission with only one functioning arm and a fracture in her right shoulder that made it nearly impossible to move her right arm either. It was over. All that work and planning for nothing.

After a few minutes, she reached the steel hatch, which was, as expected, locked from the inside with a robust locking mechanism like those on bomb shelter doors. With her somewhat functional right hand, she turned the long handle counterclockwise, carefully opened the hatch, and crawled out into the darkness on the quay. Max's head immediately popped up from the water, followed by his upper body. He handed her the harness to secure her to the sled while he used his other hand to offer her the oxygen mouthpiece.

The quay was completely deserted, and they could whisper quietly. Max secured Ina to the sled and fastened the oxygen mouthpiece an inch before her mouth. All she had to do was tilt her head forward and grasp the mouthpiece with her teeth and lips.

"I'll go in instead," Max whispered. "I know the way as well as you do. Just wait here."

Once inside the tunnel, he turned on his headlamp. There was no need for night vision goggles, and he felt more comfortable with regular light. Everything looked exactly as it did in the VR environment, so he continued as he had during the training exercises.

After half a minute, he reached where Ina had fought the enormous Rottweiler. He paused for a moment, stunned by the beast's incredible size. The floor was covered in blood, but thankfully not Ina's. My God, what a monster. How did she survive this? he thought in amazement before continuing through the door and into the Passage to Helgeand's Islet.

After two hundred feet, he took the door to the left, just like during VR training. Now, he just needed to take the first door on the right and follow the passage to the wall mirror in the meticulously cleared Royal Treasury. As he approached the back of the mirror, he could clearly hear the conversation inside the Treasury. It seemed like someone was giving a presentation to the others, who only interjected with approving and affirming words. The aroma of the sumptuous Arabic feast served in the Treasury was tantalizing. He suddenly realized how hungry he was but knew he wouldn't be welcome to join their meal.

Max gripped the handle with his left hand, as he needed his right hand free to quickly lob in the two M60/B fragmentation grenades, each containing one pound of pressed TNT—more than twice as much as the army's standard M56/B model. He had exactly five seconds once he threw them, longer than typical grenades.

He took a deep breath. Would the mirror slide smoothly to the left as it had during VR training? He dared not pull the safety pin from the grenade until he knew the mirror would open. If the mirror jammed, Plan B was to shoot out the wooden panel holding the mirror with the mini carbine slung around his neck, then kick in the remaining wood splinters with a single heavy kick and throw the grenades through the hole.

He took another deep breath as he heard cheerful laughter on the other side of the mirror. The heavy and solid mirror slid surprisingly easily to the side, considering the small rail was over three hundred years old. Fine old craftsmanship, he thought as he pulled the pin from the first grenade with his teeth and lobbed it into the room to the right with a backhand throw. In the same motion, he pulled the pin from the second grenade and threw it to the left before sprinting back down the corridor.

Max barely made it around the corner and threw himself to the floor, covering his ears, when both grenades exploded in a single powerful blast, amplified by the stone vaults enclosing the room. Even though Max was pressed to the floor a hundred feet away from the Treasury and behind a massive stone wall, the shockwave almost knocked him unconscious as it hit his body like a giant fist, making him feel as if he were being torn apart and propelling him six feet forward. For nearly ten seconds, Max lay stunned on the stone floor, wondering if he had survived or was seriously injured. But soon, he was on his feet, and less than a minute later, he was on the underwater sled, gliding away beneath the surface.

Max had been so completely focused on handling the grenades that he hadn't even glanced at the group sitting around the long table. Still, out of the corner of his eye, he had seen chaos erupt as the conference participants tried to stand up, many shouting in Arabic, likely warnings or calls to take cover. The enclosed shockwave from the two grenades in such a small space was enough to kill everyone in the room, and the doorway was naturally blocked as everyone tried to rush out at once. However, it couldn't be ruled out that one or at most two people escaped to the other side of the thick stone wall. He hoped they were not Ahmed, Mahmoud, or the Syrian Colonel Mohamed, their most feared adversaries.

Now, there was just a relatively comfortable twenty-mile journey at twenty miles per hour, submerged a few feet below the water's surface, to the support boat in Waldemarsviken. Navigation and throttle control were fully automatic, so he only needed to hold on to the sled and breathe through the mouthpiece. If a boat keel unexpectedly appeared in their path, the system ensured the sled made an elegant turn to the most suitable side.

When they surfaced, Max saw Ina looking at him questioningly, and he responded with a thumbs-up, which made her light up and almost laugh.

"Ina is injured. Lift her carefully, but do not touch her arms. Lift her by the harness!"

The RIB boat sped off, and at a relatively calm forty knots, they set course for Vaxholm, where the army's medics would have something to keep them busy on the longest night of the year.

Mission accomplished.

Chapter 48

The liberation of Stockholm

December 24, 2032

Katerina Kutepova-Andersson's analysis of the Russians' long-term strategic plan for the Baltic region was correct. The Russian elite troops quickly advanced to the Muslims' lines, stretching from Jönköping at the southern tip of Lake Vättern down to Ystad, but they chose not to engage in combat with them, halting instead at the boundary line.

Kutepova-Andersson was also right about Stockholm. Before the Swedish defense staff even requested Russian help to liberate the capital, the Russian ambassador to Sweden, Iosif Vissarionovich, contacted them.

The Russians' offer was non-negotiable. The liberation of Stockholm would be carried out solely by Russian troops without Swedish involvement to avoid complicated and demanding coordination and the risk of Russian and Swedish units ending up in conflict. Vissarionovich also asserted, with ill-concealed schadenfreude, that the Swedes lacked adequate armament and would mostly be in the way and a nuisance to the Russian elite forces. The Russians estimated it would take a maximum of three days to gain full control of Stockholm, after which the city would be handed over to the Swedes, who would then march in as the Russians marched out. Did the Swedes want to liberate their capital? Vissarionovich gave Gyllenstierna twenty-four hours to respond with a decision, emphasizing that this was the only chance they would get.

The liberation of Stockholm began on Christmas Eve morning at 9 a.m., with a column of Russian armored vehicles advancing toward Stockholm from the north along the European Highway, starting from the Swedish positions in Rotebro. A handful of Russian helicopters hovered over the city and its suburbs, but no shots were fired. The Swedish observers were surprised by the small resources the confident Russians used. No more than about five hundred Russian soldiers were involved in the operation.

The column of armored vehicles moved slowly forward without being fired upon. They didn't seem in a hurry, occasionally taking breaks for an hour or so while the Muslim forces withdrew. On Christmas Day, the Swedes could see from their high-altitude drones how the column of armored vehicles reached the old northern customs station of Stockholm, Norrtull, and slowly wound its way via the long avenue Sveavägen into the city center. In contrast, smaller parts of the column took the streets of Valhallavägen and Sankt Eriksgatan.

On Boxing Day, the Muslim troops embarked on the big cruise ships Silja Serenade and Silja Esplanade at the harbor of Värtahamnen. The ferries set sail for Gothenburg and were filled with elite soldiers, *Holy Warriors*, and vehicles. From Stadsgårdskajen, the cruise ships Viking Cinderella and Viking Grace also set sail for Gothenburg.

From their positions on Tynningö, Rindö, and Värmdö, the Swedes watched as the four giant ferries left Stockholm. Sinking the ferries would have been easy at any point in the channel, especially in the narrow strait called Oxdjupet between Rindö and Värmdö. Still, the Swedes strictly observed the ceasefire agreement with the Russians.

On Monday morning, December 27, the Swedes received clearance from Ambassador Vissarionovich to enter Stockholm without reservations. Sweden's capital was liberated after 159 days of occupation. Sweden, or at least what remained of the old—and since 1660, continually shrinking—the Kingdom of Sweden, seemed to have a future as a free and independent nation once more.

The hostilities had subsided and finally ceased on all fronts without a formal ceasefire agreement. The sporadic skirmishes were more like involuntary clashes but quickly resolved.

Putin's propaganda machine went into overdrive, letting the world know that the noble Russians had rescued the Swedes and liberated their capital from the Muslim occupiers. Following the successful liberation of Stockholm, Ambassador Vissarionovich contacted the Swedish defense leadership. Apparently, the Russians no longer saw any use for the exiled government in Sveaborg. The ambassador then presented a surprising but appealing proposal: Russia would return about ninety-five percent of its occupied zone if the Swedes signed a peace agreement guaranteeing the Russians the remaining five percent as thanks for liberating Stockholm.

"We have no interest in Swedish territory per se," said Vissarionovich, "and we want Sweden as a stabilizing factor in the Nordic region. We only need the islands in the Baltic Sea and a narrow strip of the Swedish Baltic coast from Karlskrona down to Ystad to secure our legitimate security interests in the region. Plus, a small enclave in southern Halland adjacent to the Skåne border, covering seventy-seven square miles, where we will build a combined naval, air, and missile base. This area is sparsely populated and represents only 3.7 percent of Halland's area. The Swedish population must leave the Russian areas to make way for patriotic Russians who will move in."

Vissarionovich sweetened the deal by promising massive Russian support whenever the Swedes felt ready to attack and reclaim the Muslim-occupied zone, making the defense leadership dream of a bright future despite everything. The ambassador explained that Russia would never, under any circumstances, recognize a Muslim state in the Nordic region and that Russia saw Sweden as a future ally.

"We can offer one-way tickets to Siberia if Sweden wants to finance the deportation of the Muslims," Ambassador Vissarionovich concluded with a booming laugh.

The Swedish exile government in Helsinki, through Prime Minister Margot Wallfors, expressed its gratitude to the Russian leadership for liberating Stockholm, emphasizing the importance of maintaining good bilateral relations between Sweden and Russia.

Shortly thereafter, Margot Wallfors was surprised by an unknown assailant who encountered her and her companion Annika Strandberg during their daily walk for afternoon coffee at Café Valimo and shot them both dead on the bridge between Vargön and Sveaborg. The assailant calmly jogged the five hundred feet to his boat, which he had moored earlier that morning below Café Valimo, and left the island without leaving any other traces, except for a dozen shell casings left on the bridge.

It was never determined who the perpetrator was or on whose orders he acted. There were two witnesses in the form of an elderly Finnish-Swedish couple who had previously lived in Sweden and claimed to have spoken Swedish with a mysterious person speaking unmistakable Gotlandic earlier that morning. But at Café Valimo, the cashier claimed to have served a person speaking Russian at lunchtime, who had asked about the Swedish exile government, and she unsuspectingly told him that Wallfors and Strandberg were daily guests who could be expected at any time. The cashier was certain this Russian must have been the assailant since there were no tourists at that time of year. Other rumors spoke of a short and slender man, observed by several people, who spoke on the radio in Arabic with his face hidden under the hood of his jacket.

The Finnish security police concluded that the two Swedish women were murdered by a professionally managed organization that planted numerous false witness statements to complicate the investigation, which proved to be a successful strategy, as all the testimonies were deemed highly credible. The only thing that could be established with one hundred percent certainty was that the two women had indeed been shot dead on the bridge between Vargön and Sveaborg and that the unknown assailant had escaped.

Chapter 49

New Year's Eve at the Defense Headquarters

December 31, 2032

Alfred Baksi swept the pointer across the seventy-five-year-old map of Sweden that had been pulled down from the ceiling.

"The UN mediation commission proposes a ceasefire, freezing the situation in three zones. In practice, a ceasefire has existed since Stockholm was liberated. No fights between the Russians and Muslims have occurred, supporting Katerina Kutepova-Andersson's theory that the Russians assured the Muslims they wouldn't attack them in exchange for leaving Stockholm without a fight. The Swedish zone includes all territory north of the Göta Canal," Baksi said, sweeping the pointer from Söderköping to Motala. "This means that all Russian troops north of the canal will evacuate, which the Russians themselves suggested. We tried to extend the zone to Linköping, but the Russians were adamant. They apparently want to ensure we can't rebuild our air force. But eighty percent of our weapons factories are fortunately in the Swedish zone. They said we would return all the landscape of Östergötland in the future, within five to ten years. I think they want to ensure our capability as builders of combat aircraft is definitely obsolete before they leave Linköping. They really have no use for the rest of Östergötland, so I think we can get back the entire province, adding a couple hundred thousand more residents."

"I don't think we'll ever be able to build combat aircraft again," said Air Force Chief Wennergren sadly. "We'll have to buy on the world market like all other small nations."

Baksi responded with a barely audible sigh, "Yes, that's probably true, but the Air Force can still be strong," he concluded before continuing his presentation.

"Between the lakes Vättern and Vänern, the Göta Canal also applies. This means Zone 1 falls on our side, which wasn't the case in the original proposal. We can commend ourselves for our good negotiation tactics here. West of Vänern, the European Highway 18 becomes the ceasefire line, which matches the current situation well. Minor movements of both Swedish and Muslim forces will be required. Looking further south, the European Highway 4 from Jönköping west to Östra Ljungby serves as the ceasefire line between the Russian and Muslim occupation zones. From Östra Ljungby, it's Highway 13 all the way down to Ystad, which falls in the Russian zone."

The twenty conference participants tried to understand the mediation commission's proposal, and there were many questions.

"How long-term is this division? What will it look like after a future peace agreement?" These were the questions most of the audience had.

Gyllenstierna summarized the situation to answer the questions before they were asked.

"I feel optimistic that Sweden has a future as an independent nation, albeit in a smaller form. The liberation of Stockholm was necessary to even talk about a remaining Sweden. It doesn't feel like we should thank the Russians for anything, but we can acknowledge that it's thanks to the Russians that the fighting has stopped. The long-term outcome is hard to predict, but we can assume that peace negotiations concerning Western Europe will eventually happen. What we have achieved is probably the best possible in the current situation. We stop the killing and destruction and can start rebuilding what's left of Sweden, which is relatively intact in infrastructure and industry, with Stockholm and Luleå-Boden being the major exceptions. There aren't many undamaged buildings in Stockholm, north of Slussen, excluding Östermalm and the northern suburbs."

Gyllenstierna poured a glass of water from the pitcher on the table and turned to Björn Väster. "Björn, as our energy expert, could you say a few words about the situation?"

"Of course," Väster replied, standing up. "Even though it's been a while since I was the energy minister."

"A major long-term problem is the power supply," Väster began. "It will take at least a decade to rebuild the fifteen power plants in the Lule Rivers. However, new gas and coal-fired power plants can be built in a few months with international help. China has promised to build ten coal power plants in less than three months, entirely for free, in exchange for concessions to operate our six largest ports for ninety-nine years. The Swedish people are freezing and cooking on open fires, and I think we must take the Chinese offer. A high-priority task is to rebuild the hundreds of switchgears that have been destroyed."

"One could argue that the Civil Contingencies Agency should have protected the switchgears instead of engaging in unconstitutional censorship and persecution of patriots on Facebook," Baksi interjected. "Switchgears powering entire cities are protected only by six-feet-high fences without roofs. Not even barbed wire. If you know what you're doing, it takes just a grenade, a Molotov cocktail, or even a wrench."

"That's true, and it's actually even easier than that," replied Väster. "A few bursts from an automatic weapon can shatter the insulators into a thousand pieces. Now, it takes months to get spare parts because no one expects so many switchgears to fail in such a short time. The nuclear power plants in Forsmark can probably be restarted, but that will take even longer."

"Energy supply is probably our biggest concern," Gyllenstierna noted. "We need to appoint a special group or council to focus solely on that. It's important to get a clearer picture of the new Sweden, which our newly formed 'Future Council' knows much more about. So, I'll hand it over to Lilian Ceder from the Ministry of Industry, who will lead the future councils' work."

Lilian Ceder stood by the old flip chart, took a thick black marker, and quickly sketched a map of Sweden divided into three zones.

"As you understand, we've just begun our work and have only started the analysis in broad strokes. But we have fifteen ambitious employees working around the clock, so we should be able to give a good picture of the remaining Sweden within one to two weeks."

She pointed with the marker to the Swedish zone.

"The remaining Sweden is certainly truncated but still significant. Our new Sweden consists mainly of all Svealand and Norrland, as well as the northern parts of Östergötland and Västergötland. The population before the war was 6.24 million in this area. We don't know how many were killed within the new Sweden, but we estimate the number at just under half a million, leaving a remaining population of 5.8 million. Broadly speaking, the new Sweden is comparable to one of our neighboring countries, Finland. We have a larger GDP, population, and area than Finland. Like Finland, we have large forestry and high-class engineering industries and excel in IT, particularly the Internet industry. The new Sweden remains the largest in the Nordic region in all respects, but one could say that the Nordic region now consists of four equal countries—plus the occupation zones, of course."

Ceder paused dramatically and tapped the back of the marker a few times on the flip chart to emphasize that she was about to say something very important before she continued speaking.

"One very difficult question remains, and we must address it now. The major challenge is, for natural reasons, the composition of the population. Let's not shy away from calling things by their proper names—a shovel is always a shovel—what are we going to do with the 1.2 million Muslims who survived the war and now inhabit the new Sweden? They make up about twenty-two percent of the population, and considering what has happened, it will be hard to see how we can create peace and stability between Swedes and Muslims. I'd like to hear how Sweden's leadership—those of you in this room—feels about the matter."

Brännström was the first to speak, with a little speech, as always, honest and straight from the heart.

"I consider it impossible for Sweden to host a Muslim population. The fourteen-hundred-year history of Islam clearly shows that wherever there are Muslims, sooner or later, there's war. It always ends with Muslims conspiring and eventually trying to seize power by force. Surely, we've learned something from the horrific war we just went through."

"I agree with Brännström," said Bianca Popovic. "We in SÄPO advise against any Muslim presence. We know far too much about them to recommend anything else for the future. The saying goes, 'A country is built on law,' and Muslims only follow their own laws, making any cooperation impossible."

"Islam is incompatible with any other ideology," Wennergren said. "It's us or them."

"Deportation of the entire Muslim group, absolutely," said Bergström. "All mosques on Swedish territory have already been blown up—with great pleasure—and they damn well shouldn't be rebuilt! We've had enough of hate preachers and secret Muslim weapon caches."

"Kick them all out!" said Wiklund. "Just get them out! I don't care how it's done, just if they disappear from our country forever. It must be a final solution!"

Gyllenstierna raised a hand to halt Wiklund.

"The issue isn't quite that clear-cut," Gyllenstierna said. "People like Baksi and myself might be considered Muslims in many eyes, but we're more blue-and-yellow and more Swedish nationalists than the Swedes themselves. Should we be thrown out, too?"

"No, of course not," came the murmurs around the table. "That's not what we mean. We want all good Swedes to stay."

Lilian Ceder stood up and returned to the flip chart.

"I wanted this spontaneous discussion here to highlight the issue's complexity. Our future council has naturally already started working on the matter, which we've come up with so far: Our fundamental premise is that Sweden should be a multiethnic society based on Western values rooted in Christian foundations and our Nordic cultural heritage. Sweden should be a Western society where citizens have the right to express themselves freely, form opinions, political parties, and all that we've been accustomed to, but with a clear—and very important exception: Islam must be criminalized and labeled as terrorism, which means banning all forms of practicing Islam, banning mosques and all forms of Muslim associations, possession of the Quran—in essence, banning all Islamic symbols and attributes. Traditional Muslim clothing, veils, and so on are, of course, prohibited. From my discussions with everyone, I interpret that there is consensus on what I just said?"

Brännström took the initiative again.

"Yes, there is undoubtedly full consensus. The question boils down to what we should do with the estimated seven to eight hundred thousand Muslims who are hostile to Sweden within the new Sweden's borders?"

"Yes, it does," Ceder replied, "but it's important to note that not all Muslims are hostile to Sweden. Many are too afraid to deviate from the group, as it's a death sentence. With adequate protection, we have many friends among them. The future council proposes that Muslims who sign a conditional contract with the Swedish state, agreeing to cease all practice of Islam, should be allowed to stay and integrate into society. The contract is lifelong, and those who break it, for example, by wearing traditional Muslim clothing or dealing in halal products, will immediately lose their citizenship and be deported for life. Special courts will be established in every municipality, with experts on the regulations. For simplicity, it might be appropriate to legislate that all Swedish citizens are bound to this so-called social contract to avoid determining who is Muslim, as exemplified by the cases of Gyllenstierna and Baksi, which highlight the problem. The Legal Council is currently investigating the matter."

"What happens to the Muslims who refuse to renounce their faith?" Wennergren asked.

"The future council proposes that they be deported as soon as possible," Ceder replied. "Nearly all Muslims are already interned, thanks to the commendable efforts of the National Task Force and the Nordic heroes of the Viking Battalion. They will remain interned until it is determined, on a case-by-case basis, whether integration or deportation applies. It's fortunate for the Muslims that they've been interned so we can protect them; otherwise, they would probably be massacred by enraged Swedes. We've already seen thousands of cases where Muslims have been beaten to death by Swedish mobs, so I think most Muslims prefer to stay in their internment camps for now, under the protection of the National Task Force and the Viking Battalion."

"Even more Swedes have been lynched by Muslim mobs, which is important to point out in this context," Popovic added. "And it started several years before the war broke out."

Gyllenstierna interjected with a comment.

"One possible scenario is a population exchange between Sweden and the Muslim zone. We send the Muslims who are to be deported to the Muslim occupation zone, and they send an equal number of Swedes here in return. That would solve the housing issue smoothly."

"Just like the population exchange between Greece and Turkey in 1926," Bergström noted, always ready with historical references. "Christians and Muslims are as incompatible as water and fire, so both sides collaborated in the operation."

"Yes, that's exactly the example we've studied in the future council," Ceder said. "It was a rare, successful population exchange of similar size. However, the risk is that we might cement and permanently establish the Muslim occupation zone by filling it with perhaps half a million Muslims."

"A more dramatic and bloody exchange occurred between India and Pakistan following the British withdrawal in the late 1940s," Bergström said. "That involved millions of Muslims and Hindus. Now we're dealing with Swedish Muslims and Christians. Always these damned Muslims! Forced displacements and deportations are much more common than orchestrated population exchanges and have occurred if there have been humans on Earth," Bergström continued. "Europe's largest population movement, which most people don't even know about, happened after World War II, when twelve million German-speaking minorities were expelled from countries like Poland, Czechoslovakia, Hungary, and Romania, including the Volga Germans in Russia. Simultaneously, there was a spontaneous population exchange between Poland and Ukraine."

"More recently, we had the ethnic cleansings in the Balkans during the 1990s, which were quite successful, though they cost a couple of hundred thousand lives," Brännström added. "Yugoslavia was like an unpinned grenade, destined to explode sooner or later. The Balkan war was as inevitable as our own war, so it was just as well that it happened, but it was never fully resolved, so there's more to come. Just like here in Sweden, I fear."

"The future council believes that the approach should be a population exchange rather than outright deportation, but if the Muslims refuse, then deportation it is," Ceder said.

"The important thing is that we achieve a final solution, with a permanently Muslim-free Sweden," Brännström stated.

"Yes, a society where there are no shootings and bombings every day. A Sweden like we had before the Muslims flooded in by the millions!" Popovic agreed.

"A society where we can let our children grow up safely," Wiklund added. "All Swedes have the right to live in a Muslim-free society, and it's our duty to make that happen."

Baksi summarized the situation. "We all agree on the direction for the new Sweden. Our negotiating group will immediately take up the issue of population exchange with the UN mediation commission, but if the Muslims want a population exchange, it will be carried out, regardless of the UN's stance. The UN has been a joke since the US withdrew, so why should we care about them?"

"With that, we'll adjourn the meeting," Gyllenstierna concluded. "Let's enter the new year at least in a ceasefire. If you hear any bangs, pretend they're fireworks."

Gyllenstierna stood up, signaling silence. He slowly swept his gaze around the conference table, making eye contact with the other nineteen people for a moment.

"Well, we've been holed up deep in the Swedish bedrock for over five months, first in Zone 1 and then in Zone 2. Now that the war is over, at least there's a ceasefire, we can finally crawl back into daylight. The next meeting will be the day after tomorrow, Sunday, January 2, in Stockholm City Hall, which is one of the few large buildings that isn't demolished. I've arranged accommodation for all 198 people currently here. We must remember that no communication will work for a long time, except for small sections of passable roads. Bridges, subways, commuter trains—everything is destroyed. Therefore, we will make City Hall a Zone 3, where we will stay for months ahead. It might seem easier to set up governance in a city that isn't in ruins, but the symbolism of the government being in its capital outweighs that. It gives us legitimacy."

"Legitimacy, yes," Wennergren said. "That's the question we should ask ourselves. How long should we maintain control, which is effectively military rule? Should we reinstate democracy and call for elections, or what?"

"We in the future council believe it would be madness to even discuss such ideas within at least the next year and probably much longer," Lilian Ceder said, looking at Gyllenstierna. "The situation is unstable; armed militias are everywhere, and we don't know what they'll do now that an official ceasefire has been declared. Besides, some of them still fight. And we never know when the war against the Muslims might flare up again, not to mention the whims of the Russians."

"Whoever controls the military resources is the one who effectively governs, and that's us," Brännström said. "We must absolutely maintain control over the country and, most importantly, bring the militias under our control. We'll see how things develop over time."

"Our top priority now is to build a strong defense," Baksi said. "Many want to see a stable Sweden in the Nordic region, not least China and Russia, and we are already negotiating large arms purchases on credit. By the way, China demands the right to protect the ports if we grant them the concession to operate them, and that might not be such a bad idea. A militarily engaged China could fill the void left by the USA and become a deterrent against new invasions; even the Russians wouldn't dare challenge the Chinese."

"Brazil wants to export their upgraded version of the JAS Gripen F to us," Wennergren added. "They're offering very attractive discounts and credits. The Indians are also eager to introduce their fighter jets here. Times are changing."

"Population exchanges and deportations of Muslims must begin immediately," Björn Väster said. "The interned Muslims are starving because we have difficulty getting supplies to them. So, we should give them a helping hand and kick them out of the country while they're still alive," Väster continued with a wry smile. "I see it as a necessary aid operation. 'Generalissimo' Väster will personally oversee this via the National Task Force with assistance from Brigade Viking. We will conduct a nationwide and thorough ethnic cleansing."

"Yes, it's crucial that the ethnic cleansing starts quickly," Popovic said, "and this cannot be carried out within a democratic framework."

"I agree," Baksi said. "The issue of ethnic cleansing is urgent. And we must never forget how the betrayal of our country was carried out and who was behind it. It was politicians elected through democratic means. Democracy is dangerous, and we must not give them the chance again."

"Traitors to our country must be captured and brought to justice," Väster said. "This will be one of the National Task Force's main priorities, involving up to fifty thousand people who have committed various degrees of treason. Most of them should be stripped of their citizenship and exiled for life for simplicity's sake. The most important thing is to get rid of them, not to seek revenge, except for perhaps a couple of thousand who should face severe punishment."

"Those who caused the destruction of our country and the maiming of Sweden must, of course, be brought to justice and given appropriate sentences," Gyllenstierna said, nodding toward Väster. "But that will be a matter for the so-called National Council, which will govern Sweden moving forward, with me as chairman. We'll see if any civilians will join the NC, as we call it. The NC has a massive task ahead; the first question is who will be on the council. Before we all go our separate ways, let's have a little champagne, which happens to be conveniently available in the storerooms," Gyllenstierna continued. "Evacuation and relocation start at 6 a.m. tomorrow, so pack your belongings, as you'll never return here. We'll meet at City Hall on Sunday. Cheers!"

"Cheers!" the group replied in unison, raising their glasses.

"For peace and the new Sweden!"

"For the National Council!"

The door opened in the middle of the toast, and Baksi's closest intelligence officer entered and whispered something in his ear. They turned their backs to the group and spoke quietly for a minute under the curious gazes of the others. Baksi turned around, took a teaspoon, and clinked it against his champagne glass until quiet.

"Unfortunately, I have to dampen the good mood with some bad news," Baksi said, suddenly tired. "I just received information that the Flottsbro force's ingenious attack on the Muslim leadership in the Castle wasn't as successful as everyone thought. The initial information was correct in that none of the fifteen people in the Treasury survived the explosion. However, the top leaders, Ahmed Ben Barka and his right-hand man Mahmoud were in another part of the castle having a phone meeting with their leadership in Cairo. Our infiltrator reports they're walking around the Castle, alive and well without a scratch."

"Well, that's just fantastic!" Väster exclaimed in frustration. "Those two seem to have at least nine lives, and we haven't taken one yet."

"Additionally, the master chef Hassan survived, if that matters," Baksi continued. "He was apparently in the kitchen when the explosion happened."

A low, disgruntled murmur spread through the room. The champagne glasses were emptied and placed on the table, and the participants left the room to pack up for their departure the following morning.

Chapter 50

The first meeting of the National Council

January 2, 2033

City Hall was bustling with people who had made new homes behind curtains and on mattresses in the Blue Hall, the Golden Hall, the Hall of the Three Crowns, and even the Vault of the Hundreds. The building offered comforting warmth, thanks to air heat pumps powered by the first delivery of a thousand diesel generators promised as Indian disaster aid. City Hall's warmth was an inviting alternative to the icy, bomb-damaged homes, especially on days like today when it was down to ten degrees.

Hundreds of Stockholmers sat around the wide staircases, waiting for the next serving from the soup kitchen. Warmth and scheduled meals felt like pure luxury after the stressful and hungry months of war. However, many still shivered and broke out in cold sweats from anxiety, haunted by dreams of suicide bombers infiltrating City Hall. The five psychologists stationed at City Hall were busy, but with no anxiety-relieving medications available, they relied on talk therapy as best as they could. Restraints and confinement in the basement vaults were sometimes necessary, where anxious screams wouldn't disturb others.

Since Stockholm had been liberated on December 26, there had been no suicide bombings, and the nervous security guards hoped that all suicide bombers had left the city for good. In the heavily guarded Council Chamber, however, no outsiders were allowed. The Council Chamber was reserved for the National Council, which had established its operations there. The chamber had space for about a hundred seated members, with galleries that could accommodate twice that number. Previously used by Stockholm's city council, the Council Chamber was perfect for a smaller parliament, complete with spectator galleries.

None of the four men now ruling Sweden intended to introduce any form of democracy. It was the degenerate democracy that had led to Sweden's destruction and the deaths of an estimated 750,000 Swedes within the old borders of Sweden. People generally viewed democracy as a repulsive farce controlled by anti-Swedish forces. The main responsibility for the collapse of democracy was generally attributed to the media, which had caused decay through misleading manipulation of the public, driven by the media owners who always seemed to strive for the dissolution of European nation-states.

Like most Swedes, the men in the National Council saw the governance in countries like China, Russia, and Singapore as ideal. No one could deny that the so-called benevolent dictatorships were the countries that had developed the best, providing their citizens with peace, law, and order and the fastest-growing welfare over the past half-century. No one could deny that these benevolent dictatorships had advanced their positions in international geopolitics by quickly filling the void left by the imploding Western democracies.

The men in the National Council agreed that countries should be run like businesses. It's no coincidence that the business world can never be democratized. It's all about making quick, decisive decisions and ensuring that subordinates are loyal to those decisions, that everyone is in sync, and that those who aren't are removed as quickly as possible.

The men of the National Council saw themselves as the board of directors for Sweden Inc. Like all corporate boards, their task was to chart the course for the future and ensure that the strongest and best leaders had enough room to drive the company toward its goals. There was no doubt that it would take a firm hand to get Sweden Inc. back on its feet, and there was also no doubt that the men of the National Council would use whatever means the situation required. A given prerequisite was that the council would quickly establish a complete monopoly on violence, which required control over the free forces and extensive purges of leftist activists within the authorities.

Even though the National Council had no intention of pretending to run Sweden Inc. democratically, the Council Chamber was still seen as perfect. It was large enough to hold information and pep meetings on a larger scale, with over four hundred people fitting in, including the galleries. Since the parliament building was in ruins, there was no good alternative. The fact that Sweden Inc.'s board was sitting in Stockholm City Hall, known abroad thanks to the Nobel Prizes, was a heavily weighted symbol.

The 'Gang of Four', as they came to be called, consisted of the previous leadership trio of Gyllenstierna, Brännström, and Baksi, with the addition of Björn Väster, who was invited into the inner circle of power due to his operational ability, impressive decisiveness, and inexhaustible energy. However, the most important reason was that Väster would be responsible for the purges of Swedish Muslim collaborators and the deportation of Muslims who did not meet the requirements to stay.

Väster was given control over the police, the National Task Force, and the Viking Battalion, also known as the Lagerbäck Battalion, which the Nordic soldiers preferred to call their unit. Officially, the National Council consisted of eight equal members, with Gyllenstierna as chairman, but since the Gang of Four made all decisions in their own small forum, things always went their way. The council members rarely dared to question any of the four insiders, but when they did, the combined pressure from all four's arguments was always too much, and the opponent quickly backed down. Everyone knew they would be ousted if they opposed the real leaders. At their appointment, Gyllenstierna informed them that their positions were temporary and could be adjusted based on circumstances.

The National Council consisted of eight people: four effectively ruled Sweden, and four mainly acted as information providers and advisors to the four with real power. The other members of the National Council were the heads of the three security services and Commander Captain Fridolf Palmquist, who had been promoted to navy chief after the less competent Fred Bergström was ousted by Gyllenstierna, who had also received intricate information that Bergström might be spying for the Russians. The Air Force Chief, Stig Wennergren, was also ousted since Sweden no longer had an air force to manage.

Army Chief Anton Brännström was promoted to Supreme Commander at the National Council's first meeting. At the same time, Gyllenstierna stepped down as Supreme Commander to take the position of Chancellor and Chairman of the National Council. Brännström announced that Major Gunhild Svartenbrandt, who had led the Swedish troops' operations in Stockholm, would immediately succeed him as army chief.

All power was now concentrated in Gyllenstierna's hands. Gyllenstierna's friend and confidant, Anton Brännström, entirely controlled the military. The heads of the three security services reported to Alfred Baksi, Gyllenstierna's right-hand man. Björn Väster, now given the title of National Order Councilor, controlled the police, the National Task Force, and the Viking Battalion, and of course, Väster reported directly to Gyllenstierna.

However, Chancellor Gyllenstierna was not satisfied with this alone. He took another step to strengthen his grip.

"Besides the three existing security services, the National Council needs a special guard force and security service independent of the other three. Therefore, we are now forming the National Council's Special Security Service, NRSS, which is tasked with ensuring our security and overseeing the other security services. The leader of NRSS will report directly to the Chancellor, that is, to me. I will soon announce who will head this service."

The National Council's first meeting lasted eleven hours and resulted in a list blending strategic direction with urgent operations. Just as often happens in business, speed took precedence over formality. Most points focused on establishing law and order and gaining full control over the country.

- Ultimatum to the leaders of all free forces to subordinate themselves to the Supreme Commander within forty-eight hours or be subdued and tried as traitors. Responsible: Brännström.

- Program to purge leftist activists within authorities and municipalities. Responsible: Väster.

- Program for the deportation of undesirable Muslims. Responsible: Väster.

- Ultimatum to the leaders of free citizen militias to subordinate themselves to the police within forty-eight hours or be arrested and tried as traitors. Responsible: Väster.

- Establishment of a special tribunal for traitors. Responsible: Baksi.

- Creation of a legislative package regarding various degrees of treason. Responsible: Baksi.

- Ban on independent media operations. Purge of leftist activists within all media. State expropriation of all media within the Bonnier and Schibstedt spheres. Responsible: Baksi.

- Total reorganization of the military. Responsible: Brännström.

- Begin negotiations with the Russians regarding their proposal to return most of the occupied territory in exchange for a peace treaty accepted by the Swedes. Responsible: Gyllenstierna.

- Negotiate with the Chinese regarding the concession to operate ports in exchange for aid focused on energy reconstruction. Responsible: Gyllenstierna.

- Initiate the adaptation and amendment of the constitution. Responsible: Lilian Ceder.

- Establish a national budget and financial management agency. Responsible: Lilian Ceder.

It was almost midnight, and all participants were hungry and exhausted. Chancellor Gyllenstierna stood up to conclude the meeting.

"Sweden is now a constitutional monarchy, with King Carl Philip as the head of state and the National Council as the government. New constitutions are being prepared. No one can legitimize our rule stronger than the king. Remember that we are unknown to the public, while the king is hailed as a leader and war hero, especially among the free forces but also internationally. The king has promised to open doors and assist with international contacts and negotiations for disaster aid, which we will undoubtedly receive and desperately need.

"This Wednesday, January 5, King Carl Philip will hold a press conference here in the Council Chamber, with most of the world's major media broadcasting live. This will also give the National Council a chance to present itself. The press conference will give us a strong start. Then everything is up to us."

The fate and future of the new Sweden now seemed to lie in the hands of the Chancellor and the National Council, but it would soon become apparent that stronger forces beyond the Swedes' control would shape the future. The great European war for freedom had erupted in full scale, and Western Europe was ablaze.

Afterword

As I write the afterword for the English edition of Perfect Storm, I can observe that a great deal has changed in Sweden over the six years since the book was written in 2018. Back then, public debate was tightly controlled, with mainstream media and the anti-Swedish organization Expo systematically harassing and shaming anyone who dared to criticize the country's insane immigration policies. Critics and debaters were silenced out of fear of being labeled and ostracized, which could lead to social exclusion and, in the worst cases, loss of livelihood. At least some hundreds lost their jobs and positions because they did not align with the prescribed values. This method seemed copied from the communist regimes that ruled Eastern Europe until the fall of the Berlin Wall in 1989. Today, the pressure has slightly eased as more wise and brave individuals speak out, supported by a rapidly growing array of independent media. But Sweden's Security Service, SÄPO, recently officially stated that independent media threatens democracy, which aligns with what the President of the European Commission, Ursula von der Leyen, also formally declared.

However, the persecution of dissenters continues with full force. A clear warning sign for all friends of democracy and freedom of speech is that eight successful Swedish regime-critical authors have been put on trial, myself included. In contrast, the Swedish PEN, the Authors' Union, the Publicists' Club, the Press Club, the Newspaper Publishers' Association, the Journalists' Club, and the Journalists' Union remain silent, along with our Minister of Culture, the Iran-born Parisa Liljestrand, who claims that there is no such thing as Swedish culture.

Those who most loudly proclaim the importance of free speech are the very ones who stifle it. The mindless mass immigration to our country continues unabated. Meanwhile, politicians and media claim that Sweden has the EU's strictest immigration policy.

Another way to persecute dissidents is to block them from using banking services. Today, June 24, 2024, my company and I were suspended as customers of SE-Bank (SEB), one of Sweden's largest banks controlled by the Wallenberg family. Several Swedes have been blocked from banking services, and the same thing is happening internationally, for example, the famous English critic Nigel Farage. The first time the banks were used to punish critics was, as far as I know, when Canadian President Justin Trudeau used the method against demonstrating truckers.

When I decided to write this, my first novel, I knew from the outset that it would be a dystopia, which, according to dictionaries, means roughly a bleak depiction of a future inhumane society.

Perfect Storm is a story about Sweden in 2032 that can be read as pure fiction about an imagined situation that will never happen. However, it can also be read as a warning about a problem that could indeed occur and, unfortunately, has become significantly more likely since the book was written. Some sections of Perfect Storm are drawn to extremes that may seem too severe to be authentic. However, reality often surpasses fiction.

I want to extend my heartfelt thanks to my author mentor, who chooses to remain anonymous out of fear of personal persecution.

Finally, I thank my dear wife Sorina for tolerating a husband who sometimes dwells in a dream world instead of being a present and attentive partner.

Nothing in this story is autobiographical.

Djursholm, Sweden, June 24, 2024

Arne Weinz

www.ingramcontent.com/pod-product-compliance
Lightning Source LLC
Chambersburg PA
CBHW051102030726
47504CB00006B/1741